About th

Alan Hescott was born into a working-class family in West London; his grandfather was a local road-sweeper and his dad worked as a labourer at a paper mill. He left his secondary modern school aged 15 and a few years later went to drama school. Alan trained as an actor and worked in theatre and television. He was a member of Richard Eyre's company at the Nottingham Playhouse. During this time Alan began to write. His plays have been produced by Derby Playhouse, Leicester Haymarket Theatre, The Arcola and Nottingham Playhouse.

Alan has written extensively for screen and for radio. He was nominated for a Writers' Guild award, and has written for BAFTA award-winning television. *Wolf Trap* is his first novel.

Wolf Trap

Alan Hescott

This edition first published in 2020

Unbound
6th Floor Mutual House, 70 Conduit Street, London W1S 2GF
www.unbound.com

ISBN (eBook): 978-1-78965-084-6
ISBN (Paperback): 978-1-78965-083-9

Cover design by Mecob

Printed and bound in Great Britain by Clays Ltd, Elcograf S.p.A.

To Sue, Tom and Guy

With thanks to Bill Nighy, for years of encouragement and help, and for being my First Reader

Major Patron

Sue Nott

Super Patrons

Geoff Adams
Jaymie Addicott
Mike Ashcroft
Trish Ashcroft
Marnie Ayres
Mike Batting
Gregory Boardman
Jeremy Booth
David Braithwaite
Louise Bucknole
Dean Burke
Ruth Caleb
Tony Chapman
Julie Cheung-Inhin
Harry Cooke
Alan Cork
Sherri Cork
Tom Cork
The Corkies
The Corkies
Kate Day
Tuyen Do
Donald P Doe
Fred 'Kipper' East
Agnes Ellington
Richard Elson
Sara Feilden
Ola Ferraro
Joe Ferrera
Julia Gilbert
Anne Gilchrist
Peter Grange
Jack Green
Haydn Hades
Clementine Hescott
Guy Hescott
James William Hescott
Louise Matilda Hescott
Lucy Hescott
Ned Hescott
Thomas Hescott
Jane Hodgson
Anna Home
Anne Howick
Teresa Jackson
Neil Jones
Lionel Joyce
Ian Kirkby
Bernard Krichefski
Diana Kyle
Cinthia Lilen
John Maclean
Billy Macqueen
Davina Moon
Chris Murray
Tom Nott
Mark Oosterveen
Carla Pastorino
Major Patron
Nigel Pickard

Mark Pitter
Jeff Povey
Emma Reeves
William Rycroft
Steve Ryde
Steve Sheen
David Smith
Elizabeth Smith
Fergus Sturrock
Neal Sussman
PQA Sutton
Joe Talbot
Rhys Thomas
Lexi Thomas & Marcus Potter
Ana Torre
Chi Tudor-Hart
Anita Turner
Eve Turner
Dan Usztan
Mark Vent
Rik Warren
Jonathan Watts
Mike Watts
Jacqueline Wilson
Francis Wright

CHAPTER ONE

Gabriel had taken two bullets for his betters; the first for a fat bishop in Spain, when Gabriel had been serving in the Condor Legion fighting for Franco, the second for a Gruppenführer, when Gabriel was serving in the SS Nord Division, fighting Ivan on the Finnish border. The Spanish bullet had shattered his shoulder; the Russian round had made a mess of his stomach. But now, Gabriel thought, as he fitted the telescopic sight to his British-made SM Lee–Enfield sniper's rifle, it was his turn to squeeze the trigger, and he was going to aim for the head.

The ring of mountains about Gabriel watched his actions. He tore a tuft of grass from the Alpine hill, held it at arm's length and let it drift. There was a movement in the air – too soft to be called a breeze, but enough to bend the round on its journey to the target's head. Gabriel had grown up further south-west, over the border in Switzerland, and his father had told him on their hunting trips, *When there's a gap in a valley wall there'll be movement, even on the stillest day*. And this was a still day. Beyond the mountains the world was tearing itself apart in war, but the mountain range seemed neutral, an island, an oasis, baking slowly in the late August heat.

Gabriel looked along the path. Soon Wolf would be coming. It was his habit; the same time every day, sleep late then stroll to the Mooslaner Kopf tea-house. Today was the same as every day except today the target wouldn't get his tea and toast. Today the war was coming to those quiet mountains in Bavaria. He looked down his sight and the crosshairs focused on the path. Soon they'll focus on Wolf, he thought.

They'd focus on the forehead of the Führer, Adolf Hitler.

Gabriel saw Hitler below him on the track, setting off on his stroll. The Führer had spotted August Korber, clumsy August, who, when he was off duty, wore Bavarian sandals, Gabriel remembered with a shudder. The Führer hated discovering any of the Leibstandarte, his close bodyguard, dogging his tracks, so August had been sent packing. Gabriel pitied him; Hitler was going to die on August's watch so August would be lucky to survive. But then they were all living on borrowed time, all the Old Hares; the war was lost.

The Führer continued his journey and Gabriel slid into position. Around him the Bavarian Alps reeled up and away. Choughs soared and called their dismay; below them a man cradling a rifle was going to bring blood and chaos to their kingdom in the clouds.

The Führer moved into the killing zone. Gabriel scrutinised him through the sights. It was like tracking an image on a cinema screen, akin to aiming at the head of Mickey Mouse or Charlie Chaplin. He had an icon in his sights and he was going to obliterate it. He tracked the Führer, feeling the man's pace, moving with him, the crosshairs meeting on the target's temple. Gabriel breathed out and tightened his finger on the trigger.

A shot from somewhere else, from an unknown source, cracked and echoed in the amphitheatre of the mountains.

Gabriel flinched and almost saw the passage of the round as Hitler's head flicked around to follow it.

'Didn't allow for the breeze,' he admonished the unknown shooter, the other would-be assassin who had fired first and missed.

Gabriel's finger completed its journey and a second crack followed the still-echoing first. It was no good; Corporal Hitler had served four years in the trenches and was too old a soldier to stand gawping under fire. The Führer was full length in the dirt and crawling for cover as Gabriel's round passed harmlessly overhead.

'Put your weapon to one side. Roll over slowly,' said a voice from behind Gabriel.

Gabriel froze on the rough grass, angry that he'd become too focused on his target. He pushed the rifle away and turned. The man behind him was Volfgangu, a French waiter from the tea-house. Volfgangu was shaking, not from fear but rage. His face was like a ripe berry about to explode.

'You tried to kill the Führer.'

Volfgangu was a big man, an ex-Legionnaire. Soldiers have two ways of moving: they can stamp about, smacking parade grounds with their heels, or they can slice through the air as silent as hunters. The Frenchman moved like the latter. Gabriel, in the deep concentration of trying to make a kill, had not heard him approach. In the enraged waiter's hand was a Walther PPK. Gabriel waited for the pistol to bark; he had gambled and lost. He couldn't have been discovered by anyone worse than the waiter; Volfgangu loved Hitler. The sun glinted on his enamel PPF badge, the French Fascist Party emblem that Volfgangu was wearing on the lapel of his suit. He had also been a member of the Milice Nationale, the French Gestapo. Gabriel remembered Volfgangu using his oath of loyalty to that organisation as a drinking toast. 'I swear to fight democracy, to fight De Gaulle's insurrection and to fight Jewish leprosy!'

'Obersturmführer Zobel, you're a fucking traitor, I should kill you now – but I'd rather watch them hang you up by your balls with piano wire.'

Gabriel's mouth was dry and he tried to swallow but his nerves wouldn't let him. He couldn't think; small things were distracting him; the SS tabs on his collar rubbed him under the chin. It had all gone wrong.

'Get up.' Volfgangu reached into his belt and produced a knife with a serious blade, the sort of dagger Gabriel's father would have used to skin a wolf. 'If you try anything I'll open you up.'

He waved the knife. Gabriel nodded and hauled himself up. As he rose he screamed at someone behind the Corsican, 'Now!'

Gabriel saw Volfgangu spinning round, the Walther tight into the Frenchman's side where it wasn't exposed and he could fire accurately pressed against the platform of his hip. The knife was held straight out, securing the space in front of him from any charging enemy. But there was no one, and Gabriel was no longer watching; he was up and hitting the treeline, weaving to dodge the expected rounds. None came; instead he heard the crash and smash of the Corsican's frame bisecting the wood in a straight line, a line that led to Gabriel's exposed back. Both men were fit and strong and both were warriors; not soldier-citizens but professionals from hard regiments, and only one of them was armed.

Gabriel ran, knowing he needed to be assembling with the rest of Hitler's bodyguard. Instead he was being chased by a Corsican who should have been serving tea, not waving a blade. Gabriel knew where that knife had to go, and quickly. His lungs worked like bellows. Gabriel could run forever up the mountain, but time and circumstances were about more than just getting away; he needed to organise an ambush.

Ahead of him, viewed through the trees like the cottage in Hansel and Gretel, was a chalet. Its owner, Gabriel knew, was not unlike the wicked witch of the fairy story. Around the chalet was a small, neat, Alpine garden, laid out like a military parade. He hit the precise ranks of blooms like the Goths storming Rome.

Let it be empty, he thought. Let the witch who lives there be on duty at the hospital, he prayed, as he raced towards the door.

Gabriel smashed into the door of the chalet. Ahead was an interior with the ambiance of a Swiss bank. There were many kind and compassionate nurses at the hospital but the chalet's owner, Iron Arse, wasn't one of them. Her taste was as bleak as her humour, Gabriel thought; cold, distempered walls. He ran through the lounge, threw the door to the kitchen open but didn't go through; instead he ducked behind an armchair.

A beat later, Volfgangu crashed into the sitting room and raced for the open kitchen door. Gabriel poised himself, ready to spring on the ex-Legionnaire's back, when the moment of ambush was spoiled by barking. Iron Arse's miniature dachshund, a turd on legs, snapped at Gabriel in fury at his trespass.

Volfgangu skidded to a halt and, following the rat-dog's nose, pointed the knife and pistol to where Gabriel curled ridiculously behind the chair. Gabriel grabbed the dog and threw it with all the strength in his arm at the Corsican, who batted it away. The dog howled.

Gabriel was across the room and running up the treads of the exposed staircase in the corner and Volfgangu started off after him. At the top of the stairs there was just one door and Gabriel ran through. It was Iron Arse's bedroom and he was pleased to see the paranoid bitch had fitted a lock to the door. He turned the key and rushed to the window. Sweeping a world of Dresden shepherdesses from the sill, he threw it open and climbed through it, as behind the door reverberated to a kick.

He lowered himself till he hung there by his fingertips, the strength needed to do this almost betraying him as his fingers locked and he saw Volfgangu's blade flashing towards his knuckles. Gabriel unclenched and a second later the knife raked the wood. He dropped and rolled like a paratrooper up on to his feet and then off, running again and hearing the Corsican behind doing the same.

Gabriel was suffering. He'd trained hard to regain battle fitness after his wounds, but he knew he couldn't train for fear, and, as his first sergeant had said, fear adds another pack to the back, one full of bricks. His legs and lungs were slowly betraying him.

Gabriel knew he needed to bring this to a conclusion. Ahead he saw what he needed: a tree nearly uprooted growing out of the ground at a 45-degree angle and, under it, branches sprouting like a screen. Gabriel ran into one and bent it back with the force of his velocity, and held it as it twisted and fought to escape his grasp. Volfgangu charged after him through the gap in the evergreen curtain as Gabriel released the bough and heard it smack into the Corsican's face.

Gabriel followed the branch and launched himself into the blinded man. He grabbed Volfgangu's hands, keeping the Walther pointed skyward with one, and the other wrestling for ownership of the knife as they struggled on the rocky platform. Gabriel raised the heel of his jackboot, brought it down hard on Volfgangu's foot and broke it. As the ex-Legionnaire gasped in pain, his grasp of the knife loosened and Gabriel had it. He stepped behind Volfgangu and slid the blade in under the Corsican's earlobe and up into his brain.

It wasn't the first time Gabriel had killed someone in this

fashion, yet it always caused him a moment of amazement when a victim went from life to meat in an instant. He had been convinced the first enemy he had killed this way, a Spanish Republican, had only been pretending to be dead. It had been a comrade in the Condor Legion who had made him drop the cadaver, shouting at him to *Stop dancing with it and fucking ditch it!*

Gabriel let go of Volfgangu and let the body slide to the ground, the knife still protruding from under the ear, where it cauterised the wound. He knew it was a good way to kill someone if you wanted to avoid a lot of splatter; the Corsican was pretty much a dry corpse and Gabriel was grateful – he couldn't be seen later covered in gore. Dishevelled yes, bloody no. But now he knew he had just minutes to hide the body.

Gabriel slipped the small Walther PPK into his tunic pocket. He tried to calm his breathing and to stop trembling. He removed both Volfgangu's belt and his necktie. He hoicked the body over his shoulders. Sucking in oxygen, he began a steep climb up the angled tree. When the bough intersected with another vertical tree Gabriel exchanged trunks. He began, with a superhuman effort, to climb up into the canopy. He switched into the soldier mode of dealing with a huge physical ordeal; he sent his mind somewhere else. Gabriel focused on the bark under his hands and feet, the amazing greenness of it, like climbing an overgrown billiard table. The moss was a testament to the torrential rains of the mountains. The deciduous tree he was climbing was green; the firs standing around it wore their lichen grey like splashes of paint.

It took willpower and a back-breaking, lung-bursting effort for Gabriel to carry his passenger to where the last of the sturdy boughs left the main trunk. He gratefully lowered the body onto a junction where two branches grew out horizontally. Taking out Volfgangu's belt he secured its owner to the main trunk, pulling it tight. He pulled the head up and the Corsican stared him in the eye, but Gabriel ignored him and instead attached the lolling head to the trunk using the tie. He then arranged Volfgangu's legs carefully, one on each bough, and, removing the laces from the Corsican's shoes, tied them in place around the ankles. Finally, he stuffed the hands down the front of the trousers, making the whole edifice seem obscene.

Even when winter came the body would be hidden from the ground; Volfgangu's grave in the clouds was secure. Gabriel scrambled down and looked up – the body was invisible. Up in the canopy it would rot privately – what more could any old soldier wish for, Gabriel thought. They had practised sky-burials in the fir forests on the Eastern Front. When the earth was too iron hard with frost to inter a comrade's corpse. Up with the bird nests, safe from predators and desecrating Ivans. Of course Volfgangu would be reported missing, but Gabriel hoped just maybe the missing waiter would be blamed for the botched assassination attempt.

He set off and ran fast and low, his knees bent the way Swiss boys are taught to run downhill in the mountains. Tourists bounded down Alpine slopes with long leaps that carried them away until, out of control, they tumbled and crashed and broke legs and ankles. Mountain people ran with a low centre of gravity and short, controlled steps. Gabriel tore down through the pine forest, aware that by now news of the attempted assassination would be out and the Leibstandarte would be up on the hills, hunting the would-be killer of their Führer. Gabriel knew he had to re-join their ranks without raising suspicion.

He saw them through the trees, the Leibstandarte, the Old Hares. They could have been men slightly gone to seed, surrounding a favourite doughnut stall; men attending a sporting event, comfortable with each other and suspicious of strangers.

Instead they were grouped around a rifle that one of them, Bruno Gesche, held.

'British,' Bruno was saying.

Gabriel stepped out of the bushes and bent double to regain his breath, as if he'd run all the way up from the valley floor, rather than having run for his life and killed a man in a knife fight. Bruno called to him. Although Gabriel was of equal rank and younger than them, the Old Hares deferred to him; he was a veteran, had seen action, and they had merely killed in alleys and bars.

'We've found the weapon, Scar,' said Bruno.

Their inevitable nickname for him. He almost touched his face where the disfigurement itched whenever it was mentioned. Instead he took the weapon and inspected it, as if seeing it for the first time in his life.

'Sniper's rifle,' he said.

From below came the sound of the Begleit Kommando, Hitler's second and larger tier of bodyguards, setting out on a more organised manhunt, divvying out radios and quartering the valley floor. From closer at hand, more members of Hitler's personal bodyguard arrived. Eight were now present; only Kurt Gildisch, their CO, was missing from the Old Hares. Gabriel looked at his comrades; they were all commissioned officers in the SS, but the rank was more of a compliment to their Führer than their merit. They did not lead men in battle and in a regular regiment they might have attracted the military nickname *uncle*, denoting an officer old for his rank and past his best. Most of the Old Hares had beer bellies and bleary eyes, but they weren't soft – just padded the way experienced gangsters get, living off the fruit of their crimes. Gabriel knew every one of them was dangerous.

'How is Wolf?' asked August.

'In a fury,' said Bodo Gelzenleuchter, who'd been the last to arrive. 'And Scar,' said Bodo, 'Wolf wants to see you.'

'What?'

'The Führer. He wants to see you – now.'

He knows, thought Gabriel, *Hitler knows*.

CHAPTER TWO

It felt like coming to from an operation, as he had that time in his childhood when he'd had his tonsils removed; befuddled by the dregs of the anaesthetic and being shaken awake by a nurse. The confusion and panic were the same. Two figures loomed over his bed. They were made shadows by the smoke that was attempting to smother him. He was pulled roughly out from under the sheets and upright, and the sudden heat made him want to crouch back down. He was drowning in air, in thick, clogging air. He felt his lungs working like bellows, desperately seeking to fill him with fresh oxygen, only to be frustrated by the smoke.

They pulled him to the door in the corner of his basement bedroom that led to his tiny courtyard garden. The door was open already. Jago was bundled through and a great waft of smoke followed him, as if it too were trying to escape the blaze. He had seen no flames but the scorch in the air had made the assumption of fire inescapable. As he bent double and threw up, supported by the firemen, he realised he had been rescued and that he had been bombed.

Suddenly the two silent firemen, under their wartime-issue helmets, were lifting him over a neighbour's fence into another yard. They clambered after him and one of them produced a blanket that smelled of other fires and wrapped it around him, rushing him through next door's flat. He wondered about the blanket. Why? It wasn't a cold night; September was proving to be as warm as August had been. Was it for modesty's sake? He was in his pyjamas after all. Or was it part of a ritual, its reason and meaning forgotten? All bombed-out victims to be wrapped in a coarse wool blanket and given a cup of tea. Sure enough, on the pavement in front of the house, a concerned neighbour pressed a cup into his hands.

An emergency tender was parked on the blacked-out street, and an Indian file of firefighters led from it down the basement stairs to his front door. They held and controlled a wilful snake of a hose. Someone moved between him and the scene. It was a man in a real fireman's helmet, one with a crest.

'Captain Craze?'

Jago tried to answer in the affirmative but merely croaked. He quickly took a sip of the tea and found it to be, quite simply, the best tea he had ever sampled. He remembered a fellow agent in the Special Operations Executive, a Czech, saying when they had dined on hedgehog during an escape-and-evasion exercise that hunger was the best chef. Possibly, Jago mused, nearly being fried alive put one in the best mood to imbibe tea. He took another gulp.

'Are you Captain Jago Craze?'

The man was becoming impatient.

'Yes.' His voice was back, but fruitier than usual. More bass notes. Richer and sexier than his usual shrillness. He wished Nicky could hear it. 'Craze, that's me. Was it a V2?'

The fire chief shook his head and said something strange.

'Do you have any enemies?'

Jago was confused; there was a world war occurring. 'The Germans…' he tried. The wrong answer, and Jago could hear the man's impatience in his tone. 'Not the Nazis. Closer to hand. Do you have a personal enemy?'

Jago was at a loss and returned briefly to the tea, as if an answer might be found there. 'I can't think of any. I'm not involved in anything cloak and dagger.'

Jago thought of his dismal days in the shabby office in Whitehall; his semi-penal job in what was mockingly called *the Forgetting School*. He silently raged at the deliberate monotony of it, the punishment for failure. Eking out his war to the ticks and tocks from the overloud clock on the wall in his sight line, so he would always know the time. His twin enemies were boredom and shame, but he didn't think the fire chief meant those.

'No,' he said. 'No enemies that I can think of.'

He finished the tea, and the neighbour, waiting for this moment, bobbed forward and recovered the cup. 'Thank you,' Jago said to the dressing-gowned back as it disappeared down the street.

The fire chief made his announcement. 'This isn't the result of enemy action; someone deliberately set fire to your front door. Petrol was poured through your letterbox.'

All Jago could do was wonder where the unknown assailant had got the petrol – it was on the ration.

'You were fortunate, Captain Craze; we were on a call-out earlier, a V2 rocket down by the river. We were on our way back to the station when my driver spotted you were ablaze. A lucky coincidence you might say.'

Fear came to him for the first time. Now Jago understood the blanket. He pulled it about him.

'Otherwise I might have been burnt alive?'

'Suffocated first,' corrected the fire officer.

A fireman clattered up the metal steps from Jago's flat.

'All damped down, Chief,' he said, before turning to Jago.

'I'm afraid the place is a write-off; the front room and kitchen are wrecked. The bedroom escaped the flames but the smoke damage is extensive.'

Jago felt a sense of loss as his memory presented him with a casualty list of objects that he had owned and were now no more.

'Why would someone do something like this?' he asked.

A look passed between the two firefighters. The chief spoke.

'There used to be more of this sort of thing, back in the Blitz. Fire excites some people, arsonists. They'd start their own blazes under the cover of enemy action.'

'As if we hadn't enough on our plate,' the other fireman said.

'Arsonists?' Jago echoed the word. It seemed insane to him that when a city burnt, some idiot would add to the conflagration to feed their own ego.

'Life goes on, and some of those lives are bad, rotten. War doesn't stop that,' said the fire chief.

It was a strange new thought for Jago and he considered it. So much was changed by the conflict; the men going away, people's attitude to each other, pulling together. But of course, he told himself, it would be naive to think that the enemies of society had declared an armistice for the duration. That the robbing of banks would only begin again when peace broke out. Jago remembered that he himself was still acting criminally and was, of course, an enemy to society, war or no war.

'You need to lock this gate,' the lesser of the two firefighters said, and swung the gate at the top of the basement stairs to illustrate its unsecured state.

'Yes,' agreed Jago, 'I have a key.'

'Then you might think about using it in future.'

Jago nodded at the advice. To begin with he'd always locked it, but then idleness had set in.

'Do you have somewhere to stay?' The question came from the chief.

Jago pointed to the house rearing up above the basement flat. 'That's mine as well.'

The fireman nodded and probably wondered why any young man would want a decaying four-storey pile in Pimlico. He still had some advice. 'You might find the ground floor a little smoky, but further up won't be a problem. And there's no structural damage.'

Smoky or not, the ground floor was destined to be his domain, Jago knew. Upstairs was the realm of Christine, his wife, and the stairs were no man's land.

'We'll be off, then.'

The crew were retreating to the tender.

'Thank you,' said Jago, then raised his voice to include all of them. 'Thank you.'

Weary hands were raised in acknowledgement as they climbed aboard, and Jago's blanket went with them. The requisite term of the loan was apparently over.

Jago knew Major Smedley from his pre-war days in Oxford; they were both fellows of the same college. He'd been hoping the summons to Smedley's office meant that at last he had read the report. But after barking *Enter*, and exchanging a curt salute with Jago, the major turned back to his papers.

'Give me a moment, Captain Craze.'

Jago gave his moment, which stretched in the airless office, and the non-regulation wig that Smedley wore itched Jago's head vicariously. The suffocating place intensified the smell of smoke coming off his uniform. He'd had it laundered twice but to no avail. Possibly the aroma disturbed Smedley and he looked up from his file.

'No injuries I hope from the conflagration?'

Jago shook his head.

'No, sir.'

'Has Mrs Craze recovered from the ordeal?'

Jago answered before he thought. 'She sleeps on the top floor, a long way from the basement.'

Smedley was a bachelor and a stranger to the doings of a married couple. Nonetheless he was aware that, by and large, married people slept in the same room if not the same bed. His face registered a confusion that Jago rushed to banish.

'Christine has a fear of air raids.'

'And yet she sleeps at the top of the house, not secure in the basement?'

With you, he meant, Jago knew.

'She's terrified of being buried alive.'

Of course this didn't explain why they slept apart but Smedley wasn't going to turn that stone over. Instead he produced from a drawer the folder that Jago recognised as the one containing his report.

Smedley looked across his desk. Jago suspected the phoney peace was over and that war was about to break out. The major opened hostilities. 'May I ask who tasked you with writing this, because it certainly wasn't me.'

Jago went on to the defensive. 'No one, sir, it just seemed – propitious.'

'Propitious?' Major Smedley looked at the junior officer standing before him in the vain hope that he might expand his explanation. Not for the first time, Jago thought the major looked like an illustration from Lewis Carroll; an elegant grasshopper. He was impossibly skinny, and the skin on his face seemed two sizes too small to cover his skull comfortably. Then there was the wig. Jago resisted the urge to snatch it from Smedley's head and to thrash him with it. Smedley was one half of a set of identical twins; both had lost their locks to alopecia brought on by the traumatic loss of their father in the Great War, but only Jago's Smedley covered his dome with someone else's hair.

The noise of the traffic outside on Whitehall seemed muted; there was certainly less of it since the V2 attacks had started. It was a scorching September and Jago felt sticky. A fly was buzzing and trying to escape the sterile office by using its own head as a battering ram against the tall window. Jago felt like joining it. Major Smedley squeaked into life once more.

'Explain.'

Captain Craze sighed; a verbal explanation of a written report required the sort of expansion that sabotaged insight. In Jago's opinion it was akin to explaining a joke to someone without a sense of humour.

'It occurred to me, sir, during the euphoria the other month, when Adolf had his trousers blown off at Rastenburg and we all mistakenly thought for an hour or two that he was dead, and the war might be over, that...'

'What? Spit it out, Craze.'

'Well, it might not be a good thing; Hitler being dead.'

Smedley twitched; the startled insect. 'Not a good thing? You a fan of the Nazis or what?'

'No, sir, quite the opposite. Someone has to shoot him, but the question is when and who. It certainly mustn't be the general officers from the Wehrmacht. They can't be allowed to buy their way back to the negotiating table via a bullet in their Führer's brain. That's what I say in my report.'

Patience left the major and the report quivered in his hand. 'You say that do you? Have I missed something here, Captain Craze? Have you recently been appointed to the Imperial General Staff? Has Field Marshal Sir Alan Brooke taken you to one side and said forget your appointed task, take yourself off on a self-indulgent mystery trip?'

'No, sir.'

'No, sir! Good grief, Craze, you've only been here two minutes and you're going your own sweet way again. May I remind you, Captain, you came to Army Intelligence under a cloud? The report of your funk in SOE did not make pretty reading.'

Major Smedley stared at Jago. There was no answer. Jago knew why he meandered from one backwater to another, and what had been written in his report when SOE had dumped him back in '41: *Due to a lack of moral fibre this officer is unsuitable for special operations and is unfit to lead men in battle. It is therefore recommended that he undertake administrative duties for the duration of the war.* He wished they'd just shot him, but over the previous three years he had been trying to live with it. He breathed out slowly and spoke that monosyllable that served the military so well.

'Sir.'

Jago knew that Major Smedley, in his other life at Oxford, was a classicist whose tiny specialisation was to research sheep husbandry on a single Greek island during a century of the Mycenaean period. To do this, Smedley spent his summers collecting fossilised sheep turds, and the long Oxford winters slicing the fossils with a grinding tool and dissolving the dissected turds to reveal the small grains and seeds that were so important to his research. Jago liked to think that this dissolving of shit to reveal the truth was a practice that so deliciously replicated the activities of an intelligence analyst that Smedley had been swept out of his gown and into a uniform as soon as war broke out. The real reason had been duller; Smedley volunteered.

'Explain your conclusions again, Craze.'

'You've read the report?'

'Of course I've read it, but I can't say I've digested it. I do have other duties.'

He hadn't read it.

'Of course, sir. Well, sir, we have to ask ourselves what makes Germany the foe it is. What essence of Germanic culture is it that we're fighting?'

'The Nazis,' said the major, as if the answer was obvious.

Jago, like all men with an original idea, warmed to the task of making a believer of the sceptic. 'With all due respect, sir, the Nazi party, beastly though it is, is not what makes Germany such a dangerous threat. It's militarism. Did Hitler make Germany or did Germany make Hitler?'

'Are you about to deliver a lecture, Captain?'

Jago chose not to hear the heckle and pressed on. 'Go into any public house and you'll find a table of shabby men in the corner planning world domination. The extraordinary thing is, in Germany, this table of postmen and hysterics did indeed take power. Now this wouldn't have mattered to the world if the country had been Bolivia or Tibet, but these clowns gained control of a great manufacturing nation at the heart of Europe. And this prize marches to the beat and was organised by a Prussianised culture.'

Major Smedley decided to score a point. 'Craze, the Nazis crawled out of Bavaria, not Prussia.'

Jago wouldn't be diverted. 'That's Geography and I'm talking about Philosophy. Germany is a Prussianised country; it's organised on military lines from top to bottom; they even give medals to mothers for breeding.'

Jago wondered if he'd detected a slight shudder from Smedley at the word *breeding*.

'You object to a state run along disciplined lines?'

'I object to a military dictatorship that believes the state exists principally to wage war. Germany is an incredible tool, a weapon. Today madmen control that weapon. We can remove the current batch of madmen, but the weapon will still exist until we occupy Germany and demilitarise it.'

Smedley sat uncomprehending behind his desk, as dull and slow witted as only an Oxford academic adrift from his specialisation could be. Jago tried to prod his brain along. 'With Hitler dead and his rat's nest of Nazis cleared out, the regular German military will seek to make peace with the Western allies.'

'Surrender,' said Major Smedley.

Now they were at the nub, Jago thought. 'But not unconditionally. No, they'd want an armistice along the lines of the one that ended the first show. Germany relinquishing all occupied land and retreating behind its pre-war borders in the west.'

Smedley's hands, moving like spiders, led his eyes to his own work before him on the desk. His tone was that of a tutor admonishing an undergraduate for making a basic error. 'Churchill and Roosevelt won't accept anything less than the unconditional surrender and occupation of Germany.'

Jago took a sharp step forward to emphasise his words.

'Mr Churchill won't be prime minister if Hitler dies. Without that demon we won't need our own demon king. Reasonable men will say reason has returned to Germany; reasonable men now rule it once more, men we can reason with. The so-called Guilty Men, the appeasers, still sit in the Commons and the Upper House. Do you think they will stay silent if the German generals offer a limited surrender, sir?'

Smedley abandoned the tempting file before him and, fuelled by his irritation at a fly buzzing somewhere in his office, snapped back.

'Good grief, Craze, the appeasers are yesterday's men.'

'Yesterday's men have a habit of coming back tomorrow.

We all read the draft surrender document the German generals were circulating in July when they thought they'd killed Hitler. If the appeasers managed to make that public, don't you think there'd be dancing in the street? Can you imagine one mother or wife who wouldn't demand the government accept the terms of a German semi-surrender just to have their boys come home safely? If Churchill defied their wishes, he'd be out of office faster than he came into it.'

'Haven't you forgotten the Americans?' asked Major Smedley.

Jago tempered his words, speaking gently to try and make his superior listen. 'Roosevelt is ailing, and of course most Americans see Japan as their main enemy. It's doubtful they would even be waging war in Europe if that idiot Hitler hadn't declared war on them.'

For a beat or two they held each other's eyes and it seemed at last as if Smedley was being swayed by Jago's argument. Then the major stood with a tut of impatience and, picking up a file, launched an offensive against the buzzing fly.

Jago spoke desperately to regain the initiative. 'Churchill will be replaced by an appeaser, Roosevelt will be bullied by public opinion, and France will explode,' said Jago.

The mention of France seemed to catch Smedley's attention and he abandoned his pursuit of the fly. 'France? For heaven's sake, why?'

'The French have hardly contributed to victory. Another year of war and they can sit at the victors' table. But if the war ends now – well it's possible that they might find themselves prosecuted for collaboration and war crimes. Internally they'll be subject to unrest and disorder, if not all-out civil war. Who's to be in charge, the Vichy collaborators or the communist resistance?'

'General de Gaulle.'

Jago knew that after five years of war Smedley, like most of the British, had forgotten the other France, not the France of De Gaulle's Free French, but bourgeois France with a police force that outshone the Gestapo in its persecution of the Jews, and a government of generals that identified with their conquerors and despised the weak democracy they blamed for their defeat.

'General de Gaulle is an outsider, not part of the establishment. If he's not merely to be an unelected generalissimo he'll need to legitimise his claim as leader by planting French Army boots on the German side of the Rhine. France needs to regain its honour and to do that it needs time.'

'No accounting for the French,' muttered Smedley, his attention drifting back to his desk again. In desperation Jago played the card he now thought he should have led with.

'Then there's Britain's inevitable defeat and destruction if we kill Hitler prematurely.'

This had the grasshopper's attention. 'Defeat? What are you talking about? It's the death of that madman that will end this war.'

'I don't think so, sir. Germany is a Hydra. If we cut off its head others will replace it. Men who are perhaps more deadly than the Austrian Corporal. Consider the enormous talent of the Germans. Their scientists and engineers have a genius for weaponry; look at the V1.'

'The doodlebug?' said Major Smedley.

Jago felt he could almost see inside the other man's mind, see Smedley picturing the ridiculous start-stop buzz bomb that farted its way over the Channel, like a Gothic flying machine made of brass and rivets, and stolen from a *Flash Gordon* episode.

'Absurd I agree,' said Jago. 'All that time and effort wasted on a device that carried a small bomb and our people shot them down in droves. But then last month came the V2 and no one laughs at the V2.'

Invisible, silent, with no warning of any kind, the V2 announced its presence with an ear-shattering explosion that demolished streets and wiped out communities. The fearful V2 had emptied London in a way that the earlier Blitz had failed to.

'Which brings us to what the V3 will be like,' said Jago. 'As tall as a block of flats with one of those city-smashing bombs in its cone? You remember the panic we had in Intelligence over that heavy water in Norway at the Norsk hydro plant? We stopped the Germans developing an atomic city-smasher that time, but if we let them off the hook and give them the space – well of course they're going to go straight back and make it. Then in, say, 1948, one afternoon, Portsmouth stops being Portsmouth and becomes a hole in the ground. And the German generals say, *The next one's on London unless you surrender – and surrender unconditionally.*'

Outside, Big Ben chimed eleven times, long and slow. Smedley extended his neck to glance around Jago towards the door. He wanted to know where his mid-morning coffee was.

Jago attempted a classical allusion: 'This offer from the German generals is a wooden horse; we'll think we've won and then, in their own time, they'll take us.'

A look of distaste arrived on Smedley's face and he passed it on to the report in his hands. It was as if an undergraduate had given him an essay with a tad too much salacious detail.

'It's your arrogance that takes my breath away, Craze. You know what they say; so many brains in London these days it's only the barrage balloons that stops Whitehall sinking. And yet out of all this conscripted talent and grey matter, whole colleges emptied and denuded of their brightest talent to feed the war effort – only you, Captain Jago Craze, undistinguished scholar and soldier, has had this insight and subsequently written this conclusion.'

Jago was at a loss; what Smedley had just said was akin to George Bernard Shaw embracing capitalism. From the moment he had gone up to Oxford it had been pressed on him that thought matters. And indeed, that insight and discovery often came from lowly sources; the obscure chemist or a vicar who watched worms every day for forty years and made notes. Smedley, he realised, is that other sort of academic, not one seeking brave new worlds, but one whose research is a blanket, something to hide his head under.

'Sir,' Jago said, 'I'm sure other people in other departments are reaching similar conclusions, but we can't rely on that. My report can at least stimulate debate and if my betters feel I'm wrong they can slap me down.'

Smedley twitched angrily. 'I also will receive a rap over the knuckles if it's believed I allow my staff to waste their time fabricating whimsy.'

Jago rode the moment in silence and eventually the tension eased and the Major sighed. Like Prometheus tasked with stealing fire from the gods and knowing that eternal damnation would surely follow, against his better judgement he asked a question. 'Alright, Captain Craze, what am I supposed to do with this report of yours?'

Jago seized the moment. 'I'd like you to pass it up the line, sir. I think it's vital. I assume that somewhere in the Allied war effort there's a department tasked with Adolf Hitler's assassination. You see, I think they must be told to desist, to stop. Further, I believe they must be told to reverse their role. They should be tasked with protecting Hitler. They must prevent his generals from killing him. Otherwise, sometime in the next few years, the phoney peace will be broken and we will lose the war, sir.'

Major Smedley's decision hung in the air between them. The sudden buzz of the fly was like a burst of irritated static in his head.

'I'm terribly sorry, Craze, but this really isn't our business,' said Major Smedley, reaching across his desk as he might to return an essay to an undergraduate who hadn't understood the subject. At the window the fly gave up trying to escape and fell back dead.

CHAPTER THREE

Gabriel stared out of the huge picture window of the Berghof, across the valley to the mountain of Untersberg opposite, and then let his gaze drop to the foot of the Obersalzberg, to the small town of Berchtesgaden. Down there was another world, a fairy tale land of cobbled streets and houses painted with *luftmaleres* frescos, the village at the bottom of the beanstalk. Gabriel was viewing it from the castle of the giant and he was Jack with a giant to kill.

The man by his side spoke. 'My father used to say you can't eat scenery.'

Gabriel smiled; his memory jogged. 'Mine said the same, sir.'

'It's hard to be a parent when you live in the shadow of these gods. Never underestimate geography.'

'I won't, sir,' said Gabriel.

'These mountains enter a man's soul and draw him up. It's why the desert peoples will only ever be the grit and dust of history.'

Even this proclamation was delivered gently, softly, in the warm accent of an Austrian. Gabriel thought this was a different Hitler from the one in the newspapers. He'd seen the press photos; the close-up, the famous face always wearing the same expression, as if someone was at that moment stamping on his toe. In newspaper print, in black and white, the eyes were always dark, but in real life they were blue. He'd recovered well from the generals' attempt to blow him up in the Wolf's Lair, his headquarters on the Eastern Front. The failed coup. That had been in July, but a couple of months later and the Führer seemed as confident and in control as ever. Was the man indestructible, Gabriel wondered?

In the month Gabriel had been at Obersalzberg, he realised there were two Hitlers, sometimes literally. He knew there was another Hitler in Berlin at that moment, his photograph appearing in papers giving out gallantry medals to servicemen. But Gabriel didn't mean the Führer's use of doubles, rather his two personalities. There was the Hitler of the mass rally, of Barbarossa, of blood and fire and iron. Then there was the Hitler of the Berghof, his home, surrounded by his close staff and bodyguard. The gentle Hitler who would appear unannounced in the kindergarten to watch the children play and smile, while the teachers adored him. Hitler was the second world leader Gabriel had met and he preferred him to the Holy Father. Pope Pius didn't connect with people. The Führer made it his mission to do just that.

'Call me Wolf,' the Führer said. His intimate name, reserved for friends; not the Führer, not Adolf Hitler, but Wolf. Wolf, with his Alsatian, Blondi, in the conference room above the world; Wolf like an Alpine shepherd watching out for his flock. The room was decorated with regional beer steins, the odd atlas indicating grand strategy, and, on an SS drum used as an occasional table, there was a copy of *Mein Kampf* bound in gold and Moroccan leather. A massive, six-metre-long, marble-topped table gave out rumours of meetings that dealt with destinies. On the walls were paintings of very naked women, and, Gabriel was distressed to note, one where a swan seemed to be raping a woman. The Pope had better paintings, he decided. Like an orphan interested in other children's homes, Gabriel decided this was not a room he'd ever be comfortable in. One picture did draw his eyes and call to him; it was of a woman holding an ermine. Gabriel had a peculiar feeling that the animal was him; the whiteness of it like him with his white-blond hair, and the feeling that under its camouflage of fur the mask would be scarred. It was a predator, a killer, but it was controlled by the woman, her pet. Just as he was owned.

Blondi sniffed at Gabriel's crotch, and he resisted the temptation to ruffle the dog's ears. Bruno Gesche had warned him, 'Leave the dog alone. Wolf's a jealous man and he loves that dog more than any woman. The umbrella-man made too much fuss of Blondi and Wolf didn't like it.'

The umbrella-man: Neville Chamberlain. Gabriel speculated that had the British prime minister preferred cats, then a world war might have been averted.

Heinz Linge, the Führer's valet, slid in with coffee and toast, and a plate of Mohnklosse – poppyseed cakes, Hitler's favourite.

Hitler took Gabriel's arm and guided him to the refreshments. 'Usually I breakfast at the tea-house, but this morning – he fired twice you know. He had two goes at murdering me. I heard the first shot pass my ear and I knew what it was immediately. You never forget.'

The Führer indicated that Gabriel should sit at the low drum table where Heinz had left the tray before silently departing. As he sat, Hitler reached out and touched the scar on Gabriel's face. It was something Gabriel noticed and didn't like; the scar made his face common property, the way a pregnant woman's stomach is patted by complete strangers, he thought. Old ladies would cluck in concern and stroke it. He wanted to slap those hands away but he tolerated it in silence.

'My scarred seraph,' said Wolf. 'It's a mark of the warrior. Another medal.'

The hand came away, and Gabriel breathed out.

The German leader served Gabriel tea and toast. Then with the sly smile of guilty indulgence he gave them both a poppy-seed cake.

Suddenly, and alarmingly, he declaimed; '*Here thou, great Anna! Whom three realms obey, dost sometimes counsel take and sometime tea.* The English poet, Pope; my old schoolmaster gave it to us as an example of anticlimax. It's typically English and typically wrong. There are no anticlimaxes in history and Pope was a homosexual, yet he was almost right about those of us with special duties; sometimes counsel we *give* and sometimes tea.' He handed a cup to Gabriel.

Hitler pointed to a ribbon on his own chest. 'I got mine on the Western Front. Yours?'

Gabriel knew Hitler was tying them together with the bonds of comradeship. 'I was awarded my Iron Cross on the Eastern Front, at Karelia.'

The Führer smiled. 'You would have known what it was, that drone in the ear, like a lazy bee – but…' he pushed the sugar bowl in Gabriel's direction, 'but if the assassin had been shooting at any of my bodyguard, my Old Hares, then the target would be dead, flat on his back with a hole in his forehead, his last thought: that's a bee with a punch.'

They both laughed, one of them politely, as the generators whirred and the clouds went by.

Gabriel had a sudden terrifying suspicion that he was being toyed with. That Hitler knew he was an assassin. That after the poppy cakes would come pain.

But the Führer continued without accusation. 'They're good men, my Old Hares, they've been with me since the beginning of my struggle, but they're sad in their way. Too young for the first show and now too valuable to serve in the front line in this one. They've not been there like we have, Gabriel, none of them.'

Gabriel nodded and nibbled his Mohnklosse.

Wolf, with a sigh, abandoned his. 'The truth is I spoil them – like Blondi.' The dog wagged her tail at the mention of her name. 'I sack my generals and spare my Old Hares and that's a mistake. They've got fat and slack. Kurt Gildisch – do you know where he was this morning while a sniper was attempting to end the life of his leader? He was unconscious, drunk, intoxicated at eleven in the morning.'

Gabriel put down his plate as Hitler continued.

'He's going. Gildisch is going, one of my oldest friends, been with me since the beginning, a founder member of the Leibstandarte, but he's going. I cannot tolerate this dereliction of duty. He let me down so he's out. But who is to replace him as officer commanding the bodyguard? The others aren't drunks but neither are they sharp and I need someone sharp, someone who has been there, someone who, if it became necessary, would put the life of the Führer before his own. Obersturmführer Zobel, I've read your service record, I know what you've done; in Spain and in Russia. It was me who ordered you to be treated in the military hospital here on Obersalzberg. I wanted to take a look at you. I wanted to see at close quarters this man who twice has put his body between his superior's and an enemy. Well young man, I liked what I saw and had you transferred to my close bodyguard. Even your name is appropriate; Gabriel, the angel charged by God to lead the angelic war host.'

The leader slowly rose and, across the table, Gabriel mirrored him. 'I want you to be the commanding officer of the Leibstandarte, with the rank of Hauptsturmführer.'

It was absurd, insane. Gabriel had told himself that he was on Obersalzberg to assassinate Hitler, not to protect him. The berserker in Gabriel wanted to laugh and tell the Führer the truth.

'It will be an honour, sir,' said Gabriel. He remembered what the sergeant in charge of ceremonial duties at the Vatican had said: *Some say Michael Angelo designed our uniform, some say it's older, I say it doesn't matter. What matters is how deep it goes. For some a uniform is a set of clothes you wear, but for us in the Guard it should go deeper. It should become our bones.* Gabriel had worn the uniforms of three nations and each had gone so deep it had almost suffocated him. While part of him celebrated the knowledge that the most elite soldiers had always been guards and he had just been appointed the duty of guarding the Führer, down at the bottom of the well was a man who was finished with uniforms, and this man was going to kill Adolf Hitler.

Heinz was showing in another man, a Luftwaffe major. Like Gabriel this man's holster was empty, his sidearm handed over before entry. No guns were allowed in the Führer's presence. Gabriel read the other man's blue-grey uniform; not a pilot – no wings, an artillery flash – so an anti-aircraft gunner, but a gunner wearing a cloth edelweiss on his cuff and a Silver Class Close Combat Clasp on his chest, signifying the major had taken part in thirty hand-to-hand battles. Gabriel's own Close Combat Clasp was gold.

From the doorway the major saluted Hitler and approached. As he came, he limped. Gabriel studied the major's uniform; the edelweiss, the sign of an elite Gebirgsjager, a mountain soldier, on the cuff of a gunner. Like Gabriel the man had been wounded and he too had been given a cushy number, transferred from a front-line unit to a support arm in a rear area; an anti-aircraft gunner somewhere that had never been bombed.

'Major Max Adler,' said the Führer, 'Hauptsturmführer Gabriel Zobel.'

Gabriel replaced his cap and responded to Max Adler's salute. They were of equal rank but Gabriel was SS and that gave him the seniority. Honours done, they waited. The Führer didn't invite them to sit and Gabriel knew that, for this meeting, he was no longer Wolf.

'Hauptsturmführer Zobel is a hero, Major Adler.'

The Major listened to the Führer's words impassively. Gabriel got the impression that he had met many heroes but had yet to be impressed.

'Not once but twice he has placed his body between a bullet and a superior. He has paid the blood price for his medals.'

This time Gabriel was rewarded by a slow glance from the major. It was a look that still reserved judgement. Hitler had no such reservation.

'This is the sort of man I want by my side.'

'Yes, sir,' said the major dutifully, but the Führer wasn't listening.

'Gentlemen, do you know who the most dangerous man in the world is?'

They decided they didn't and stayed silent.

'The man you trust.'

The Führer walked to the huge picture window. He stared out silently. Max and Gabriel stole a glance at each other and glided as smoothly as staff officers to stand by him.

'The mountains are full of legends and superstitions. One of them gives us the expression *turncoat*. It's an Alpine superstition. The story goes that on a dark night a lonely traveller in the high passes, finding his footsteps dogged by an evil spirit, took off his coat, turned it inside out and convinced the evil spirit his rightful victim was someone else. He reversed his luck by turning his coat. Certain elements in the Reich have decided that I am that evil spirit and that to save themselves they must turn their coats, as the Italians have done, as the Finns are about to and as the July plotters did.'

The Führer turned from the view and looked at the two junior officers.

'I thought I was safe here in my home mountains, surrounded by my friends and comrades, but I was wrong; there is a turncoat here. What to do? To open up the investigation would bring in outsiders and we would have tittle-tattle. The assassination attempt is not only attempted murder but bad for morale. It tells the folk that, even here, the Führer is not universally loved, that there is dissent, weakness, betrayal. That even one of those closest to me has decided it is time to turn his coat.'

They waited while Hitler gathered his thoughts. It was a pause the world knew well; as if he were conducting a deep trawl to places further inside him that shallower men could only imagine. He mined what he was looking for and brought it to the surface with a long exhalation from his nostrils.

'I need a detective. My people would like me to believe that the assassin is the missing French waiter. They'd like that, they'd like it to be him; French, different, not one of us. But I knew this man, he served me coffee and cake every day; he was as intelligent as a house brick. He might have been a traitor, but if so, he was the sort of traitor who obeyed orders; therefore even if he was the trigger man, the brains of the gang are still at large, still out there.'

Gabriel found his eyes drawn to the huge window as if the chief assassin might be floating by, ready to try again.

The Führer continued, 'The brain is someone I trust, one of us. He will be almost certainly a member of the SS, and a party member, so I don't need the service of the Gestapo, who will be inclined to trust their own comrades; I need the services of someone outside these organisations.'

'Someone who might even be antagonistic to the Party, sir,' said the Luftwaffe major.

The Führer studied him for signs of insubordination as he contemplated Major Adler's choice of words before continuing, 'And men of that description are few and far between in Obersalzberg. Only in the batteries of anti-aircraft guns do I find men who are not in the Party. So I look through their records and what do I find?'

The Führer turned his eyes on to Major Max Adler, flicked a switch in his head and made those blue eyes twinkle. 'Before joining the Gebirgsjager the major here was an inspector in the Bavarian State Police. So he is going to lead the enquiries, and you, Gabriel, as head of my Leibstandarte, are going to assist him.'

Breakfast was over.

The ex-Bavarian detective clumped along by Gabriel's side as they retraced the Führer's footsteps that morning. The limp didn't prevent Max from moving across at a mountain soldier's pace. The fast step of the Jaeger.

'Did you inspect the rifle?'

'Yes, Major.'

'What about if you call me Max? We're the same rank. I know you're SS but he put me in charge of the investigation – so honour is even I reckon. If we're going to work together, standing on ceremony isn't going to help. What do I call you; Scar, like the other Old Hares?'

Gabriel said, 'Gabriel.'

'I can manage that. How did you get the scar?'

'Gardening accident.'

Max came to a halt on the track and looked at Gabriel as he might have once given an uncooperative suspect the once-over. 'You're a real pin-up for the SS aren't you? Six foot?'

Gabriel decided to be exact and hold his ground with inches. 'Six foot one.'

Max mocked him with a nod of acknowledgement. 'Lean and mean, hair ash blond like a Swedish whore. Dye it yourself?'

Gabriel had been born with this colouring. The only anecdote that had come down to him about his mother had her saying, as she held her newborn son, that his head had touched the clouds. Shortly after, her soul had gone in the same direction.

Gabriel spoke. 'Do you want me under your feet? In spite of what he said, I'm SS and as such I'm here to watch you. Wouldn't it be best for me to knock the Old Hares into shape and let you do the detecting?'

Max turned his attention from Gabriel and plucked a tuft of grass from the hillside as Gabriel had done earlier, tossed it into the still air and watched it catch in the warm föhn wind from the south. He turned to inspect its source; the pass in the hills. He turned to Gabriel.

'The Old Hares, bit of a joke, eh? I know them better than you, Gabriel. I knew them back in the old days, before the world took a shit without a shovel. To get into the Mountain Jaeger you have to pass climbing and skiing tests. To be one of the original Leibstandarte you also had to pass a test. They had to display an aptitude for murder. There's not one of those jovial bastards who isn't a killer. There isn't one who hasn't shot, stabbed or strangled a personal enemy of the Führer. We knew them all back in Munich, and so does Hitler. Sharpening the guard might just mean training up an assassin. He doesn't trust them; the Führer doesn't trust them any more. They're survivors; they killed to get into the Leibstandarte, which kept them out of the front line. Now maybe, they're thinking, *How can I survive the war?* SS membership, a member of Hitler's close bodyguard, it doesn't look good. It's not the ticket it once was. So – they killed to get in; not such a big jump to kill to get out. Wolf is frightened one of them is starting to find the coat itchy.'

Max started to walk again, and Gabriel followed. 'I'm an Old Hare?'

Max shook his head. 'Not yet, sunshine. Not until you've killed a personal enemy of the Führer. Once we've identified the would-be assassin the Führer will want you to kill him. Then you'll be an Old Hare. Until then he wants you on the outside, working with me. Watching me.'

'And if you fail to unmask the traitor?'

Max gave him a happy smile. 'Then you'll be on hand to kill me; it's how he punishes failure. Either way you'll end up an Old Hare, good and proper.'

They continued uphill until they reached the place the rifle had been found, Max whistling, Gabriel silent.

Finding a natural break in the tune Max stopped and spoke. 'Tell me about the weapon.'

Gabriel made his report. 'A British Lee–Enfield number 4 with sniper modifications.'

'With Australian modifications; they were the sods who turned it into a sniper's weapon. Did you serve in the desert?'

Snow, not sand, had been the stuff to soak up Gabriel's blood. 'Eastern Front.'

Max tasted the air as if it were champagne and he was dying of thirst. Then he said, 'Got posted to the Sahara after Crete; bloody stupid place for mountain soldiers but you serve where you're sent. The best soldiers the Allies had in the desert were their Australian troops, the so-called Diggers. At Tobruk their snipers took out more of our officers and signallers than was feasible, bloody bastards.'

Gabriel nodded. 'We all hate snipers.'

Max bobbed as well, as they both considered their private experiences with the invisible men who had taken their friends suddenly, the sound of the shot lasting longer than the last breath of their comrade.

'Weird bastards,' said Max. 'You can put a soldier on a small arms course, but just because he becomes a marksman, that doesn't mean he'll have the cold hands of a sniper.'

Gabriel possessed those cold hands. He knew the target in the crosshairs couldn't become a real person with a wife or mother. A sniper needed the heart of a hunter. That was the heart he had inherited from his father.

His thoughts were broken when Max swore under his breath. 'Shit. So here we are at the sniper's den and of course it's been trampled to buggery by the Old Hares. How long have you been with the clowns?'

Not long, Gabriel thought, but it had seemed longer. Waiting for acceptance from men who didn't like strangers. Now he was their commanding officer and that wouldn't make things easier. They'd watch him, waiting for a mistake. They just might see something worse. The best opportunity is the first opportunity, and he'd failed to take it. Trying for a second shot while being watched would just about make the job impossible.

He snapped to; Max was waiting for an answer. 'A month. Discharged from Platterhof military hospital and ordered to stay on here. Thought they were serving me up some healthy mountain air.'

Max snorted. 'Convalescence and easy service for us cripples. Unfit for further active service?'

Gabriel knew he'd recovered from his wounds – he'd made

sure of it, running up mountains and swimming lengths in Albert Speer's swimming pool. 'I'm battle fit,' he said.

Max circled the site slowly, looking into the centre, then he reversed the journey looking out.

'Mmm,' he said.

'A clue?'

'Not a thing.' Max turned his stare to Gabriel again. 'So why you? Why would Wolf choose you?'

'Does he let you call him Wolf, as well?'

'No, he doesn't like cops, especially not the Bavarian kind, not after the failed putsch. He calls us police-apes. Mind you, we always called him the Gob.'

Max stared at Gabriel as if trying to divine how deep the blood oath to the Führer went under the field-grey Waffen-SS uniform. Then he swept his eyes over the peaks that circled them, the three mountains surrounding the Obersalzberg Plateau: Kehlstein to the east, north of them Untersberg and the mightiest of them to the south, Watzmann. 'Throne of the gods. So, Gabriel, once again, why you?'

The air was warm and carried the scent of mown meadow grass up from the valley. Clouds moved the floor in and out of shadow. The bottom lands where the fat farmers lived, Gabriel's dad had said. The man had sometimes been a shepherd, sometimes a hunter and sometimes a soldier. He knew how to do a lot of things in a way lesser men never could. He used to spit in contempt at the farms and villages below. He carved a living out of an unforgiving world. Gabriel had tried to learn all the skills of his father, those of the shepherd and the hunter and, in the fullness of time, those of the soldier. But he knew he had learned one military skill particularly well.

'They believe I take my duties as a bodyguard seriously.'

'Meaning? What's your crime sheet?'

Gabriel sighed inside and made his report. 'After national

service in the Swiss Army, I joined the Papal Guard at the Vatican.'

'I had you down as Swiss,' Max said as he might have said in his previous life, *I had you down as a petty thief.*

Gabriel ploughed on. 'As a Catholic I went from Rome to Spain fighting for General Franco. I was in the Condor Legion. Then, because I learned English at school, they moved me sideways to coordinate with the Brigada Irlandes, the Irish Republican brigade fighting for the fascists. One day outside Madrid, a bishop came to bless the Irish. I was escorting him when, out of the crowd of watching peasants, steps this old man with a shotgun.'

'And you took the shot?'

Gabriel nodded. He saw the old man's face, the hatred carving it like a church gargoyle. Gabriel knew what he was going to do and so did the Spanish bishop. The bleating prince of the church tried to use Gabriel's body as a shield. It ended with Gabriel nearest the gun and taking its hit in his shoulder. Then there was the sound of the Irishmen's rifles as they blasted the old man out of existence. Shot after shot, as if every man in the brigade wanted to be able to go home to the Emerald Isle and boast they'd killed their atheist.

'Most of the blast missed, but one part of my arm parted company from my shoulder. No permanent damage.'

Max looked out across the valley. 'And Russia?'

Gabriel moved in his head from the stifling heat of Spain to the paralysing cold of Russia. 'I was in the Nord Legion, fighting alongside the Finns, sometimes above the Arctic Circle, and I took a couple of rounds in the belly for my divisional commander.'

Max turned his eyes on Gabriel again. 'And the thing on your face you say happened gardening?'

Gabriel almost touched the scar that ran from under an eye

down to where it dissected his top lip. He said, 'I got hit in the face with a shovel.'

He had a flashback to the Ivan running towards him with a short-handled spade in his hands, already raised, already swinging. He had known these things were called Stalingrad shovels and he had a moment's indignation as the blade descended that they weren't in some rat-infested cellar in Stalingrad, but an open snow plain. Somewhere clean where men should fight with clean weapons. Then the razor-sharp blade of the spade had hit his face.

Max spoke, 'None of us gets a sword through the heart these days; it's a piece of flying metal here, or the flame from an exploding fuel tank over there. Industrialised death on a grand scale. Nothing personal, nothing poetic. What's that word our masters love? Total. Nuremberg was total theatre. Blitzkrieg was total war. Now we get total death; death in an instant, no last words or laments or even a body – just a heap of crisped ashes next to a piece of machinery that's exploded, brewed up. And the tin on your chest?'

It was a question that civilians asked when they wanted a war story in a bar. They knew no better but Max should. 'Got the Knight's Cross for saving my Gruppenführer's life in the land of ice, and a Spanish Military Medal for saving the bishop in the land of fire.'

Max moved closer and touched the medal Gabriel had deliberately ignored. 'And let's not forget this little bugger, a Close Combat Clasp in gold; top of the class, good boy. Shit knows what that feels like; the other gongs, well maybe you got lucky, had a good day or buggered your officer, but a Close Combat Clasp – you can't magic one of them up. In my part of the war it was the tin we all respected, and you've got one in gold. Over fifty horrible, nasty, gut-spilling hand-to-hand shindigs with an enemy you can smell. Shit knows what that feels like.'

Gabriel didn't enlighten him. Max watched him for a beat, nodded in the silence, gave him a smile as wide as an Autobahn and spoke.

'Two shots. The Leader heard two shots and he should know, he's been shot at often enough. He heard both rounds pass by close to his head. And that's confusing.'

'Why?'

'The first was an easy pot; plenty of time to get it right, a soft day – so how come he missed? The second shot was at a moving target and yet the sniper still managed to place a round inches from the target's head. He misses with a shot a geriatric from the Volkssturm could have pulled off and then nearly hits gold with a shot a Stalingrad sniper would win a cigar for. Confusing.'

It wasn't to Gabriel, but he played along. 'A lucky shot?'

Max turned to Gabriel.

'Gabriel…'

'Yes?'

'Why did you do it?'

The ice on the mountain tops reached down and squeezed Gabriel's heart. Max the ex-Bavarian cop stared him down, waiting for a confession.

CHAPTER FOUR

Captain Craze left the War Office in Whitehall with the other desk warriors and walked north, through Trafalgar Square into the West End. As he progressed, the crowd of uniforms and the bowler hat brigade thinned as they took their own routes to get home, but Jago didn't feel like going home to Pimlico. The knowledge that Pristine Christine, his wife, would be there made going to his club seem a better idea. He'd recently joined – Nicky's idea; he still wasn't sure it had been a wise move. It was the sort of establishment he usually avoided.

The day was still hot and dusty and he wished it would rain. He liked wet weather, liked walking through a London of drizzle as the streets and the air were washed. He wanted to dissolve his disappointment in a slow, steady soaking, but the sun thought otherwise.

Civil servants fanned themselves with their bowlers as they strode, older men by and large, and feeling the heat. Some of them displayed Great War ribbons on their chests to prove that once they'd done their bit. There seemed to be a collective guilt among all who were not in uniform, who had not served overseas and heard shots fired in anger. Everyone wanted to prove that in some way, some small way, they had made a difference and *done their bit.* Jago had even witnessed a clippie on a bus refuse to let a paratrooper buy a ticket. 'I'm not taking money from a para!' she'd said and men had called out 'Hear-hear!' and 'Bravo!' Jago, in his uniform and Intelligence Corps cap badge, felt a total fraud. He felt he could say with absolute certainty that so far, after five years of war, he had most definitely not done his bit.

Jago scanned the streets; since the V2 attacks that had started the previous month, the West End had emptied again. For a couple of years, the streets had been crammed with servicemen on leave, arm in arm with good time girls, but Soho had become a ghost town once more. He knew Londoners had accepted the first Blitz with fortitude and humour but this second one was causing a bitter resentment; the whole world knew that Germany had lost the war so why did they go on fighting? People were wearier, less cheery, dirtier – as if the brick dust in their clothes had entered their souls. They just wanted the whole thing over.

Jago passed a closed playhouse with padlocked doors. He loved plays and had read that only eight theatres in the West End were still open and they were each playing to a handful of audience. The vengeance weapons were killing the cultural life of the capital as well as its population, though given the sort of show Jago enjoyed, he wondered if *cultural* was quite the word to describe it.

His mother had loathed the theatre: 'People I don't know shouting things I don't want to know.' His real mentor had been his honorary Aunt Esme, his mother's friend. Esme loved literature and believed the theatre only justified its existence when it staged good writing. But Jago had a guilty low taste, adoring musicals and camp farces. He'd seen Lilian Braithwaite in *Arsenic and Old Lace* earlier in the year and still found himself chuckling over the two murderous old lady protagonists. There was something so neat and orderly in the elderly sisters' home that felt almost Germanic. He speculated that Nazi Germany was indeed this household, where Miss Hitler and Miss Himmler and murder were dressed up as respectability.

Possibly because the West End was so deserted as Jago entered the Charing Cross Road, he became aware he was being followed. Footsteps behind too in time to his own, and too close. An amateur. He checked the shop windows on the opposite side of the street and identified his tail. Jago sighed; he just wished to walk and clear his head, but now he needed to wake up and lose the seedy young man in a suit that was too big. Jago recognised him; a cockney lowlife with whom Jago had had a very brief encounter, and had now come back to haunt him. The man was obviously a leech. Jago was nearly at the Rockingham, his club, and he decided that after his drink there he'd slip out the back way.

The Rockingham wasn't some grand eighteenth-century gaming and dining house. Its undistinguished entrance was almost invisible; a simple doorway in a Victorian house that had been in its time both a brothel and a bistro and now looked faintly bohemian, with peeling paint and loose guttering. Jago ascended a short flight of stone steps, chequer-boarded with black-and-white quarry tiles, while before him the door swung open as if by magic.

The guardian who had granted entrance was a creature of pathos and flesh; Jago went in past Mildred, the towering club porter, and headed for the bar across the small dance floor. In the ballroom someone was playing 'I'll Be Seeing You' on a gramophone and, early as it was, there were half a dozen couples swaying in time through the dust motes, illuminated by the overhead skylight. Most of the dancers were in uniform, some in suits, all were men. On the edge of the music a dancer stepped out in front of Jago, his arms wide, the invitation clear.

'Fancy a jig, ducky?'

Jago swerved around him.

'No thank you.'

He heard the mocking laughter and comments following him.

'Hark at her!'

'All that beef going to waste.'

'Yes, and meat on the ration.'

Jago hated the campery, men dancing with men. He disliked all of it; the total acceptance they were inverts and then revelling in it without shame. He wondered again why he'd joined such a place but as he came into the bar, he saw the reason waiting for him. Nicky looked as gorgeous as ever in his naval uniform, with his brilliant blue eyes seeking out Jago in the gloom like twin searchlights. The light from the bar behind him turned his blond hair into a nimbus. Jago had never seen him first thing in the morning but he suspected that Nicky had a fair stubble that would shimmer in the early light. Jago reminded himself, Nicky was a temptation he had to fight.

'Jago, splendid news, they've got some gin in from god knows where.'

Jago, not much of a drinker, nonetheless grinned at Nicky's announcement. He seemed to take his first full breath of the day. This was Jago's home, he realised, wherever Nicky was. Then he stifled the thought; that couldn't be so, not in the long run, or even in the short term. 'Gin it is,' he said.

Nicky signed for the drinks, nudged a pink gin along the bar to Jago, while listening to his problem with the leech. Nicky knew all about Jago, as did Jago of Nicky. They'd shared their guilty secret – but that was all.

'So, who is he?' Nicky asked.

'Rough trade. God I hate giving in to it; why can't I be stronger? What could be more unpleasant than hanging around a gents' toilet looking for some temporary relief from a lowlife?'

Sometimes Jago thought Nicky's principal attraction was that he was a nicer person than Jago. As now: 'They're not lowlife, Jago, they're people.'

Jago knew Nicky was right and wondered why he played the snob when he felt shame and guilt. They sipped their drinks and pondered the problem, and as usual when Jago was faced with an imminent threat he prevaricated.

'It just isn't fair. I never asked to be a queer. Things might have been different if I'd had a proper father, or I'd been sent to a boys' school. I grew up surrounded by women and girls; by the time I went up to Oxford I was ruined. Sissified.'

Nicky tapped the bottom of his shot glass on the bar impatiently. 'Yes, you've said before, quite often.'

Nicky drained his glass and indicated to the barman, whose shirt was alarmingly unbuttoned, that he'd like it refilled.

Jago sipped his gin and said, 'I must just stay light on my toes till he latches on to some other mug to blackmail.'

Nicky cleared his throat. 'You don't know he wants money. Why not hear him out?'

Jago sighed. 'He's bound to be on the cadge. Just my luck, just my rotten run of fortune.'

Nicky reached and squeezed him across the shoulders, manly reassurance – and something more. He said, 'You do seem to be in the wars; wars personal, not the big one we're all stuck in. Nearly fried alive in your own rooms, and then that time you all but ended up under the Tube at Baker Street.'

Jago finished his gin. 'That was nothing. An accident.'

Nicky looked at him. 'Was it, old man? Can you be sure? You said you distinctly felt a hand in your back?'

Jago remembered; the awful, sudden, all-consuming shock and terror as he felt himself pushed off the platform. 'I know I was pushed, but I don't think it was deliberate. There was an awful crowd and I expect the owner of the hand was jostled and reached out instinctively and caught me one. After, he was probably too ashamed to come forward, especially in front of the Yanks.'

The wonderful American airmen, one of whom had seemingly plucked Jago out of the air and landed him back on the platform. They had been irreverent, loud, back-slappingly raucous. Their voices were a magic carpet ride of America; dialects from everywhere but, in that refreshing way of the New World, accents that told where the speaker came from, not what his father did for a living.

Nicky was speaking. 'You don't think your report has anything to do with these incidents?'

Jago shook his head. 'I've been accused of being arrogant today, but I'm not that deluded. I've put my theory out there, but I know it's probably the week for steam engines.'

The allusion foxed Nicky. 'What?'

'The steam engine was invented by three different men in three different places in the same week. The information was available to all and the inventors just joined up the dots. Same with my report. I don't doubt that other bods are coming to the same conclusion as me. Killing Jago Craze will not stop the hypothesis. It would serve no purpose. I won't be the only one to see things this way.'

Against his better judgement, Jago ordered another drink. He didn't want to go home half-cut. He needed to be sober in Pimlico while dealing with the problem of Christine. Even when he had a clear head, his wife had a way of making him say things he regretted as soon as they were out.

'And the said paper? Had your CO read it?'

'Binned.'

Nicky suddenly seemed as angry as Jago. 'The idiot! Your Major is a third-rate academic in a fifth-rate wig. I don't know why you bother, Jago.'

But Jago knew. 'You've been there Nick; the Spanish War, Norway, Crete, the Atlantic. Lord, you've even been torpedoed...'

'Overrated.' Said with a smile that almost sank Jago.

He blundered on, 'I've never been at the sharp end, Nicky. I've tried but it's no go, so I do every job that comes my way as conscientiously as I can, and this report is my way of trying to do a little bit more.'

'Above and beyond?'

'If you like. I just want it to be read by someone with more imagination and insight than the turd slicer.'

In the ballroom next door, someone put on a record of Billie Holiday singing 'Night and Day'. Nick sipped his gin.

'I'm very fond of you, Jago. You were the scruffiest queer at Oxford. It took me five days in an open lifeboat to get that look, but you've buffed up quite nice since. What say I get my admiral to look at it? After all, he is one of us.'

One of us. A queer. Another invert, thought Jago. 'Can you do that? Will he read it?'

'When he gets back. Currently he's on a tour of naval shore establishments in the East Midlands. Where are the East Midlands?'

Jago let his sense of defeat leave him. 'Will he be able to do something with it?'

'My admiral has sufficient scrambled egg on his sleeve to sit on various combined committees. If there's something in your concern he'll get it to the right chap. Old queers' network. What did Churchill say in 1940? Something about arranging any resistance to a Nazi occupation around the homosexual community, as we already were a secret society.' Nicky gave another smile that was a further assault on Jago's heart. 'Shame your place met a fiery end, you never did take me there.'

The word *take* lingered between them.

Jago broke the moment and raised his glass to sip, hoping it wasn't obvious to Nicky he was being shaken off. But Nicky was persistent. 'I could always visit you in your upstairs. You own the whole house, don't you?'

Jago almost snapped back, the suggestion was so shocking. 'Where Christine and Veronica might hear us?'

Nicky turned away from Jago and spoke to him via the mirror behind the bar. 'You're always welcome in my set.'

Nicky's set was his apartment in a mansion block off Piccadilly. Doing it in a bed, overnight, would be further into queerness than Jago had so far ventured. Nicky was dangerous, a temptation too far. Jago knew that one day he had to get himself straightened out. A love affair with another man would complicate that process.

Jago flashed the false smile of the coward. 'Let me think about it.'

Nicky finished his drink and the conversation seemed to be at an end.

Jago went and his fear went with him; Nicky was proving addictive. He left by the rear of the club. Mildred, an old NCO from the Coldstream who sported the ribbon of the Military Medal among his Great War haberdashery, checked to see if the coast was clear.

'No sign of the weasel, sir.'

Jago joined him in the doorway; the alley was empty and the dustbins were full. The early evening light seemed abashed and threatened by the shadows. It was a lurking Soho light.

'Good luck, sir,' said Mildred and closed the door behind Jago.

Jago came down the concrete steps and set off up the alley. The head appeared silently from behind a dustbin, like a marionette being pulled from above on a string. The seedy young man in the overlarge suit grinned at Jago. 'Watcha cock.'

Jago was suddenly filled by a rage fuelled by snobbery. He was superior to this lowlife and it seemed simply wrong that he should be persecuted by someone who was, as his mother would have put it, NOCD: *Not our class, darling*.

'Come on guv, I just want a word, can't we have a little chinwag? You won't shake me off, I'm – tenacious.'

His use of a word that didn't fit his mouth tipped Jago over the edge. He kicked the dustbin the leech was standing behind. It knocked him off balance and, as he staggered, Jago remembered the training in unarmed combat he had learned in the SOE – never fight unarmed, always improvise a weapon. He snatched off the dustbin lid and hit his tormentor with it. Like a discus, the rim caught the leech in the temple. Jago hit him again with the rim, in the middle of his face, and his nose exploded with blood. He made a noise of hurt surprise that a small boy bullied in the playground might. It sounded bewildered, as if Jago's attack had been unprovoked.

Jago stepped back, his rage leaving him as swiftly as it had arrived. This wasn't him; this violence wasn't him – he was an appeaser. He turned and walked away quickly up the alley. The man's words following him.

'What d'you wanna do that for?' And then quieter. 'Why couldn't he speak to you himself?'

It froze Jago as he marched away and turned him back, but the leech was retreating himself, back up the alley and around a corner into Soho. What had the seedy man meant? Who should speak to him?

CHAPTER FIVE

Jago had bought the house in Pimlico with his inheritance that came from the sale of his mother's school in Huntingdon. It was a late-Georgian stucco-fronted terrace, with a basement and three other floors above. It was London shabby and in need of some paint, but Jago liked it all the more for that. Battered and bombed London could take it, and so could his home.

The basement flat still sent up the scent of burning. He could see the remains of the front door hanging off twisted hinges. Instead of descending, he went up the three steps to the front door and, still feeling like an unwanted visitor, let himself in. He went straight through to the back, where a previous owner had knocked the small kitchen and back scullery into a large sit-down kitchen of the sort found in farmhouses. As such it had a rural feel, encouraged by his wife, who yearned to be a countrywoman. The shelves groaned like a blood bank under the weight of jars and jars of jam. Christine and the sisterhood had discovered foraging early in the war and now there was barely a fruiting tree or bush on common or heath they didn't know of and visit to strip of its bounty at the appropriate season. Of course, one couldn't forage the sugar, and Jago had no idea where that came from; black market, he suspected.

Christine was sitting at a long mahogany dining table that was surrounded by mismatched Windsor chairs. The table was scratched and stained and had been his mother's work base, the huge surface being the desk she'd run her school from; the coffee rings her halos. His wife sometimes talked of having it restored, of getting in a French polisher, a *little man*. To Jago it would have been like expunging his mother.

The Windsors had arrived with Christine; high backed, elm, with seats polished by generations of country bottoms. The table and chairs were a collision of taste, or a compromise, thought Jago, like their marriage.

Two women sat at this *compromise*, like a tribunal, with Jago the object of their judgement. His wife Christine sighed by way of greeting, while Veronica lit up her face in a brief smile of welcome. A Martian anthropologist, Jago speculated, coming across the women together, would assume from their respective appearances that they were from distinct species. Christine had the ability to suck the life out of her auburn hair. Her Titian locks became drab hangings attached, as they were, to the personality beneath. Podged out by stodge in girlhood, she wore her lumpiness like an extra cardigan. Her complexion was sun scorched rather than tanned, and, Jago knew, she had been born to weariness. Veronica, the other woman, was very different.

Jago had spent the ages of five to eighteen as the only boy at the girls' boarding school his mother owned and of which she was the bursar. There had been a pretence that he was a full member of the student body; he dined in one of the houses with the girls and played tennis in the summer, but of course he was an outsider. Sitting alone at a table one lunchtime Jago had witnessed Veronica's *divorce*. It had been a particularly nasty and female form of punishment at the school; when a girl upset her peer group they would wait for a meal and when the offender sat the others would instantly gather up their plates and leave the table for another one. The girl would know she was divorced and henceforth on the outside, not invited to treats, not spoken to, forever after – alone.

At this divorce the girls had risen like a silent flock of birds and brought their crockery to the table Jago sat at, it being sparsely populated with just him and the Jewish girls. Behind them, Veronica stewed in the horror of realisation: she had been divorced, a terrible penalty within the school, from which there was no coming back. From that time she would be excluded socially, not invited to tennis, unpassed to on the lacrosse field, without a partner in a crocodile. There was no remittance of sentence for good behaviour, indeed rumour had it that at an old girls' event a woman had approached some ladies she had been at school with only to see them turn and walk away, cutting her – she had forgotten she was divorced, they hadn't.

For reasons still unfathomable to Jago, he stood and left the settling girls and went and joined Veronica. 'Hello,' he said.

She looked up from her misery, saw him. 'Hello, Jago.'

So had begun their confederacy of the lonely. They had weathered those awful years together. Veronica become his closest and now oldest friend. She was also his wife's partner and was sitting next to blowsy Christine like a Cleopatra.

Jago had been with her when she transformed. They had left school after Highers and Jago was waiting to go up to Oxford, while Veronica was destined for a typing course in London, the last grudging gift from her guardian. In her new home, a bedsit in Paddington, she began the change to become a totally new creature. She started by plucking every last hair out of her eyebrows, swimming in tears from the pain, but ploughing on. Then Jago was sent away and told to come back later when she'd completed the metamorphosis.

He went to a news theatre and watched cartoons for an hour. When he returned, the old Veronica was gone forever. Her mousey hair now resembled black Chinese lacquer with a severe centre parting. Her face appeared to have had cream poured over it that had stuck. Her eyebrows were now two diagonal painted lines, while her lips looked like his mother had used her rubber stamp on them, the one dabbed in crimson ink before marking a document *urgent*.

'I'm never going to be invisible again,' said the animated chinois.

Now the Queen of the Nile sat next to the pudding. They had been studying a pamphlet on laying poultry. Christine's passion, Jago suspected. 'Evening Veronica.'

'Jago.' Smile. 'Tea?'

'Coffee?'

'I think we have some – no sugar though.'

No, his sugar had gone into the wretched jam, he thought bitterly.

Jago sat at the table and, as if on a counterweight, Christine rose; gathering up the chicken literature, she went upstairs. He heard her on the stairs; she was a clumpy little woman, he thought. 'What am I to do, Veronica?'

'She's frightened of the flying bombs.'

'Then she needs some fortitude.'

'She needs a home in the country. Her nerves aren't strong.'

'I won't stop her if she wants to go.'

The coffee arrived in front of him. Veronica spoke reasonably to him. 'Jago, you know – Christine has no resources, no money of her own.'

It was the old argument and Jago was tired of having it. He was tired of everything. He felt as bitter as the unsweetened coffee. 'I'm not selling this place, not for a wartime price. And even if I could sell it for a thousand pounds, I won't. I don't like the country.'

'Don't be selfish.'

'I hate being resented in my own home. I shouldn't have married.'

'Not one of my better ideas,' said Veronica, sitting down next to him with her coffee.

Jago, as he so often did, speculated on why he had allowed Veronica to persuade him to marry. It made no sense. He knew that when he could, he would sort himself out and become a proper man, one that wouldn't want a lesbian wife. Yet he had married Christine. He knew it was because of the terror, the accusation flung at him that he could deny with the proclamation he was a respectable married man. Fear, not love, had been the poison on Cupid's arrow.

They sipped in silence. Veronica was a clever woman and knew something else was bothering Jago besides the domestic arrangements. 'What progress on your report?'

'Nil. He hadn't read it and when I told him its contents he binned it. The thing is...'

'What? Drink your coffee while it's hot, Jago.'

He took a sip. 'I think it's important. I think it's so very important.'

Veronica's hand slid over his. 'Jago.'

He looked at her, smiled and said, 'I should have married you.'

She laughed and took her hand away. 'Darling, you'd have got the short straw if you had; I'm virulently anti-man, the very word Mrs is an acid in my mouth. Now what are you going to do with the report?'

Jago perked up. 'I'm using the old queers' network to get it onto someone important's desk.'

'Oh lord, Jago, you're going to get the sack again.'

'I don't really care. D'you know what I'm doing at Military Intelligence? I'm going through the files looking for Indians who might object to going back under the imperial yoke after the war, and that's just about every one of them. Millions of them and why not? There's a famine in Bengal that's probably killed between three or four million men, women and children. We could alleviate the suffering by delivering food, but this would take cargo ships away from the war effort, and so, because they're brown, we let them die. I don't know what the Nazis are doing to the Jews, but I do know what the British are doing to the Indians, and I want no part of it. Good grief, Veronica, I'm not fighting this war any more – I'm poisoning the peace.'

Veronica nodded and got up; he knew she'd stopped listening to him, silencing him in her head so as not to listen to one of his rants. He shut up and she went to the jams and ran her finger down the line of them, almost as if she expected this action would create a long, slow note of music. No one ever ate the jam; sometimes a jar went to a child's birthday party, but that was all. They were too important to be eaten; they were a symbol of frugality, of Christine doing her bit. Jago knew why she gloried in the war; it allowed her to be the shabby hoarder she so desperately wanted to be, to wear old clothes and never have to dress up and go to a dance. The parsimonious behaviour, considered eccentric in peacetime, was transformed by war into a fanfare of duty and patriotism. But it wasn't the war, he thought, it was Christine and all the people like her who found the idea of enjoying themselves an ordeal too far. There had been dozens of girls like that at his mother's school, girls who coped well with academic excellence and rigorous marking, yet who would be discovered in a heap of tears at the thought of having to go to a party.

Veronica abandoned the jams and came back to the table.

'Jago...'

'Yes?'

'Is there any chance the German generals, the Wehrmacht, might be receiving aid and encouragement from this end?'

'What d'you mean?'

'People sending out peace feelers and perhaps even joining in on the plot to kill Hitler.'

Veronica had Jago's total attention. 'What makes you say that?'

'I don't know – something at work, something at the House. Ever since that book came out in 1940, *Guilty Men*, and everyone turned against the appeasers, well the so-called guilty men have kept a very low profile in the Palace of Westminster.'

Jago looked at her. 'And now they're not?'

'The last five years they've been going around like depressed ghosts, now suddenly their heads are up. But I don't understand why. The appeasers always wanted to make a deal with Hitler; why do you think they now want him dead?'

'Think about it,' said Jago. 'The appeasers wanted peace and Hitler stabbed them in the back. They won't trust him twice. Without him they believe there's a real chance of stopping this war.'

Veronica took an abandoned mug to the sink. 'Isn't that a good thing?'

Jago knew what she meant; the promise of peace was seductive. But it was a hollow promise. 'Hostilities won't cease just because Hitler's dead.'

'The appeasers think they will.'

'The appeasers are a group, Veronica. Groups spread. Within the ranks of the appeasers are true pacifists, like the Quakers, who are against all wars. Then there are the liberals who believe enough is enough. They'll settle for an armistice. The total defeat and occupation of Germany has too high a blood price, in their thinking. Finally, there are those who are not against war, in fact they rather approve of it. They just don't like this war. They think we're fighting on the wrong side. The far right would like to fight alongside the Nazis against the Soviet Union. To get that war they'd sacrifice Adolf Hitler.'

'So the question is, where do the appeasers at Westminster sit on your spectrum?'

'Precisely.'

Veronica eased her bottom onto the table and sat there swinging her legs. Jago knew his mother would be appalled.

'All I know,' she said, 'is they're going around as happy as Larry.'

'Any idea why?'

'Oh yes. I suppose it's two and two. If I hadn't read your report, if I didn't work for the appeaser in chief... well, I wouldn't know what four was.'

'And four is?'

'My boss, the Viscount, received an invitation marked personal and, after reading it, let something slip in front of me; it's very easy to do. Anyway, he rang the person who'd invited him to the function, and said something...'

'What?'

'He asked the bishop – it was George Bell, the Bishop of Chichester – what it was about. The bishop said something and my Viscount nearly exploded with excitement. *Really*, he said, *is that true, George? One of the Old Hares is prepared to do the dirty?*'

Jago was surprised to discover he'd been holding his breath – now he let it escape, slowly. 'He said the Old Hares?'

'I wouldn't have known what it meant if I hadn't read in your report that Hitler is vulnerable to assassination as his close protection is entrusted to a dissolute band of Nazi Party fanatics known as the Old Hares. That's right, isn't it?'

'Veronica, is it possible to get me that invitation, the one your boss read before ringing the bishop back?'

Veronica replied as if Jago had made an immoral suggestion that she was only half prepared to comply with. Her very red lips pursed. 'I can get you into the House; getting into his desk will be up to you.'

Jago had trapped himself. He heard his own inner whine that he wanted to do his bit, and now he had a chance to turn intention into action. But was he that man he wondered, or did he just write reports for others to act on?

'How will you get me in?' he heard a voice say and was surprised to recognise it as his own.

CHAPTER SIX

The pub was old, and there was history of course, but history in Westminster is something a wise building doesn't boast of. It did have one tiny unique feature; all public houses had a bell but the Two Chairmen had a second, a bell that rang to warn those of its patrons who were also Honourable Members that their presence was needed in the House. Next to the pub an alley ran straight to Parliament Square. It was known that even a fat and farty MP could manage the dash in time to vote in a division. During dull debates the Two Chairmen became known as *the third chamber*, as it swiftly filled with Commoners and Lords escaping the tedium. But in September the House was still in summer recess and consequently the bar was half empty.

Veronica sat with a man who was wearing a Scottish Rifles tie and a distinctive eyepatch. As agreed, she was ignoring Jago. Her handbag was at her feet, also as arranged. Her companion had been on a Dunkirk beach when a German bomb had exploded next to him. The shrapnel, in the mysterious way of explosion and blast, had missed him, but the sand hadn't. Around his missing eye his face had the texture of an Aertex vest.

'Douglas is harmless,' Veronica had said of him. 'Doesn't try his luck as he thinks his disfigurement puts him out of the running with the ladies. As a man, he's almost human; just wants, as my guardian would have said, the rustle of silk petticoats.'

This confused Jago. 'What?'

Veronica shook her head. 'It means the proximity of a woman, the waft of her scent, someone who doesn't smell of trench foot. He's Clem Attlee's speech writer and personal secretary. Douglas does his work conscientiously and feels a cad that he's not still with his regiment. It won't be him, will it? Dougie won't be your victim, will he?'

The smoke in the bar spiralled up in the lazy, post-work atmosphere of the bar. Jago had been able to assure Veronica that Douglas Strachan, late of the Cameroonians, the Scottish Rifles, would not be his target. Not because Veronica had described him as a *baa lamb*, but because of his eyepatch and disfigurement; Douglas was just too memorable. Jago remembered his SOE training; his mark had to be anonymous, therefore no one who was disfigured, or even too tall, or fat, or ginger haired, or famous; just a faceless pawn in Britain's war effort.

A man in a pin-striped suit, with trousers held up by braces, put down his half pint of mild and made his way to the gents'. Veronica picked up her handbag from the floor and started to root in it. Jago now knew the man was an employee of the Palace of Westminster, so he followed him into the lavatory. The man was standing at the urinal so Jago aborted the mission and stood next to him and passed water. Jago followed him back into the bar. Veronica's bag was back on the floor.

There was one more false alarm at the urinals, and another where Jago didn't even follow the would-be mark into the gents' due to an absence of braces, but then the handbag was picked up again as a man with a face like a soft-boiled egg, and necessary braces, had Jago on his feet again. Jago prayed this one was a goer; he couldn't keep following men into the gents' without arousing the suspicion of the landlord that Jago was a queer looking for a cottage.

As he entered, Jago heard the bolt on the cubicle door being shot across. Jago took up his place at the urinal but didn't unbutton. His heart was starting to race. It was now or never; he needed to crack on before another customer entered to use the facilities. He heard the small discharge of gas and echoing splash and Jago turned and acted. He moved quickly and reached over the door. He grabbed the neck of the jacket hanging there. He knew it would be there thanks to the braces. Wearing braces, the mark had to take his jacket off to drop his trousers. What fun they'd had practising this at Beaulieu. Jago hefted the jacket clear of the top of the door and out of the cubicle.

'What the bloody hell...!' came from inside the smallest room, but Jago already had his hand in the jacket's top inside pocket and was lifting the wallet. He dropped the jacket and left the gents' as he heard the frantic sounds of redressing. Moving quickly, but not in a panicked way that would have drawn attention to him, he crossed the small bar and was outside. He now accelerated and threw himself onto Pristine Christine's bike, which he'd borrowed without permission, almost a bigger crime than stealing another man's wallet. He began pedalling furiously and in a few turns he was lost in a maze of small Westminster streets with names like Old Pye Street and Perkin's Rents. Ten minutes later he was back home in Pimlico. An hour later Veronica joined him.

'Poor chap's Adam's apple was going up and down like a lift on elastic,' she said.

'Did he make a fuss?' Jago said.

Jago was strangely anxious for the victim.

'That was the extraordinary thing. Having gone outside and ascertained you were nowhere in sight, he went back to his drink and didn't say a dicky bird to anyone.'

'The embarrassment of being caught with his trousers down.'

Veronica winced. 'Too pictorial, Jago. Now, did he have one?'

Jago produced the Palace of Westminster pass.

'Splendid,' cooed Veronica. 'Was that all he had in his wallet?'

Jago showed her the pound notes. 'Two pounds,' he said. He felt wretched about the stolen money. 'I suppose I can donate it to charity?'

'Nonsense.' Veronica reached out and took the notes, folded them and put them into her purse. 'My fee.'

Jago was shocked but not surprised. Like his wife, Veronica had convinced herself that she was hard done by. That life had dealt her a low blow by not creating her rich, and rich in Veronica's estimation was a wide category that included anyone who had something Veronica hadn't. Jago sometimes came home to find the whole house a blaze of lights and no one in. It was their way of telling him he could afford it.

They made their way to the Palace of Westminster along the north embankment of the Thames. Behind them were white stucco Georgian houses, twins of Jago's abode. They stood like more white cliffs looking out across the water at the foreign country that was south London, working-class London with its factories and cranes and derricks and tugs and lighters. The vast Battersea Power Station seemed like a battleship moored in the midst of the city. Its four huge chimneys reached into the sky defiantly, like the battle standards of the men and women who poured into it to work impossible shifts and who weren't awarded medals. Behind the factories were the countless streets of tiny soot-stained terraced houses where these people lived. Posh north bank, poor south bank; a tale of one city, Jago thought.

A fairy tale appeared before them; the mock-Gothic extravaganza of the Houses of Parliament doing its best to ape the abbey. It was on the north bank, of course.

Veronica and Jago separated at St Stephen's Porch, with Veronica going in first just ahead of him. Jago was to follow her to her boss's office. It had been agreed between them they should not appear to be together. Because of the war, security was concentrated at one point, so both Members and staff entered at St Stephen's Gate. The guard barely glanced at the pass Jago held steadily in his direction. He didn't do anything that would have upset his old SOE trainers, such as hold his thumb over the name. The guard accepted the pass, and the suit, and the right sort of haircut, and looked at the name through a glaze of indifference. It was why it had been important not to steal the pass of someone memorable, something to jerk the face into focus. Jago was nodded through.

St Stephen's Hall was a corridor of murals of significant moments in British history, fronted by a twin honour-guard of statues that lurked like dangerous butlers in a horror farce. As the hall led inexorably to the flamboyant entrance to the Central Lobby, Jago's heart began to pound uncomfortably in time with Veronica's clacking heels, beating out a tattoo on the tiles underfoot.

Jago entered the Central Lobby, which had that sense of pique all great and momentous spaces have when they are ignored on a daily basis. It was emptier than Jago had hoped; he wanted crowds of bustling politicians surrounded by hordes of circling party bees. Instead the summer recess had decimated the Palace; as in the rest of the country there was the usual selection of uniforms blending with the suits, but far too few.

A sprinkling of the Sergeant at Arms' security men in their ceremonial rig of frock coats and tights were there to frighten the SS if they invaded the Mother of Parliaments, plus of course an overweight policeman whose neck was bigger than his head.

Most of the pedestrian traffic turned right towards the Upper House, because left, to the Commons, was out of bounds, with builders' scaffolding across the entrance of the Commons corridor. The Lower House had been bombed out of existence three years previously and now awaited the outbreak of peace to be rebuilt. Jago kept six paces behind Veronica and followed her. But then disaster.

'Ah, Miss Rawling, just the person. I assumed the Viscount would be in the House, but apparently he's off somewhere hush-hush, and I must have a brief word with him on the telephone – pretty pronto, actually. I have a scrambler line if you could come and dial a number he can be reached at.'

Without a backward glance Veronica was gone with the patrician and Jago was left without a guide, with the maze of Parliament before him. He came to a halt and felt the panic start to brew in his heart. The very design in the mosaic of the stone floor alarmed him, resembling as it did the Star of David, as seen on so many poor Jews, as they were tormented on the streets of Berlin in pre-war newsreels.

Jago knew he should keep moving, he knew he should be striding out with a purpose as if he belonged, not hovering stationary, lurking even, as guilty as sin. He tried to move his feet, to blend in, but he was frozen in a funk. His father would have breezed across the Central Lobby, the way he breezed into clubs he wasn't a member of, but Jago was a conformist; hopeless at team sports but someone who nonetheless played by the rules. And now he was going to get caught. He even met the eye of one of the Sergeant at Arms' men who was standing by the small post office in Central Hall. The man looked at Jago with a helpful, questioning face. When he looked again there was more suspicion and he started to walk in Jago's direction.

The stolen pass felt like a siren going off in Jago's inside pocket.

He was going to get caught, he thought hopelessly. Yet again Jago Craze was turning out to be pathetic. A coward. How did the military put it? A lack of moral fortitude.

CHAPTER SEVEN

As briskly as she'd gone, Veronica came back from her errand, cutting across Jago like a yacht stealing another boat's wind. Jago set off behind her, leaving the guardian in tights in their wake. Jago followed Veronica as she moved with a brisk efficiency that swayed her skirt from side to side. It was a skirt that, in spite of wartime austerity, had weight and style. From somewhere within it came the sound of silk stockings. She had a way of getting things like that, Jago knew. As befitted her Cleopatra mask, she had an authority over some men. Men who bought her presents as sacrificial offerings to a goddess, even if they half suspected she batted for the girls' first eleven. So, heads turned as she passed, which was good, Jago thought. Veronica's bottom and seamed stockings soaked up all the passing curiosity. It had been a Frenchman of course, a resistance leader, who'd advised the SOE trainees that if they wished to be invisible to walk behind a beautiful woman.

They left the Central Chamber and made their way smartly to the Lower Waiting Hall, where Veronica turned right and climbed a staircase to the next floor. Ahead of them stretched a long corridor with doors on either side. It was panelled in undecorated wood that, after the Pugin extravaganzas below,

Jago found soothing. They passed no one and, shortly, Veronica took a left down another, shorter, corridor. Soon Jago felt lost in meandering wood tunnels with doors that could have led to Alice's Wonderland for all he knew. Veronica swept into an office and left the door open behind her. Jago walked in behind her.

'It's up to you now,' she said and promptly left, closing the door behind her.

'Up to me,' thought Jago. Was he up to it, he wondered? But he was there now and, the sooner he started, the sooner he could get away to a nice cup of tea at home.

The owner of the office, the Viscount, was away on war work. Of course, like everything in a government at war, it was graded *secret*. Secrecy, Jago had learned early in the conflict, was a form of currency. The more a man's documents were decorated with red TS stickers – *top secret* – the richer he was in prestige. Real secrets were few and far between. The office was a large single room without windows. The oils on the wall were of various creatures in various glens, all suggesting the occupier of this den was a masculine hunter-gatherer. It housed two desks and numerous filing cabinets, all in woods that had responded well to polishing. Jago went to the largest desk, which sat like a toad in the middle of the room.

Veronica had seen the Viscount lock the note in the top right-hand drawer of his desk before she'd been banished. Jago knew there was no guarantee it would still be there but he needed to look, before searching the rest of the office if it wasn't. This was the bit Jago hated; the shaking hands when he needed them to be steady, his ears pounding with the sound of his rushing blood when he needed to listen for sounds in the corridor. Fighting the desire to take deep breaths, *the quickest way to hyperventilate*, he'd been told in training. Instead he went into a fantasy that this was his own desk in his own home, that he'd lost the key to and needed to open. All very innocent and no cause for panic and it worked: the hand that produced his set of picks from his pocket had ceased trembling. The picks he'd held on to when dismissed from SOE.

Jago inspected the lock and chose one of the thinner picks. Picking locks was something he'd excelled in at Beaulieu. Possibly he'd artist's hands, as had his father. He remembered a beefy, ruddy-faced ex-rugby international, who, working with picks against the clock to open a locked door, had suddenly lost patience and kicked it down. He'd been returned to his unit, Number 8 [Guards] Commando.

A satisfying click told Jago he'd done it. The drawer sighed for him as he slid it open. There, on top of pencils and green treasury tags was the invitation card. Jago took it out, quickly read the brief contents and knew he had what he wanted. The Viscount hadn't transferred the invitation to a safe, obviously believing the best security was openness. An innocent card in a drawer becomes an object of suspicion when discovered locked away. Conspirators have to be plausible if they wish to stand on the same steps as Caesar.

Jago pulled a notebook from his coat pocket and began jotting down a copy of the document. He put the completed copy and pad into the file he'd carried as disguise. The original went back into the desk and Jago locked the drawer with his pick. He turned to stand and leave as the door to the office swung open and the man with the face like a soft-boiled egg, the man whose pass Jago had stolen, stood there.

Touché, thought Jago. Now he had been caught with his trousers down.

'What are you doing?' the man demanded, but didn't wait for an answer. 'I knew it was you when I saw that hand come over the door. I recognised your hand; I'd seen you at the bar and I noticed then you had fine fingers.'

Jago knew the man was jabbering because he was scared. 'I don't know what you're talking about,' Jago said.

'Yes you do. I came straight here to report the theft of my pass, and I saw you crossing the Central Lobby, as bold as brass. So I followed you.'

Jago responded softly so as not to spook him. 'Right.' Jago slowly got to his feet. He knew he'd need to use another lesson he'd learned at Beaulieu, a skill that the commando had been rather good at. The man in the doorway read his intention and turned and ran, but this time he did make a fuss.

'Stranger! Stranger in the House! Security!'

Jago followed him out into the corridor and walked away up it in the opposite direction. He fought the temptation to run and so draw attention to himself. He walked briskly; a man going about his lawful business. His face a calm and thoughtful mask covering the bush fire of panic inside, unable to think, to reason, to plot his escape. He tried to remember his training and, incongruously, could only remember the flavour of the tea they served in urns, which always tasted metallic. He thought about that taste, concentrated on it, and slowly his fear left him as he became preoccupied with the memory of tea.

In control once more, he stopped blindly striding down passages and tried to engage with his sense of direction. Captain Clark on survival exercises had taught him to be aware of it. Not at the front of his mind, but further back, was a voice that read out the compass points to him at each change of direction. He played Nobby Clark's voice back and discovered he was going away from the river and that he needed to go towards the Thames to find the very long corridor that led to the stairs. An ever-present sense of direction was one of the more useful skills he had learned at the *Finishing School.* Even on a moonless night or in a London pea-souper he could relocate any geographical feature he'd passed and find his way back to it. He knew now which direction to take to find his way back to the stairs and freedom. Of course getting out was another problem, as would be evading the various search parties out looking for him. He needed to change his appearance.

Jago dodged into an empty office and pulled off his coat. He hung it on a peg behind the door. He retrieved his notebook from the file, stuffed it into his trouser pocket and placed the empty file into the back of a crammed filing cabinet. He forced himself to leave the false comfort of the office and, out in the open, made his way towards the long corridor. He heard the noise of excited voices and even 'tally-ho!' coming from various corridors ahead. A puzzled-looking face peered out at him from an office.

'What's going on?'

'Armed intruder,' said Jago. 'He's already shot Black Rod. Go back inside and barricade yourself in.'

'Good grief!' The door slammed.

Jago broke into a run and sprinted towards the sound of his own hue and cry. He prayed the man who had caused the hue and cry was being passed up the chain of command, making his report to every Napoleon with a chevron. Jago ran around a corner and saw a party of half a dozen younger members of the House, some in uniforms, piling towards him in a pack.

'Quick!' he yelled. 'He's in my office. Follow me!'

They did. Jago pointed out the room he'd told the nervous man to barricade himself inside and, unnoticed, slipped away, as the hearties went berserk trying to kick their way in. He continued to run when he got to the long corridor, and from there found the stairs and got back to the ground floor. He moved through the palace at a smart pace, across the Central Lobby, down St Stephen's Hall and carried on until he found the Porch guarded by one of the Sergeant at Arms' men in tail-coat and tights. Jago knew he had to pull rank quickly, to assert his class and crush any opposition. He yelled at him as he ran up.

'Have you been told there's an intruder?'

'Yes, sir…' began the porch keeper.

'Has anyone told the constables?'

Two police officers traditionally stood outside at the New Palace Yard gates.

'I don't know, sir.'

'Typical,' Jago said. 'Don't work up a sweat will you? You might ladder your stockings.'

Leaving the doorkeeper to stew in his own resentment, Jago raced outside and, instead of bothering the constables, ran home to Pimlico.

'Rotten luck the little pansy being an amateur poet.' Veronica sipped her tea and filled Jago in on events at the House after his departure. 'He was quite brazen, telling all and sundry that he'd spotted the tapering fingers and alabaster sheen of your hands, and had decided to add their description to a poem he was composing about hands in a public house.'

'There is an arrogance in surveillance that leads one to believe that one can watch the world unobserved. One should always be alert to the possibility that someone is returning the favour.'

'Bravo Jago for remembering the lesson, but detention for not remembering it sooner. He even saw the way you stared at me.'

'I was just watching for your handbag signal.'

'Anyway, when he came to the Palace and saw you following me across the Central Lobby, he assumed the theft of his wallet and pass was an elaborate ruse of yours to follow me and leap on me in a lonely office. Malcolm thought you wanted your wicked way with me.'

Jago was appalled. 'He thought I was going to rape you?'

'He's a poet.'

Jago let this pass. 'Did he see you take me into the Viscount's office?'

'No, he'd lost sight of us down a corridor, so he started checking offices and opening doors.'

'And found me on my knees at the desk.'

Veronica tutted at Jago's recklessness. 'Anyway, the good thing is he maintains he prevented you from tampering with it. He's quite the hero. Did you get a peek?'

'Yes.'

'And?'

Jago wondered how far to involve Veronica. 'Do you really want to know?'

'You're right, I don't. I've done my bit. You left the place in uproar; they're used to perverts in the House but a possible enemy agent trying to tamper with a government minister's desk is quite major. Black Rod has sent for the Box.'

The Box, MI5, was being called in. Jago realised it had been a shambles. Instead of invisibly visiting the desk and obtaining a quiet look at a note contained therein, he couldn't have been more noticeable if he'd arrived on a fire engine ringing its bell. Worse, he'd alerted the Viscount to the possibility that someone this side of the Channel knew what he and his other appeasers were up to.

Veronica finished her tea and put down her cup. 'What a swine you were putting the dragoons on to poor Toby Sweet.'

'Who?'

'The schmuck you got to barricade himself in his office.'

Jago had a sudden flashback image of a startled Piglet face peering round a door. 'Good lord, I'd forgotten about him.'

'The heavy brigade burst in and roughed him up – broke two of his ribs. That's the problem with having Honourable Members in uniform; if their regiment is on home duty they hang around the Palace as if it's their club, even in a recess. A bit of gin and excitement and they revert to the bullies they were at school. Captain Tubby Cooke, the Honourable Member for a hunting shire, stamped all over Toby, cheered on by the others.'

Veronica glanced at the wall clock and abruptly changed the subject, 'Where's Christine, she should be home by now?'

Jago had seen her in the hall as he entered, passing like the couple in a weather house. 'She fled upstairs as soon as I came in,' he said.

Veronica sighed. 'I'll go to her. These new Vengeance rockets have just about finished her nerves.'

'None of us likes them, obviously.'

This got a glare from the black-lined eyes under the punkah-fan lashes. 'Jago,' Veronica spoke sharply, 'You know it's not the same for Chris. She lost her parents to an air raid. She lost her family home. She's a penniless orphan and very, very frightened, so don't pretend it's the same for you as it is for her.'

Veronica looked at him, her face suddenly hard as if the make-up had frozen instantly in the harsh late afternoon light. Her features were pointed and sharp, more like a predatory rodent than a goddess, Jago thought. At the corner of her eyes there was the suspicion of crow's feet.

We're getting old, he thought. When the war started we were children.

'I went out on a limb for you today, Jago. I risked my job and I need that job, I need *my* wages.'

The old story, the old resentment. 'D'you mean I don't?'

'I mean you should perhaps be a little generous to those around you, to your wife. What's so wrong about the country? You lived there as a child. Air that doesn't smell of bomb damage and brick dust. A sky that isn't home to rockets that just suddenly drop and simply evaporate you as if one has never existed. Stop being so bloody selfish.'

Veronica stood up sharply, strode to the door and went through it. A second later she was back. The face that peeped around it might have belonged to another woman; the weasel was gone and Veronica was back. She looked at Jago softly.

'Sorry.'

He smiled back through the dust motes. 'Thanks for today.'

She nodded and was gone. Jago settled down in the kitchen with the copy of the Viscount's note before him amongst the halos on his mother's table.

THE IZAAK WALTON SOCIETY
10th Sep 19.00 Post evensong in the Lady Chapel.
Chairman: Chichester.
[Attendance by invitation only.]

It wasn't in code; instead it was open and therefore deniable. There was a resistance group in the French Alps that circulated details of their meetings under the cover of a botany society that had been in existence since 1850.

Jago mused as to what the Izaak Walton Society was. Stamp collecting? A group dedicated to listening to classical gramophone records? It rang a bell and then Jago remembered; Izaak Walton had written some biographies in the seventeenth century that he had read, but then he remembered that Izaak was celebrated more as a fisherman and had written *The Compleat*

Angler. The Guilty Men were meeting under the cover of a fishing club; the chairman, Chichester, was obviously George Bell, the Bishop of Chichester, infamous for his views in support of appeasement and someone who'd never got behind the war effort. The Lady Chapel would be in his cathedral where the society would meet at nineteen hundred hours tomorrow, Jago thought. There they'd hear news from their German friends and their asset in the Old Hares.

On the Chichester train Jago struggled to find a seat, even in First Class. The train left twenty minutes late. It was overcrowded and uncomfortable and Jago quite failed to notice he was being followed.

CHAPTER EIGHT

Chichester Cathedral was smaller than the cathedrals of Jago's youth: Ely, Lincoln and Peterborough. It was a pocket cathedral, seemingly without room for its bell, which stood in its own tower to the north-west side of the cathedral. Inside, quiet soldiers drifted as slow and as silently as dust motes, in and out of the shafts of light from the great doors that were left open to aid the candles in giving light to the dark, sombre interior. The windows were sandbagged and boarded up and quite blind. The wartime tourists wore flashes on their uniforms that informed the world that the wearers were from places such as Poland, Canada or the USA – rather than Arundel and Bognor. Jago thought the uniforms suited the sombre thousand-year-old air of the Cathedral Church of the Holy Trinity.

Jago quietly located the vestry. Just as in his school and college chapels, the room was equipped with an enormous timber cupboard for the choir to hang their cassocks. He intended to use this facility later but for now Jago moved on.

As always in a religious space, be it the parish C of E church his mother had attended, or the Quaker meeting house of Aunt Esme, Jago had a sense that the thick, complacent silence was about to be broken suddenly and loudly by something enormous; that God would roar. It made him nervous.

Security in the cathedral seemed to depend on faith rather than locks and Jago knew he was about to abuse that faith. He approached a door in the south transept bearing a notice: *NO ADMITTANCE TO THE GENERAL PUBLIC. AIRCRAFT SPOTTERS ONLY*. Did they still try to spot enemy aircraft now they'd disappeared from the skies over southern England? Jago wondered. He tried the door and, as he expected, it wasn't locked. He glanced back at the few lady volunteers in faded frocks and utility turbans, flitting from visitor to visitor, ostensibly to answer questions but really to say thank you, thank you to these boys from overseas who had come to save this tired old nation of cathedral builders. Thank you, with polite whispered explanations of Doric columns. No one was watching Jago. He went through the door.

A twist of stone steps curled before Jago, like the set of an exciting American film purporting to be the true history of Robin Hood. He climbed the steps and left them at the first opportunity. He went through a heavy wooden door, acned with studs, and his world widened again as he entered the upper aisle that looked down on to the choir and presbytery. Keeping as far from this view as possible and hugging the shadows of the south wall, he continued to the end, where he looked down on the altar. Another door led Jago into the narrow passage above the Lady Chapel. The Lady Chapel where the Guilty Men would receive news from Germany, news of their asset in the Old Hares.

Jago checked his watch; it was 16.30, three hours until the meeting. He knew that afterwards he might well find himself locked in for the night, until the tourists returned the next day and he could mingle and slip away with them. He slid down onto the floor and waited. The ritual of the institution carried on beneath him; at the appropriate time, evensong was celebrated, and afterwards Jago felt the cathedral start to empty, the ladies gently ejecting the last of the visitors. None of them would remember a British Army officer who'd arrived late afternoon, spoken to no one and who'd quickly merged into the shadows and silence of the ancient church. Jago heard the great door being closed in a last solemn slam, followed by the juddering clunk and clicks of a monstrous lock being turned. Jago was alone.

There were times of the day when Jago was prone to anxiety, such as waking up when the night incubus still had control of his brain and poisoned it with morning paranoia. Another enemy was the late afternoon, when work started to dwindle and an empty evening stretched ahead. He was at the mercy of any time when he found himself alone and when he counted the tally of his life and discovered he was a failure. The worst were those times when he discovered he was alone in a crowd, pretending to be a member but knowing he was an outsider. Yet this depression was currently almost an anaesthetic, as the blues stopped the sharper emotion of terror from grabbing his being. He was spying on some of the most important men in the land; their power was immense, and if he were discovered he was in the right place to be crucified. So he contained himself and calmed himself in a mild, familiar melancholy.

A key turned, a door opened – not the massive fanfare from the great doors creaking and grumbling their age, but a secret and more private invasion from a more modest side door. There was the odd subdued scuffle, the odd mumble from below, as men stealthily entered the cathedral. They lit candles as they progressed like a masculine coven in suits and uniforms. They appeared in the Lady Chapel. Deep in the shadows, Jago watched them; his melancholy fled, replaced by curiosity.

There were a dozen or so men. Jago recognised some of

them; the Viscount of course, Bishop Bell by his cassock, others from newsreels and pictures in the press. Most though were strangers to him. He knew they were probably eminent men in public life; politicians, civil servants, general officers, the good and the great. Yet, he thought, he didn't know their faces and how strange that was when he knew the faces of the leaders of Nazi Germany so well. The British Empire was led by anonymous men in well-cut suits.

'Are we all known to each other?'

The bishop standing in front of his subversive flock addressed them in the true and tested formula where no register of written names could be kept. It was a security that rested on fellowship and belonging and where the stranger had no place. The men did indeed all know one another. They probably had done since prep school.

Jago stared down at Bishop Bell, a man Aunt Esme had considered to be a saint. *The most significant Christian in the land.* An opponent of Churchill with his policy of carpet bombing and total war with Germany. Jago saw that the two antagonists resembled each other. George Bell was no vicar from a stage farce. He had weight and gravitas. Amongst the mighty below, he still dominated with voice and personality.

'I'll open this meeting with significant news. I've received a letter from a fellow pastor of the late Bonhoeffer's Confessing Church of Germany. Pastor Bonhoeffer, as you all know, was a decent German who shared our values, before he was executed by the Nazis. The pastor who wrote this letter, a certain Grunwald – forgive me if I remind you not to bandy his name around…' Grunts of assent were given. 'Tells me he was left desolate by the failure of the July Plot, and was resigned to the rape of Germany. Which means of course, not just the eradication of evil but the destruction also of all those institutions and values we share with him.'

The men nodded their agreement.

'Hear, hear,' said a man in a spotted bow tie. 'We can't sanction the destruction of Europe to save a few Jews.'

There were some tuts of disagreement at this Jago was pleased to note.

'Horace, please,' said the bishop.

'Well really, George,' said Horace to Bishop Bell, 'have you ever met a Jew you liked?'

'Yes, he's hanging on the cross in front of you. Anyway, if we stop the war now that would mean more Jews saved.'

Horace wasn't encouraged by this. 'I expect they'll all come and clutter up the civil service. One can't move for them at the moment.'

The Viscount spoke impatiently, 'Horace, do you mind if we press on?'

'Be my guest,' the man in the bow tie mumbled back.

The bishop reclaimed the meeting. 'Let us remember, we toil together to save those parts of German life that we ourselves hold dear.'

A colonel amongst them agreed. 'What's the point of this war if we can't save civilisation? That means the true Germany of Prussia and discipline. I've always admired the Germans far more than the French, for whom the benchmark of civilisation seems to be over-rich cooking sauces.'

This caused a small murmur of laughter that drifted up to Jago through the dense, incense-laden air.

'I couldn't agree more, Colonel,' said the Viscount, 'but this we all know. So what has happened to reignite the pastor's hopes?'

The bishop nodded silently. All, including Jago in the heavens, leaned in closer to hear George Bell's words. 'An SS officer on leave sought out the pastor in Munich. The pastor was wary, and why not – the man confessed to being a loyal tool of the Nazis, a member of the Leibstandarte, Herr Hitler's close and personal bodyguard. These men are known colloquially as The Old Hares. They are Hitler's closest guard. This man shared his fears, he could see that the war was lost. He was consumed with worry for his mother and sisters; what would happen to them when the Soviets arrived.'

Above, like God on a cloud, Jago felt his conscience cross-examined. He was the man striving to extend the war.

'What was this… Old Hare proposing?' asked the Viscount.

'He said that in his privileged and trusted role close to the Führer, he would be able to do successfully what the generals had failed to do in July. He could assassinate Hitler. However, he wanted assurances that the generals would do the rest: round up the remainder of the Nazi gang and make peace with the West. Our pastor has his contacts. He knows there are many on the German General Staff who, relieved of their oath to serve the Führer unto death, would immediately send out peace feelers to us. They would be prepared to quit all occupied lands, including Poland. They would release and repatriate all Western POWs. Further, they would make reparations to all members of the Hebrew faith who have a legitimate claim against the German state. All they wish in return is to be allowed to condense their forces into a defence against the red menace of Stalin.'

The generals were not men of peace, Jago believed. Replacing their Robespierre with a Napoleon, they would rebuild their factories and laboratories. Go on to develop their super-weapons, then obliterate their enemies in turn; Russia, Britain, the USA – the war relaunched with a rocket. Jago saw the men below turn to the Viscount to gauge his response. He kept them waiting while he considered the bishop's words.

'Winston would never agree to it and he may be right – he was right before. In 1940 he was right and we were wrong.

He had the mark of Herr Hitler and we and Mr Chamberlain didn't. Since then I've devoted my energies to fighting this war. I accepted an invitation to join this group with reluctance and considered hesitation.'

'I'm sure we're all grateful that you did.'

'Thank you, Bishop. Well, Winnie was right in 1940 but this is 1944 and times change. Without Hitler and his evil gang, it would be a sin of the highest order to march on. To smash innocent Germany back into the Stone Age. For what end? An unconditional surrender?'

Nays and noes rumbled out.

'At the conclusion of my war,' said the colonel, 'we marched proud on our victory parades with the wit that our war had been won and concluded with an armistice. We didn't need to rub the other chap's face in it, we respected him too much.'

The Viscount spoke as if sharing his spontaneous thoughts, but Jago suspected he'd been preparing for this moment since the invitation had arrived on his desk.

'Winston isn't popular in the party. Remember, the Conservatives hold the majority of seats in the Commons,' said the Viscount. 'He's still a hit with the public but they're war weary. The opportunity for peace now with a limited victory would unite both the party and the public. With Hitler dead and the German generals' reasonable proposals on the table, the tide would flow in our direction.'

A man Jago thought he recognised spoke for the first time.

'What's your reading of the Yanks?'

The Viscount answered him. 'No different from ourselves really, Clive. Perhaps a little less war weary, but many of our cousins remember it was the Japanese that attacked them at Pearl Harbor. They wonder why, therefore, their leaders insist on a Germany-first war.'

The man called Clive spoke, and Jago's memory supplied his identity; Clive Roberts, deputy controller of MI6.

'That's what my chaps have been picking up. Plus, I consulted one of my men who served in Tokyo in the 1930s. He assured me that in Japan the perceived enemy to the Chrysanthemum Throne in this century is Russia. They've been to war in 1905 and 1939, with honours even. It's no secret the Nipponese government has been putting out peace feelers of its own via neutral diplomatic missions. Not to mention the Black Dragon Society, its secret service. Believe me gentlemen, it is not beyond the bounds of possibility that, with the model of Germany before him, the Japanese Emperor Hirohito might arrange a coup. Dismiss his war leader General Tojo; make the same offer to the Western Allies – the retreat from all occupied lands in return for the sanctity of its home islands and monarchy.'

Peace in the East, the empire saved. Jago could feel their silent enthusiasm rising up to him.

'Won't they still be empire hungry?'

'Possibly Colonel, but who of us here really cares if they turn their attention north? Does it matter to the West if Siberia flies the Soviet red flag or the Nipponese rising sun? Let the hounds of Germany and Japan tear at the Russian bear from either end. We would be well out of it.'

The colonel agreed. 'And then we can get back to some proper soldiering; policing the empire and riding to hounds.'

'Peace,' said Bishop Bell, declaiming it like a war cry. 'Our people have earned it. Sudden and surprising peace, as unexpected as Noah's rainbow. We must prepare, gentlemen, we must make sure our side is ready to respond positively when the deed is done.'

Peace. The word resounded in Jago; he had very nearly been a pacifist like Aunt Esme the Quaker. He had certainly been an appeaser. He wished he could join them below but, as always, he was the outsider. He saw what they cherished as a false dawn.

'We must seize the moment,' the Viscount agreed. 'Winston will try one of his ponderous speeches, announcing that the chief bully is dead but the toil continues until we have weeded the bed – but he must be shouted down by the Commons. We must have a new leader in waiting. There must be a vote of no confidence called and we must control the whips. Simultaneously our people in the press must thunder headlines: *Peace Now* and *Bring our Boys Home*.'

'I can get the bells rung throughout the land!'

'Good for you, Bishop. Churchill and his cronies will be yesterday's men. We all know what that feels like. Does Pastor Grunwald give any indication when it will happen?'

The bishop shook his head. 'Post has to make its way to these shores from Germany by a most circumlocutory route. It comes via friends in neutral countries who readdress and send on the letter. Time has passed since it was penned – so we must expect a result at any time.'

'Then we must be ready. We must mobilise,' said the Viscount.

Then Jago heard a name said from down below. Clive Roberts of the Secret Intelligence Service MI6 was speaking. 'Jago Craze. Captain Jago Craze of the Victoria Rifles currently assigned to Military Intelligence…'

Jago listened to his own name entering the debate below him. He felt as if the shadows hiding him were being banished by a searchlight, that he was trapped in a powerful beam of light. That soon he would be shot down.

'He's a busybody. He's done a report that fortuitously fell into the hands of a friend of ours. This Captain Craze is trying to get his document read by all and sundry. In it he argues that anything less than an unconditional surrender will leave Germany a militarised state, able to regenerate itself. Then, armed with new super-weapons, will attack us a year or two down the line. He wants no opportunity for the German generals to make a separate peace with the West. To that end, he argues that Adolf Hitler must be preserved until the bitter end.'

The appeasers growled their disapproval and Jago had to swallow the urge to apologise.

'Is he listened to, Clive?'

'He's a nobody George, but it might be an idea to nip him in the bud.'

'Can't he be returned to his regiment for active service?'

'No, Colonel, Craze has plenty of brain but no backbone apparently. He was with SOE but funked it. His papers are marked *Lack of moral fibre*. His regiment won't want him back.'

'Leave it to me,' said the colonel. 'I'll use my influence to find the biggest administrative hole in the British Army. I'll have this Captain Craze dropped into it. He'll be out of Whitehall into a tedious job in a dull part of the war effort. There let him rot.'

Jago raised his eyes from the men below, considering what he'd just heard. The anger and shame he felt anew at the SOE incident. As he did so, some tiny movement from directly opposite him on the gallery on the far side of the Lady Chapel caught his eye. He saw a face watching him. He looked again and she was gone.

CHAPTER NINE

Jago tried to stop breathing, although he knew this to be absurd. Neither the men below nor the mystery woman opposite would hear him, even if his fear caused him to gasp. He scanned the far side of the cathedral for her, but there were only shadows looking back. Jago dropped down. He curled into a corner and shut his eyes, as if to make himself invisible. Was she a watcher for the appeasers, he wondered? But why then hadn't she raised the alarm?

An immediate exit was required. Jago knew he had to put as much distance between himself and the opposition; the larger the area of search, the thinner their resources to scour it. But there was no escape from the cathedral: he was locked in. The windows were sandbagged or boarded up. There was just one way out, and that door was locked. He considered trying to infiltrate the men when they eventually left, joining them quietly at the back, but he knew it would never work. They were all known to each other. One glance from any of them and he'd be exposed.

It occurred to Jago, as he huddled on the ground, that if the woman wasn't with the appeasers, she too was faced with the same problem: how to get out? As a woman, Jago hoped, she'd be even more scared than he was at that moment. Wouldn't she be feverishly working out how to avoid him now Jago had spotted her? Who was she? Possibly a reporter, spying. Had she thought Jago was a fellow journalist chasing the same scoop?

Jago knew he had to move. He couldn't wait in the last place the woman had seen him. He consoled himself she was only a woman, while he was a man who had been trained in hand-to-hand combat on the commando course at Arisaig. He decided to stick to his original plan. He had a place in mind to spend the night. Next day he would join the other early morning worshippers for matins. Afterwards he would leave with them.

'Gentlemen, thank you for coming.' The Viscount was winding up the meeting. 'The bishop will let you out; leave quietly. Horace, will you lock the door after them? George, I'll drop the key back off with you. Perhaps Colonel, you would delay your departure by a few minutes? Clive and I have something we need to discuss with you.'

Above, Jago heard the meeting dissolving. He knew that he too should be leaving or at least changing his lair.

'We'll just hang on for Horace to return. Thank you for waiting,' said the Viscount.

'Not at all,' said the Colonel, 'I seem to have done nothing but wait since the Japanese invaded Burma. Thought I was doomed to sit out the war in Siam. Good to have something to do again in the old country.'

The Viscount glanced at his watch. 'Yes, tempus fugit – well, perhaps I can make a start. Ah, here's Horace back with our new chum.'

Horace returned with another man. Clive introduced him to the group. 'This is the Inspector. He's of my world but not exclusively. In fact, he's a very useful chap who fulfils a number of vital jobs for government. Those tasks that need to be done but can't appear on paper anywhere.'

Glances were cast at the silent figure. Jago tried to make out his face but he stood deep in shadow.

'We'll get to the Inspector's role shortly,' said the Viscount, 'but first of all you need a proper briefing, Colonel. Things we couldn't share with our queasier colleagues.'

Horace snorted. 'Bunch of Hebrew-loving pacifists. Someone should string that bishop up.'

'All in good time, Horace,' said the Viscount. 'Now, Clive, perhaps you can explain. After all, espionage is more your world.'

'I suppose it is. Well, here goes. Jerry isn't a fool. He'll know that we have a dedicated unit tasked with killing Hitler. The codename for this department is Foxley and it comes under the remit of SOE. Now the Old Hare who wants to save himself by bumping off his Führer has a price. He's one of life's survivors. He wants to be around for some time to come after he's pulled the trigger. He's also aware that his worth to the generals dies with Hitler.'

'So, what does he want from us?' said the Colonel.

'What he imparted to the pastor was that he wished to make contact with our Operation Foxley. To receive aid and succour from them. He assumes Foxley is more effective than it is in reality. That it has assets in Bavaria if not on Obersalzberg itself. He wants SOE to help him with an exit strategy that would see him removed promptly from the scene of the crime. Soon after delivered safely to these shores.'

'And will SOE cooperate?' asked the colonel, 'This Foxley Operation?'

'The problem, Colonel, is Foxley. No one has ever taken Operation Foxley seriously. Not the fault of the chaps in it but events generally. To have killed Hitler while he was still a demigod would have unleashed the wrath of the SS on our POWs. By the time Hitler became a liability, all the talent had left Foxley for more active departments. I very much doubt they have an agent on Hitler's own personal estate, Obersalzberg. It would take time and time is something we don't have. We can't wait until Ivan is at the Brandenburg Gate.'

'What's to be done?' said the Colonel.

'Foxley is part of SOE and SOE is one of Churchill's wild-arsed outfits. I'm sure you realise the true objective of a subversive force behind enemy lines is information – not blowing up the odd telegraph pole. I can't tell you how many genuine intelligence operations have been compromised by these mufti cowboys.'

'Intelligence as in 6?' said Horace.

'Of course, MI6. The Intelligence Service's activities are buried deeper and are sown over years rather than weeks. Churchill wants results yesterday; he's not interested that we can tell him what might happen next year. You are all aware that the previous chief of MI6, Sinclair, was a friend of Germany first and Soviet Russia last. Sinclair filled 6 with like-minded men.'

'Ah, blessed Quex of fond memory,' said the Viscount.

'And because we tried from the pre-war period to make contact with conservative Germans, we landed a big fish. We in 6 have something we cherish. This really is top secret, gentlemen. We have an asset up that mountain, an asset into whose ears the Führer drips gold. If it were for anything less than ending the war with a single bullet, we wouldn't dream of compromising this asset. It goes against the grain to curtail a superb clandestine operation to turn it into a swash-and-buckle B feature.'

Jago felt himself pulled to his feet by the desire to discover this asset's name. He didn't care if the woman opposite was watching him. This was a big secret and he needed to hear it.

'I think under the circumstances, Clive, such a re-tasking would be justified,' said the Viscount.

'Very well, the codename for our operation in Hitler's lair is the Three Graces. I'm sure you don't expect me to supply the names of our people.'

His audience muttered their *no, of course not.* All, including Jago, wished the deputy director of MI6 could have been a little less discreet.

Clive Roberts was speaking again. 'This stays an Intelligence Service operation and won't be given to Foxley. I don't want the Baker Street Commandos anywhere near it. I will run it from my desk and report to this sub-committee. We will aid the Old Hare using the Three Graces. We will get him away when he has completed his task. The German generals can then clean out the Augean Stables of the Nazis.'

The Viscount spoke. 'That of course will be the dangerous moment. Not the peace Bishop Bell craves, but to swap horses mid-race. Gentlemen, there will be no sitting on the fence in this conflict, no middle ground. Peace will not break out with the death of Hitler. We have two choices: help Soviet Russia to annihilate German civilisation, or help German civilisation triumph over Bolshevist Russia.'

'And the bishop's peace?' asked the Colonel.

The Viscount shrugged. 'Fool's gold. We are either for or against Germany – that's how their generals see it. If we step aside and don't join in their crusade, then that wretched Captain Craze is correct; when they have the weaponry, they will finish us.'

'You see?' Horace echoed to the Colonel, who nodded, but asked a question. 'And if we let things roll out as Churchill wishes?'

The Viscount rolled his eyes. 'You're the soldier. You know that in less than a year in all probability Allied troops will come face to face with Soviet forces over the ashes of Germany. Do you imagine, Colonel, the Russian steamroller will apply its brakes? Of course not. They will carry straight on until they are situated just across the channel from Dover. We all remember what 1940 felt like.'

The Colonel did and nodded his agreement. 'You're right, our only chance is to throw in our lot with the German generals.'

'We'll play the bishop's game,' the Viscount said. 'Kill Hitler, get the peace crowd out on to the streets. George can ring his bells. We can topple Churchill in the House. With our man at the helm he will, like Chamberlain, guarantee the sovereignty of Poland. No one can complain about that.'

Horace burst into life. 'Hear, hear. After all, it's why we got into this shindig in the first place.'

The Viscount took back the baton. 'When the Soviets fail to vacate Poland, the new PM will regretfully announce that a state of war exists between His Majesty's Government and Uncle Joe.'

The man from the Intelligence Service broke his silence. 'Then for the first time since 1939 we can fight on the correct side. But for things to pan out as we hope, we are going to need your help, Colonel. We would indeed like you to dump Captain Craze in a backwater, but he's more problematic than that. The fact is he's in possession of something that doesn't belong to him.'

'Oh?'

In his head Jago echoed the colonel's question, *Oh?*

'I suppose it's Jerry's mind. Give the British General Staff the weekend off and they'll go hunting. Do the same for the Prussians and they play war games. They got together and came up with the Walpurgisnacht Plan. Now, unfortunately, Captain Craze has a copy of it.'

Jago vehemently denied this accusation in his head.

'What is this plan?' the Colonel asked.

'It's the template and timetable for events after Hitler's demise and it has two eventualities. One, that the British are with them in their crusade against Ivan, and it plots our order of battle into the German lines. Two, we've played the pacifist card and are neutral. This latter supposition is the damaging section, because in it they speculate which of our cities to demonstrate their atomic bomb on, prior to our surrender. They debate the merits of obliterating Windsor or Croydon.'

'Croydon please,' said Horace.

The Colonel asked his question, 'Not London?'

'No, absolutely not. They want to keep things simple, clinical. They don't want anarchy. No headless chickens running amok, please. Just a big hole in the ground to concentrate our thinking.'

'And they put all this down?'

'Yes Colonel, it's all in the Walpurgisnacht Plan. Not a problem if the document had stayed in a filing cabinet in Berlin. But a clerk, who happened to be a Red fifth columnist, copied it down and sent it to this country. Probably by the same circumlocutory route that Pastor Grunwald sent his letter to Bishop Bell. I have it on good authority from my sources over the Rhine that it was hand delivered to Captain Craze.'

Jago wanted to deny this at the top of his voice, shouting down at them from above.

'What I don't understand,' said the Colonel, 'is if this document validates Craze's hypothesis – why hasn't he gone public with it?'

Clive shook his head. 'Not that simple, Colonel. Captain Craze is a nobody. If he popped up waving a German plan he couldn't account for, he'd be charged with fraternising with the enemy. End up at the Tower in a cell next to Herr Hess. He needs a big gun to broadcast it and so far into the game he's isolated and alone. We've searched his home and office to no avail. Two attempts have been made to deal with the problem permanently, but he's had the devil's own luck. That's why we want you to have him posted somewhere remote. With luck, he'll take the Walpurgisnacht Plan with him and we can find it in his scant possessions. Failing that, we'll dump Captain Craze into a more permanent hole than his posting.'

'Promoted to glory.'

'If you like, Horace. Anyway, the problem my agency has is that we're all brains and not enough muscle. I've had to enlist the help of an outsider who is rather good at the wet work.'

He beckoned the figure in the shadows, who dutifully stepped forward. 'This is Billy Grogan. He's an inspector with the Metropolitan Police, but as I said, he works for the more interesting government agencies.'

The man stepped into a circle of light from a candle and shook hands slowly with the other conspirators.

The Viscount was summing up. 'I admire the German leader. But if we want to preserve his values, we must say goodbye to him. You might almost say that, by killing him, we are saving Hitler.'

They were in agreement. The meeting was over. They were on the move, snuffing candles out as they left. As a deep velvet blackness surrounded him, Jago prepared to make his way to the hiding place he'd chosen. He knew now that it was more important than ever to get through this night and take what he'd heard to the War Party, people he'd despised before 1940. He stared into the black space opposite; there was no sign of the woman. The door closed from somewhere in the cathedral.

The conspirators were gone. Jago made his move and shuffled, like a blind man, through the black soot of the church.

It was as dark as a cave. There was no light, no seepage from the stars creeping in through cracks in the blackout. Jago knew that even if he waited a year, his eyes wouldn't get used to this darkness. He shuffled along as quietly as he could. He guided himself with one hand on the wall as he set out to make a blind man's journey back to the tower. There he would face the nightmare journey down the spiral stairs, disorientated in the blackness.

Once on the ground floor, he was going to retrace his steps to the vestry, to the huge cupboard. With an armful of cassocks on the floor to make his bed, Jago would spend the night there. Inside the cupboard, with the door closed, there was little chance of the woman stumbling over him. Even if she did come looking for him.

Snail slow, Jago made his way along the galleries. He kept his breathing even and his nerves under control. In a strange way the utter blackness was comforting, like a large blanket he was hiding under. Suddenly that blanket was ripped aside. The cathedral was turned into a microcosm of the world outside. A powerful torch beam erupted from the floor of the nave, like a searchlight seeking enemy bombers. It swept in Jago's direction. He dropped below the balcony as a separate beam cut horizontally across from the opposite gallery. Both beams crept over the wall above and behind Jago as he crouched on the floor. His heart went wild.

'He's up there somewhere,' said a man's voice from below.

'He saw me, so he knows we're here.' The woman's voice followed her torch beam in Jago's direction. 'Come on, Captain Craze, show yourself, you're not getting away.'

The beams tracked back and forth, while below them, on his stomach, Jago inched towards the tower door. His heart was thumping. He was angry with himself. He'd stayed too long listening to the last important details of the meeting. He'd been told: *Once you're compromised get out. Whatever the temptation to stay, don't. Run.* Jago hadn't run. He'd made the assumption he was just facing a lone woman. He'd been wrong.

'Where are you, Austen?' the woman said.

'At the bottom of the tower in case he manages to get down.'

'He's not moving; he's gone to earth across there.'

'You're right, Lavender,' said Austen. 'I'll get up there and winkle him out.'

Jago was frozen with indecision. The odds were two to one, and his exit was cut off. If he hid, they'd find him with their torches. He couldn't go down to where the one called Austen was coming up. There was only one option, a rotten one. He too had to go up. Ascent was the worst direction when being hunted, this Jago knew. It was the false security of the tree – until the hounds are under it, howling. Guns being pointed up. Nowhere else to run. Yet even as Jago stretched his muscles and prepared to sprint, an idea came to him. Not much of an idea, but he remembered the sign on the tower door: AIRCRAFT SPOTTERS ONLY. The idea terrified him, but at least it was an idea.

Jago stood and sprinted for the door, running through the beams like a blinded Lancaster trying to find invisibility and safety in the clouds.

'He's going for the tower!'

Austen's voice followed him as Jago raced up the stairs for the roof and the aircraft-spotting station. From below, light bounced off the walls; Austen was coming up the stairs. Jago reached the top of the spiral. He threw the little narrow door open, grateful that it wasn't locked. The medieval masons who'd built the church had been sparing with the wicked expense of locks.

Once outside, with the stars dangling like a camouflage net above him, Jago slammed the door. He looked around desperately for something to barricade it. A couple of deckchairs were folded under an overhang of ragged stone. They were there for the spotter team to sit back in and observe the sky above for bandits. Jago grabbed one and smashed it against the wall again and again. The wood splintered. Still attached to this shaft was a rag of the striped cloth that drooped like the flag of a defeated army. He pulled it out of the way to reveal the now jagged end of wood. He rammed this point under the door like a wedge and kicked it home.

Now he searched the walls. He found what he had hoped would be there; the forlorn hope. The rope ladder that was to provide an escape route for the spotting team if all about them went to flame and fury in an air raid with all other exits destroyed. He'd seen them in operation on the newsreels at the cinema. Silhouette men, swinging precariously and slowly, step by step making their descent, backlit by raging fires. Sometimes they made it.

Jago threw the surprisingly heavy rope over the crenellations and heard it slap and flap against the cathedral walls. The upper end was secured by bolts. Behind, someone hit the wedged door and yelled.

'He's put something in the way!'

The more Austen shoved, the deeper the point went under the door and the firmer it held it shut. Seconds are vital, Jago had been taught. The wrecked deckchair had bought him the time to gingerly climb over the wall and onto the ladder. The swaying ladder was trickier than the single rope lines he had scrambled down on training courses at various quarries. He kept his weight central and got a rhythm going. From above he heard the door taking a battering, but below him was a wonderful silence. His arms ached. The cathedral was tall, but not as tall as the cliffs he'd clambered down. He was going to hit the ground running.

The circle of light that caught him had a perfect circumference on the unbroken wall. He dangled helplessly, like a convict caught escaping down a bed sheet.

'Only a few more rungs, Captain Craze,' said Lavender, 'and please don't try anything funny when you're down. Listen to this...'

Jago heard the distinctive click of a firing hammer being pulled back.

'It's a Webley, British Army issue. Heavy as sin but it makes a hole an elephant could fall in. When your feet touch the ground, keep going. Lie down and stretch out face down, there's a good boy.'

Jago heard someone else arrive and assumed it was Austen, but when he spoke Jago realised his mistake.

'For god's sake Lavender, you don't need the Webley. Put it away.'

Then there was a pause and Jago's head swam with confusion and hurt.

'Evening, Jago old man,' said the voice.

Jago swallowed. 'Nicky?'

CHAPTER TEN

Jago glanced up from the ground at Nicky. He wasn't wearing the uniform of an officer with the King's commission in the Royal Navy; instead he looked more like the volunteer he'd been in Spain. He was in voluminous trousers and up top he was sporting a grubby white roll-necked jumper that looked like it had belonged to a submariner.

'What's going on, Nicky? Is it a joke?'

'Wish it were, old man; let's wait for Austen.'

Jago looked at the girl called Lavender. Her lips were as red as sin, while her hair was free and fair. She flicked it; Jago, raised amongst girls, knew this was a sign of vanity. 'You should cover it up,' he said.

'What?'

'You should cover up your hair on ops, it reflects the light. It gave you away in the cathedral.'

Nicky spoke, 'Lavender doesn't need any advice; she's done tours on the other side.'

Operations on the other side of the channel. Something Jago had never managed. He shut up and condemned again his delusion that he was the stuff of agents. Half a dozen half-arsed courses in living off the land and eating rat had not removed his inappropriateness.

The man called Austen arrived. 'Got him then,' he said.

Twisting his head up, Jago realised he knew this man too, but not as Austen. It was the leech he'd hit with the dustbin lid. 'What is this? What's he doing here? Is it blackmail?'

'I should coco,' said Austen.

Lavender seemed to take offence at Jago's words and snapped at him. 'Stand up Captain Craze – you look like a drunk lying there.'

Jago stood. 'Are you one of them, Nicky? A collaborator? Or do you play on MI6's team; a secret agent under the cover of a Royal Navy gentleman?'

'All in good time. Did you stow away the ladder, Austen?'

'All shipshape, skipper.'

'Alright Lavender,' said Nicky, tossing her some keys, 'fetch the Daimler, will you? It's at the front of this God-shed.'

He turned to Jago as Lavender beetled off. 'Austen and I motored down together, Lavender came on the train with you.'

'I didn't see her.'

'You weren't meant to.'

Another confirmation of his amateur status. 'Where are you taking me?'

Jago saw the attempt at reassurance in Nicky's smile. 'Nowhere exotic, just back to the Smoke. I'm afraid you're going to waste your return ticket.'

The levity failed to amuse Jago. 'What's this about?'

For the first time in this bizarre incident, Nicky seemed to be serious.

'Someone wants a quiet word with you. It's important you listen.'

'Then your approach might have been a little less dramatic.'

Nicky smiling again, a lazy grin. 'We tried, old man; turns out you can get rather violent. Ask Austen.'

'Too right.' Austen's face floated into view, the nose and cheekbone still purple with bruises.

Jago looked at the young man in the baggy, double-breasted suit. 'Do you normally try to start a conversation by offering your body in a gent's toilet?'

The bonhomie left Austen and something hurt and harder took its place behind his eyes. 'That's how you see me, don't you? Some bit of shit on the fiddle, not a someone. Not a someone who might have thoughts and ideas just as clever as you. You might have more shrapnel to clink in your pocket and folding stuff in your wallet but that don't make you a better man than me, Captain Craze. It takes two to make an immoral congress, two. Or does your willy let itself out and go cottaging on its own? Maybe I'm as moral as you, Captain. Maybe I've got principles too.'

'Maybe Austen has more *principles* than you, Jago,' said Nicky.

Austen poked Jago with a finger. 'You look at me and all you see is a tuppenny-ha'penny bum-boy, and so when you see me again you reckon I've got to be on the cadge. But maybe I'm involved in great works, a great struggle, but you don't give me a chance to explain, you hit me with a dustbin lid. A bloody dustbin lid.'

They stood there, not speaking, as the sound of a car drew closer. Nicky broke their stand-off. 'Here she is, good girl.'

Lavender wound down the window and leaned out. 'All aboard.'

Nicky took command. 'In the back, Jago. Austen up front, please.'

Nicky climbed in beside Jago. 'Off we go, Lavender.'

They drove off into the night, and Jago felt the panic of the prisoner who, in an instant, has lost his freedom and is now controlled by others whose motives are hidden from him.

The silent drive seemed to last forever. The night was overcast and the blackout made the world blind. There was no reassurance of road signs, just endless blank choices that Lavender seemed able to make. His father had once told Jago why he never painted nightscapes: *The night is a different dimension; I paint light and life.* His father had been right for once, Jago thought: in daylight the drive would have been through one of the softest landscapes in Britain, but in the dark it had become a world of sinister shapes and grotesque silhouettes, of tree tunnels that seemed to slide past the car as if the Daimler was stationary and the shadow world on the move somewhere.

London, when it finally came, was a graveyard; tombstone-type buildings shuffled together in disapproving streets that stared at the passing travellers like the wounded left behind by a retreating army. The bombed, blind buildings with cataract eyes; smashed windows misty from the night sky behind. They were missing roofs, missing walls, missing people. Jago caught glimpses of another time – the garish wallpapers now muted and fading into something blurry and softer, washed by the rain. The missing pipework, still remembered by dark lines that crossed the exposed interior walls like lines on a blueprint. Jago felt his fate and reputation shared a similarity with the bombed buildings; destroyed, exposed. Exposed, destroyed.

The drive affected them all in the same way, as if the smell of brick dust cemented their minds into the same thought.

'Think this is bad, you should see the East End,' said Lavender.

'At least we're hitting the bastards back. We shouldn't stop till Hun-land's as flat as a pancake.' Austen turned to speak into Jago's face as if to challenge him to disagree. 'Every sodding church, hospital and orphanage; let's drive what's left of them out into the wilderness to live in ditches, like animals.'

Jago met Austen's look. 'I'm surprised you're not in uniform.'

'Piss off, Captain Craze. You know nothing about me.'

'Leave him alone, Jago; you're on dodgy ground,' said Nicky. 'And he's right, isn't he? He subscribes to the same set of beliefs you do, doesn't he? He voices it, puts it into words, the actions you advocate in regard to Germany – every home and hospital; that's what unconditional surrender is going to mean isn't it, the rape of the people and the eradication of their way of life? Or are you still an appeaser?'

Jago gave them the answer he gave himself. 'I know that after this monstrousness there shouldn't, mustn't, ever be another war like it.'

Nicky laughed. 'How convenient. Regarding the future, every man takes an idealistic view, but it's the here and now that requires practical answers.'

Jago had another attempt to explain his shifting beliefs. 'I thought what happened at Munich, when Chamberlain brought back that paper – well I thought it was wonderful. I thought he'd been brave and noble to reach out and seek a reasonable solution to our differences. With another personality to deal with, it would have been the correct action, the action of a great statesman – with Adolf Hitler, it turned out to be a mistake. I still think it was worth attempting; to try to talk.'

'So did we.'

And something in the way Nicky said *we* made Jago realise he was talking about more than his three captors in the car.

'Park by the bottom of the Heath, Lavender. I'll deliver the captain by foot.'

Lavender parked the car and then leaned over the seat to speak to Jago. 'I just wanted to say, Captain Craze…' Jago was sure she was going to say something innocuous such as *Driv-*

ing you has been a pleasure, but she didn't. 'I just wanted to say, Captain Craze, that the way you treated Austen was really horrible, and that makes you rather nasty in my book.'

The car was abandoned and Lavender and Austen set off south with gas-bags swinging. Nicky and Jago headed into Belsize.

'Lead on, old man.'

Blacked-out North London loomed about them.

'I don't know where to go.'

'Don't worry, I'll tell you if you take a wrong turn.'

Jago didn't know this part of London well, and the situation in which Nicky had become a stranger made the walk weirder and the night seem darker than it was.

They went barely a quarter of a mile before Jago's captor pointed down an alley that ran through a parade of shops. 'He's waiting for you at the other end.'

'Who?' said Jago.

Nicky shrugged. 'We don't know his real name. We call him the Don.'

'Spanish?'

'Academic. And, Jago, he'll be armed, so no silly buggers.'

Jago paused and looked into Nicky's brilliant blue eyes. 'I'll go and see him – you leave me no choice – but you do understand Commander Godwin, that after this there can't be any communication between us. No friendship, Nicky.'

Jago walked off down the alley, stepping around coke-bins and dustbins, past doors that led to flats above shops, where families grouped around their wirelesses. He walked on, trying to ignore the lump in his throat that seemed the size of a cricket ball. It was over. No more Nicky. No more liaisons at the club, just loneliness after work in the house where he wasn't welcome.

At the other end of the alley, in the slit of the buildings, the silhouette of a man appeared almost theatrically. The shadow raised an arm and Jago saw it wasn't a greeting but that the man was displaying an automatic; not as British as a revolver, thought Jago – more sinister. As Jago reached the man, the automatic was pocketed but the threat was clear.

The man was silent but smiled. In late middle age, portly, dressed in a houndstooth check suit and Madder paisley tie, he wasn't London, Jago thought. He smelled of Oxbridge. Some insane don who would kill Jago and giggle into his sherry at the memory. Someone ultra-bright, but not quite human. The Don.

'Across the road and turn left,' he said.

They walked on into Belsize until they arrived at a low block of modernist flats that Jago recognised as the Isokon Building. He was herded inside and up the stairs into an apartment that resembled the exterior; cold, aware of itself and not wanting company. The Don in his country squire clothing was at odds with it, but then it was the sort of room that might have made Salvador Dalí feel a little conservative.

The man took himself to a Butaque armchair and indicated its twin for Jago. When they were settled, the Don finally spoke. 'So here you are, Captain Craze.'

'Yes, here I am.'

'Can I get you anything?'

'An explanation?'

As the Don considered Jago's request, he played his stomach with his fingers as if it were a piano. The silent tune finished, he finally spoke. 'Of course, a reasonable request. Let me assure you, although I'm armed that's for my defence in case you go mad; I'm not one for fisticuffs. As for you – well you can go whenever you please, but I would be grateful if you would give me a little of your time and all your attention. Now, an explanation…'

'Who are you?'

The Don sighed. 'If I told you my name it would be a lie. I have many names. Would you like one? I can offer you a choice. And if later you want to sneak to the beak, I am so very happy to tell you this ghastly furniture showroom is not my home.'

Jago sat silently. The Don continued, 'As to why you're here, think about it. Who brought you and more importantly how many of them were there?'

'Three.'

'Ah, I can see the penny has dropped.'

'A cell,' said Jago.

'A cell as you say, and who operates in cells?'

'Communists.' Jago was annoyed and felt like an undergraduate again, some new boy being patronised by a don into answering a series of simple questions.

The Don smiled. 'If only we could teach the cell system to the French Resistance, with their insistence on a centralised command and everyone knowing everyone – so French and so deadly. Such a gift to the fascists.'

'So why do you want to see me? I'm no one.'

The Don tried to snuggle down into the vicious armchair. 'We've been interested in you since you trained at Beaulieu with the SOE. Oh yes, we know all about the Finishing School, the permanent training staff: Ralph Vibert in charge of codes and ciphers, Killer Green in charge of housebreaking and safe-blowing, Nobby Clark in charge of living off the land and field craft, and Kim Philby in charge of black propaganda. We know about the house system; you were in Drokes House and Captain Carr was your housemaster – so wonderfully public school. We know everything about you. We've read your military service record, we've been told about your peculiar childhood, the world knows about your degenerate father. Then there's your sham marriage and – of course – your homosexuality. Have I missed anything?'

Jago stood up. 'So what's new? We all know the Communist Party is a vulgar little organisation, full of seedy people who feed their self-importance by uncovering sordid secrets.'

'Sit down, Captain; I'm not trying to blackmail you. I'm just trying to say we know everything and we still want to work with you. Would the British government say the same?'

They held each other's eyes like gangsters at the Brighton races. Jago sat back down and the Don leaned forward.

'I'm here to tell you, Captain Craze, that we admire you. We are all in awe of your analytical skills. Your report on the undesirability of assassinating Adolf Hitler, of reaching an armistice with the German generals, has reached the highest levels of Soviet government. The highest.'

'Did Nicky give you a copy?'

The Don smiled and stayed silent.

'Why did you kidnap me?'

The false joviality vanished, the face became hard, the eyes cold. 'The Soviet Union cannot be abandoned by the West. I cannot stress how strongly this is felt in Moscow. No one will gain from a premature armistice.'

'Well the Jews might.'

The Don found his humour again and sniggered. 'The Yids? The Kremlin wants their persecution to continue. Consider the resources the Nazis waste rounding up the Jews, transporting them on trains that could be taking soldiers and tanks to the Eastern Front. Think about the trained SS personnel guarding them and murdering them, men of crack legions wasting their training cooking Jews. The Final Solution, as they call it, is a considerable drain on the fascists' dwindling resources; long may it continue. As Stalin himself said, *Better the Yids get it than the Soviet Union*. So don't talk to me about the money lenders.'

Jago realised he had moved from listening to the far-right wing to the extreme left and that he couldn't tell them apart. 'You have almost convinced me that it might be worth going for peace now.'

The Don roared at him. 'Rot! You know that's sentimental twaddle; for the West a premature peace now means a bigger war tomorrow. If you're a Jew-lover – well it's tough, but it doesn't alter the fact that what the German generals are offering is a mirage, a false image of water in the desert. They're not offering peace, it's not in the nature of these Prussians; war is their blood. What they want is a breathing space to deal with their enemies piecemeal; first Russia and later the West. And believe me, in the German Empire there'll be no place for the Jews, with or without the Nazis. But I'm talking to the converted, aren't I? You wrote the bible.'

Jago accepted the compliment uncomfortably. 'And I'm to do what with it?'

'Get it read and acted upon.'

'I believe I'm about to become yesterday's man; I'm to be transferred to a mobile bath unit or something. That's if I'm not murdered. The opposition believe I have the grand strategic plan for the Fatherland to deal with little England.'

'What?'

Jago explained and the Don pondered and sighed. 'Yes, almost certainly purloined and sent by a comrade. Some silly little over-conscientious sod of a clerk who believes in the cause, sings the Red Flag, but has neglected to officially join the Party. If he had, he might have known to give the plan to his contact and not launch it into the ether aimed at Captain Craze, a report writer. And you haven't received it?'

'No.'

'Bugger. Where's it got to?'

'No idea, and it probably won't find me now I'm to be shunted into the long grass.'

The Don shook his head. 'Possibly, possibly not, we'll see. I think we see more in you than you see in yourself, and we're not sentimental when it comes to judging men. We followed your progress through the Finishing School at Beaulieu; we even thought of tapping you on the shoulder, till you disgraced yourself. Plus, there was your political naivete; far from setting you against the Establishment, your Bohemian father and your own deviant sexuality have paradoxically made you more desperate to belong to it. We lost interest in you, but thanks to your report, we could be persuaded to change our minds.'

Jago discovered he was tempted. He'd been an outcast, uncherished for so long that even an offer from the Communist Party, that murdered almost as many as the Nazi Party, flattered him. But it wouldn't do. 'No thanks.'

The Don snorted. Jago was pleased to note it was with displeasure. 'Shortly you will find yourself in a position to serve both our ends. Don't let us down, Captain Craze. You have to save Hitler.'

'And if I fail?'

The man smiled but left his eyes out in the cold. 'We will blow the cover off your little secret. As you know, it's a criminal offence to be a queer in this country. The world you want to move in, be accepted by – the Establishment – will not welcome a membership enquiry from one of – how do they put it, one of the pansy fraternity?'

CHAPTER ELEVEN

'I thought he meant why did I try to kill Hitler?'

'What did he mean?' said Lorelei.

Gabriel turned his attention from the naked woman lying next to him on the bed. Her apartment, filled with the soft scents and scanties of a woman, both enflamed and embarrassed Gabriel. It was a secret world, made more enchanted by the apartment's peculiar location as the only habitable part of the ruined Theaterhalle Obersalzberg. He thought back to that scene on the mountain with Max, and his confusion.

Max: 'Why did you do it?'

'Do what?' he'd said, his heart thumping.

'Take the bullet – for the bishop and the top brass?' said Max.

Gabriel remembered the relief, flooding him like – what was that word Lorelei used? Flooding him like a tsunami.

Lorelei brought his thoughts back to her boudoir with a small kick.

'Well, what did you tell him?'

Gabriel remembered Max scrutinising him, as he waited for an answer and decided not to lie. 'The truth.'

That was the strange thing. After years of letting others

shape and retell his story, he'd told the ex-Bavarian policeman the truth. 'I'm not a hero. In Spain I had the measure of the old guy as soon as I saw him. He didn't even have his shotgun up and pointed but I knew what he was going to do. I had a second to act and, believe me, I was thinking of myself – I knew I couldn't outrun the blast and he'd get me even if his target was the bishop. So I moved in to disarm him, and I would have too, if the idiot bishop hadn't also spotted the threat. He had hysterics and grabbed me and tried to hide behind me. This was a fat bishop; like a castrated bullock the Spanish breed for meat, twenty stone if he was an ounce. I tried to shake him loose but it was like waltzing with the village spinster – he wasn't going to let go. And when the old man let us have it, I wasn't the lucky one; I took the blast.'

Gabriel remembered it flicking him aside, the way a truck might dispatch a careless pedestrian.

'Hurt like hell I expect?' said Max.

'There was a blow like someone had hit me with a club, but not much pain, just shock.'

'And the bishop?'

'Unhurt.'

The blast had careened Gabriel into the bishop and they both lay in the dust, the bishop's eyes rolling in terror at the sight of Gabriel's blood gushing out of his shoulder. He'd thought that a priest that close to death would exhibit a sort of serenity; not so. The Prince of the Church had cried like a baby, and, looking into his eyes, Gabriel had seen no belief, no promise of eternity. Just a fat face, covered in fat hands, covered in large, garish rings, rings that had a thing about rubies.

'The man wasn't fit to stoop and tie my father's bootstraps. Yet had this bishop visited our village church, my father would have knelt on his entry.'

Max looked at him. 'Are you a Catholic?'

A breeze rustled a bush on the hillside like a soft roll on a snare drum. 'Once.'

'What happened in Russia?'

The breeze died. The bush shut up. He thought back to the white waste, without trees or foliage. The snowscape moving slowly in the wind as if it was one material, not a billion crystals, but a vast cotton sheet. Russia was a shroud.

'It was a mess. The divisional CO shouldn't even have been up in the line with us.' Gabriel remembered the absurdity that had brought the Gruppenführer forward to shake some morale into the near-mutinous soldiers. He heard again the idiotic order read out by an NCO at roll call. It was an instruction meant for somewhere like Italy but, in the way of the military, was delivered to all front-line troops, even to men of the Nord division serving above the Arctic circle, where it grew so cold that the fillings in men's teeth contracted and fell out, where ice ate the bones. The NCOs had barked the instruction from Army HQ in Potsdam that sunbathing was a military offence, and any serviceman reporting unfit due to sunburn or sunstroke would be deemed to have a self-inflicted wound, and would be punished accordingly. In another unit, at another time, the crazy order might have occasioned some gallows humour, but the Nord, most northerly of the Axis forces, had long considered themselves similar to the Tommys in Burma, who called themselves the Forgotten Army. The Nord felt forgotten too, passed over regularly for proper winter clothing. Many of the troopers on that parade still wore the fur coats donated by German ladies. Standing in the snow and wind, it had been a humiliation too far. Men had become insubordinate. The Gruppenführer, new to the Nord, but a proper soldier who wore tin from the first war, rushed from Division to calm the situation at the front line.

'But there was no line really,' Gabriel continued, 'and sometimes Ivan got amongst us without warning, and that's what happened when the general pitched up. Shit and shells out of nowhere and the grey ghosts rising up out of the snow at our feet. We all grabbed weapons and set about earning our corn. Herman was a friend. He has a misfire so I move in to cover him while he clears the blockage, and I walk into one of their Stalingrad spades.'

A look of understanding came across Max's face. 'Ah, the gardening accident. Didn't come across them in the desert. Ivan sharpens them so they're like an axe?'

Gabriel nodded and fought the desire to touch his scar when it was mentioned. 'I put a pattern of two in his chest and finish this Ivan. But blood is pouring from the gash in my brow into my eye. Another Cossack has brought down Herman and is moving in to finish him off so I shoot this Russkie as well. I stand over Herman, yelling at him to hang on. Then Ivan's gone as suddenly as he came; in their white snow clothes it was like fighting spooks. I look down and it isn't Herman I'm protecting; it's the Gruppenführer. I've got blood in my eye and I've cocked it up – Herman's a dozen feet away and dead.'

'The confusion of close-quarters combat.'

'As a parting gift, Ivan sent some rounds back. I'm still standing there over the divisional CO when I get two in the stomach and fall over. The Gruppenführer is telling everyone I saved his life. I get a battlefield commission and an Iron Cross first class, but best of all I'm airlifted out and back to Germany. On the downside, I have more pain than there should be in the world.'

'I've heard you don't know pain till you've got a stomach wound,' said Max.

'Where did you get your leg?'

'Africa, traffic accident.'

Max had shut up after that and they'd walked back to the barracks.

Gabriel looked around at Lorelei's apartment, at the art on her walls. He had no experience of people's homes: his father had almost been a hermit, so they never visited. In the army, barracks were kept bare. At home, there had been a couple of religious effigies on the walls, but Lorelei had framed prints of Berlin cabaret shows; grotesque, sexy, decadent and Jewish. She confused him. A German girl with a love for all things oriental. In her early twenties, she seemed older and she looked at him when they made love. He found this disconcerting; the soldiers' women he'd previously been with had always turned their heads to stare at the wall.

His dalliance with Lorelei had the taste of sin. His first real girlfriend, one he didn't have to pay, was turning out to be different to what he'd imagined a sweetheart to be. More sensual than sweet. Lorelei wore underwear that hadn't started life on a sheep. Her perfume would have breached a gas mask filter. He discovered he didn't just like *doing it* but also kissing her, and stroking her skin, which was as soft as satin. Sometimes it was hard to tell where her pants ended and she began. Gabriel loved her little shows when she undressed for him, epoch slow, one garment at a time. 'Shoes off last,' she'd say. Why did that work on him the way she knew it would? Female mystery. When they finally embraced, Gabriel discovered he hadn't the cool head he had for combat but rushed at the obstacles like some idiot from the cavalry screaming *charge*! Lorelei had retrained him. *Nothing tastes better than slow*, and she proved it with fingernails and feathers.

Lovemaking was a patrol in depth and she took no prisoners. After the initial action, Lorelei wouldn't let him rest or retreat.

She'd exchange passion for sensuality again and tempt and tease him into another assault. Once, she left the room and came back dressed as a Japanese girl with her hair held up with chopsticks. She put a record on her gramophone and slow, crazy, Eastern music had filled the bedroom. To the sound of that music, Lorelei said, 'Let me introduce you to the back of my neck.'

Once she suggested she open her curtain and undress by the window.

'There's a guard post up the hill. The guys are always trying to watch me – I could give them a show?'

Gabriel was confused by his arousal at this suggestion but his shock won. 'Lorelei!'

Words of his father came out of his mouth. 'That's depraved.'

She'd smiled lazily at him. 'Yes.'

He'd pulled her back to the bed before she could suggest anything else.

'Alright, I'll leave the bedroom curtain closed.'

Then, in the way of their strange romance, she'd stopped being compliant and taken command, become Control, the team leader. 'The curtains. We need to establish some warning signs for each other. Listen, those curtains stay closed from here on in, so whenever you visit, check. If they're open, that means danger, stay away. Understand? Now, would you like a little fun?'

And that was their pattern; moving from sex to plotting and back again.

All passion spent, they shared intelligence and Gabriel was almost like a new recruit, needing Lorelei to tell him what had happened.

'How do you know to do the things you do?' he asked.

Lorelei gathered his arms and made a nest for herself. 'I

could reverse the question, soldier. Why don't you know about them?'

'The working girls never do this sort of thing.'

She sighed and nuzzled his chest with her hair. 'They don't make love because the men don't ask them to. They have sex because that's all men know.'

'But don't you feel like one of them when you do this stuff?'

She snorted. 'How can I feel like one of them when what I do is what they don't do? I refuse to open my legs mechanically, like a Hausfrau...'

'Lorelei!'

'Europe is a miserable continent for sex; withered wives and brutalised whores. In the East it's different. Have you ever heard of a Dakini?'

'No.' The word made him nervous.

Lorelei stood on the bed and unpinned a drawing from the wall. She presented it to Gabriel. 'This is a Dakini.'

He looked at the picture. It was of a girl, not Japanese, perhaps Indian or Middle Eastern, he thought. She seemed to be dancing; her head going one way on an impossibly long neck, and her arms the other. One foot was lifted and one breast was exposed. Gabriel wasn't shocked; he'd seen more tits on the Vatican's walls. 'So?'

Lorelei's head came next to his, looking at the illustration. 'She's a Dakini; a sacred prostitute. The Dakini would ply her trade on the temple steps, raising money for that institution by selling her body. She'd come from a good family and, for one season of her life, she'd take men in the perfumed garden put aside for that purpose. Or, if the weather was inclement, offer her charms in a candlelit chamber filled with incense. Being, as it were, an amateur and high class, the Dakini was much in demand and commanded a big price – which meant I suppose she was protected from the low and dirty. Of course she could always bestow the blessings of the temple on an impoverished young man if he seemed especially – devout.'

Gabriel took his hand from the picture. 'Her family let her do this?'

Lorelei sighed. 'Her family weren't Swiss postmen. They understood that sacrifice transcends respectability. A Dakini brought honour to her family and when her season ended she returned home almost a saint.'

Lorelei's head rose on her long neck as she said this, and her eyes closed, almost as if she was savouring some spiritual essence in the contradiction.

He snorted. 'But could she get a husband?'

Her eyes snapped open. 'A Dakini fetched a higher bride price than a virgin.'

Lorelei stood and pinned the picture back on the wall. Gabriel dismissed the artwork with a shake of his head. 'Everyone is different I suppose. I don't judge…'

'You do.'

'Swiss girls wouldn't care to do it.'

Lorelei lay next to him again and looked at him with those eyes that sometimes seemed to him to be as old as sin. 'Don't be too sure, soldier. You're too pure. I think an awful lot of nice girls, given the Dakini option, would embrace it in preference to a tedious little finishing school. Come on, I want a cuddle.'

She opened her arms to him and her nakedness almost caused him to turn away. He felt a shame for her she didn't seem to feel for herself.

'Lorelei, I'm trying to treat you with respect. I know women, real women – not Dakinis in pictures – don't like it. My father told me. I know you do – sex – for us, not because you enjoy it. I understand we mustn't humiliate women, that we have to let you get up and get dressed as quickly as possible after the act. My father said, *Don't rub her nose in what she's just done for you. Turn away, show some respect*, so I'm trying.'

'What else did he tell you?'

'Not to behave like a Frenchman.'

Lorelei laughed. 'Did he know any?'

'Plenty; one of the armies he served with was the Foreign Legion.'

Lorelei slid off the bed, wrapped herself in a Japanese silk kimono and slid into Gabriel's arms. 'You have more scars than you realise.'

She trailed a finger down the line from his brow over his cheek from just below his eye to where it dissected his top lip. She reached up and ran the tip of her tongue over the crevice, then tilted her head to do the same to the wrecked skin on his shoulder. Simultaneously she tucked two of her fingers into the two circular puckers on his stomach and worked them.

'And our Frenchman, Volfgangu, he's all tucked away neat and tidy?' she asked.

'All neat and tidy.'

Still stroking Gabriel, she went quiet as she thought back over his story of the botched attempt on the Führer. 'So, who the hell was the other shooter?'

She'd been asking this since he'd escaped the Luftwaffe major, Max Adler, and reported in to her.

'I don't know,' he said, again. 'But Hitler wants me to find out.'

'And so do I,' she said.

The lovemaking began again but then something else occurred to Lorelei. 'The Frenchman's pistol...'

'The Walther PPK?'

'Do you still have it?'

He nodded towards his clothes. 'In a pocket,' he said.

'Not safe. Better let me have it – after...'

'After what?'

'This.'

She took Gabriel's hands and ran them over the slips of satin that barely covered her. And he found the touch of her skin through silk released in him a desire that defeated his scruples.

'Come back to bed,' she whispered in his ear. The breath of the whisper in his ear, on his shoulder, set off more explosions in him. 'Come back to bed – that's an order, soldier.'

He obeyed, but then someone knocked on the door to the apartment.

'Shit!'

A young soldier stood there, the grin on his face frozen when he saw the girl he had come to see metamorphosed into a scarred SS officer.

'Who are you and what do you want?' demanded Gabriel.

'Trooper Berger, sir, I bring the mail up from the station in Berchtesgaden.'

Gabriel looked round Trooper Berger's head, before eyeing the boy again. 'Does this look like Obersalzberg post office to you?'

'No sir!'

'Well?'

'I've dropped off the sack. I just popped by to see if the Fräulein needed anything from down in the town.'

The boy was smitten, Gabriel thought. 'What's that?'

The young soldier was trying to make a portfolio under his arms disappear by ignoring it. 'Nothing, sir.'

Gabriel stared at him. 'You know there's a shell hole on the Eastern Front waiting for a certain Trooper Berger, don't you?'

'No sir, yes sir!' the boy burbled.

'Well?'

'It contains a drawing, sir. I was an art student before the war.'

'Show me.'

Reluctantly the would-be artist opened the portfolio and drew out a sheet of cartridge paper. On it was a pencil drawing of Lorelei. She was dressed – just – in a light frock that, in a breeze, caught every curve of her body. There was even a suggestive Y at the top of her thighs.

'Oh, I like that, is it me?' said Lorelei, coming up by Gabriel and taking the drawing.

'Yes,' said the boy simply.

'I'll pin it up in my bedroom,' she said, and the boy, pleased, escaped.

They went back in and Lorelei held up the paper by finger and thumb.

'Oh dear,' she said, 'I'm afraid he's drawn me with his penis.'

She crumpled it into a ball and dropped it into a wastepaper basket.

Gabriel approved.

CHAPTER TWELVE

Max brought another shovelful of topsoil to the garden sieve Gabriel was holding. Around them the peaks ignored them, but Gabriel knew; the mountains missed nothing.

'Steady,' Max said as he tipped the earth, and Gabriel shook the sieve gently back and forth till the loose debris was gone.

'Anything?'

'No, Max, just stones and a snail shell.'

'Snail shell?'

'It's empty, no one's home.'

'Must belong to a Jewish snail.'

Gabriel wiped his brow; it was hot on the hill. Max brought over some more dirt from the ground the Führer had dived onto to save his life. 'Try this lot.'

Another shovelful hit the sieve and this time they both saw it immediately; a glint in the matt of the soil.

'Here's one,' said Max as he reached into the sieve and picked out a small spent shell. He held it up and inspected it. 'Lee–Enfield round.'

Gabriel nodded, but Max was already turning back to the soil. 'Right, let's find the other.'

Gabriel felt the September sun burning his uncovered arms

in the thin air of the mountains. He could have been a child again, working with his father on the poor soil. What had his father said? *I swear the only things we can grow here are stones. This is a stone farm.* His father had been a soldier, a hunter, a shepherd, but never a gardener.

A noise stopped them working. A car was coming along the track towards them; a giant, open-topped Mercedes, known locally as the Swabian Colossus. The Führer sat in the front next to Erich Kempka, his chauffeur; in the seats behind, like giant errant schoolboys, sat six of the Old Hares. On the hill opposite, a line of armoured cars and motorcycle combinations rode the skyline, like American Indians in a movie. These were vehicles of the RSD, another of Hitler's personal protection units that specialised in his security when moving on road or railway.

Max and Gabriel came to attention but, not wearing headgear, they didn't salute. The engine of the Mercedes died and Adolf Hitler climbed out and called to them. 'That bastard, the assassin, he's ruined my walk. Is it too much to ask: a quiet walk to the tearooms each morning? Now I must go like an invading army and goodbye privacy.'

The Führer came over to them. 'What are you doing?'

Max, still at attention, explained. 'Looking for the spent cartridges, sir.'

'To what purpose, Major?'

'We've found one; if we can find the other we can compare them, see if they both came from the same weapon, or...'

'Or what?' said the Führer.

'Or do we possibly have two assassins? A team, sir.'

Hitler became silent and went into himself. He looked around the mountains but Gabriel knew he wasn't looking at the scenery. Then he was back with them and looking at Gabriel. 'Do you like these late summer days in the mountains?'

Gabriel answered promptly. 'I prefer the mountains in winter. Christmas.'

The Führer's face crinkled into smiles. 'Ah, Christmas Eve in the mountains is special. How did your folk celebrate?'

Gabriel threw his mind back to childhood, a time before wars. 'We'd ski down the mountain in the pitch black, holding up flaming torches. Wherever you looked, all you could see were other communities skiing to the church with the flaming torches.'

Hitler nodded. 'It was that mountain tradition that I used in my Olympics. Berliners have no eye for art, or should I say, dramatic art. I took that image of the flaming torch and imposed it on the games. I made the Berlin Olympics into total theatre.'

'Yes, sir.'

'Wolf, not sir, I told you.'

'Wolf.'

The Führer leaned his head in close to Gabriel as if he was going to share a state secret. 'And when you all arrived at the church in the valley, did you do the play?'

The play, thought Gabriel, he'd forgotten the play. 'Yes, we did.'

The Führer laughed and looked at Max, still standing to attention and trying to be invisible by the miracle of soldierly rigidity. 'This one doesn't know what we're talking about; flat foot from the city.'

Divide and rule as always, Gabriel thought, and of course – Hitler was no more a man of the mountains than Max. Gabriel knew his father would have called him a valley boy, brought up in the shadow of the hills. Another delusion of the Führer's he decided, but Gabriel played along. 'I was a shepherd in the mystery play.'

'So was I! I always wanted to play one of the three kings,

or to be your namesake, the angel. But I was passed over, held back to allow lesser boys from more privileged backgrounds to play the biggest roles, and they did it badly.'

The Führer's eyes turned dark as he remembered these childhood slights. Gabriel tried to bring him back to the present, before he fell into the well of resentment.

'What shepherd did you play, Wolf?'

The Führer brightened again. 'The deaf shepherd, the one who can't hear the good news and keeps saying *What, what*? I used to get all the laughs.'

The Führer cupped one of his ears with a hand and approached Erich in the Mercedes. 'Erich, what time is it?'

'11.30, sir.'

'What, what?'

'11.30, sir.'

'What, what?'

'11.30...'

'What?' Hitler turned and laughed with Gabriel and put his hand on his shoulder. 'I was a very good deaf shepherd. Everyone said so and they were right.'

He looked up at the mountains and sighed, 'I'm still a Bohemian at heart, not a soldier – but that was a lifetime ago, the time before I answered my calling. Now it's my generals who pretend to be the deaf shepherd when I try to correct their mistakes.'

He turned suddenly to Max. 'Find the other shell.'

Then he was back in the Swabian Colossus and continuing his journey to tea and toast at the Mooslaner Kopf. Across the valley came the sound of many engines starting up. As the Mercedes drew away, it was followed by another limousine carrying the rest of the Old Hares, and after them an enclosed black car with a section of Begleit Kommando armed with machine pistols. On the hill opposite, an armoured car manned by RSD soldiers puffed busily along, bringing up the rear. The circus left town.

Later that afternoon, Max found the second shell. 'From a Kar 98k. Two weapons, we're looking for two assassins.'

Gabriel and Lorelei picked their way through the wrecked theatre. It was like being inside a giant egg that had been cracked from above by a huge spoon. The roof was still complete but lined like a spider's web. Below, everything was perfect, except in places the ceiling met the backs of the chairs. In others, it was still high enough to pass under, but spotlights dangled in front of their faces and they had to move around them. The stage was still intact.

'Snow damage, not bomb damage; the weight of snow brought it down one winter,' said Lorelei.

'Who constructs a building with a flat roof in the mountains?' said Gabriel. 'What was it used for?'

Lorelei stopped working her way forward through the shambles underfoot and looked at Gabriel. 'It was for putting on plays, that's what they do in theatres; they put on plays. Even the tots in the kindergarten know that.'

'I know they put on plays here, I meant what else? You can't have a building this size just for plays.'

'Yes you can. Anyway, this was Hitler's theatre, built specially on his country estate for cultural extravaganzas and edifying spectacles. Only the snow wouldn't obey even his orders.'

They stood and looked at the destruction in the auditorium. They'd come through the door that led from Lorelei's apartment, which had once been the home of the theatre manager, and in front of them was the wrecked dream. The roof had collapsed from the centre and beneath it the seats were crushed, but the side aisles were still untouched. The stage itself looked like fairyland, covered in cobwebs but perfect, waiting for the lights to go up and a princess to appear.

'What's the idea?' said Gabriel.

'Come on stage and I'll tell you. But what I will say now is, you've only got yourself to blame. Did you get the Führer reminiscing about his childhood days appearing in the local mystery play? He told Eva all about when he used to be one of the wise kings.'

'He wasn't a king; he was a shepherd.'

'If Adolf Hitler wants to rewrite history and say he played the Mother of God in a play then he was the best Mother of God there's ever been. Correct?'

'Correct.'

They arrived at the stage and climbed onto it, using a short flight of steps to one side of the orchestra pit.

'Lorelei, what's this about?'

'It's about killing Hitler and getting it right this time.'

She no longer spoke like Gabriel's lover. Now she spoke like Control. 'He's coming here to assess the damage; he's talking about having the place repaired. He wants to get a professional company to come and perform for the kindergarten children and the community at Christmas.'

The puritan in Gabriel was shocked. 'But the enemy is at the gate, he doesn't have time for plays.'

'He has time for procrastination, though. Eva says when the war was going well you couldn't get him out of Berlin. He had the generals running to him every day. Now things are not so good for Germany, he hides away here and the generals can't get to see him. Goebbels, Himmler and Goering come and stay in their houses on the estate but he avoids them. Field Marshal Model comes specially to speak to him, and when he finally gets to see the Führer he gets shouted at.'

'How will we do it?'

'Hitler will come here with Eva, or, if she's irritating him more than usual, he'll come alone. If he comes with Eva, I'll deal with her.'

'Bullet or a blade?' said Gabriel.

Lorelei shook her head. 'Neither, I'll break her neck. I want to keep the shooting to the minimum and a blade can go wrong. If you miss the throat, there's all that screaming and blood. If it gets on my clothes, it's going to delay our getaway.'

'Take me through it.'

'Hitler arrives and I show him around. Once he sees the stage he'll want to get on it and, being him, he'll go centre stage to show off. You're going to be in there.'

Lorelei pointed at a square box on the stage, situated in the line of footlights.

'What is it?' said Gabriel.

'It's called the prompt box but, as they mainly put on musicals and opera in this theatre, it was used by the second conductor. The first conductor would be in the orchestra pit, there. This meant he was out of sight to the performers on the stage, so a second conductor would conduct the singers from this box. There's a small room underneath for him to stand in. Go and see.'

Gabriel climbed off the stage and dropped into the pit. Under the prompt box he found a door, and let himself in. He stood on a box that was there for that purpose and suddenly there was Lorelei in front of and above him; a perfect target. He spoke to her.

'If he stands there, that's where he'll die. What about the sound of the shot?'

'The theatre's soundproofed and, even in this wrecked state, the shell of the building's still intact and the sound shouldn't carry.'

'Right, he's dead, what happens next?'

'We hide him in a cupboard in the chorus dressing room – that's the one on the lowest level under the theatre. They'll find him eventually but by that time we should be in Switzerland. What do you think?'

Gabriel looked at her peering down at him, framed by the perimeters of the prompt box. 'I can do this.'

'I'll send the message via the usual route. London will be told – Wolf is going to die.'

CHAPTER THIRTEEN

If someone sitting behind a desk could be said to be soaring in triumph, then, Jago thought, Major Smedley was up with the eagles.

'You've done it now, Craze.'

'Sir?'

'I've had a phone call. The paperwork is on its way apparently, but the gist is: Captain Craze is to be sent down, finished in Military Intelligence. So clear your desk and pack your pens, you're not coming back.'

It was the sack – again. Jago had not liked the job, but he hated the humiliation of losing it even more. Smedley was still fussily attacking him.

'You wouldn't be told, would you? Even after I binned that wretched report of yours, you tried to go over my head, which is typically arrogant of you. Well, its contents have upset someone. You're going to be jumped on from a great height. They're sending a car.'

They were moving quickly, Jago realised. Barely two days had elapsed since his Chichester trip and he was about to be sunk without trace. Smedley must be a happy man, he thought.

'I can't work you out, Craze: all you had to do was keep your head down to see out this war and then return to Oxford.'

Jago looked at Smedley the survivor, and knew he'd work diligently for saint or sinner, for Churchill or Hitler. Jago thought he was a slave in all but title. 'If Jerry had marched up Whitehall in 1940, you'd have done that, wouldn't you, sir? You'd have kept your head down and tried to see out the war? I do believe you're one of life's collaborators, Major Smedley.'

The major stared at him. Jago realised Smedley wasn't triumphant, he was disappointed. Jago had disappointed him. And as the major was a shit-slicer by trade, he now sliced shit, and the turd was Jago.

'I called you arrogant because you are. You can't settle to any task given you and work at it diligently. You have to step back and try to grasp the bigger picture, not allowing that that might be someone else's job, higher up the chain. Someone older and wiser. You're like a lot of modern young men, you want to start up the top. True research calls for humility, a putting aside of assumptions, opinions, even beliefs, and getting down on your knees to investigate the dirt under your feet. You're all head space, Craze, no knees. And there's something else. Plenty of undergraduates turn up at university to find themselves; there's something about you that makes me think you arrived to lose yourself. You're an army in retreat, a shambles.'

Jago wanted to be away, out of the office, away from the lecture, but Smedley hadn't finished. 'I've met your sort before, so frightened of being labelled you sabotage your own life. No job is worthy of you because by doing it conscientiously it might define you. You have a first-class brain, Captain Craze. Unfortunately, it's attached to a will-of-the-wisp.'

Jago went quietly. Outside, a Riley saloon car, painted khaki, was waiting for him. The driver was a FANY, a member of the

First Aid Nursing Yeomanry. She was one of the bright young things that ran errands around London. The same girls who sometimes parachuted into occupied Europe as secret agents. She was also unmistakably Lavender from the Chichester debacle.

Now Jago felt he was lost in Alice's Wonderland. The White Rabbit had turned up in the Riley to drive him down the rabbit hole. He hovered on the pavement, with too many questions jostling for position to allow one of them the opportunity to be asked. Then Lavender forestalled him.

'You can ride up front or in the back, sir,' she said, without any acknowledgement that she knew him.

Jago climbed in beside her and stared at her in daylight. She looked young enough to still be at school; fresh in stale old bombed London. That the Communist Party had assets in uniform didn't surprise him; that they could pull strings to make sure Jago was *supervised* by one of their number did. He wondered who would spy on him in his next posting, and how low he was going to fall; was he to be banished to Army Postal Services or the Catering Corps? And what then – a fatal accident? A hit and run in the blackout? He felt so angry; to be murdered for a mistaken assumption. He hadn't got the bloody Walpurgisnacht Plan. He turned on the driver irritably.

'Do we talk about the other night?' he said.

Lavender changed gear with an alarming cry of protest from the throttle. 'Best not, sir. Think of it like a play at the theatre; when I'm in these togs I'm playing Lavender, the brave young lass in the FANY. When I'm pointing the Webley at you, I'm another creation on the stage. Two separate characters played by the same actress. Get it?'

Jago did and entered the play. He understood. Lavender was leading two lives, just like him, and with a second secret life, discretion wasn't just required, it was mandatory.

'So where are we heading, a mobile bath unit? Where are you taking me?'

'Sorry, sir, I've taken a vow of silence.'

She stared at the road ahead and didn't for a second glance in his direction. Jago knew this lack of cooperation came from the fact she hadn't forgiven him for the treatment of her comrade, Austen.

Jago brought his mind back to his present crisis. He knew how these things played out; first he was going to find himself on the carpet for a bollocking, followed by a formal dismissal. Then he'd be back in the car for a drive to a seedy backwater of the war effort, where the officer commanding would tell Jago how unhappy he was to accept him and how he'd be keeping a close eye on him. Then he'd be handed over to a semi-criminal sergeant, smelling like an ashtray, who'd find Jago a desk with one leg shorter than the other three. Behind this rocking monstrosity, Jago would spend his days chasing plumbing supplies and facing a large wall clock that would tick his brain into despair and move as slow as death.

'Here we are, sir,' said Lavender, pulling up at an office on Baker Street.

Phase one, he thought: the bollocking. He presented his military pass to the redcap on the door. He was asked to wait in the lobby and a few minutes later Lavender reappeared.

'If you'll come with me, sir; we're on the second floor.'

'Lavender...'

'Sir?'

Jago looked up and down the corridor; he needed to talk to her. The place seemed deserted apart from a military policeman on a corner staring into infinity and wondering whether to put it on a charge. Jago stepped into an alcove that housed two red fire buckets, one containing water, the other sand. Each to be used on their own specific fire hazard. After a beat, Lavender reluctantly stepped into the alcove with him.

'Austen, is he your – young man?'

Lavender huffed; it was the only word that Jago could find to fit the noise of her impatience.

'Is he my young man? Are we walking out? Do we have an understanding? Are his intentions honourable? You really have wafted in from the shires, haven't you sir? Anyway, I think you know for a fact in what direction Austen's sexual appetites lie.'

Jago was irritated to discover he was blushing. 'I suppose I do.'

Lavender stopped mocking him and looked coldly into his eyes. 'Austen's my brother, sir.'

And the way she said it, the weight she gave the words, told Jago that Austen would always count more in Lavender's life than any gentleman caller.

'Oh, right,' he said weakly.

Her answer was brusque. 'Let's get on, shall we sir? We've got a war to win, a revolution to organise, a population to agitate, a worker's paradise to bring about and a load of toffs to put up against a wall and shoot.'

She marched off out of the fire-point alcove and Jago followed her, knowing that, as far as Lavender was concerned, he was going to end up with his back to that wall.

They reached a solid mahogany door with a military plate screwed to it, bearing the legend, *KNOCK AND WAIT*.

'You don't have to wait, sir,' she said, reaching for the handle to open the door for him. 'And by the way, sir, I hope you won't take it amiss if I tell you,' she whispered, 'you're improperly dressed.'

Jago entered the office in confusion.

'Major Craze,' Lavender announced to the assembled group of three, all wearing headgear, Jago noticed. They brought their right arms up into a salute as he entered, longest way up, shortest way down. He returned their salute. As he did so her words registered: *Major* Craze.

He caught her eye and she glanced at the rank pips on his shoulder. 'Said you were improperly dressed, sir; there are pips where there should be a crown.'

A captain of the Dorsets stepped forward. 'I'm Captain Thomas, sir, outgoing CO. This is your staff.' The captain waved a hand at the others.

Jago saw all three services were present, both sexes and officers and other ranks. By way of welcoming him, those with commissions smiled, and the elderly naval rating straightened his back. There was a sophisticated woman, in glamorous early middle age, who looked like she'd been poured into her RAF squadron leader's uniform. The sailor looked like his skin had been removed, sent to a leather factory and only returned to him when suitably tanned. Lavender was looking at Jago with scorn. The rabbit hole had just got deeper.

The captain of the Dorsets continued, 'I'll do the honours after I've briefed you, if I may. Come through to my – your office, I should say.' He turned to the ancient naval rating, who bore a striking resemblance to a dissolute old vampire Jago had seen in a pre-war German film. His memory supplied a name: Max Schreck as Count Orlok in *Nosferatu*.

'Tea and biscuits, Nightingale.'

'Aye aye, sir,' the rating said, as he lumbered away leaving an audible grumble, 'Biscuits he wants, and them on the ration', to float behind him.

The office was that wartime mixture of heavy old wooden furniture, clashing with contemporary metal storage. It was not a room that seemed harmonious to Jago.

'Well, this is it,' said Captain Thomas.

He seemed to be waiting for Jago to speak, to comment, to

ask a question, but Jago was lost; there wasn't even a carpet underfoot for him to receive a bollocking on. 'Please forgive me, but what the hell's going on? What's this all about? My sudden promotion to major? Frankly – I'm totally lost.'

'I take it you've not been filled in, sir?'

'I'm in the dark.'

They caught each other's eye and, in that look of shared bemusement, betrayed their joint amateur-soldier status. Inside they relaxed slightly.

'What a way to run a war, eh?'

'I thought I'd been brought here for the sack. What is this place?' said Jago.

'I'm told you're SOE?'

'Was,' said Jago. 'I've been with Military Intelligence for the last two and a half years.'

'But in the beginning, weren't you interviewed here? This is Station X; SOE headquarters.'

Jago remembered the chaos of the times; the radio call-up of the Reserve, two days before war was officially declared. The guard sergeant at Victoria Barracks had missed the wireless broadcast and, not having been briefed, had tried to send him away again. But then others had turned up, other TA men with their kitbags, and the sergeant had muttered quietly, *Christ, there's going to be a war.* And the chaos had continued; his regiment had gone to France but thanks to his degree he'd gone on a commissioning course, then instead of returning to his regiment he'd been sent to the newly formed espionage service. There hadn't been any interviews in Baker Street, just a posting to a stately home.

'No, I was sent straight to the Finishing School, at Beaulieu.'

Captain Thomas nodded. 'I see. Well sir, 64 Baker Street is SOE headquarters; designated Station X. Up here on the second floor we run just one operation, known as Foxley. And actually I'm in the same fog you are. Yesterday I was informed I was standing down as CO as a Major Craze was taking over.'

'I'm sorry,' said Jago.

The captain smiled. 'Don't be. I'm going back to my regiment – at last.'

'Are they giving you a company?'

'No such luck. I'm to be battalion intelligence officer – but I'm going to be there, I'm going to be there at the end. I've spent the war in an office and I thought I'd missed my chance, but now I'm re-joining my regiment.'

He smiled the smile of a happy soldier. Jago knew how he felt and what he meant by he was *going to be there*. The captain was going to be at the sharp end, the place where the real war happened. It would be something he could tell his grandchildren, *strip his sleeve and show his scar* and explain Grandpa's part in the great adventure to free the world – if he survived *being there*.

'And Foxley is?' asked Jago.

'Well, truth to tell, it's been a bit of a dead duck, sir. We've been charged from virtually day one of this war to devise ways to kill Adolf Hitler, and Foxley is our assassination team on Obersalzberg.'

'And is Hitler too well defended to pull it off, an impossible target?'

'There's no such thing as an impossible target, sir, but for most of the war we've been ordered to hold our powder. You see, when Hitler was a demigod to his own people, we daren't bump him off, for fear of what they'd do in revenge to our lads in the POW cages. The generals' botched attempt told us that possibly the time is right for us to have a serious pot, and, as we have a team in place, upstairs has given us the go.'

Jago felt like one of the heavier pieces of old oak furniture in the office had just dropped on him. 'You've been given the green light to kill Hitler?'

'If the German generals take over, the thinking is they'll respect the Geneva Convention and look after our boys until they can repatriate them.'

At that moment Jago didn't care about the POWs. 'And is this assassination attempt – imminent?'

'Well they've already had one pop.'

Jago felt a surge of panic. 'They tried to kill Hitler?'

'Well he is the enemy, sir.'

Jago was astonished to find that he was relieved that Herr Hitler had survived. He realised this must have been the attempt the collaborators had discussed.

'So, this team we have…?'

'Four strong; an Anglo-German nurse is Control, a turncoat SS officer who'll carry out the kill, a Swiss businesswoman on radio in Switzerland, who then hand delivers to our so-called postman, who has regular access to Obersalzberg and gives the messages to the nurse.'

Jago sorted the facts in his head. It didn't make sense. Clive Roberts, of the Secret Intelligence Service, had told his fellow collaborators he didn't believe that SOE had any assets on Obersalzberg, but in fact they had a whole team, while the traitors just had one, and he was to come under the Control of the MI6 asset, the Three Graces. The answer came to Jago: there were two subversive groups up that mountain, each planning to shoot Hitler, one answering to SOE and the other to MI6. It was worse than Jago had imagined, but at least he was now in a position to block the SOE assassination.

'And there's about to be another attempt?' he asked.

'Everything's in place. My last order as CO was *Go, go, go! Kill the beast.* Ah, here's Nightingale with the char – and three biscuits. Excellent foraging Nightingale.'

'Aye,' said the lugubrious Nightingale, bearing the tray before him like a high priest bearing reliquaries at a pharaoh's funeral. 'Digestives, and I had to go cap in hand to get 'em.'

'Well done Nightingale, now beat it.'

'And begging your pardon, sir, Commander Godwin is back and wanting to come aboard. He's in the lobby. The lady dressed as an RAF officer has gone to fetch him up.' Nightingale went.

Captain Thomas turned to Jago. 'We don't like bodies wandering around unescorted in Baker Street. Do you know Commander Godwin?'

Jago lied, which he had been taught was a mortal sin the last time he'd worked for SOE. Only lie when there really was no alternative, had been the maxim. Lies trip an agent up. 'No, I don't know Commander Godwin.'

Had he failed to tell the truth because, at heart, he felt he hadn't really known who Nicky was, ever?

'Neither did we, till yesterday; then he turned up with the milk. He had the correct authorisation so we stood back and he went through everything with a fine-toothed comb. Finally, he announced you were to be the new CO and I was to be returned to my regiment.'

The door opened after a courtesy knock and the smart female squadron leader looked around. 'Commander Godwin is here, sir,' she said.

'Thank you, Mrs Cambridge – Squadron Leader I mean – show him in.'

Nicky entered. 'Hello Jago, good to see you again.'

The lie was exposed. The wisdom of SOE training revealed. But this was London and not Berlin, and Captain Thomas was too much a gentleman to ask an embarrassing question of a superior. Jago stewed in mortification and blamed Nicky and refused to acknowledge him.

Nicky broke the silence. 'Good morning, Captain Thomas. You may go.'

'Sir,' said the captain. He stepped through the door and out of Jago's life.

Nicky stared at Jago. 'I expect your head's spinning?'

Jago didn't want commiserations, he wanted explanations. 'What's going on? How did the Communist Party become aware of me? Was it you who gave them my report?'

Nicky had a poke at the biscuits in a desultory fashion, and then abandoned them. 'Believe me–' he said, but Jago hadn't finished.

'Did you betray me, Nicky? Did you tell them what I am?'

Nicky sighed. 'I didn't have to, old man. They know all the queens who come down from Oxbridge. They keep close tabs on the cottages. Your toilet habit betrayed you.'

Jago's embarrassment made him angry. 'Do you know the Don is threatening me with blackmail?'

'Don't judge us all by the Don. He's old school. The Party wants to own you and will use blackmail to that end, but not me. I want a new world, not the old one with new masters.'

'Don't be naive.'

'I don't think I am.'

But Jago wasn't listening. 'When we bumped into each other again, was that arranged by the Party?'

The sudden near-collision in a Whitehall corridor. The surprise and pleasure when he recognised Nicky. Their decision to have a drink after duty, not their decision at all, Jago realised. It had been ordained by the Don.

Nicky had the decency to look shamefaced. 'It was a set-up, I admit. But what happened after wasn't politics.'

'Nothing happened.'

'No. Quite.' And Nicky shut up.

Jago hated that he was a thing to be moved around the world

at the whim of other people and their plans. 'Can the Kremlin arrange promotion within the British Army?'

Nicky succumbed to the biscuit and bit into it. 'On night watches on the Murmansk run, we dunk these in cocoa and rum. Keeps out the cold. The Arctic convoy is the worst of them all. But no one complains, none of the men. Everyone knows the Russians are shouldering the lion's share of the war effort against the Nazis. Anything we can do to help Uncle Joe we do. There are people here, in London, who feel the same and some of them have a lot of scrambled egg on their sleeve. One of our high-ranking friends arranged for your transfer and promotion, and in the process scuppered the collaborators' plans for you. Poor Captain Thomas has inherited that destiny.'

'What do you mean?'

Nicky finished the biscuit, brushed his fingers and shrugged. 'Captain Thomas is a good man and, as so often in war, bad things happen to good men. He thinks he's on his way to re-join his regiment in Northern France but he's been lied to. I lied to him, and sadly he's about to fill the role others had designed for you. Captain Thomas is going to see out the war in a Pay Corps depot outside Peebles.'

'Is that necessary?'

Nicky stared at the tea growing cold in the cups, and then he looked at Jago. 'Oh yes, quite necessary I'm afraid. You have enemies, old man. This way there's a chance they'll believe that it is you who has gone to Scotland. Now, down to business. You should know there's an imminent attempt on Hitler's life being planned by Foxley…'

But Jago hadn't finished. 'We'll work together, Nicky. I accept that. But our friendship, as I said before, is over.'

Nicky met Jago's eyes. 'Alright, Jago. If you say so.'

'I do. Now, the attempt by Foxley?'

'I set wheels in motion yesterday and I hope I've scotched

it. The problem is, one can't just pick up the phone and say *Scrub it, lads*. Our radio contact is in Switzerland, which makes wireless communications easier and safer, but then this Swiss national has to travel to Munich to give the message to the Postman, who in turn has to deliver it to Control, and then she has to inform the trigger man to put his safety catch back on.'

'But we do have assets close to Hitler?'

'Very close, why?'

'Then, if they haven't already killed him, they must not just be called off, they have to be re-tasked. They must reverse their role. We know for a fact there is at least one other team operating in Obersalzberg and their mission is to kill Adolf Hitler. So our team must be told in future they are there to protect him. They must be told to save Hitler.'

CHAPTER FOURTEEN

'This should never have been allowed to happen.' The Führer was treading angrily across the rubble and debris in the wrecked auditorium. In the prompt box Gabriel could hear but not see him.

Eva Braun's voice joined Hitler's, 'Darling, it's no one's fault; you can't control the snow. The theatre just needs a new roof.'

'Plus the replacing of wrecked and ruined equipment,' he said, making the obvious sound like insight.

'The stage is undamaged.' Gabriel heard Eva climb onto it.

'And that's the important thing,' he said, 'because the stage is the battlefield where the great deeds are done; tragedies are enacted, and victories unfold. Everything in a theatre points to the stage. It's the soul of the building, the way a great leader is the focal point and soul of the nation. Drama and leadership are both realised in conflict; all endeavour feeds this elemental need for struggle and triumph. First comes reality, history, where the real man tosses his hat into the maelstrom of events and asserts his destiny against weaker, punier men. Then, in the centuries that follow, come the great plays and operas, as the talented but lesser men, the artists, take inspiration from the great man to make great art.'

Gabriel could feel Eva's confusion coming down through the stage. 'But it's a children's play you're planning, isn't it, for the kindergarten and the Goebbels children?'

'Yes.'

Gabriel heard their feet above him, the hollow clomping, so different from the drum-tight beating of his own heart. He stood rock still in the shadow of the box, cradling a Kar 98k.

'What's it called again, dear?' she said.

'*The Shepherds' Play*, but I might have it rewritten as something more relevant, more twentieth century, more total; not just peasants but engineers and draftsmen, modern men waiting for a modern messiah.'

As they talked, the pair moved, unaware, into Gabriel's field of fire. He was going to take them both out and drag the bodies down to the chorus dressing room on his own. Lorelei had disappeared. She hadn't been in her apartment but, as the curtain had still been pulled across the window of her bedroom, Gabriel knew there was no emergency. These things happened in the fog of war but the good soldier still tried to carry out his original orders, even under changed circumstances. Hitler and his woman were going to die and perhaps, by the time he'd stowed their bodies away in a costume skip, Lorelei would turn up and they could escape together. Otherwise he'd open her bedroom curtains to warn her and hope she'd follow him.

Now both the targets were before and above Gabriel, side by side, heads floating together like balloons on string, the perfect target. Gabriel breathed out, cradled his rifle and lined up on the Führer. Hitler was chattering about the legend of Barbarossa, how Barbarossa was supposed to live under the Obersalzberg, waiting to be recalled to life at Germany's greatest moment of peril. 'The old man under the mountain.'

There was never going to be a better time. Gabriel's finger

began the gentle squeeze to bring about the end of the monster.

'There you are, Gabriel!' Lorelei's head suddenly appeared, framed in close-up by the box. His finger sprang from the trigger; he dropped the rifle to his side, masked by Lorelei's mop of hair.

'Hauptsturmführer Zobel?' he heard the Führer say.

'I'm here, sir,' Gabriel called out, as if it was the most natural thing in the world to be secreted in a prompt box.

Lorelei moved to one side and Adolf Hitler glared down at him. 'I know what you're doing, you can't fool me.' The Führer's heavy brow lightened and he turned to the women. 'This is the good Hauptsturmführer doing his conscientious duty. He's being my bodyguard. He knows I hate the claustrophobia of close protection so he tries, out of sight, to do his duty and protect his leader. Good man – of course I'd already seen you. I decided to spare your blushes.'

Gabriel heard hurrying feet on the rubble.

'Sir?' came Heinz the valet's voice.

'What is it?'

'Sir, Field Marshal Model is here.'

'Right, I'd better see him,' he said to them and left with his valet.

Eva's pink face appeared before Gabriel. 'What a cosy sentry-box, but you can come out now. He's gone and I want some tea and toast.'

Without the considerable curves on her sensual body it would almost be, Gabriel thought, like being invited to tea by a child. But the last thing he wanted was tea; he wanted to know what was going on.

Lorelei's head appeared by the smiling Eva's. 'Come on, soldier, time for tea.'

Her smile inflamed his confusion. He'd been to the edge, put his life on the line, pointed the weapon and then been blown with a grin, with a simper, with an invitation to tea.

'I'd love to go to Japan.' Eva was trying on a silk kimono that hung from the wall of Lorelei's apartment, almost as a decoration. She sighed. 'Perhaps after the war is won. Mr Hitler has been invited, you know, when General Oshima, the Japanese ambassador, was here in May.'

Eva thought it was sweet to refer to her lover as Mr. She always did, never the Führer. It was her nickname for him: Mr Hitler. On a good day it amused Gabriel, but today it added to his anger.

Lorelei came in with a tray of tea things and Eva cleared a space for it. Gabriel wanted the charade over, he wanted to be alone with Lorelei. He was desperate to find out what she was playing at, but Eva wasn't going anywhere. Instead she held out her arms, heavy with the kimono, so she looked like a flowery letter T. 'It almost looks art deco,' she said.

'It is,' Lorelei said. 'Japanese ladies love to copy the West, but when then do, they do it better.'

Eva lifted the hem and inspected the embroidery. 'Red camellias.'

Gabriel found his impatience moving towards anger. They were talking flowers. He needed to know why he had been prevented from completing his mission. Why was Hitler still alive?

Lorelei joined her at the silk and stroked it. 'The red camellia is a special flower; it signifies dying with grace – for love.'

In his mind, Gabriel crushed teacups under his heels and incinerated satin frocks with a flame-thrower.

Eva inspected an Eastern print on the wall. 'How did you come to be born in Japan?'

Lorelei explained as she handed out the tea things. 'My father was in the Kaiser's navy in the Great War. In the Pacific his ship was sunk by the Japanese Imperial Navy and he was taken prisoner.'

'Didn't he come home after the war?' said Eva.

He knew these women could talk forever. Their chatter was stoking his confusion. He needed answers.

'There wasn't much to return to. The British blockade was still in place, even after the armistice. People were starving. In Tokyo the Japanese were so kind to the released prisoners of war that my dad and a lot of other Germans decided to stay on. He sent a ticket for my mother, and she left Europe for a new life. He opened a beer cellar in Kyoto and the locals loved it. I was born there and I was lucky, I had a happy childhood. I didn't realise it was exotic until I left it behind.'

Eva slipped the kimono off and hung it back up. She took her tea. 'You know, I'm surprised at Mr Hitler getting so excited about Christmas.'

'Especially as it's only September,' said Lorelei.

And they'd still be talking come the New Year, Gabriel thought bitterly.

'Normally he hates that time of the year. Clara, his mother, died just before Christmas – he was very close to her. Usually he just shuts himself up, or walks that bloody dog, endlessly. I think this Christmas is different. I think he has plans.'

'Yes, the play,' said Lorelei.

'That's the icing, the celebration I think. He has a bigger plan, I'm sure. He believes his luck is turning again; the July plot against him failed, and the Allies in Normandy are not as tough as they were in the desert and Italy. He thinks they've become cautious, that they lack the political will to take the sort of casualties outright victory will require. So he has a plan, which he won't tell me about, but he's chuckling again, and he's sent for Field Marshal Model.'

More reason to kill him now. Gabriel fumed. Why had he been stopped?

There was a pause in the babble.

'More tea, Eva?'

'Thank you, more tea. Golly, hark at me; I just rattle on.'

Another awkward pause followed, as each of them sought to find a subject that might draw the silent man into the conversation. Lorelei glanced at Gabriel, whose sullen presence was suffocating the ambiance. It was Eva who took up the burden of small talk again. 'So, where did you two meet?'

Lorelei responded gratefully with a gush of words. 'Platterhof Hospital, here. Gabriel was on the general surgical ward I help out on some nights. He was as helpless as a newborn babe, weren't you?'

Gabriel met her look the way a boulder meets rain, but inside he remembered his despair, the black cloud, of not wanting to die but also of not wanting to go back to the Eastern Front. And of a darker shadow still, that he had made an error: he had served the ghost, but he was not his father, he was different. The women waited for an answer, but as Gabriel tried to find clumsy words to contribute, he had a sudden moment of clarity. It terrified him. He'd made a mistake. That had to be it. Everything was unravelling. Hitler's death would have been his death as well. They were closing in. That was why Lorelei had come between him and the target. Abandon the mission. Escape. He had no words.

Lorelei tried to cover. 'I had to do everything for you, didn't I?' she said.

Silence, his tea growing cold. He wasn't in the room. He was back on the ward. She had rescued him from that despair, by teasing and flirting with him, by her scent and smile and touch. But it was the things they talked of that finally saved him. Apparently sometimes, with special women, a man could talk, open his heart and be understood. The trust that came from treachery was stronger than that of pure affection. Now he needed to talk to her again. What had gone wrong?

Having tea with a stuffed male was becoming increasingly embarrassing, so Eva tried to do her bit. 'And how do you like being an Old Hare?' said Eva.

Eva looked him in the eye. She was the Führer's mistress. Gabriel knew he couldn't be rude to her. He needed to play his part again. He reached for his lukewarm tea, poured it down his throat and said, 'I'm not an Old Hare yet. Not accepted.'

Those were the only words that came to him. The women waited for more but there wasn't any. Eva worked with what she'd been given. She gave a small laugh, and said, 'They're such poppets. They're just like honorary uncles; they make such a fuss of me.' She lowered her voice as if to impart a state secret. 'And they don't like Blondi, either.'

'Ah,' said Gabriel, finally.

The tea party was dead and Eva stood and continued with her dog theme. 'Well, I must go and walk the boys.'

She meant her Highland Terriers, which she adored and the Führer didn't. They were like a couple who had children from previous marriages, Gabriel thought, where neither cared for the other's offspring.

Alone at last, Lorelei said, 'We need to walk as well.'

'And talk,' he almost screamed at her.

But she made him wait until they were outside. Away from people.

'What's happened? Do we need to go? To get away?' Gabriel felt the relief of finally demanding some answers. Lorelei tried to walk on. He boiled over and grabbed her. 'Why didn't you let me kill him?'

'Let me go.' Lorelei squirmed from his grip and stepped away. It was another sun-swept day in the false peace of the mountains. She turned from him and scanned the horizon, seeming to take it all in; the peaks, the taste of the air, the warmth of the sun baking her skin through her thin cotton dress.

She looked over her shoulder back at him, as if fearing that to face him fully might heighten the confrontation. 'Our orders have been changed; that's why I had to go to Munich suddenly.'

This confused Gabriel. 'You don't meet.'

She turned, and sought to placate him with detail. 'Ordinarily, no. But this was an emergency and the usual delivery system was considered too slow. London's in a panic, they've changed their mind; we're no longer to kill Hitler. In fact, our orders have been reversed: we're to spare no effort to protect the Führer from any further assassination attempt by the German generals.'

Gabriel felt as if he was falling off the mountain. As if he was slipping and sliding into nothingness.

'What?'

'They have their reasons I suppose.' Lorelei turned to walk on, hoping to take Gabriel with her. But Gabriel was going nowhere.

'I don't understand.'

Lorelei spoke impatiently. 'It's official, you really are to become the Führer's bodyguard.'

Gabriel took it in. They hadn't been found out. There was no need to escape. But instead of relief came rage. 'I'm here to kill Adolf Hitler and I will kill him, whatever you or London want.'

CHAPTER FIFTEEN

Gabriel looked around Max's new office in the Berghof barracks. On the wall, of course, was a photograph of the Führer, but it was behind Max's desk where he wouldn't see it when he looked up. Instead, in his eyeline from the desk, there was a grandmother clock on the wall with an audible click that sounded like an old lady tutting. On the walls either side of the door were two maps; one of the whole Obersalzberg estate, the other covering a larger area from Salzburg to Munich.

Gabriel was interested in rooms. Before his quarters in the officers' mess, he'd never slept alone. The log cabin he'd grown up in had been one large room that he shared with his father. Barrack life had been communal. On the battlefield, slit trenches were always shared. Like all soldiers, he personalised his uniform where he could, but a whole room was daunting. Lorelei's apartment had impressed him; she had put herself up on the walls with the pictures and things in a way that Gabriel knew he couldn't. Most of what he had or knew about himself, he wanted to forget or keep hidden. Max's room seemed a good compromise; it was a uniform with four sides. What was underneath was out of sight, unlike Lorelei's chemise of a room where you could virtually see everything. But then Lorelei's room had lied to him; it had told him she was a freethinker, when in reality she just obeyed orders. He banished her from his thoughts.

'I need to be at the heart of things, if I'm to protect Hitler,' said Max.

'Supposing there's an air raid? Won't they need you at Battery HQ?' said Gabriel.

'There's never been one so far.'

'Never say never.'

Max sighed. 'I've got a contingency plan. The first sign of a terror bomber over Munich will result in the officer commanding Spotting Unit ringing the Obersalzberg HQ and the NCO on this end of the line setting off the siren. Whereupon I will jump astride my trusty BMW bike parked outside, to roar up to my battery to be ready to receive our guests.'

Gabriel nodded and went to the source of the aroma that had been tormenting him since he'd entered the office. Screwed to a wall, by a stained pine filing cabinet, was a coffee grinder with a jar underneath to catch the grains. On the filing cabinet was a coffee maker with an electric plug that was attached to a socket in the wall.

'Electric?' said Gabriel.

The machine was bubbling and purring like a mechanical cat. Max hovered; the proud owner.

'Perk of being an old cop; confiscated this from an undesirable source.'

'But where did you get the beans?'

'Another old contact, a smuggler, brings it in over the top – from your part of the world.'

'Switzerland?'

'Probably why we never invaded, in spite of there being a sizeable population of German-speaking folk for the Führer to unify. Think about it; an adjacent neutral country makes life tolerable for a nation at war. You can smuggle in luxuries, sneak out the loot and if your war goes tits up you've got a convenient bolthole. Coffee?'

'Thought you'd never ask,' said Gabriel.

As they drank the black syrup, Gabriel went into a sort of minor ecstasy that he knew soldiers were prone to when dirty and dangerous service was relieved by some small comfort. The flavour of the beverage spread through him and the aroma toasted his head and took him over. He groaned internally, almost as if he were enjoying sex. But coffee, real coffee, was more reliable; sex was just ersatz, and he was finished with ersatz.

'Right, let's have a look at the problem,' said Max, and went to the map of Obersalzberg on the wall. 'Once, this was a village that enjoyed the reputation of being an air cure resort; good, clean oxygen. It attracted the Führer and he lived here with his neighbours until, in 1937, the Party bought out the locals by compulsory purchase, and constructed a further ninety buildings. Obersalzberg became a sort of high-class camp for the Nazi privileged; they became concentrated here behind a wire fence, guard towers, roadblocks and pickets.'

'It's a big space to police,' said Gabriel.

'Yep, by any standard this is a large estate and its acreage is dotted with targets, luxury houses; the Berghof, Adolf Hitler's home, is here, Goebbels' is over here, Bormann's is down here, Himmler's – though he never visits – is here, and Speer's is just there with his studio next door. This is Goering's with its swimming pool; this splash of blue, see?'

'I was given permission to swim there – when I was recovering from my wounds. Trying to regain battle fitness.'

Max stared at him as if he'd farted audibly on parade. 'For fuck's sake, why? So they can send you back? My limp is my best friend.'

Gabriel himself had wondered the same thing as he'd slogged up mountains and swum endless lengths of the pool. Why? It was the soldier's vanity to be A1, he'd decided.

Max was speaking again. 'There's also a community of support staff, both military and civilian, with their families, which means there's also a hospital, a kindergarten, tearooms, hairdressers, bomb shelters and barracks. That means a population of over twelve hundred.'

'And the problem?'

'Everything is geared to prevent a threat from getting in. Look...' Max banged the map at various points. 'Wire fences, picket-posts, patrols, barriers, but if Obersalzberg is Troy, then the walls and their guards are fuck-all useless if the wooden horse is already inside. And all these uniforms, and comings and goings in armoured cars, make everyone think someone else has got it covered, and they relax. It's so slapdash it would make you weep. The pickets have stopped checking the passes of people they think they know; the milkman sails past three checkpoints every morning with no more than a cheery wave. A blind one-legged burglar could knock this place over and make off with Mrs Goebbels' pearls!'

'So what's the plan?'

'Tighten up security; we need to guard against external threats, even though we know the bandits have got a team on the inside. Then we need a second circle of eyes; a cordon of pickets looking in, not out. My Luftwaffe gunners have had sod all to do in this war so far, except try to send themselves blind. The batteries circle Obersalzberg, so instead of scanning the sky with their binoculars for non-existent terror bombers, I'll get them to follow every move our leader makes. Plus, each gun will have a different Old Hare to watch.'

Gabriel forgot his coffee and became alert. 'You think the Führer is right to suspect one of them?'

'Why just one? We're looking for two assassins. Probably two old sods doing it together to give each other confidence, like two little girls holding hands when they walk home after dark.'

Gabriel sipped his coffee and then spoke. 'But – the Old Hares, they've been with him since the beginning.'

Max looked at Gabriel. 'Listen to what the Gob says, friend. Listen to what our dear Adolf declaims. He has a talent for survival. He watches the world without any sentimentality, without any softness, without any charity or kindness. I'd go with his suspicions because he's the expert. If he told me to brain his dog Blondi because she was planning to kill him, I'd go and look for a suitable brick. Right?'

Gabriel finished his coffee. 'Right,' he agreed.

'My gunners will keep a logbook recording any move they make, even if it's only to go to the ablutions.'

'I'll stick to Hitler,' said Gabriel.

Max shook his head. 'He's the target, you don't want to take another bullet. We're going to use our heads and check some back stories. Let's see if any of the Old Hares has a cast-iron alibi that rules him out of the attempt on the Führer. If we can get the numbers down a bit, we can saturate the scrutiny. We'll get the bastard, then you can justify your membership of the Leibstandarte by sending him to Valhalla.'

'And what will you be doing, Max?'

Max grinned, 'Me? I'll be watching you, sunshine, watching you like a hawk.'

Gabriel hadn't seen Lorelei since the sabotaged assassination attempt and it left him with nowhere to go in his off-duty hours. He found himself rooted outside his mess, unable to go one way or another, not knowing where to spend the next hours. Carousing in bars had no appeal, nor did walking the hills, or even an overnight in Munich with a visit to a soldier's woman thrown in. Nothing worked for him any more and he was angry with Lorelei; she'd lied to him, deceived him when he'd been at his most vulnerable, when he was lying helpless in a hospital bed.

He'd liked life on the ward; it was clean and warm and soft service. The disabled and amputees tainted the air with a euphoria that they were going home soon. Those recovering lived for the minute, day by day, grateful for the holiday, fighting off the thought they were going back.

Lorelei came to him by night when the ward slept. He'd watch her at her desk, lit by a lamp, glowing as she wrote up her notes. Finally, she'd clear them away and make her rounds. He was always last.

'Still awake, soldier?' she'd whisper.

She'd sit on the chair by his bed and lean in and they'd talk together. Inch by inch they'd moved from small talk to dangerous talk, oiled not just by like minds but by desire. It was a courtship born of danger, and plots, and the scent in her hair, as she moved her face close to his while she began to whisper treason.

'Every country is like the kindergarten; there's a dressing-up box and in it is all their history. Sometimes the folk try on one set of costumes, sometimes another. When I was a teenager, the Japanese folded away all the lovely legends I'd grown up with and got out all their cruel Bushido stories. They changed, and their attitude to me changed. I can speak Japanese, I understood when they called me *giraffe woman* because I'm taller than them, I understood when the men called me *whore* because I was born with blonde hair.

'One day a gang of girls surrounded me in the street and started to kick me and then, while I was trying to hold them off, they produced a giant bottle of school ink and kept splashing me with it, trying to get it in my hair. And when they did, they cheered, not raucously but in sweet high oriental voices and they clapped delightedly with their fingers spread like children's. Respectable older women came forward with their nail scissors and gave them to the girls and encouraged them to cut my hair off. Men watched silently; no one did anything to help me. I broke through and ran away – this wasn't Japan, not the Japan I knew, not the Japan that had been so kind to my father. You see, they'd taken out a new set of clothes and a whole people had changed.'

Most days Lorelei worked at the kindergarten and escaped the tyranny of the hospital matron, Iron Arse. She was one of those Germans who thought final victory could be brought closer if she could be just a little bit harsher than she had been the day before. As it was an officers' ward she was outranked, so she saved her bullying for the visitors.

'Only two visitors per patient and one chair. No children. No sitting on the bed.'

She was a cow of the first order and Lorelei had explained to Gabriel how she'd got her name, Iron Arse. 'She wouldn't let a man see his little girls and he was due to be discharged back to the Eastern Front, with no saying if he'd ever have the chance to hold them again. So he got at her coffee substitute; he put a really powerful laxative in it. She drank the lot and the men waited for the – *fireworks* – but nothing happened, the laxative had no effect. The men decided she must have bowels of steel and called her Iron Arse.'

As Gabriel improved, Lorelei would come after kindergarten to rescue him from Iron Arse and push him in a wheelchair around the gardens. In among the flowerbeds, where only the mountains above seemed to be trying to overhear, he'd share his own guilt.

'I came across some of our men – they'd caught a bunch of Russian kids stealing from our supplies. We were going hungry a lot by then and there wasn't much pity in the air. These men had got an old truck with no engine and locked them in the back and then...'

'What? What did they do, Gabriel?'

'They rolled the truck downhill into a minefield. Everyone was silent as it ran through the mines, you could hear the kids screaming and crying in the back – they knew what was being done to them. Then it hit a mine and, as it went up, the men I thought I knew all cheered and clapped each other on the back, as if something had been achieved or a goal had been scored. It was a fireball and out of it stumbled this kid in flames. He moved like he could put out the fire if he ran fast enough, but he trod on another mine and the explosion sent him up into the air like a firework. As it happened, the men laughed as if it was the funniest thing they'd ever seen. You think the roar of the guns or the blast of a bomb is the sound of war – but to me it's the laughter of those men.'

She held his hand. 'Could you have stopped them?'

Gabriel shook his head. 'Some of them outranked me. I just stood there and, for some reason, I remembered my village priest telling us of the time he'd nearly lost his faith, how in the shadows he'd heard the devil laughing, and at that moment I knew I had too. I thought of my father. He never told me this was war. He must have known, he'd been four years at the front, but he came home afterwards with a love of medals and uniforms and camaraderie, and a desire for me to follow in his footsteps, and I wondered why he never mentioned the burning kids. When my comrades drifted away and the flames died down and the boy went out, well, the last of the soldier in me went out with him.'

He'd lied to her. It wasn't because he was outranked, that

wasn't why he hadn't intervened. Gabriel, who could do the business of war, said to have balls of brass, feared being an outsider. His uniform was his skeleton, he knew that – it held him up. He needed the acceptance of other men and breaking rank to go soft put that in jeopardy. In this respect Gabriel knew he was a coward.

Her eyes had looked at him then, not just at him but into him. 'What do you want, Gabriel?'

He thought for all of his life he'd done what his father wanted; even after his death he'd served the ghost. Now he needed to write up orders for himself and this was new. So he thought and he considered. 'I want to go home. I want this war to be over. I want to cross that mountain into Switzerland and go home to my hut.' But not alone, he thought but didn't say.

She nodded and touched his forehead with her own.

When Gabriel was strong enough and could walk, she'd taken him to her little apartment in the ruined theatre. He'd seen her Japanese mementos.

'When my father died, we left Kyoto. We were barely tolerated by then; we came back to Europe.'

'To Germany?'

'My mother's English. We went to London and I started my nurse training, but it didn't feel like home. German is my first language and I'd be hard put to say whether Japanese or English is my second. I couldn't settle. I visited an aunt in Heidelberg and found it resembled Kyoto; cultured, medieval, clean – everything that London wasn't, so I finished my training there.'

'So you're German?'

'No.'

The small word that hung between them.

'Something happened – and I went back to London.'

Gabriel wondered if he should ask what? Instead he stayed silent and wondered where his infatuation for the nurse was taking him. He supposed it was a strange courtship but he wasn't really sure; it was all new to him. He'd only known camp-followers and soldiers' women before. When Lorelei fussed around him, she'd put her face close to his and he thought that maybe she was waiting for him to kiss her, but kissing was the one thing prostitutes never allowed and he was lost. He couldn't be sure he was reading the map of her actions correctly.

'What are you thinking?' she said.

'About a comrade who'd been a bank robber in another life.'

'He robbed banks?'

'Yes.'

She scooched closer to him. 'So why were you thinking about this bank robber?'

'He told me why most bank jobs fail. When the robbers' car pulls up at the bank, no one will get out first. They sit there in silence or argue and then they drive home in shame. Apparently every gang needs a member with the balls to get out of the safety of the car and cross the pavement. He said, *That's what you are, Gabriel, you're the nutter who crosses the pavement. When we're all hugging the mud, you get up and do the business.*'

'And this appertains to what?'

'To this – I'm about to cross the pavement.'

Gabriel kissed her.

The kissing thrilled him in a way he hadn't expected. He'd seen it done in parks and on the screen at the cinema, and he thought kissing was for the ladies. It was why working girls never kissed; the man had paid, so the stuff done was for him and men didn't pay for kissing. He'd been wrong. He hadn't realised how intimate it was; her lips touching his, the taste of her, the soft skin of her face in his hands, trying to express all the pent-up passion in his body through his lips.

Things progressed, sometimes at Lorelei's instigation, which both shocked and thrilled him. By the time they made it to the bed there was only one thing left to do, but she stopped him.

'I want to, Gabriel, I really want to, but I have to say something first. I don't ever want you to think I trapped you or bribed you with my body.'

She told him. 'Making love to me might be a death sentence; you might be having sex with a coffin.'

His arousal didn't want him to listen, just get on and do it. 'I'm a dead man anyway; this war will kill me.'

She stopped him, even looked around nervously before she whispered to him. 'Hear what I have to say, Gabriel – please.'

He stopped fumbling with her and she spoke. 'When I found the Germans were doing the same thing with their dressing-up box as the Japanese, I went back to dirty old London. I saw it with different eyes; I fell in love with it because no one got spat at on its streets. I worked as a nurse, but when the war started I was approached and asked to come back to Germany as an agent – and I agreed.'

The night outside froze, stars stopped moving, fear gripped Gabriel. 'You're a British agent?'

She didn't answer but reached under her clothes to her armpit. She winced as she detached something there and then produced a tiny metal box in military green. It clicked open and inside was a single tablet.

'What is it?' he asked.

'Suicide pill,' she said. 'Do you believe me now?'

He did.

'Still want to have me?' she asked.

Gabriel kissed her and felt her trembling not from passion but from the fear of what she'd told him. He made his confession to her. 'I don't have a side any more, I just want the war to be over,' he said.

'That's what I'm trying to do, soldier.'

She carried on, 'One man stands in the way of peace; Adolf Hitler. I want to kill him so all the boys can go home.'

'Then so do I.'

And they made love to seal the deal.

But now that deal had been broken.

CHAPTER SIXTEEN

Gabriel used the only significant bend on the narrow road to the Kehlsteinhaus to view the party as it edged around it and disappeared ahead of him. The cavalcade was led by a Panzerwagen light-armoured car from the RSD. Behind the armoured car came a Mercedes carrying half the Old Hares. Third in the column was the Swabian Colossus with Hitler and three of his adjutants, Colonel Nicolaus von Below, Gruppenführer Albert Bormann and Konteradmiral Karl-Jesko von Puttkamer. Next were two more Mercedes ferrying the ladies, and behind them came Gabriel with the other half of the Old Hares and Max. Last was another armoured car. Up ahead, and unseen, was a section of RSD on Zundapp motorcycles with sidecars, while another motorbike section, also out of sight, was bringing up the rear.

The Führer was well protected, Gabriel thought. There was no chance of finishing the job, not in the motorcade, nor at the Eagle's Nest, where they were heading. The noise of the engines rolling off the mountains exhilarated Gabriel, and deep within him he knew he was excited that Lorelei was in one of the cars with the other ladies. His excitement made him angry. She was in his past, he told himself.

Startled choughs flew up and off, shrieking alarm calls, their black plumage almost marking them as SS, another military wing of the Führer's elaborate protection. A movement behind Gabriel made him turn; Emil Maurice was taking potshots at the excitable birds with an imaginary shotgun. Gabriel was tense; the expedition to the mountaintop folly was fraught with problems and he was not in the mood to pretend-shoot anything. He tried to relax, lullabied by the steady growl of the carburettors and the warmth of the autumn sun through the windows. The mimed shotgun dissolved and disappeared as Emil forgot it and tugged at his dress uniform. The party was to be semi-formal, with the ladies in tea dresses and Hitler's close guard in their number ones. Gone were their soft forage caps, replaced with coal scuttle helmets brought to a mirror-bright shine.

The angle of the ascent increased and the engines growled in ratio. It was, thought Gabriel, the fashionable fanfare of the great; the roar of the motorcade. Ahead, like weasels slipping into a rabbit's burrow, the cars entered a tunnel into the mountain without breaking speed. The column became a mole, an underground creature, with the way ahead lit by a sinister dull glow. All around them, grey walls flashed by.

'Very German,' said Max, who was sitting between Gabriel and August Korber, who was driving.

'What is?' Gabriel asked.

'Those walls. Can you believe this? They're made of marble. Now marble is an expensive stone and it's right that a tunnel used by the Führer on a regular basis isn't lined with brick – like a sewer.'

Gabriel could feel the other occupants of the car tuning into Max; was he about to commit treason and compare the Führer to a turd?

Bodo Gelzenleuchter challenged from the back, 'Doesn't look like marble to me.'

'Of course it doesn't. Marble is an effete stone, the sort of rock an Italian, who shall remain nameless, might use to line his mistress's bathroom.'

Small laughter, mostly relief; Max was tilting at the soft underbelly of the Axis. No one cared what he said about Mussolini. Max continued his lecture as they sped on deep into the mountain. 'So, here's the thing, the German thing. Having clad the walls in shiny marble – they brought in masons to rough it up and make it look like granite.'

Gabriel looked at the fake granite. August, behind the wheel, shook his head. 'That's incorrect Major Adler. This part of the tunnel *is* lined with granite, it's only the final chamber, where the Führer alights to enter the elevator, that is lined in marble. But you're right; the marble there has been scoured to disguise it as granite.'

Gabriel looked at August's profile where it protruded beyond Max's. 'How do you know that?' he asked.

August was off, the cleverest boy in the classroom. 'I know, Scar, because I was one of the volunteers who constructed the Kehlsteinhaus. We worked for thirteen months. All volunteers, no slave labour.'

Max clapped his hands slowly, almost silently. 'Bravo,' he yawned.

August glanced at him as he changed down the gears and slowed the car to a stop, while still chattering. 'Day and night, summer and winter we laboured, to build the Führer's fiftieth birthday present from a grateful Party.'

August and his memories were ignored, as the doors were open even before they came to a halt. Protocol demanded the bodyguard got out of the car first and secured the perimeter. The vanguard of motorbikes formed a roaring corridor from the Swabian Colossus to the elevator doors, then, on a signal, fell silent as one, their engines cut simultaneously. As the fumes from their bikes rose, silence came through the memory of the revving. Gabriel looked around. The Old Hares were in place, upright, their polished helmets catching the glow of the underground lighting. He crossed the cavern, the echo of his steps coming back at him from the walls. Ahead, Von Below was already out of the car and standing alert alongside it. Still inside the Mercedes sat the Führer, staring ahead.

As Gabriel passed the cars with the ladies, he heard a mocking voice say in time to his march, *Left right, left right*, and then giggling. It was Gretl, Eva's younger sister. As he reached the Führer's vehicle, Erich Kempka, his driver, shot out and opened a door, as simultaneously the remaining two adjutants let themselves out the other side and stood at the apex of the motorbike guard at the very doors of the elevator. Gabriel came to attention, saluted, called out the salutation, bent and spoke to the figure in the shadowy interior. 'The perimeter is secure, sir.'

The Führer nodded, slid out and stood upright, looking about him as Kempka closed the door behind him. 'The hall of the Mountain King,' Hitler said, looking about him. 'Did you hear about the Japanese?'

Gabriel hadn't been expecting this and he wondered what the Japanese had done now. 'Sir, no sir!'

The Führer smiled. 'Your little lady told me. I think it was Korea – but somewhere in the Orient. The occupying Japanese had suffered some insurrection from the local populace and had decided, by way of retribution, to kill the mountain the people worshipped. They forged a six-foot nail and took it midway up to the shrine that was the focal point of the worship and which, they'd been told, covered the heart of the mountain. There, two of their biggest men took turns to drive the nail into the heart, using sledgehammers and accompanied on each stroke by a great beat on a gong. The Koreans wailed and wept and the nail went home and the mountain was killed. Total theatre. Primitive superstition – but I think Wagner would have approved. And here, in the belly of this mountain, who can say for sure it is not a living thing.'

Gabriel followed Hitler's scan of the tomb about them. The cavern was a great stomach, glowing dimly, seemingly powered by its own constitution. He wondered if it was aware of the parasites in its gut?

Hitler frowned at Gabriel. 'Why should one be afraid of a mountain just because it's big? It's stationary, one knows where it is and it's easy to kill. Just like shooting an elephant and it makes less fuss dying.'

'Difficult to mount the head – as a trophy, sir.'

'Wolf,' the Führer corrected.

'Wolf.'

The Führer looked at him, searching for some sign that he had just been mocked. Gabriel went behind his face and sat out the search, reminding himself of the time before his commission; an officer could be friendly to an enlisted man – but he was never a friend. Hitler smiled and pinched his cheek; humour had been detected but it hadn't offended.

'My dear, scarred seraph, the mountain *is* the trophy. I live in a world where little men are frightened of giants; gigantic countries like Russia, gigantic wealth like the Americans. I say they are merely mountains, big, fat bits of rock, too obese to move. Easy to kill with the right sort of nail.'

A sad, flat ping echoed about them as the elevator arrived. Gabriel stayed at attention as Hitler left him abruptly. The Führer swept on, turning back briefly to do a two-arm wave at the women in their cars, releasing them. They exploded like racing pigeons from a basket and banished the gloom and ponderous silence calling to each other, their dresses bright splashes of colour against the grey, scoured marble. About the chamber, the men stood at attention, staring ahead, while the women combined and moved through and around each other like a shoal of fish. Only one woman stood apart from the others, a balance to Hitler by the elevator doors, Ilse Hess. She'd travelled with the women but scandal, and her own personality, kept her separate. Frau Hess viewed the gossiping of her sisters with a disdain that wasn't remotely concealed. Rumour had it she was the one woman who made the Führer nervous.

Hitler radiated his desire to be the focal point with one of his long, silent stares, and the chattering ceased as all eyes were turned to him. The doors to the lift opened and revealed another opera set. The elevator resembled a golden cave, its walls covered in polished brass. Hitler went into it and stood waiting to ascend. His three adjutants joined him and dressed the interior with their poses, like spear carriers around a medieval presence. The doors slid shut, a small light above indicated Hitler's journey to the heavens and chattering returned to the waiting masses. The crowd breathed out and moved to wait their turn to follow the Führer.

A strange military quickstep took place. The men of the RSD abandoned their Zundapps and sidecars and marched to the walls, where they exchanged posts with the Old Hares, who marched to the vortex of motorbikes. On Gabriel's command, they came to a halt and were taken to the at-ease position, before being dismissed. The Old Hares infiltrated the ranks of the ladies, in compliance with their further duties that afternoon to be on hand and host Eva's tea party.

Max lumbered over to Gabriel. 'What about me? Do you want me down here or up with the eagles?'

There was only one way up to the summit, the elevator. Any outside assassin would have to take on and wipe out the troop of RSD to get access to it. Gabriel didn't care if someone wanted to kill Hitler, he just didn't want it to happen on his watch. A bullet behind the ear would be the best he could hope for if that happened. Better that than a transfer to a penal battalion on the Eastern Front, he thought grimly.

'I want you up with the Old Hares, Max. That's where any threat is going to come from.'

'Ride with us, Mr Scar!'

The elevator's lights proclaimed its imminent arrival and Gretl wanted Gabriel to travel with the ladies, one of whom was Lorelei, demurely ignoring Gabriel as he tried to ignore her. He wanted to refuse but the party of women staring at him robbed him of his confidence. He nodded mutely and stepped forward.

'Good luck,' Max said.

Gabriel, like all the soldiers who were to ascend to the summit, had one last task to perform before he did. Erich Kempka, the chauffeur, waited by the lift doors with a tray. Gabriel unclipped his sidearm and put it on the tray.

The doors to the elevator reopened. As before, it was as if the hills had parted and revealed the treasure trove of a dragon. The polished brass shimmered and Gabriel assumed that the only reason a grateful people had not made the walls of gold was that the precious metal might be too heavy. He followed the ladies aboard and, amongst their bright plumage, felt he was entering an elaborate birdcage.

As the doors closed behind him, the smell of the women was intensified. Gabriel had dealt with many overpowering aromas in his life – the incense of the Vatican, the gangrene gas of the battlefield – but he wasn't sure he had the strength to deal with their perfume. It was as if they'd bathed in flowers. Their scents came off their bodies and entered his and aroused him. In the lift everyone was too close. He could hear the sounds of their silk stockings rubbing together as they moved. Lorelei was in front of him, with her back to him, and Gabriel had a sudden memory of her standing in that position wearing just her scanties. The claustrophobia of the space intensified his desire. He stared at her and then realised she was watching his reflection in the polished brass and she was smiling.

The doors opened and the mountaintop, like a puritan, blew away the scent of the women in a gust of intolerance. He followed the women and their giggles out of the lift, like a dog on a lead. There was a brief impression of staring mountains, a collision of peaks, before they were in again out of sight, out of mind, as the party entered the tearoom in the sky.

In the Scharitzkehi room, the ladies were making for a long table loaded with coffee and cake and under the control of maids in traditional dirndls. The room was as big as a barn or a large parish church; in Hitler's Germany nothing was cosy, Gabriel thought. There was a monstrous fireplace with an angry expression and the Führer stood by it. He looked like he was waiting for someone to take his photo and Eva obliged. The flash went off suddenly like the glare from an incendiary shell. The ladies set up a patter of small arms fire with their clapping. Then Eva arranged the ladies around Hitler. Of course, Frau Hess wouldn't permit her photograph to be taken and Hitler didn't try to persuade her. Annelies von Ribbentrop placed herself to the right of the Leader, fractionally before Magda Goebbels could secure that position. Gretl held back, while Gerda Bormann linked arms with Lorelei on the left of the Führer. Two of Hitler's young secretaries, Christa Schroeder and Gerda Christian, stood in the second row, peering through gaps in the front rank of Nazi womanhood, while the third secretary, Traudi Junge, was prevented by the Führer from joining them.

'Fetch a chair,' Hitler called to Emil Maurice. 'Set it in front of me.'

Protesting, Traudi was led in her widow's weeds to sit before Adolf Hitler, and he placed a hand on the shoulder of her black dress. Her husband had been killed the month before in Dreux, France. Rumour had it that the Führer had broken the news to her personally. The sacrifice of the husband had promoted the widow above the grander ladies of the Reich. Lorelei had told Gabriel that Hitler's three secretaries were the closest things the Führer had to daughters.

Eva began to take pictures, labouring away diligently. She had been a photographer working for Heinrich Hoffmann, Hitler's head of press, when the Führer had first met her. As she snapped and moved and snapped again, all the coquettishness and cuteness seemed to vanish, leaving a confident, professional woman. As he watched this transformation, Gabriel wondered if all women were actresses. His suspicions were interrupted by the growing awareness that someone was standing close behind him. He turned and discovered it was Ilse Hess.

'You are Zobel, commanding officer of the dead bunnies?'

Frau Hess stared at him with eyes that he felt had not blinked since the Fall of Troy, or perhaps since her errant husband had taken himself off to Britain. They were very dry eyes.

Gabriel clicked his heels to acknowledge she was correct.

'Do you know who I am?'

'Frau Hess,' he said.

Her scrutiny of him continued. 'You're here for a purpose. You'll find out what later, so don't get too hot under the collar with the floozies. By the way, which one is yours?'

Gabriel broke her stare to look away. 'None of them – any more.'

She almost snorted with impatience. 'Alright, which one was?'

'Lorelei – the girl by herself.'

'The woman looking sad?'

'Yes.'

Frau Hess stared at her and Gabriel, surprised at his own feelings of protectiveness, was pleased that Lorelei seemed distant and reserved, not as silly as the other women at that moment.

'Is she political? A woman is just a tart if she isn't political. They lie to little girls and tell them that romance and love legitimise the handing over of their bodies to a husband. Not true. It is the meeting of minds and for that a woman needs a brain. Romance is a decadent Jewish invention. A botulism from Hollywood.'

Laughter exploded amongst the women, which they tried to suppress by filtering it through fingers held over mouths. One of the Old Hares had apparently said something funny.

'Don't be fooled,' Frau Hess said. 'These women are an elite. You might think they are as brainless as they are pretty, but you would be in error. They are quite as murderous, sinister and as vicious as any you'd find wearing trousers. Don't be fooled by the pretty print of their frocks. The Reich wastes them, they are a wasted resource. But beware, young man.'

Then she was gone, before he could answer, gone as the group by the fireplace fragmented. Lorelei came out of the throng, took a cup of coffee from a passing tray and came at Gabriel with it held towards him as a peace offering. He wanted the coffee but not the obligation of unconditional surrender. 'No thank you.'

Hitler swept from behind Gabriel like a fighter out of the sun. He lifted the cup in one sweeping movement and held it out. 'Take it,' he ordered.

Gabriel did.

'A little more gallantry I think, Hauptsturmführer Zobel.'

Lorelei stood by Hitler's side, watching Gabriel sip his beverage. 'Would you like some cake to go with that coffee?' she asked.

He risked a refusal but this time the Führer supported his decision. 'No cake for a soldier, young miss. A uniform hates an ounce of flab more than any other article of clothing. You don't want Gabriel here to end up like Lilac Pants, do you?'

He meant Hermann Göring, who encased his huge frame in pastel-coloured silk uniforms.

Lorelei pretended shock before giving out a delighted laugh. 'Sir, you mustn't,' she said.

'Wolf, not sir.' He gave her his avuncular twinkle.

Lorelei, to mark the moment of this great honour, stopped laughing, adopted a sober expression, bowed her pretty head and said quietly, 'Wolf.'

Gabriel thought she was a good actress.

'Let's get some air,' said the Führer, taking more coffee from a maid before he led them out onto the terrace and into the best scenery in the world.

Gabriel's father had told him there was music in the silence of the peaks. It was easy to believe in gods when you lived among them. Far below was the meadow-green water of Lake Königssee.

The Führer seemed to share Gabriel's thoughts. 'Only Wagner could have captured these mountains in sound. Listen.'

They did and they heard what wasn't there; the horns and deep melodies of rock and water.

'I will be buried under a mountain,' he said. 'Not in Berlin, not in some warehouse of superstition, but under a mountain, like Barbarossa laid to rest under the Untersberg.'

They finished their coffee in silence and placed the cups on the flat surface of the terrace wall. A maid appeared and, as gracefully as one of the circling birds, swooped to carry off the crockery. As she went, a sudden breeze caught the hem of her dirndl and lifted it, showing a little more of her leg than she might have wanted. The girl gave a small bleat of dismay and, hindered as she was by the cups in her hands, gave a little sideways skip of desperation to try and rescue her modesty from the wind. It was, Gabriel thought, an intensely female move, containing all the decency of a German girl.

The Führer had also witnessed the maid's mishap and he turned to Gabriel with a look of male conspiracy. The man who had launched a war across the world wanted to have a naughty moment, and so Gabriel relaxed his fixed expression just enough to curl his lips into a smile. Lorelei played her part in the little charade; putting one hand on a hip, she wagged a finger on the other hand at them.

'Boys,' she said, as if shocked and dismayed.

The Führer loved being included in this female censure and Lorelei ticked him off like a naughty boy in the kindergarten. But Gabriel was thinking about the maid who had now disappeared inside. Disappeared from history. Had this been her one moment of immortality, the only significant anecdote to survive her life; how when granny had been a girl, her skirt had blown up in front of Adolf Hitler? Books would be written about him but all she could bequeath posterity was a small incident, magnified by the stature of the man who had witnessed it. She wouldn't even get a medal. Life was, he thought, like being in a play or an opera; everyone had a role to play – but who gave out the parts? At the Vatican the cardinals would say God. Hitler would say you take the part you want to play. Gabriel didn't know. Yet he did understand, in the depths of his being, that the maid was as important as the man of destiny, it was just the books that were wrong.

'There are no mountains in England – if there were I'd kill them,' the Führer laughed and Lorelei looked puzzled but Gabriel understood.

'There are mountains in Scotland and Wales but England just has hills. This presents me with a problem; where to base myself when we have conquered them. I refuse to live in London which, I'm assured, has become a nigger town thanks to their black empire.'

'Windsor is outside London,' said Lorelei, 'and it has a castle.'

'I don't like old architecture, I'm a modern man. I'll have land cleared and Speer is going to design me a home.'

'Where?' Lorelei asked.

'A place that resembles Bavaria, a miniature Bavaria, the Welsh borders. There's a small town on the Welsh side – Bridgend.'

'Bridgend is very picturesque,' Lorelei gushed.

'You know it?' Hitler asked her.

'Oh, yes.'

'Would you recommend the High Town or the Low Town?'

And in that moment Gabriel saw that Lorelei had been lying. She didn't know the town and now she was lost; she didn't know what to say.

'Well – they both have things to recommend them. I'm not sure but…'

The small but blatant lie finished the small talk as far as the Führer was concerned. Flattery he perceived as false irritated him.

'This has been pleasant, but now the war intrudes. Thank you, my dear.'

Lorelei knew she was being dismissed. She gave a small bob and retreated back inside. Hitler turned to Gabriel. 'Destiny has placed you at my disposal.'

Destiny, he thought, destiny that raises a maid's skirt or kills a man.

'We are not here for the coffee and cake and to listen to the silly, false flattery of your girlfriend. Go back inside. Shortly you will be sent for. Today on this mountain there is going to be a meeting, a very secret meeting, one that you will attend, Hauptsturmführer Zobel.'

CHAPTER SEVENTEEN

'Englishmen can't be trained,' said Annelies von Ribbentrop.

In the classless world of National Socialism, Gabriel thought, this woman still had class. Her clothes looked French, and whereas he felt he could picture every other woman present in a traditional dirndl, his imagination broke down when faced with the wife of the German foreign minister; there was nothing peasant about her. Lorelei had told him she had been everywhere and met everyone – everyone who mattered – and by her manner Annelies von Ribbentrop suggested that some present didn't. Eva and her sister Gretl kept well away from the *von* camp and chattered to some captive Old Hares.

'How do you mean, Annelies?' asked Magda Goebbels. The other women in the group leaned in to catch her answer. Gabriel pretended interest but swept the room, counting Old Hares, trying to ascertain if they were all present; that none had gone out onto the terrace where Hitler was now, with his adjutants and with Frau Hess.

'I have German friends who, to their misfortune, married Englishmen. You know how it is, ladies: a German girl marries a German boy. She then has to roll up her sleeves and spend the next two years converting him from a son into a husband.

It's hard work but she doesn't stint on the effort. Finally, she is rewarded with a man who may be left alone in the house for short periods without catastrophe. No one encumbered with an English husband would dare undertake anything so reckless.'

The female audience laughed but were still curious. Gabriel also laughed but wasn't listening. He had misplaced a Hare but had caught the eye of Max who, reading his mind, nodded towards the lavatories. Sure enough Willy Herzberger, the missing man, emerged from them and went back to flirting with the three young secretaries. Gabriel breathed again.

'Why can't they be trained?' asked Gerda Bormann. 'Have they less intelligence than dogs?'

'Possibly. Probably.'

More light laughter.

'My friend has tried for years to persuade her English husband to take off his outside shoes when he enters the house but he never does. She says he always apologises and says he will in a second and then he forgets. She tries to have a really good row with him, shouts at him and throws things – well we know how good that feels, don't we ladies?'

The ladies apparently did. Gabriel wondered if Lorelei was expecting him to play the German man with her. To have a really good row.

'But the Englishman, he won't play, he won't fight back. He apologises and is disgustingly reasonable and that is the Englishman's secret weapon; he apologises while he does what he wants and damn the world.'

Gabriel's formal uniform rubbed at the throat and itched him. His helmet felt heavy and he saw that his comrades had removed theirs – but he was waiting for a summons from the Führer so he suffered his.

'Is your friend still in England?' Frau Goebbels asked.

'Still in London, Magda. A woman's country is her husband's. It must be very hard for her I think.'

Lorelei nodded. 'My father married an Englishwoman; my mother spent the first war in Hamburg among strangers, and this war she's in London – among strangers. A woman who marries a foreigner is in danger of becoming stateless, unless she embraces her new country as passionately as a son born to it.'

'No more about marriage, here comes Traudi,' said Frau Bormann.

Coming towards them was the young widow, glowing like a bride but her dress as black as her late husband's SS dress uniform. Behind her, Gabriel saw a whole block of the bodyguard head for the lavatory. He felt a sense of relief; he knew now they had a bottle stashed in there, something to invigorate the tea.

'Hello Traudi,' said their unofficial hostess, who then scanned the room. 'Where's Ilse?'

'Frau Hess is with the Führer,' Gabriel informed them.

'You do speak after all,' Frau von Ribbentrop said, to laughter that included Lorelei's.

Gabriel clamped his mouth shut as Magda Goebbels became tutty.

'That Frau Hess – why can't she leave him alone?'

Her petulance carried her off towards the cake. It was an open secret on Obersalzberg, Lorelei had told Gabriel, that Magda Goebbels loved the Führer in quite the wrong way. 'Always rattling her ovaries near Hitler,' was what she actually said.

Frau Bormann spoke from a mountain of smugness. 'Goebbels has taken another lover you know, half his age of course.'

'Joseph Goebbels has both a genius for propaganda and for

seduction. Which is a wonder when he has a leg he drags behind him like a damaged dog. Traudi, how are you?'

Annelies von Ribbentrop gathered the young girl to her.

The young secretary smiled bravely. 'Every day a little better.'

'So beautiful, so tragic. You should have taken some time away, gone home.'

Traudi shook her head at Annelies von Ribbentrop's words. 'I couldn't leave him.'

Him, the Führer, Adolf Hitler.

Frau Goebbels sailed back from the cake and into the company. 'Who says there's a war on? The chocolate sachertorte is divine.'

Gabriel found himself watching the Reich's three leading ladies – Annelies von Ribbentrop, Magda Goebbels and Gerda Bormann – as they consoled and fussed the young widow. A trio of women married to the most powerful men in Germany. Was there any seed of dissent there, in their eyes, in their thoughts? Any treachery that came with their wedding rings; a husband who now wanted out of his blood oath, or to get the ultimate promotion over a dead body?

'We are blessed with our beloved Führer,' said Frau Bormann. 'Look at the men who lead our enemies – a fat drunk and a cripple.'

'What about Stalin?' Lorelei asked.

Annelies von Ribbentrop scoffed. 'A disgusting man, my husband told me. His photographs flatter him; often it's a double. He never brushes his teeth, they're brown and green. He never bathes, so he stinks. And worst of all – he likes young girls, very young girls; twelve-year-olds.'

Gabriel thought Frau Bormann was going to cross herself. 'Dear God, is that true?'

'My husband told me in confidence.' She whispered to give

her words weight. 'They have these ghastly Mother Russia festivals where girls from all over the Soviet Union flock to Moscow in peasant dress and wave bunches of red flowers, unaware the secret police are scrutinising them, looking for the most beautiful and virginal. These they select and, when the other girls go home, they are kept on. They stay for a year in the Kremlin. The parents are proud, and the girls are guaranteed Party membership and a place at university when the time comes. The little girls stay behind to decorate the Kremlin with their sweet presence. To go to Uncle Joe when he sends for them. They spend a year in Moscow but they don't go home virgins. It's a great honour apparently.'

Max was by Gabriel's side. 'You're wanted.' He nodded towards the door to the terrace where the adjutant, Colonel von Below, waited and beckoned to Gabriel.

Out on the terrace there were two Hitlers. The Führer was intimidating one of his doubles.

'You are dismissed, Weler. Go to Berlin and be me. Hold your head up, stiffen your spine; your task is an important one.'

'Yes, my Führer.'

Martin Bormann was there and Gabriel wondered where he had sprung from; possibly the small study Hitler kept in the Kehlsteinhaus. He knew this Bormann to be one of life's plotters, unlike his brother Albert, the adjutant. Gabriel watched him carefully as he spoke to the double, Gustav Weler.

'After the party breaks up, I will accompany you to the Chancellery. In Berlin, we don't want you to make speeches, just be seen – hand out some Iron Crosses.'

'Yes, sir.'

'My presence with you will validate your assumed identity. Now wait in the study till the ladies have departed.'

Weler, Hitler in every way but charisma, scuttled off. The

Führer watched him go and shook his head. 'Perhaps every man expects more from his doppelgänger.'

Frau Hess glanced at Gabriel. 'This one's here.'

Hitler regarded him and said, 'Send a section of the Old Hares with Weler; that will help the deception.'

And clear out some possible traitors, Gabriel thought. He signalled compliance with a click of his heels.

The Führer addressed them all. 'Operation Watch on the Rhine has been delayed again.'

Frau Hess growled. 'Your generals are contemptible shits, the lot of them. You should have shot them years ago, I always said, but you're too soft. The military pretend to listen to you but don't let their supposed attention fool you. Come down hard; fear is better than flattery – shoot a few generals.'

During her speech, the Führer had turned to inspect the mountains again, as an officer might review a line of soldiers. His back said, I'm not listening to you Frau Hess, but his tension said he was.

'There will be time to shoot the General Staff after Watch on the Rhine – if it fails.'

'It mustn't,' said Bormann.

Hitler pulled the trick of letting his voice swell softly. It drew them in. He included them in destiny. 'If I succeed, the United States and the British Empire will be swept off the continent of Europe into the sea. They will not get a chance to return, not across the Channel. They can't pull the Normandy trick twice. Speer will use his slave armies to build an impregnable wall down from Denmark to the Spanish Pyrenees. France will then know there will be no rescue and therefore they have two choices; sit on their arses and wait to learn Russian, or join the crusade against Slavic Bolshevism.'

Bormann agreed. 'They've collaborated on a grand scale; given us their Jews, children as well. They won't want the humiliation of occupation a second time, on this occasion by the Russians. The French are like women; they'll change their minds and pretend it's what they intended all along. The Yanks and the English will go away, defeat the Japanese in the East and have their victory there.'

Hitler brought his clenched right fist into the palm of his left hand. 'Leaving us to fight the real war and defeat the Soviets.'

Everyone now followed his gaze into the mountains. Hitler barked up at the clouds, 'We will have broken the ring of steel.'

The old German nightmare; the ring of steel, the encirclement of the Fatherland by a coalition of enemies.

'We will have done it, gentlemen,' the Führer said.

Suddenly the mountains gave their blessing. The mist that masked the peaks broke and revealed a stone feature, the way a gap in theatre curtains reveals one aspect of the scenery, highlighting it, giving it significance. A shaft of sunlight illuminated a peculiarity, and the two things together – the gap in the clouds and the shaft of sunlight – showed what had been there for countless ages but never noticed before – a chiselled twist of rock like an eagle's head. Below, two cliffs swept out and up like giant wings. The German Eagle soared above them, out of the mountain. Gabriel felt the hairs on the back of his neck rising to attention. He heard the majesty of Wagner.

'Do you see it?' von Below whispered, as if frightened he might spook the bird of stone.

Hitler spoke softly and let his voice rest on the wind, 'I see it.'

The clouds closed and the show was over.

'But,' said Frau Hess, ignoring signs from on high, 'if the assault in the west fails?'

Gabriel almost felt the resentment as her words grounded their exhilaration.

'Then this war,' said the Führer, 'will be lost. At that point we will have to find some way to divide our enemies. We will have to seek terms with the Western Allies.'

Frau Hess stamped her foot in anger. 'How? We tried in 1940. When we had the British at our mercy. My husband, at your secret instigation, flew to that island with peace proposals – and Churchill had him locked up in the Tower of London. Frankly he was the wrong person to send. It should have been me; I'd have rammed peace down those British necks!'

'Ilse,' Hitler murmured.

'No, I'm right – if the British wouldn't negotiate when they were beaten, why should they now, when they must be able to smell victory?'

The Führer took her arm and spoke to her gently. 'Because they're not like us. Because they're not like you and I, Ilse. They haven't experienced our struggle. Because their nation is not like our nation. They didn't live through the turnip winter of 1917, the ice winter of 1918, the starvation of 1919. They haven't tasted defeat. We will fight forever to avoid that terrible drop into the pit of shame again – but how much stamina have they for war? They were young in 1940 but now they're old and tired. Offer them an armistice at Christmas and who knows? They're sentimental about Christmas.'

Frau Hess clapped her hands once but it wasn't applause, it was the sound of despair. 'If the assault in the west fails, they'll be over the Rhine by Christmas. By the New Year they will have started to find the camps. Once those pictures make their way onto the newsreels, they will find the vigour for war again.'

Hitler took a short walk that took him nowhere. He came back to where they silently waited. 'So – if we lose the next battle, we lose the war.'

'The men will fight to the doors of the Chancellery,' said Martin Bormann.

His brother shook his head impatiently. 'Yes, yes – but the result will be the same, defeat.'

The brothers glared at each other. Hitler ignored them, following his own line of thought. 'Germany will be defeated and the Western capitalist democracies will face communist Russia, nose to nose, over our corpse. If they went to war over backwaters like Belgium and Poland – why not Germany? Germany is Europe. Germany is the heart of Europe. It is the commanding economy. Russia can't afford to give us to the capitalists and the capitalists can't let the communists have us. We are the treasure that will undo their victory. Greed will tear them apart like robbers fighting over the loot.'

Martin Bormann took up the theme. 'Germany, lost and humiliated, will need a king to rise up from under the mountain to rescue her honour. The Fatherland will need a Napoleon to return from exile and rally the folk. We will fight against the Soviets of course, and our men are better soldiers than the weaklings from the democracies. Germany will rise from the cinders, from the brick dust and ashes.'

Bormann's words had energised the Führer. 'We will defeat the Red Menace and, in the fullness of time, there will be a reckoning with the Jew governments in the West. With German technology and genius there will be a reckoning.'

'You are that leader,' said von Below.

'Of course,' he confirmed, and then continued. 'The problem is where I base myself until the moment of resurrection. Berlin would be a death trap. So – where is to be my Elba?'

Colonel von Below stepped forward. 'We initially explored the possibility of Spain. Plenty of out-of-the-way places and a sympathetic government – or so we thought. The Generalissimo however isn't enthusiastic. He's like an old woman; he doesn't want a scandal.'

The Führer reached out his arms in what, Gabriel thought,

was almost a Jewish gesture of despair. 'Gratitude, where is the gratitude?'

They could all feel Hitler was on the edge of a rage. A storm that would take hours to blow itself out. Bormann spoke quickly, indicating his brother. 'Albert, make your report.'

'I investigated the feasibility of turning part of the Bavarian Alps into a redoubt. The Western Allies don't like attacking well-defended positions; look at the mess they got themselves into at Cassino. We discovered we could certainly make somewhere impregnable here, and we could build deep shelters that would be proof against bombing. However, the problem, as always in a siege, is supply. A redoubt is in fact a trap; all they would need to do is sit outside for a year until the garrison starved to death.'

'It was always a ridiculous idea,' said the Führer. He turned to his naval adjutant, 'von Puttkamer?'

The admiral stepped forward. 'I think this one might work. Technically Argentina is at war with us, but this is a paper conflict forced onto the Argentinians by the United States. In reality, the country is fiercely pro-German, the army especially. It is in fact the perfect state in which to start the fightback. They are anti-British, loathe the Americans and have locked up their communists. All that's needed is discretion. Property has been acquired by Nahuel Huapi Lake in Patagonia. This is a remote area peopled with emigrant Germans. A ranch on similar lines to the Berghof is being constructed there, miles from anyone. This is a place where even the most celebrated man in the world could disappear.'

Hitler paused and thought. 'It's the best idea,' he said finally.

'It always was,' agreed Frau Hess.

Hitler nodded decisively. 'A lot to think about, gentlemen. Now I must return to the Berghof, where my generals will be waiting to explain why Watch on the Rhine must be delayed again. Hauptsturmführer Zobel,' Hitler turned suddenly to Gabriel, 'you will come with me.'

They left the terrace and avoided the tea party, stepping back into the building through a door near the elevator.

'Tell me about your hut in the clouds,' he ordered Gabriel.

Gabriel, who had been scanning the corridor for any persons lurking without reason, changed the direction of his mind.

'It's just a log cabin, turf roof – one room with two sleeping compartments. There's an open fire and chimney made from the rocks that my great, great grandfather cleared from the land. It's in the high country for summer grazing. In winter it's often snowed in, but it's warm and well stocked.'

The Führer paused by the open lift doors. 'That's all a man needs. Without women, that's all a man needs. I wanted the Berghof to be like that, but – it grew.'

They stepped into the garish interior of the elevator. Gabriel pressed the down button and the doors slid closed. He breathed deeply now they had left the threat of the Old Hares. The lift floor gave a small jump as it commenced its descent. Gabriel heard a distinctive ping and watched a small black iron ring slide across the gold walls like an insect. It was attached to a thread that led out of the lift, where the electrics exited in the dome of the roof. Gabriel knew what it was and located where the ring had started its journey. Behind the gilt telephone, housed in a cubbyhole, was the black bulk of the stick grenade the ring had come from. It was now armed, and in seconds would explode. There was nowhere for them to shelter in the brass coffin. They had seconds to live.

CHAPTER EIGHTEEN

'Mrs Cambridge, not Squadron Leader, please,' she said as she sat, at Jago's request, in the upright chair opposite his desk. 'At the beginning of the war, they liked to give everyone a rank and so bring us under military authority – but Nightingale is quite correct when he refers to me as the lady dressed as an RAF officer.'

Jago smiled. 'I know what you mean – pre-war I was in the TA but whenever I come across an old sweat such as Nightingale, I still feel as if I'm in fancy dress.'

Mrs Cambridge stared at Jago. 'Major, do you ever wonder if they too might be suffering a minor crisis of confidence in your presence? Do we, the citizen soldiery, make them, the regulars, uneasy?'

Jago couldn't imagine why. 'How do you mean?'

'Take Nightingale, all carved oak and whittled in battle, but read his papers and what do you find...'

'Yes?'

'You find that Nightingale is a country of one. I suspect he became that the moment his mother dumped him, as a baby, on the church steps. That act put a sea around Able Seaman Nightingale. Donne is wrong – the odd man is an island.'

Jago had expected a superficial male-type briefing on his team; Mrs Cambridge obviously had other ideas.

He tried to debate with her. 'Surely the Senior Service gave him a sense of belonging, a family?' Jago had joined his TA regiment with just such a hope.

Mrs Cambridge looked down her nose at him. 'We have the habit of handing over our orphans, when they reach the awkward age, to the military. But under the tradition and tattoos, believe me, Nightingale is still not a joiner. Nightingale will never go above and beyond the call of duty, because at heart he doesn't believe he has a duty. Duty is the burden of those who belong and Nightingale's mother made sure he never did.'

'Can he be trusted?'

She shook her head sharply and closed her eyes as if to cut herself off from the very idea. 'Of course not. He knows how to wear the uniform in a way we never will. He knows the slang of belonging, but Nightingale's loyalty belongs to no one but himself.'

It was a devastating broadside that had wrecked Jago's first impression of the able seaman. Jago had asked Mrs Cambridge her opinion of the tiny team he'd inherited, hoping for some honest answers. She'd let him have her honesty with both barrels. He tried to lighten the exchange. 'Well he is good at liberating biscuits.'

But Mrs Cambridge had no intention of dropping the body of Nightingale's reputation. 'Nightingale's talent isn't biscuits, but manipulating authority. He trained your predecessor to believe that he, Nightingale, is a *character* – a Dickensian matelot, a sketch by Boz come to life. Nightingale saluted Captain Thomas, but in the fullness of time, Captain Thomas bowed to Nightingale.'

'Well what are Nightingale's duties, exactly?'

Mrs Cambridge tutted at the question. 'Whatever you want

them to be. Make the old lead-swinger work. Give him an order and stick to it, in spite of his sighs, his small shake of the head, his muttered asides that, believe me, you are meant to hear. Make him work for his corn.'

Jago nodded and pretended to ponder Mrs Cambridge's words before he asked the question he'd really invited her into his office to ask. 'And Yeoman Bangle, what are her qualities? Tell me about her.' Lavender. He needed to know more about the young communist who, one day, could point a Webley at his heart and then next turn up, as honest as the day, in the King's uniform.

'Worth her weight in gold. Two tours behind enemy lines in France as a radio operator – a damned good one apparently. Can you imagine that, Major Craze, a girl from a humble background, who'd never even had a holiday abroad before, adrift in an alien world, lugging around a transmitter in a suitcase? Then, having made contact, living like a mole underground beneath churches and barns; only coming up to tap out her messages on the *music box*, aware during every beat that the enemy are monitoring her effort and homing in on her broadcast.'

Jago found he could imagine that degree of fortitude. He remembered his own female radio operator looking at him with concerned eyes and trying to persuade him to join her aboard the Lysander.

'I trust,' he said, 'Lavender was never – entertained by the Gestapo?'

'Nearly, but no. All the fault of those wretched Frenchmen of course.'

'What did they do?'

Mrs Cambridge glared at Jago as though he was one of the guilty Frenchmen. 'Machismo, that's what they did. Male pride is the most redundant quality in a modern industrialised war;

that pathetic, pale, historical reflection of the warrior. Instead of being discreet, they have to be manly and swagger, and become such awful show-offs. We try to train them not to but they will stick themselves in photos – you know, posing in the mountains, cradling a Bren gun and swathed in bandoliers of ammo. Group photos sometimes, it's insane – Jerry raids a farmhouse, does a search and finds the snap, probably under the same floorboard the pervert keeps his filthy Parisian postcards. Then Jerry goes out and rounds up the whole team.'

Jago found himself surprised. 'Did Lavender allow herself to be photographed?'

'She did not! But some idiot man managed to get her into shot by accident. She appeared in profile behind and between two resistance heroes, posing for the grandchildren they're now never going to have. The Gestapo had her face and so we had to get her out and home again, which, with difficulty, we managed. Of course she can't go back and so she twiddles her thumbs on the Home Front.'

Jago thought that, whatever the young communist was up to on the Home Front, it wasn't twiddling her thumbs. Mrs Cambridge was off again. 'And that toad, Nightingale, tries to get her to *swab the decks* – his job!'

He didn't want her to go back to damning Nightingale. 'Mrs Cambridge, tell me about the Foxley team in Berchtesgaden.'

'Stop right there,' she said and actually wagged a finger at him. 'First and foremost, before I brief you, we must be correct regarding the geography. Berchtesgaden is a very large railway station with a small town attached. It's where Hitler arrives and once he leaves it, so do we. The town we're fascinated by is Obersalzberg, ten minutes from the railway station. It's a closed world, a Vatican City, and it's where Hitler lives, far more than Berlin. He has his home there, the Berghof...'

'Also known as the Eagle's Nest,' Jago said brightly, wishing to contribute. Very quickly he wished he hadn't.

'No, Major Craze, the Berghof is never referred to as the Eagle's Nest. The so-called Eagle's Nest, or – to give it its correct name – Kehlsteinhaus, is not, as some mistakenly believe, the Western Front equivalent of Hitler's headquarters, the Wolf's Lair, in the east. The Eagle's Nest is a very unimportant folly on top of a mountain. It's a grandiose tea-house, ignored on the whole by Hitler, but adored by Eva Braun, his mistress.'

'Good lord,' said Jago, 'I had no idea he was interested in women. A mistress?'

'She's kept secret from the German people. The fact that the Führer likes bedding a young blonde half his age might take away some of his mystique, present him as just another man.'

Jago took this in, as he stared out of the window at a flight of hungry pigeons pursuing one who'd been lucky to find some crust. The birds swept in and out of sight, like a dogfight between fighter planes; the metallic shades on the pigeons' throats their squadron colour. He gathered his thoughts as the crust changed beaks, was fought over and finally dropped.

'Alright,' he said. 'Finish briefing me on the team here, and then we can move on to Foxley on – Obersalzberg.'

A brief, if severe, smile lit her face at Jago's correct use of the Nazi town. 'We're the dregs of a much larger operation that never got the green light. Much of the talent and ambition has transferred. As a skeleton crew, we suffer a sort of passed-over peevishness and claustrophobia. Nightingale is our orderly – I've said enough on him. Lavender is officially our driver...'

'And unofficially?'

Mrs Cambridge leaned into him to give emphasis to her words, her admiration. 'She's been *there*. None of us has. Lavender knows what it's like for our people on the Obersalzberg, living a lie day after day, waiting for the door to come crashing down. Lavender advises us on how to manage our asset.'

'And Captain Thomas, my predecessor, how did he see his role?'

Mrs Cambridge smothered the look of scorn, the way a Spartan wife might smother a newborn daughter. 'Captain Thomas was an English manager. You know how the British organise these things: they appoint someone with a degree from a good university to oversee artisans in a trade the graduate knows nothing about. The captain was a nice young man without any talent whatsoever for deception, espionage and assassination.'

Jago looked around the office, his office, and considered whether to ask the question. 'Do you think I come from the same mould?'

'Probably.'

Jago discovered he didn't need this confirmation of his own belief in his inadequacy for the task. 'Tell me, Mrs Cambridge, what qualifications are relevant to being a spymaster?'

'Someone who's lived a secret life. Have you ever lived a secret life, Major? How clandestine are you, sir?'

More than you'll ever know, he thought. 'If I told you it wouldn't be secret.'

Mrs Cambridge laughed. 'Touché. Now me I suppose. Who is Mrs Cambridge, what is her role in the running of Foxley and has she ever lived a secret life?'

Jago found he was really interested to hear her answer. His initial impression had been that she was the wife of someone important in government. A committee woman, who'd nagged her way from placing evacuees into rural homes into a role with a uniform and a commission. 'Well, has Mrs Cambridge lived a secret life?'

She leaned back and seemed to shed her suburban

respectability as she crossed her legs, adopting a posture that Jago found rather wrong for a woman in a uniform. It wasn't coarse in any way, just rather too assured and not subordinate.

'To begin with, the Mrs is honorary – there is no Mr Cambridge. Do you like the theatre, Major?'

This question was so random that Jago had to think for a moment to remember that he did. 'Yes actually, I do.'

'Shaw?'

'Sometimes, if he's not being too preachy.'

'Have you ever had that experience in the theatre when it seems as if the playwright has rifled your mind and has stolen the story of your life? You sit in the auditorium dumbfounded, as you watch yourself on stage.'

'Sort of...' he hedged. The Lord Chamberlain would not have permitted the depiction of Jago's life to be given dramatic licence.

Mrs Cambridge continued. 'Shaw did that to me with his play *Mrs Warren's Profession.*'

'I've read it – never seen it. If I remember correctly,' he said, 'it's the one where Mrs Warren's daughter discovers that, far from being respectable, her mother runs a brothel.'

Mrs Cambridge smiled. 'That's the one. I never knew my mother and was raised by my father, who had a fancy-lace business. The lace was manufactured in Switzerland, Bavaria and Brussels. After his death, I thought why not manufacture some of the lace bound for Britain in Nottingham, home of English lace, and save on import duties? I travelled to Switzerland to inspect my inheritance and take advice from my managers, and...'

'Discovered there was no lace?'

She laughed a laugh that would never have graced a village bunting committee. 'Well, some – on the girls' underwear. I was like Lavender in occupied France. I was in an alien world.

A nice girl, a respectable young woman, clever, I'd worn the scholar's gown at Girton, and suddenly I discovered I was in fact not a spinster of the Establishment, but the madam of three bordellos. I almost panicked and demanded to be rescued and shipped home. My first thought was to sell up and get out, but it was pointed out to me the business would continue with or without me, and the new owner might not be so considerate an employer as my father had been. He was low church and had a Methodist's heart. And of course...'

'What?'

She smiled again. 'Well – is there anything so disappointed as a female graduate who realises the journey is over? So far my girl and no further, time to bury your brains in a compost heap and pick up the threads of your preordained life. No career for you, best marry a minor civil servant and settle in Purley. Of course I stayed in Geneva.'

'And are there really bordellos in the Cantons?'

'The only establishment more discreet than a Swiss bank is a Swiss brothel.'

In spite of the shadow of his puritan mother railing in his head at the scarlet woman before him, Jago was intrigued. 'You gave it a go?'

'I gave it more than that, Major Craze; I gave it my best shot. I gave it my considerable energy and ability. To my disappointment, I discovered the houses virtually ran themselves under the eyes of the mothers, those ladies who had risen beyond the horizontal career to the lofty heights of vicarious madams. The years rolled by and the money rolled in, and so did boredom. I understood why my father shot things – if Nightingale had been present I'd have cheerfully shot him.'

Not Nightingale again, he thought. 'Quite.'

'I bought my chalet above Lake Geneva, and took out a long lease on an apartment in Dolphin Square, and nearly went mad from lethargy. You will understand I went to pains to protect my respectability. For example, I never visited a house during its hours of operation, but I did like to rub shoulders with the girls during daylight. It's the fascination that creatures of the demi-monde always cause in us sheltered ladies. I'd sit with them at their very late breakfasts and listen, while they repeated the snippets of gossip the men had shared the night before. Indiscretion, thy name is sated man; with the cigarette smoke, they breathe out secrets. And as war clouds gathered and governments considered investing in umbrellas again, it occurred to me that here was another business even more exciting than living off the earnings.'

'Spying?'

She nodded. 'I took myself off to Bern, to the British Embassy. An indiscretion, passed across a pillow to my best redhead, had given me the name of the head of MI6 there. He was a brigadier, small in stature and mind. I was shown in and barely opened my innings when I was shown smartly out again. The problem with MI6 is that it is staffed with men like the brigadier, men who disapprove of the role they are currently playing. They are quite unable to embrace the sordid, to delight in the deception, and to lie in the face of love. They are no use at all.'

Jago knew that; the peacetime Intelligence Service had been filled by men with first-rate, third-rate brains. The real brains were in academia, the Treasury and the Diplomatic Corps. 'How did you end up here?'

'With war imminent, I travelled to London and blackmailed a diplomat, and regular user of my facilities in Brussels, into finding a berth for me where my intelligence gathering might be used. SOE came along in the fullness of time and a desk was found for me in Baker Street.'

'Switzerland and Bavaria?'

'Well spotted, Major. Yes, I run our person on the Obersalzberg. Radio communications are quite out of the question so near to the Berghof, so we *talk* via my madam in Switzerland. She travels legitimately across the border to the sister brothel in Munich. There, or in Berchtesgaden, she meets the messenger. Once the man is briefed, he delivers the message to Obersalzberg, to which he has legitimate access on a daily basis.'

'And our person on the mountain?'

'A rather brave Anglo-German lass who's a part-time nurse at the Platterhof Military Hospital, and a nursery helper in the kindergarten.'

The telephone rang on the green leather-topped desk in front of Jago and he answered it. He listened to the voice on the other end of the line, talking as clearly as if they were in the room, even though they were speaking from the lowlands of Scotland. Jago took in what was told to him. He replaced the receiver.

'What's wrong?' Mrs Cambridge asked. 'What's happened? Who was that?'

'It was a policeman in Peebles, a military policeman. Captain Thomas is dead, killed in a friendly fire accident. Blown to bits.'

The knock on the office door startled them. It swung open and Lavender stood in the doorframe. 'Commander Godwin to see you, sir.'

She stepped aside as Nicky entered and she closed the door behind him. Jago and Mrs Cambridge rose to their feet.

'Have you heard?' he said.

Jago knew what he meant. 'This very instant.'

Mrs Cambridge spoke. 'Friendly fire, we understand? An accident.'

'Accident?' Nicky said. 'Murder more like, and listen Jago – he was almost certainly mistaken for you.'

CHAPTER NINETEEN

Gabriel grabbed the Führer and pushed him to the ground. He reached into the phone cubby and took out the stick grenade. Breathing deeply, he balanced the grenade, charge down, stick up, on the top of his helmet and held himself straight. It wasn't the first time he'd done this; part of his selection to the SS had been to place a live and charged grenade on his helmet and stand to attention waiting for it to explode. The sergeant had told them that if they trembled, and the grenade tumbled, they'd blow off their legs – and fail selection: the sergeant's joke.

Even through his closed eyes, Gabriel *saw* the flash of the explosion before someone hit him on top of his head with Thor's hammer. His knees buckled but he didn't fall. Smoke and the smell of cordite were everywhere. As in training, the steel of his helmet had saved him and directed the blast upwards. The domed roof of the elevator was ripped like tin foil but the cable was undamaged and the lift continued its sedate descent. Gabriel's head throbbed, he was choking, but he was aware of no pain and he was alive. At his feet, the Führer was moving and Gabriel reached down and helped him up.

The soldier that still lived in Gabriel waited for the thanks and praise that were bound to come. Adolf Hitler's eyes met his, but his face wasn't the charming one he wore for his young secretaries, or that of the fellow man of the mountains that Gabriel had become accustomed to; this face was contorted with rage, consumed by it. When he spoke, it was a shriek and Gabriel's cheek facing him was drenched in his spittle.

'You coward! You dirty little chicken heart! Why didn't you sacrifice yourself? You should have thrown yourself on the grenade! Supposing it had toppled from your helmet? You gambled with the life of your leader to save your own existence – which is of only secondary importance to Germany! Well? What have you to say for yourself?'

Behind him, Gabriel felt the lift doors open and the air clear, as the smoke that hadn't exited via the new chimney in the elevator roof left by the open doors. 'Sir, I knew what I was doing, I've done it before – on SS selection...'

But the Führer didn't really want an answer. 'Tell me, Zobel, am I less important to you than a bishop from an archaic religion, or do you think a Gruppenführer outranks your Führer? You swore a blood oath to me, me! I want that blood; where is it? You cheated me; I trusted you and you cheated me. You're like all my soldiers. When I want you to be hard, to make the sacrifice of blood and iron, you turn into milksops! You turn into cowards. Coward!'

The Führer marched from the elevator, still quivering with rage, and erupted into his car. It left suddenly, in a squeal of burnt rubber.

So, thought Gabriel, no thanks for saving his life then.

Gabriel and Max stood shoulder to shoulder in the study of the Berghof. There remained nothing of the camaraderie of their previous encounter before those giant windows.

'You've made no progress? You're no nearer to identifying the murderous traitor in our midst?'

The Führer put his face into Max's. 'I know you from the old days. I remember you Munich policemen; lazy, shiftless, corrupt! You let the Reds run the streets, you hid from them. It was my storm troopers who swept aside the Jewish–Bolshevik filth. We cleaned up your town for you. We did your job, while you hid and took bribes from gangsters! I take you to the Kehlsteinhaus, to watch and protect, and what do you do? Sniff around the skirts of the ladies like a degenerate – don't deny it!'

Hitler stepped back to take them both in. 'The pair of you – worthless! I should strip you of the gallantry awards you most assuredly don't deserve. I earned my Iron Cross with raw courage and sacrifice and the blood of my enemies on my boots! How did you get yours? By hiding and lying and pretending to a valour neither of you possess? Did you crawl out of your bolthole and find a dead comrade surrounded by the bodies of the enemy, men he had slain alone, and did you then boast it was you who had played the hero? You're contemptible, both of you, and you're lucky you are not now travelling east to serve in a punishment battalion. I am surrounded by weaklings and men of low moral fibre. I should order Himmler to trace your families; I don't doubt he would discover you're mongrels with the taint of the Hebrew and the Slav in your veins.'

There was more, until finally they were ordered to go and to capture the assassin. They reclaimed their sidearms and went to Max's office, where they chose brandy over the coffee. When Max poured, Gabriel saw that his hand was shaking.

'Don't take it to heart, Max. He's still basically a crappy little corporal. It was an NCO rant; the sort you'll hear on any parade ground.'

Max swallowed his brandy, then the glass met the wall near

one of the maps and dissolved into a rain of shards. 'The Gob called me a coward – he called me corrupt.'

Max throttled his own hands. 'That shitty little niece-fucker called me degenerate. I saw Geli's body; kicked to buggery, back lashed to shreds and then shot with no scorch marks but they still said it was suicide. Even before his fling with Geli, two of his previous girlfriends had a bash at committing suicide. He remembers me? Well I remember him – they attempted to end their own lives just to get away from him. You know what? I'd rather be hated by Adolf Hitler than loved by him, it's a lot safer.'

'But he is the Führer, Max; be careful.'

Max nodded and looked at Gabriel. He lowered his voice and said, 'He's the Führer and I'm not a traitor, but when he nearly got blown up in the Wolfsschanze, well, I'd have been happy if they'd pulled it off. It's not for me, assassination; I swore a blood oath to serve and protect him and I don't break my oath – and – I'm a policeman. I don't take the law into my own hands. But I wish the generals had done for him. He got us into this war.'

Gabriel said, 'He's like the fat farmer in the folk tale.'

'Which one's that?'

Gabriel dredged it from his memory of the fight in the frozen north. 'A Ukrainian in the Nord told it to me. It seems in this story a German settler by the Volga wanted to expand his farm eastward. But to the east, the land was ruled by a mean old wolf. So the fat settler took some traps and laid them along a track the big wolf used. Next day he went back to check and he saw he'd been lucky. There was a big grey wolf with a leg all bloody caught in the trap. It was howling with fury.'

'Did he shoot and skin it?' Max asked.

Gabriel shook his head. 'He should have. Instead the fat

farmer danced for joy and wound up stepping into another of his own traps that snapped shut and crushed his ankle.'

'Silly sod.'

'Then the screaming farmer saw that the wolf was laughing. He shouted at it, *Why are you so happy? You're trapped too.*

The wolf looked at him and said, *You've forgotten I'm a Russian wolf and I can do this...* And the wolf bent over its trapped paw and chewed it off. Free, it loped away on three legs. Then it stopped and looked back over its shoulder. It smiled at the fat farmer and said, *Don't worry, I'm coming back.* He did come back – with all his pack. More wolves than were feasible. They ripped the fat German farmer apart. They ate his flesh, crunched his bones and drank his blood.'

'And lived happily ever after? Not exactly a bedtime story for the kiddies, is it? Bloody right though; we are stuck in a trap. The question is, which of us, the Germans or the Russians, have the balls to bite our way out?'

The two men lapsed into silence. The office smelled of the coffee Max brewed there; it was a scent Gabriel had come to associate with him. He liked him, he liked Max and coffee.

Gabriel asked, 'If the July plotters had succeeded and the war was over, would you go back to the Bavarian detective force?'

Max found himself a fresh glass from a drawer. He poured them both another brandy, sat on his desk chair and indicated with his eyes that Gabriel should join him. They sat and sipped and Max spoke quietly. 'That's over, my time of playing cops and robbers has gone. It's not about peace and going back to earlier occupations – if Hitler died I mean. It's about winning this war that he's losing for us.'

Gabriel was confused. 'But without him, peace could break out – at least with the British and Americans.'

Max warmed his brandy in his hands, sometimes sniffing it,

as if he was cooking it and checking when it was done. 'Your father served the Fatherland in the first war, didn't he?'

'Heavy artillery. Yes.'

'My father talked a lot about it. Back then they didn't say *Heil* to the Kaiser, they said *God punish the English.* It was the regular greeting in the street; not *Good morning* but *God punish the English.* And he told me about what they called the National Community. It meant all Germans together, beyond region, class, religion or politics. And it grew into something real in the dark days. To be a German is not to forget, not to forget what it was like – defeat. So, it's not on the cards; peace if Adolf Hitler is topped. God still needs to punish the English.'

Gabriel appealed to him, 'But this time it's the Russians…'

'That's what you don't understand. Being Swiss, not being German, you don't understand. There isn't a *this time* or a *that time*, there's just a long war, and to win it we have to make it longer. Sure, we can make a pretend peace with the British and the Yanks – get them off our backs while we stop Ivan and push him back beyond Poland. We need time to develop the miracle weapons Hitler's always going on about. Then God will punish the English.'

'But maybe Germany will have had enough of the fighting?'

Max smiled at him. 'In a funny sort of way, in spite of the glitter on your chest, you've never really fought in this war. The Nord Division; foreigners fighting alongside the Finns up above the Arctic Circle. A private war of your own. I suppose you heard about Stalingrad?'

'Of course I bloody heard about Stalingrad.'

'I was in hospital in North Africa, after being smashed up in a car crash. You see Gabriel, I think you had to be serving with Germans or living with them to see what happened to us after Stalingrad. It was a black day, dark news, and, just like the first war, we re-found our National Community. We didn't pack it in, sack our leaders and surrender like the Italians – we, the people, inherited the war. Before that we'd been serving in something owned by the Nazis. After Stalingrad, National Socialism became National Community. We absorbed the Nazis; they became an irrelevance, not the reason we're fighting any more. Stalingrad reminded us what defeat tastes like. We don't like that taste, Gabriel. It's our war now – it'll be easier to fight without the clown troupe, but we will fight, there'll be no surrender this time. We'll fight until we've turned the world to ashes but there'll be no surrender.'

Back in his own room, Gabriel polished his boots. He had a batman to do this but Gabriel always found he needed to polish them once more – just to be sure. He tried to ease his anxiety out onto the surface of the leather. Rubbing and rubbing, but his unease wouldn't leave him. When he thought of his free time in Munich, he couldn't remember seeing any evidence of a divided Germany. The Nazis weren't forcing their young men to the front or their women into the factories. The people were united, resolved. They were going to fight on and on, with or without Adolf Hitler. With him, they would go down under a rain of shells and bombs, defeated. But without him, there was the opportunity to fight a strategic war, a false peace, a breathing space, dealing with their enemies piecemeal.

He threw the boots to one side. Was Lorelei right? Was London right? Should he have died in that lift? Sacrificed himself to kill Hitler? He retrieved his boots and placed them neatly, the way he had been trained. He knew how to keep his room in proper military order. He sat on the bed and stared at the blank wall. Plotting was beyond him. He would follow

Lorelei's lead. She said that Hitler had to be saved. Gabriel put this thought neatly into a corner of his mind. He had his orders.

CHAPTER TWENTY

They had driven to Peebles through the night, taking it in turns to sleep in the back. Using the journey to avoid talking. Jago didn't know how to chat to her. He didn't know how to while the long miles away in banter. She had delivered him to SOE in Baker Street as a member of the First Aid Nursing Yeomanry, but on this night journey he felt he was sharing the car with the Lavender who was a member of a communist cell. He remembered her face as she left the Daimler to follow her brother; the anger in it: *What you did to Austen – I think it was really horrible*. And she'd been right.

Lying in the back of the car, pretending to sleep, he thought about his descent. It had been at a urinal he had first discovered his sexual bent. It was in an Oxford pub and Jago had become uncomfortably aware that the man next to him at the wall was staring at the side of Jago's face. He'd turned, seen a Middle Eastern man with dark eyes and an actor's sweep of hair. The man had smiled at him, pleased to have got his attention, and had turned his body to reveal his penis. He'd asked Jago if he would like it. Jago had been surprised to discover that he did. In the cubicle they'd adjourned to, Jago's world suddenly made sense.

For a mad month Jago had haunted the cottages of Oxford, until a sense of disgust slowly took hold of him, the way the smell of the urine gradually impregnated his clothes. Whether he was on his knees or standing, he started to feel his dead father's presence behind him, leering. He'd tried staying away and for most of the time he could – but then something would happen and he'd find himself seeking consolation amongst the puddles and flushing.

He'd had a row with Major Smedley and, feeling he deserved something other than the perpetual bureaucratic boredom of *the Forgetting School*, he'd gone to seek an adventure. In a gents' lavatory in Soho he looked for it, but thought he was out of luck. The place was empty, then Austen had slipped in after him and lurked in the shadows as he discreetly eyed up Jago from a urinal he was pretending to use. Jago had seen a young man as gauche and awkward as himself. There was a ritual to these encounters. With the minimum of eye contact, they moved from pretending to pee to one of the cubicles and bolted themselves in. Still in silence they began using each other, strangers, enjoying the balm of intimacy with an unknown person. Yet when it was happening, with the boyish stranger so far below him, working away, Jago discovered he yearned for something else. He wanted to reach down and pull him up onto his feet. He wanted to look into his eyes again. He wanted to kiss.

He remembered reaching down and gently pulling Austen up. In the event he'd been too nervous to try to kiss him. It hadn't been agreed, kissing. The stranger might take umbrage at an attempted kiss. Instead Jago hugged him; held him close and rubbed his cheek against his. He felt the boy respond and there they were, hugging in a lavatory that someone had stolen the seat from. After that, neither seemed to need to return to the sex. Jago had slipped out first. He went home to Pimlico, still excited by the gentle intoxication of tenderness. When the stranger had reappeared some weeks later, for what Jago assumed was blackmail, he'd felt betrayed.

Outside the car, it was growing light. A resentful day was trying not to wake up. Jago sat and looked out. They were passing through the borderlands, a place where the trees had been watered with blood. But the present war was somewhere else; now the borders were at peace.

'Do you want me to drive?'

He saw the small, silent shake of her head. He climbed over and sat next to her.

'Dawn's coming up.'

This time a silent nod.

He'd grown up with over three hundred girls; he knew she could keep up the silent treatment till Armageddon came and went. He also knew they needed a working relationship and that meant communicating. 'I'm sorry, Lavender, but we need to talk.'

There was no gesture in the half-light, but Jago knew her profile was saying she was prepared to listen to him.

'What I did to your brother was unforgivable. As soon as I have the opportunity, I intend to make a full and heartfelt apology to him.'

The blare of the car's horn blasted out three times in quick succession, causing Jago to start and some sheep in a field to lumber away.

'Bravo,' said Lavender.

'What?'

'Isn't that what you want? Approval? Do you think if you say sorry that's the end of it?'

Jago supposed he did, but this, he realised, was possibly a mistake in this instance. 'I thought he was trying to blackmail me – I thought he was after money.'

'It always comes down to cash with your lot doesn't it, sir?'

Jago wondered if he should keep trying or whether things between them were irreparably damaged. People, he noticed, were far more likely to forget a hurt done to themselves than to a friend or family member. 'I can only repeat how sorry I am.'

She snorted and pressed down on the accelerator. 'What really makes me angry is that he liked you. When he volunteered to make the contact again, he thought you'd be pleased to see him.'

It was now light enough to see each other clearly. Not light enough yet to add colour to their bones. They sat like wraiths with ivory-cold complexions.

'Do you think we might slow down a little?'

His request was ignored.

'He hasn't had much kindness. They kicked him out of the navy, put it on his papers: invert – put it there in black and white for all the world to see – an invert. No one would take him on with that on his discharge papers. He's an outcast, and the world is cruel to outcasts. Then because the Party's interested in all the young queers down from varsity, the Don tells him to try and have some sort of congress with you. So he does, follows you to a gents' and apparently, the first time, you're nice to him, so he likes you, thinks you like him back and might be pleased to see him again. And what do you do when he turns up? You hit him in the face with a dustbin lid.'

The sudden and deafening screech of the brakes sounded like Lavender's rage to Jago. The car veered wildly as she struggled with the wheel. Jago was thrown forward and, through the windscreen, saw the early morning tractor and the angry face of the farmer driving it. The wheels of the car locked and it slid sideways after the accelerating farm machine. They came to a halt broadside across the lane.

'Well done. Good control,' said Jago lamely.

'Damn,' said his driver.

They made their way in silence, and at a more sedate pace, to the police station in the lowlands town of Peebles.

A sergeant in the Military Police briefly told Jago that *The good captain had met his end in a live-firing accident. Tragic.* He held Jago's eye a beat longer than was necessary. The mute look to convince Jago there was more to it. The sergeant had then directed him to a village and the local policeman who had questioned the shepherd who'd found the body. *Or what was left of the poor man.*

In the hamlet, the small police station was attached to the larger inn that served the holiday needs of fly fishermen in peacetime. War had seen it requisitioned by the military and it was being used as a mess for officers of the battery of artillery whose guns had brought about the end of Captain Thomas. The police station was located in a house built for that purpose at the turn of the century, a plaque informed them. It was red brick and slate, ugly and cosy, and Jago knew Christine would have swapped their large house in Pimlico for it in a flea's heartbeat.

Lavender stayed in the car. The constable, after Jago had introduced himself and stated his business, had led him through to his own parlour at the back of the house. It was a service where men lived in uniform and indicated they were on duty by putting on a cloth armband of black-and-white stripes, their duty stripes. It was a world where the home was also the workplace. So, although the war posters had been left behind in the tiny front office and Jago was now sitting in the man's own back parlour, because of the distinctive stripes around the cuff Jago knew the constable was still on duty; their chat in chintz armchairs before a fire wasn't cosy but official.

'Was he a pal, a comrade, the late Captain...' the policeman struggled to recall the name of the body, 'Captain Thomas?'

Before Jago could answer, the man disappeared through a doorway, summoned by the shrill shriek of an outraged kettle come to the boil. Jago registered the man had a Scottish burr and that he was old for the police. He wore the distinctive garish ribbons of the first war on his chest and his face was as brown and tough as bark on an old broadleaf tree. Jago invented a life for him: he'd never turned to teak in the low-lands. This man had served out his time in the Empire, in the tropics. He was probably a *dug-out*, an older man called back from retirement by the advent of war for routine duties, thus releasing a younger man for more active service. The walls gave no clue to his past, being bare and distempered without even a calendar pinned up. There was a mirror above the fire-place and a coal fire in the hole. A battered bucket contained the anthracite, and a hammer and short shovel were the only fire dogs. The constable bustled back with a tray of tea things and a teapot without a cosy. So just one cup and on your way, Jago realised. Jago spoke, 'No, Captain Thomas wasn't a pal, nor was he a comrade – I stepped into his shoes and we met just once; at the hand-over.'

Jago refused sugar; he wouldn't loot the man's ration. The constable poured the tea and joined Jago in the other chintz armchair before the fire. 'It's a long drive to enquire into the death of a man you don't know.' He smiled and said, 'You must have coupons to burn?'

The duty stripe really was on. Jago felt the usual tide of snobbery sweep over him. He wanted to snap at the man that he, Major Craze, was the person asking the questions and to remember his place. But he was in the man's parlour, in his armchair, drinking his tea. So he answered the question. 'I can't go into details but Captain Thomas's last posting was, shall we say, hush-hush.'

A deep cynicism lit the constable's smile from within. 'Hush-hush? How many sins are hidden under that blanket? It's up there on the same billboard as the alibi I was home in bed, ask the wife.'

The old dug-out was seriously irritating Jago. He wanted to spring to his feet and bawl him out; but there was the problem of the teacup and the over-deep armchair.

'I'm sorry you doubt my word, Constable, but as you've already pointed out it's a long drive and heavy on the coupons. They certainly wouldn't have been issued unless the powers that be deemed my journey necessary.'

'Point taken,' said the beaming policeman, defying Jago to dislike him. 'Now sir, may I ask just one question before I answer yours?'

Jago wished he was Mrs Cambridge and able to freeze the jauntiness out of the man beside him, intimidating him into subservient obedience. 'Go ahead,' he said instead.

The constable put down his tea and pulled himself up. He loomed over Jago, so that Jago felt even weaker. 'The late Captain Thomas, I accept you only met him once, but did he seem down in the mouth, glum?'

Jago remembered his excitement at escaping the backwater of Foxley and his mistaken belief he was being returned to his regiment. 'When I met him, no, he was quite elated. He thought his next posting was to France, but I believe he was mistaken in this.'

The constable nodded. 'You don't have to be much of a fire-eater to want to be there at the finish. I was there on the Western Front at the Armistice. The eleventh hour and all that, wouldn't have missed it for the world. I remember the first Christmas we kicked a ball about with Fritz, but no one writes about what it was like at the end of the war, that November morning when we walked over no man's land for the last time. They didn't meet us halfway singing carols this time; they were still in their trenches – crying, weeping like women. They were a Prussian Guards regiment, tough bastards, and I saw one of our kids, a boy soldier, holding a great grizzled sergeant major of their lot in his arms as this giant sobbed his heart out and said they'd been betrayed. A couple of days later I watched them walk away, back to Germany, a long file of them, heads down, beaten. Dreadful: all that blood and sacrifice and to lose.'

Jago looked around the room without mementos; it was all up on the walls of his mind, he thought. 'I didn't know him,' Jago said, 'but when Captain Thomas discovered he was not returning to his regiment in France and was going to see out the duration in a Pay Corps depot, I think it would be safe to assume he would have been down in the mouth.'

The constable pulled a nugget of coal onto the shovel, using the claw of the hammer, and dropped it on the flames. 'Sorry,' he apologised. 'Only autumn but I feel the cold. Twenty years in the Shanghai Police.'

Jago felt inordinately pleased with himself for reading the man's complexion correctly.

'That might explain it,' said the constable. 'To be honest there are things that don't add up. If he was well and truly browned off, it might just explain his actions – which are frankly bizarre. We try to protect the family in circumstances where we suspect suicide.'

Jago considered the constable's words, aware of his own relief and then guilt at that relief. Tragic as Captain Thomas's suicide would be, Jago was ashamed to discover he preferred that to the possibility that the cause of death had been murder, and the victim mistaken for him; that there might still be people out there who, on discovering their error, would come looking for Jago Craze, determined not to make another cock-up.

'A shepherd moving a flock had found the captain's car partially blocking the lane. The sheep spilled past it and the shepherd squeezed around; he assumed the driver was behind the wall relieving himself. When he came back later, without the sheep, the car was still there and still no driver. Concerned, he went looking and, as there'd been a live-firing exercise earlier, he already had a suspicion. The target zone is three fields in, well away from the road. There're red flags up all around it during battery fire. The shoot was over and the shepherd arrived just before the fall-of-shot observers, so he got to the body first – or what was left of it.'

'But why suicide? Perhaps he had wandered off to relieve himself?'

The policeman stared at Jago and obviously considered this a foolish remark. Nonetheless he spoke patiently. 'We've all been caught short haven't we, sir? What d'you do? You hop out and go behind the nearest bush or tree. You don't go on a ramble across three fields, especially when your vehicle is blocking the lane.'

'Point taken – but it still seems an uncertain way to kill oneself?'

The constable shrugged, slipped back into his chair and joined Jago in staring into the flames, pondering mortality. 'Maybe he didn't want certainty. Maybe it was a way of handing over. I've heard that from would-be suicides dragged out of rivers. They jump from a bridge and wait to see if the current takes them to the bank or drowns them. They're checking out God's will. He saw the notices by the road, warning drivers not to leave the road, he saw the red flags, and he was a commissioned officer. So, sick to his back teeth at the hand he's been dealt, he walks into the middle of a field and waits to find out the Almighty's plans for him.'

Jago cleared his throat. 'And no sign of anything sinister?'

'Foul play?' The old dug-out smiled. 'No sir, though of course these things happen in the world of hush-hush and Bulldog Drummond.'

Jago felt himself blushing as he stood. 'No. Well that seems to wrap it up.'

The policeman rose as well. 'Will you be hitting the road, getting some mileage in before night?'

Jago thought. It wasn't midday – they could turn around – but on the other hand they'd driven all night. 'I think I need to give my driver a break. We'll stay the night in Peebles and go home after breakfast tomorrow.'

'As you will. You might try and get accommodation at the Tontine Inn. It's on the High Street. Their beds are dry and their breakfast hot.'

The constable opened the door to the office, where they discovered Lavender waiting. Jago felt strangely irked she wasn't still sitting in the car.

'We're staying the night in Peebles,' he said.

'Yes, sir,' she replied, but didn't make a move to exit the small office.

'What is it?' he asked.

'Permission to use the facilities before getting in the car again.'

He wondered what she was talking about. 'What?'

The policeman explained, one man to another, his voice slightly lowered in deference to Lavender's bodily needs. 'She wants to use the toilet, sir.'

Jago had sought responsibility when he applied for the officer selection course; real responsibility, leading men in battle. Now he found himself a glorified teacher, deciding if a hop-ping pupil could hold it in till break. 'Permission granted, make it snappy.' Jago had a sudden thought and he turned to the policeman. 'If that's alright with you?'

'Up you go, lass. Turn right and go to the end of the corridor.'

'Thanks.' And she was gone.

Jago felt he'd had enough of the smiling policeman and sauntered outside to wait by the car, but the old dug-out came with him. 'That's the late captain's motor.'

He pointed at a Morris. Jago, for want of something better to do, wandered round it and looked it over. He was aware of the constable going back inside. The tiny village was as quiet as a vacuum. The distant bleating of sheep only seemed to emphasise the silence. The peace was as thick as marmalade, he thought. He let himself into the passenger side of the Riley and waited.

Lavender returned, turned the car around and drove them back towards Peebles. A mile down the road, she pulled over and turned off the engine.

'What is it? You surely don't need to go again so soon?'

'There's something wrong, sir. Something odd about the propaganda posters in the front office.'

'How?'

She looked at him the way he might once have looked at Major Smedley; the look of an intelligent subordinate, trying to convince an obdurate superior officer of the facts in front of their stupid face. 'For a start, sir, some of those posters dated back to the Blitz and invasion fears.'

'Come on, Lavender; there are noticeboards all over the country covered in out-of-date bumf.'

She nodded; she'd known this would be his counter-argument. 'Yes, sir, you're right, but the thing that struck me as strange was that the drawing pins sticking them to the board were new and shiny.'

Jago had a sudden vision of the board in his old office in the Empire Office; the drawing pins were as tarnished as Wallace Simpson's reputation.

Lavender spoke over his thoughts. 'I unpinned one regarding the formation of a new unit of defence, the LDV, the Local Defence Volunteers – what later got called the Home Guard.'

'I know that,' he said, snappier than he meant. 'What of it?'

'It's at least four years old; four years on the board, but when I lifted it, the baize underneath was as green as the stuff that hadn't been covered. It wasn't marked, as if it had just been pinned up.'

Jago looked at the stone walls imprisoning the car, defining the road, masking the fields, keeping them secret. Autumn had long happened in the Borders and the dry, discarded leaves were blown up and down the lane, making a rasping on the surface that mirrored the agitation and suspicion growing inside him.

'Is that everything?' he said.

It wasn't.

'No, sir. I pretended to use the toilet to get upstairs and take a peek around.'

Of course she had, he thought. Lavender was everything he wasn't, a professional. 'Go on.'

'I thought it was funny when he sent me upstairs. When did coppers start having bathrooms inside like the la-di-das? Where I came from, the rozzers had a tin bath in front of the parlour fire, and the khazi was out back in the yard.'

Why hadn't he noticed that?

'So I had a snoop around upstairs.'

'Weren't you scared he'd catch you?'

Lavender gave him the all-knowing look of the wise child.

'In my experience, sir, when a lady goes to the lavatory, the gentlemen move away out of earshot. Apparently we're powdering our nose – funny place to keep a nose...'

'Yes, alright. I understand. Go on.'

'Short corridor, sir, door at either end, and one in the middle. The far door leads to the bathroom; pre-war of course but not by much – pretty swish. Not the sort of facilities you'd normally find in a police house. My feeling is it was installed by the hotel. The door at the other end of the corridor leads into the inn and the bedrooms of the Royal Artillery officers' mess. The final door led to what was once the bedroom of the cop-shop. Male occupant – but stouter than our grinning stick bean, if the clothes in the wardrobe are anything to go by. Hanging up in the wardrobe were the Number 2s and mess dress of a captain in the Gunners. No plod-togs at all, sir.'

Jago sat, silently thinking, trying to concentrate on the things Lavender had told him, trying not to put himself in the accused dock and prosecute himself for being useless.

'I suppose at some time in the past the village police station became surplus to needs and it was closed.'

'And the inn next door bought it, sir.'

'Incorporated it into the main body of the building and possibly as a staff annexe, or perhaps the owner used it. So today I've unwittingly taken part in a play. It's taken organisation on their part to set the scene and square it with the military up here. This is a conspiracy and I fell for it hook, line and sinker. I listened to a real or bogus policeman and believed every word he said. I'm surprised I didn't take his advice and drive straight back to London.'

Jago banged himself back in his car seat. 'I've totally ballsed up.'

She touched his wrist. He wondered if his humiliation was

what Lavender required to forgive him, because her smile was not mocking but soft, almost understanding.

'Look, sir, this isn't about who's a clever boy.'

A clever boy, intellectual vanity, that's what it really is about, he thought. His whole life, his Oxford years, had been about acquiring that very currency.

Lavender was speaking again. 'Sir, you're not stupid, but you don't have the blinkers.'

'Blinkers?'

'Blinkers, sir, what horses wear to keep them on the straight and narrow. I have blinkers and you haven't. You've got a wide-sky head: look at that paper you wrote. Nicky says it's clever stuff. You've got strategy, I've got tactics, so all's well with our world. You can see what's happening on the other side of the hill with your mind – it's just sometimes you can't see what's happening in front of your face. Now what I suggest, with respect, sir, is I drive us to the scene of Captain Thomas's death. And you look at it your way and I'll look at it my way, then we'll compare notes and that way get the whole picture. Sir?'

Jago nodded. 'Yes, drive on.'

Jago thought of the sad fact that he was brought up to believe Lavender's class was put on earth to empty his class's chamber pot. He had convinced himself that he didn't believe that, but he discovered it had gone deeper in than he realised.

CHAPTER TWENTY-ONE

'He wasn't a shepherd, sir.'

Lavender had driven around the lanes to find the local who'd discovered the body, while Jago had trod the fields – trying to wear *blinkers*.

'More fancy dress?'

'No, sir, just townie ignorance apparently. He's the greer, the farm foreman, a cut above the shepherd and don't you forget it, lass. The shepherd's gone, got his call-up papers, and the greer is none too pleased. So he wasn't in the best of moods, having to move the flock in the first place, but when he finds the lane blocked by a selfish driver he becomes a Scotsman with a grievance.'

Jago could imagine. 'Not the nicest spectacle in the world.'

'No, sir. When he came back and found the car still stuck there, his cup of wrath boiled over and he set off to find the blithering idiot having a picnic. He tells me it happens; drivers see the live-firing notices and the red flags and they stop to go and watch the bang-bangs.'

'And he found the body.'

'That's about it, sir. One thing he did say that didn't add up.'

Jago turned his attention from the surrounding fields. Even

after a country childhood he didn't really like the place. It made him uneasy and he knew if he was still there at dusk then the murky light and the hills going from green to grey would suck his soul down into despair. He failed completely to see what Christine saw in it; it was filled with the sounds of things hunting and killing each other. He'd settle any day for Soho.

'What did he say, Lavender?'

'He was confused by the other car, a Humber. He said that when he passed the Morris for the first time and was putting the flock in a field, a Humber came down the lane. I think he took a dark pleasure from the thought that it wouldn't be able to get past the parked Morris, and that one of the drivers would have a long and difficult reversal to undertake. But when he came back down the lane later, the Morris was still there and there was no sign of the Humber. He swore blind it hadn't reversed up the track again. Said he was in the field and would have seen it.'

Jago felt stupidly pleased about what he was going to say. 'I don't think that Captain Thomas's Morris was blocking the lane when the Humber came down it. I inspected it, while you were using the – facilities, and the tyres were caked in mud. Red mud.'

Lavender looked at their Riley. 'We made the same journey from London and our tyres are still clean.'

Then she looked into the field. 'Red dirt.'

'I think in the country they call it earth.'

'Earth, dirt, muck – it's all the same when it's stuck on your shoes. What's your reckoning, sir? Someone slows Captain Thomas to a halt in the lane, waves him down?'

'Someone with authority.'

'Like a copper?'

'Could be.'

Lavender stared into the distance as if to find inspiration.

'Difficult to reach through a car window and deal with the driver – permanently. But a copper could invite him out onto the lane, point to something over the fields and, while the target's distracted, break his neck. You did the unarmed combat with Killer Green, didn't you sir?'

Jago had indeed undertaken the Empty Hand course; he'd done it conscientiously, but he found himself wondering how effective it might be. To kill a man with one blow to the neck. 'Yes,' he said. 'Even tried it on a rabbit – we all had to.'

'Me as well.'

'I must admit to having doubts; to dispatch a man with one chop to the neck?'

'Oh, it works sir, I know.'

Jago stared at her; she'd been there of course, on the other side of the Channel. She'd seen action. It was a bigger gulf than gender, he thought, bigger than class; Lavender was one of that fraternity who'd done her bit, and he wasn't.

'What then, sir? He kills Captain Thomas, loads the body back into the Morris and drives him across three fields to where the live-firing exercise is to happen.'

'Meanwhile, the man in the Humber drives straight up the lane encountering no obstruction.'

'And the bastard lays out the body of poor Captain Thomas to be blown to bits.'

Of course, Jago thought, she knew the late captain, well. He suppressed the pathetic thought that she probably had more respect for her late CO than Jago. Lavender looked at him.

'This was planned – they were ready and waiting.'

The people trying to kill him were conscientious and organised.

'You're the man they want to silence, sir. Captain Thomas, he was sweet but as deadly as a dead hamster. You're dangerous; behind the professor act, you're dangerous. You won't let things go, and they've tumbled that and it's why they want to kill you.'

It's insane, he thought. In the middle of a world war, where millions fought millions, he was scared because the enemy had become aware of him and wished him ill. He was no longer faceless, anonymous; he had a vision of his forehead filling the scope of a sniper's sight. 'When they realise their mistake, they'll be after me again.'

'Back in the Smoke, that's where they'll be waiting,' she said, 'ready to bounce you as soon as you touch down.'

In Peebles, Lavender drove them to the Tontine Inn and went inside to get them rooms for the night, while Jago went a few steps up the High Street to where he'd spotted a phone kiosk. The public telephone that was a little more private than the one nestling on a reception desk at the inn. He needed to talk to Mrs Cambridge about protection and possibly dropping out of sight when he returned. Once, he'd wanted to serve behind the lines in France, but now the war had come to him, and everything he had learned at Beaulieu was going to be needed.

A step from the box he saw the woman. She was very pregnant and agitated. She was calling down into the bowels of the air raid shelter, holding on to the handle of a pushchair as if to stop herself falling down the stairs. The chair was empty and, as she was shouting *Hamish!* frantically into the lower depths, Jago assumed Hamish was the occupant and currently absent without leave.

'Need a hand?' he asked.

'That I do,' she said gratefully. 'My little rascal has taken himself off down the stairs and I'm in no state to flush him out.'

'I'll get him.'

As Jago passed her, she gave him a glance. Veronica would

have called it a look of appraisal. She smiled. 'Thank you kind sir.'

Flattered by her flirt, even allowing for its futility, Jago skipped down the stone steps into the darkness.

'His name's Hamish,' came her voice from above.

'I know,' he called back.

Jago noted that Peebles, like many towns when war came, had utilised an existing underground space and converted it into an air raid shelter. What had it been, he wondered – the cellars of the boarded-up country hotel built above? As he descended, the familiar shelter smell of Dettol rose up to meet him. The noxious smells of people crammed together brought about the habit of ladies taking handkerchiefs dipped in Dettol with them when sheltering from raids. Ahead of him, pasted to the wall facing the stairs and glowing spectre white from daylight behind, was a sheet of paper listing the shelter rules. All the usual – no smoking, no pets, no antisocial behaviour, and of course the warden's word was law.

He found a light switch at the bottom of the steps and, as he flicked it, the paraphernalia of shelter life leapt out at him. Hard chairs with dusty cushions, marking them as the property of someone. In the corner, on a small table, were some toys and a box containing a game designed for children to play while being bombed. And a poster straight ahead that always seemed to him to epitomise the spirit of the Home Front: YOUR COURAGE, YOUR RESOLUTION, YOUR CHEERFULNESS, WILL BRING US VICTORY. Jago particularly enjoyed the extolling of *cheerfulness*. It had been enshrined in law, in a bill against Gloom and Despondency.

Everything was as it should be, but for the absence of Hamish. Above, the lightbulb buzzed from a touch of damp; around him the large empty room seemed to be waiting. There was a feeling of the Mary Celeste about the place, abandoned, a mystery never to be solved. This first room was obviously the one used as the shelter, but through archways Jago could see the cellars went on and on.

'Hamish,' he said, almost as a whisper, as if embarrassed to disturb the heavy and sulky air.

'He's not here,' said a man, coming through a thin door that Jago had assumed, mistakenly, led to a cupboard.

The man was lean and sinewy, tanned and carried himself like a soldier. He spoke again. 'He's not here, because young Hamish doesn't exist.'

Jago nodded dumbly; he wasn't really listening. His entire attention was focused on the revolver in the tanned man's hand.

CHAPTER TWENTY-TWO

Jago moved to the instructions in his head, instructions delivered by the voice of Killer Green, the teacher of burglary and unarmed combat at Beaulieu, SOE's *Gangster School.* Green had advised, when the other guy had a gun, to pretend not to understand the danger, or instructions, and to keep moving away. Apparently it's harder to shoot an unarmed man walking off than one closing in. Jago heard his advice, *Don't notice the gun in his hand and, in a reasonable manner, do the opposite of what he's ordered.*

'I can't find him, I think the little blighter's gone to earth,' said Jago, walking away from the man with the gun.

'Stand still with your hands in the air. You still have a choice, Major Craze; the Walpurgisnacht Plan or a new hole in your head.'

Jago coughed and cleared his throat over the man's words; Killer Green's voice in his head still informing him. *A man on his own, covering you with a small arm, will almost be as frightened as you. A handgun is an inaccurate weapon and unreliable. He takes a pot at you and misses; you can be on him in a Jack flash.* 'His mother's going crazy up there.'

Jago heard the man coming up behind him. 'This is your last chance – stop!'

He was going to shoot, Jago knew that. But only when his target was still and he couldn't miss.

'What?' said Jago mildly as he begun to turn; then he reached out, grabbed the small table with the toys on and rammed it into the assassin's stomach. He continued to push as they both toppled to the ground, with Jago on top and the table between them. Chess pieces fell across the face of the man. He still held the gun but Jago held him by both wrists. Jago felt he was in a murderous puppet show that had gone wrong, gripping the wrists of a hand that held a deadly prop. He was leaning out over the ridge of the table but the fulcrum favoured the other man: he was pushing up inexorably, bringing the barrel of the weapon to line up on Jago's face. He tried to push it back but the mesmerising black hole of it found him and seemed to want him to stare down it. Jago wondered if, for a split second, he'd actually see the round, travelling up it and out of it, into his eye.

The explosion blinded him but he felt no pain. The strength went from the wrists he was holding and Jago collapsed into the table, pushing it up the body of the man under him. Hands grabbed him under the shoulders and peeled him back onto his own space of floor. The flare in his eyes faded.

'Never foxtrot with an armed man, Jago old boy.'

'Nicky?'

But Nicky was issuing orders. 'Shimmy up those stairs, Austen, and ascertain if my shot has alarmed the locals.'

'Aye aye, skipper.'

Jago heard his feet pattering away up into the world above.

'Was he on his own?' Nicky asked Jago.

'I think so – I didn't see anyone else.'

Nicky, in reefer coat and submariner's white roll-neck

jumper, holding a Webley that seemed to be smoking complacently, job done, moved off into the bowels of the shelter. 'Better take a shufti,' he said.

Jago found himself alone with the body. The table had shielded him from the detritus of the shattered skull. He took a deep breath and wished he hadn't – the air was thick with the smell of blood. Avoiding the gore, Jago carefully emptied the man's pockets. It was a disgusting thing to do, feeling the man through the lining of his clothes – intimate, a violation – but he'd been taught that it is a man's pockets and not his eyes that are the window to his soul. There wasn't much, a wallet and a letter that Jago put in his own pocket to read later. He finished as Nicky and Austen arrived simultaneously from different directions.

'You short of a bus fare?' asked Austen, as Jago made a small pile of the copper coins from the trouser pocket.

'Just emptying his pockets, part intelligence gathering, part covering our tracks. When they find the body with the pockets empty, they might think he's the victim of a robbery.'

They nodded, and Jago felt their silent admiration for a knowledge he was secretly ashamed of.

'Austen?' said Nicky, as Jago investigated the contents of the wallet.

'Nothing happening on deck. This is a deep shelter; I reckon it swallowed the sound of the shot.'

'Anything of interest, Jago?'

Jago was reading the man's papers. 'He's a major in the King's African Rifles. By the way, how did you two turn up so fortuitously?'

Austen laughed. 'Watching your back, wasn't we? And a good job too.'

'Yes,' said Jago meekly.

'Young Lavender told us about your rush north and we thought we'd tag along, just in case.'

'You're important to the cause, cock,' said Austen.

Jago nodded. 'What now?'

Nicky looked around at the shadowy cellars. 'I don't suppose they get many raids these days so I can't believe heaps of people visit this shelter. I think we should take him to the most distant part of these tombs and dump him there. With any luck, it might be a time before he's found.'

Jago wasn't sure. 'He has an accomplice who knows he was last seen down here – the pregnant woman.'

'Bugger, I'd forgotten about her. We saw her talking to you.'

'Plus, there's a phoney policeman, an old colonial who almost certainly arranged this attempt on my life. He'll definitely come looking for his trigger man.'

They stood in a silence that Nicky eventually broke. 'Right, that settles it. We'll have to waltz chummy to the car between us. Pretend he's had one too many if anyone's around. We'll take him out of town. I'll bury him and hike back after, stay at the inn. Tomorrow I'll travel back to the Smoke with Lavender. Austen, Jago needs to go to Hampstead, pronto.'

'I'll deliver him, skipper.'

'Right,' said Nicky. 'Let's vamoose.'

As Jago stood, something rolled out of the pile of the late major's possessions. It made a tinkling sound on the brick floor. He picked it up and examined it. It was a small enamel badge, designed to be worn on the lapel. It had writing around the rim. Jago read it out to the others. 'Perish Judea.'

Jago manoeuvred them south, down the un-signposted lanes. Austen was impressed.

'You got a good sense of direction.'

Jago put his foot down and Nicky's Daimler responded. 'It was one of the things I excelled at on SOE training. I did a lot of country running as a boy – never seemed to get lost.'

'Was that your sport, sir? Do I call you "sir"?'

It began to drizzle and Jago turned on the windscreen wipers as he considered Austen's question. Where were they on the social scale? Separated by both class and rank; Austen had been but a rating while he was a major, but there was the sex thing.

'Call me Jago.'

'Not "sir"?'

Jago didn't feel like a 'sir' any more. He was someone who needed to be rescued. 'No, "sir" won't be required.'

Of course, from that moment on, there never seemed an appropriate instance for Austen to call him Jago. The word itself seemed to have become self-conscious.

'So – was it your sport; running, not football or cricket?'

The rain came down heavier and washed away the border country outside. The windows became waterfalls and Nicky's Daimler rattled like a maraca.

'I went to a girls' school. I could have played tennis, lacrosse, netball with them but I chose to go for solitary runs.'

'Best way.'

Jago glanced across at him, the pale silhouette in profile, staring ahead through the curtain of rain.

'Aren't you curious? You're the first man I've ever met who hasn't made a salacious comment when I've told them I was the only boy in a girls' school.'

Austen gave a prudish snort and said, 'I grew up in an orphanage, a mixed orphanage. Girls down one end of the building in Elizabeth Fry Wing, boys up the other end in Horatio Nelson. I know how these things are arranged. There wasn't ever no hanky-panky. The girls were poor but respectable and that meant something. And plenty of us boys had sisters down the corridor and we looked after them. People don't always have to behave badly just because the world has. We were charity kids and they never let us forget it, but we had our standards.'

Jago supposed they must have driven over the invisible border, the line that divided the two identical moorlands. 'This seems a good moment, when we're alone, for me to apologise. I'm sorry I hit you Austen. I'm sorry I suspected you of blackmail.'

The profile beside him nodded silently.

'Can we put it behind us?' Jago asked.

Austen turned and looked at Jago with eyes as creased as his suit. 'I always wanted an opportunity to serve. To win the respect of those I'd been brought up to be grateful to. To do what Lavender's done; secret missions. That should have been me. I'm the boy. I had a dad for a bit, and he told me I should take the lead and look out for Lavender.'

The windows were becoming steamy and Austen wiped the inside of the one nearest him with the cuff of his jacket. He stared through the porthole he'd created as if he could use it to look back through time.

'Never knew Ma, she died when I was born and Lavender was just a toddler. Dad was a stoker in the Andrew, the Royal Navy. He was always away. Couldn't take care of us so we went into a home for seamen's brats. He never abandoned us though. Always came and saw us on home leave. Used to bring Lavender a doll and he'd take me out for the day. Took me to the Imperial War Museum. You ever been there...?'

Again the word *Jago* couldn't be said.

'Not one that I've visited.'

'We went there on his last visit, before the old monitor battleship he was on blew an engine and roasted Dad. We looked at this picture – big thing – of Jack Cornwell at the Battle of

Jutland. He got the Victoria Cross and he was only sixteen. He died winning it. He stayed at his post through shit and shells. He did his duty. His rank was Boy First Class.'

Austen pulled up his collar and snuggled down to sleep. 'No one has ever called me first class. Don't let it worry you – people have been hitting me with dustbins all my life.'

CHAPTER TWENTY-THREE

The air smelled of leaf dust. In the dry autumn breeze, the leaves had crumbled but still needed rain to pulp. Gabriel crossed Obersalzberg and wondered what it had been like before it had been turned into a sort of benevolent concentration camp for important Nazis. Once it had been an air resort for consumptives who came to dry out their lungs. It had always been a retreat, a magic kingdom; now it was a Camelot far from the terror bombing. The magic mountains wove an enchantment and Gabriel could imagine the war reaching the foothills below and then grinding to a halt. The peace seemed too strong to be pierced. He almost expected to meet a knight in armour, galloping his charger down the track. A warrior with shield and lance and plumed helm, just like the heroes in the stories his father had read him; knights fighting dragons, knights rescuing damsels, knights winning the hand of a princess. Even as a child, he knew his father enjoyed these stories more than he had, and as an adult, Gabriel had awoken from their spell suddenly, the glory vanished, the armour crushed, the warrior inside toasted to a crisp in the brewed-up wreck of a Panzer tank.

Behind him, the Berghof watched his every move; its giant

window a Cyclops eye, watching over the whole of Obersalzberg. The year was turning. Gabriel had hoped that Hitler would have been dead by now, the war over and he would be back in his hut in the clouds in time for Christmas. Up in his mountain, where night came as soft as the snow and the air wasn't burdened by legend. A normal mountain that the gods had never noticed.

He was going to see Lorelei and tell her he was in again. He would be the bodyguard, protect Hitler from his generals and unmask and kill the other assassin. Above, birds flew but didn't sing. Did they already smell winter? Gabriel wanted the snow, snow to cover the burnt skin of Europe like a bandage. He would go home and sit at his window, watching the wind organise the drifts, then change its mind and reorganise them in a different direction, as busy as a Swiss housewife with a broom. His nostrils would detect the faint, almost forgotten, aroma of resin that still, after a century, seeped from the logs of the hut. Would Lorelei be there with him? He thought not. He couldn't see her living there and he couldn't imagine himself living anywhere else. He was ready for the season to change and he wanted to go home. But not alone.

A figure stepped onto the path and blocked him. It was the witch and he was Hansel. Matron Irmgard Gunther, Iron Arse, waited for him to reach her. She was holding something up for Gabriel to see.

'Yours, I think,' she said, like a lawyer producing a crucial item of evidence that would hang the accused. When he saw what she flourished, Gabriel realised he was indeed in the shadow of the noose.

All the soldiers of the Papal Guard were presented with one after their standing-down parade, when they were dined out of the corps; a ceremonial wristwatch. As an object it was surprisingly austere compared with their garish uniform. A black leather strap, a steel case over Swiss clockwork and the papal arms embossed across the face. On the back was engraved the name of the recipient and their years of service. Gabriel's father had been buried with just such a watch as this on his wrist, and now Gabriel's watch threatened to bury him.

'It's mine,' he said. 'Looks like it,' and he reached for the watch.

'Oh no,' she said, snatching it away, 'this is evidence. Do you know where I found it?'

Gabriel yawned, sniffed the air and turned his head to take in the view before condescending to stare back into her eyes and speak. 'In the toilets at the Mooslaner Kopf Tearooms. That's where I left it, after I took it off to wash my hands. Now would you mind returning my property to me?'

He reached, but again she twisted and held the watch close to her. 'No,' she said.

Gabriel looked at her; a lump of resentment and menace.

'Why did you smash up my chalet?'

'Don't be stupid, woman. I've never been to your home.'

'No?'

Gabriel saw she was attempting to laugh but the action was so foreign to her that her mouth resembled a wound and the sound that came out was guttural. 'Then how is it I found it under an upturned chair in my lounge?'

She waved the watch at him like a captured standard. This time Gabriel was fast enough to snatch it from her.

'How dare you!' she screamed, and somewhere above them, in the crisp air and the mountains, her words caught an echo and ganged up against Gabriel. She was shaking with rage. 'You broke his leg!'

Gabriel was confused. 'What are you talking about?'

'Kaiser, my little dachshund. He was trembling in a corner,

whining with pain. The veterinary says his leg had been kicked – kicked hard. Some brute had kicked him – you!'

'Not me.' Strangely, Gabriel discovered he felt all the indignation of an innocent man. That Iron Arse clearly didn't believe a word he said just added to his sense of outrage. Like all men, he felt that he should be believed, even when he was lying. 'This watch went missing at the same time as that French waiter did. If your home was ransacked, it was probably him looking for more valuables to steal.'

'So why didn't he take something precious? Why did he just wreck things and leave my mother's silver?'

Gabriel moved to pass her, then spun back as an argument occurred to him. 'Revenge. He's French, a defeated nation. I expect he'd had enough of the master race and decided to go home. Kicking a German dog is something a Frenchman would do.'

'Ridiculous. Anyway, why me? Why not one of the big cheeses, why not their home?'

'Because you made it personal. Everyone knows you're rude to the waiters at the Mooslaner.'

Gabriel didn't know if this were true but it was a fair guess, given her rhinoceros nature. And certainly her eyes registered a flicker of confusion. Using this moment of doubt, Gabriel side-stepped Iron Arse. He walked on, his heart pounding and not from the altitude. To survive in Hitler's backyard he had to be invisible. Incurring the suspicion of someone like Matron Gunther was the opposite of discretion. She wouldn't let things alone. She'd dig and complain and start a very public vendetta. While he could blame Volfgangu he'd be believed, but if the Frenchman's body was found, then things could become very difficult. He glanced back – she was still there, like a roadblock.

Gabriel looked in at the kindergarten window, at the art gallery pinned to its walls. The children had contributed wild abstracts of primary colours and melting form that made the wall they covered look like a burning city. In the areas seized by adults, the countryside and peace reigned; posters of forests and meadows with a complement of fauna, apparently coexisting without the need to devour each other. In the top left-hand corner of each poster, like the eye of God, was a neat black swastika.

Through the walls, Gabriel could hear the shriek of the children, and when he stepped through the door the smell of the infants swooped to meet him; the scent of innocence infused with an essence of puke. All was chaos; it was an army up-camping to move out. Chairs were being scraped back, some children were dutifully falling in, while others sought to desert. Clara Sporrier, the head, sought to bring order to the march. She held a tearful toddler to her chest and moved skilfully amongst the others, organising them into a defence that finally stuck.

Out of chaos, she brought order, and Gabriel knew that Clara Sporrier was the sort of young woman his father would have wanted him to wed. She had the beautiful face of a Madonna, a practical bust, a trim waist that seemed to have been bolted to another's body. A large bottom lurked to her south, atop tree-trunk legs. It was a good child-bearing chassis and her thighs were what his father, in the nearest he ever came to obscenity, would have called *generous.*

Clara did occasionally glance in Gabriel's direction. Looks that suggested a life of wedded bliss awaited if he were interested. She was a woman who could definitely cope with a hut in the mountains and children underfoot. Lorelei was also in the melee, calming the horseplay, gathering the lost souls, organising the little people into an arrangement that was pleasing to adults. There was a brief question mark in her eyes when she spotted Gabriel. The look spread to her mouth, which gave a cautious smile – then she was off after an escaped child, flying down the tailwind of his scream.

Adolf Hitler watched the chaotic arrangements with the slow, fixed smile of a benevolent marionette. Beside him, Eva Braun expressed more impatience, as she tried to focus her camera on the fluid scene. The children suddenly seemed sucked dry of energy and stood still in a lethargic lump. Clara placed a chair in their midst, a chair for the Führer. Gabriel turned to him and was disconcerted to find he was the object of Hitler's scrutiny. A slow smile turned the edges of the Führer's mouth up and he shrugged in resignation. A look to Gabriel, a look between men, men in a sea of women and children. The mad, raging Hitler of their last meeting was gone. The chameleon had changed its colour again. Gabriel realised he was too trivial to be resented for long; the Führer had bigger fish to fry.

Hitler seemed to take a step towards the chair, then turned on his heel and whispered in Eva's ear. 'My dear, you need to clean up the image.'

Eva glanced at her lens, as if some dirt might have lodged there. The Führer tutted and explained slowly. 'There are too many swarthy children in the composition. The German housewife associates swarthiness with dirt. Clean up the image, only the blonde ones.'

Eva was confused. 'But none of them are Jews. All the children are German.'

'But some of them don't look German enough.'

He walked to the group, smiling and nodding at them, and moved among them as they stared up at him, curious and hopeful that all this might lead to a story. As he passed through them, he tousled heads, and the hair that he ruffled was all dark. As he indicated them, Eva scuttled forward and removed them from the group and handed them over to Lorelei. The ranks were closed and became densely blonde.

Hitler took his place on the chair in the middle of the chosen children and beamed about him. And no one pointed out to the Führer that he, like the rejected children, had dark hair. As Eva began to focus anew and then take shots, Gabriel saw Hitler's eye for the dramatic. He saw the drama of the contrast; the Führer was one of them – but different. The star in the midst of the chorus.

Gabriel followed the banished children to the other classroom, where Lorelei was in charge of them. It was another cosy room; autumn leaves pasted to walls, nuts on a nature table around an old bird's nest, a line of small beds for naps. Lorelei sat them on the floor and began to read them the 'Three Little Pigs'. As Gabriel listened with the toddlers, it occurred to him that the third little pig, the one who built his house of bricks, was a very north European pig, and the wolf some Slav or foreigner; indeed, Lorelei had given the wolf a Russian accent. It was a moral tale, where feckless piggies ended up in the wolf's belly, but the pig who made the best defence of his home would not only fend off the invader, he would defeat him and eat him.

With excellent timing, Hitler entered the classroom with the blonde children and his blonde mistress as the wolf fell down the chimney into the pan of boiling water. Everyone laughed with approval. Again he caught Gabriel's eye above the children and women and he pulled an expression of amused shock, as the toddlers laughed out loud with relish at the wolf's end. His eyes said little children were savages, and adults were more civilised beings. Gabriel wondered if fairy stories were the first round of basic training for the young future soldiers, as binding as all the military trappings were; the regimental badges, the corps flashes and the flapping colours paraded with crashing music. Perhaps it didn't begin with the anxious recruit coming through the barrack gates for the first time; perhaps this unit loyalty was begun in kindergarten, with shared stories, myths and legends. Lorelei read out the storyteller's promise: *they all lived happily ever after*. Hitler nodded.

The children were bundled into coats to play outside, where Eva wanted to take some informal shots of them. Lorelei had abandoned book for Führer and, as Gabriel moved closer, he could hear her. 'It's almost two towns, Bridgend.'

He realised she was jabbering on about Bridgend, this time a lot more knowledgeably than in the Eagle's Nest. Hitler seemed to be listening carefully to her babble, while ignoring the waving of the children being marched out into the autumnal sunshine, led by Eva. For some unfathomable reason, Hitler's rapt scrutiny of Lorelei filled Gabriel with unease.

Then Lorelei's monologue was broken as Clara approached Hitler, her face screwed with anxiousness, an advance warning that what she was about to say might be contentious. 'Sir, the children, sir – I'm not political, I can't pretend to understand these things – but the colour of a child's hair – isn't it irrelevant? Aren't all God's children the same, even the swarthy ones?'

Gabriel noticed her enormous bottom was trembling as she asked, but there was no mockery in his observation. It was one of those rare moments on the battlefield when a previously unregarded soldier does something monumentally brave. He wanted to cheer her, the brave nursery teacher who loved children and whose conscience demanded of her that she speak. Gabriel wondered what stories she'd been raised on. He realised that Lorelei had moved by his side in trepidation of what was to come. Hitler was the weather over a peak; dark, moody, threatening a storm – then the sun came out and he smiled and pinched Clara's cheek.

'You're a good woman. A good German woman. You know you have the same given name as my mother? So you see, I would expect nothing less from German womanhood but kindness and compassion, that's how it should be. I expect this from women, this universal love for all children, even those from the mongrel races. What an awful world it would be without it. But, my dear, for men it is not the same. It cannot be.'

He looked around as if to find support for his words, but it was merely, Gabriel knew, a desire to address the crowd, to buttonhole posterity even in a kindergarten.

'I love children,' he said. 'Men love children as much as women – but men have to be selective; history demands it, survival demands it. A man must feed his own children first. This selective love is a burden a man must carry and if a man is not prepared to shoulder it, he must renounce his manhood and become a priest. Listen, young lady, as you know in your position of teacher, the boys are as kind as the girls; all are born kind.'

The Führer seemed to pull himself in from the waist and clutched his hands in prayer, his eyes closed. And although he spoke softly, there was thunder in his words. 'But it would be irresponsible for a society to leave young boys in this natural state, when one day, as protectors, they must be strong and make cruel decisions.'

He looked around the classroom as he gathered his thoughts and he saw a bucket and mop in the corner. 'That bucket,' he said, and his audience regarded it with a respect engendered by the person who had drawn their attention to it.

'That bucket is the answer. I believe every child in the kindergarten should be given a kitten, a beautiful little bundle.

The girls will be allowed to play with their kittens here in this classroom, while the boys will take theirs to the hall. There, in the centre of that room, they will find this bucket.'

Again the bucket was regarded.

'It will be full to the brim with water and the boys will be encouraged, one by one, to drown their kitten. In this simple way, we will teach the boys to harden their hearts. We will teach them the true path to manhood. It will be a rite of passage, their first test. The whole kindergarten will learn their true role in life: the girl to be kind; the boy, when required, to be cruel.'

He finished and went silently out into the playground to join the children and Eva. Clara turned and looked at them hopelessly, before she too followed the Führer out into the weak sunshine.

Gabriel turned to Lorelei by his side. 'You were right,' he said.

'What about?'

He looked around at the soft room they were in, its yellow walls glowing like honey. 'I still want to kill him. I want to kill that monster – but you're right, and London's right – it would just make things worse. A new world can't rise from the ashes unless there are ashes. Germany has to burn. Everything has to go; all the old stories, all the shit. There needs to be a clean sweep. Half measures will avail the world nothing but a breathing space, before a new Hitler, or a committee of Hitlers, starts the whole fucking business again. How does it go? – purged by fire. So I'll protect him from his generals, I'll make sure he's alive to take this whole great nation down into the pit with him. I'll be his bodyguard.'

Lorelei listened and nodded and took his arm. 'We need you. London has been in contact; we're definitely looking for an Old Hare.'

CHAPTER TWENTY-FOUR

The coffee dribbled into the jug; a small, black stream that filled Max's office. As he watched the slow drip, he tried to remember when good coffee, like Max's smuggled brew, had disappeared from general life. It had been a gradual attrition. There had been no shortage of coffee, as he could recall, during his ceremonial service at the Vatican, but later, during the war in Spain, supply of all things had been chaotic. Franco's logistics had been slipshod and his colonial troops and foreign mercenaries, like the Condor Legion, learned to take what they wanted from the peasants. This had meant an abundance of cheap, gut-rot wine but not much coffee.

Max handed him a steaming mug as reverently as a priest might handle the wine that was the blood of Christ, and delivered his blessing. 'Drink it while it's hot.'

Gabriel did – black, scalding, oily. Some soldiers in Russia maintained that a good shit somewhere warm and safe was better than sex. For Gabriel it would have been coffee that triumphed over copulation – that was until he met Lorelei. She had welcomed him back into the Foxley team with a passion that still shivered him and gently shook the coffee in his hands as he had flashbacks of her on the bed of her apartment in the ruined theatre. He was back in her lap. Gabriel was the ermine again.

And after the passion, there had been the news. 'London has told us. The MI6 team is being led by an agent with the codename the Three Graces,' Lorelei had told him.

'So, are there three of them?'

She shook her head. 'Probably not. It's deception, a codename that's confusing. The Three Graces could be one old, embittered SS officer, or seven virgins in dirndls. Don't put any weight on the word three.'

'Or grace,' he said, reaching for her again.

'My, you are hungry,' she said, complying.

Suddenly Max was speaking across the blue film of his memory and Gabriel had reluctantly let his erotic images of Lorelei float away.

'So why two teams?' Max swirled his own coffee around in its mug and stared down at the mini-maelstrom he'd created, as if expecting an answer in it.

'A circle of steel,' suggested Gabriel. 'A war on two fronts; one espionage team run by the Russkies and the other by the Tommies?'

Max became agitated as a barrage of homilies shelled his head. 'Too many cooks, too many irons in the fuck-up – bollocks Gabriel – how does it go: left hand not knowing the right hand's having a wank? Two teams working simultaneously and not cooperating? Sounds like the bloody Italians and the Africa Corps in the desert.'

'Maybe that's it; allies don't always work well together, maybe they don't share intelligence. We're allies of the Japanese but they didn't tell us they were about to attack Pearl Harbor and bring the Yanks into the war.'

Max nodded morosely. 'True.'

Max sat behind his desk, eking out his coffee in small sips.

Gabriel sat in a leather club armchair that at some point, in a colourful past, had been wounded in one flank and still bled horsehair.

'Besides,' he said.

'What?' prompted Max.

'I don't think we're dealing with two teams any longer. I think the first, let's call it the British team, on account of the Lee–Enfield rifle, is now defunct. Their sniper was probably the French waiter-cum-Legionnaire, Volfgangu, and he's done a runner.'

Max nodded his agreement. 'Given his military background, I reckon he was the marksman who took the second shot. The French Resistance and British wouldn't send someone to shoot Adolf Hitler who wasn't an A1 sniper.'

'The first, rotten shot queered Volfgangu's pitch; Adolf was ducking and weaving but he did his best, tried his luck, missed and headed out for La Belle France.'

Max reluctantly put his empty mug on his desk. 'The remaining team – you think it's a Red cell?'

'The Soviets put ideology above professionalism. I can see them sending a trusted communist in spite of the fact he's also a mediocre marksman.'

'What about the second team being run by our generals?'

Gabriel nodded. 'But again, they'd send someone like me or you.'

'An elite soldier who could shoot off a midget's prick at a thousand metres. Someone with the cold hand of a sniper.'

'That's right, Max. And anyway, the generals shot their bolt at the Wolf's Lair.'

'It won't stop them trying again.'

'No,' said Gabriel, 'but it takes time to organise a plot.'

'And their leaders are dead and the survivors won't be reckless. It must have been a kick in the balls for them when we all believed the little corporal was dead and no one took to the streets cheering.'

'An attempt two months after the failed bomb plot is far too fast for the Prussians.' Gabriel leaned forward and his mug joined Max's on the desk.

Max thought and shook his head. 'I don't know why but it doesn't feel right, this Red cell thing. If this was Berlin, maybe; plenty of communists there, but Bavaria? Any man on Obersalzberg has had his record trawled through time and time again. There's only one Party up here and it's not the Workers'. And don't forget, someone put a grenade in the Führer's elevator and that someone can only have been one of the Old Hares. And their profile fits the crime; they're survivors every one of them. Faced with defeat, which of them is most likely to sacrifice Adolf to save themselves?'

Max pulled himself up, approached his electric coffee machine. For a wild moment, Gabriel thought they were in for a second mug, but Max fought temptation and paced the office, speaking his thoughts. 'Perhaps he has family, female relatives – we all know what Ivan does to women. The Old Hare has done his best, but Germany is still going to hell courtesy of a T34 tank. He's pragmatic; time to bail. He needs to trade, so what's he got in his pocket? Little Wolf. And for slaying the beast, he gets immunity for himself and his ladies and a passport out of the ashes – but it won't be the Reds, will it?'

'Why not?' Gabriel asked.

'They don't want what our generals want. They want the little corporal fucking things up till they roll over his bones in Berlin. No, if it's not the Prussians it still has to be the British or Yanks. The Yanks are still Boy Scouts, so my bet is the British. The grenade proves they haven't abandoned the mission. I bet my best boots there's a British team on Obersalzberg running an assassin in the Old Hares.'

Gabriel found his hand working the hole in the side of the armchair. 'So,' he said, 'we're back to finding which of them doesn't have an alibi.'

'Them and you,' said Max, turning to face Gabriel. 'You still haven't explained your movements on the day in question.'

'But I was in the elevator with Hitler, I defused the grenade. Why would I try to kill him one day and save him another?'

Max laughed. 'To save your own skin. And besides, this might be another two-team cock-up. Forget the grenade, what were you doing on the morning someone tried to put a round between the beloved Führer's eyes?'

Gabriel abandoned the hole in the armchair and folded his hands in his lap. He spoke primly. 'To tell you where I was would impinge on the modesty and reputation of another person.'

Max snorted with impatience. 'If you were with Lorelei Fischer that morning just say for God's sake. You're not at the Vatican now. They're running scared; the good and great of the Nazi party are shitting themselves and that makes them dangerous. The rule of law means sod all to them. I tell the Führer you're a possible suspect, he's just as likely to shoot you without further proof, just to be sure. So spit it out – where were you precisely on the morning of the attempted assassination?'

Gabriel took a breath and tried to look as if he was being made to talk under duress, but the lie he was about to give to Max had been concocted weeks before he'd squeezed the trigger. 'I'd spent the previous night with Lorelei. I was up and dressed when I heard the shots but still in her apartment.'

'What did you do?'

'Attached my sidearm, left the apartment, saw Herzberger and Schadle ahead of me, racing up the hill.'

'What did you think had happened?'

Gabriel shrugged. 'We all know Wolf's routine. There had been one attempt on his life.'

'And no one saw you till you all arrived at the picnic. Will Lorelei confirm you were with her all morning till the alarm?'

'If she must.'

'Oh yes, she must.'

Gabriel pulled himself up out of the armchair. 'Then she will be my cast-iron alibi.'

As if they were on opposite ends of a seesaw, Max sat. 'Be careful of that: cast iron has a habit of shattering.'

Max looked at Gabriel, drummed his fingers on his desk and began to lecture him. 'One of the things you discover as a copper is how little couples really know about each other. Maybe they've got better things to do than talk. But we love it in the force; having two suspects romantically entwined. One of them will always finally rat out the other. There's no honour among lovers.'

'I know Lorelei.'

'Do you? Do you really? So, what's she doing here, up this bloody mountain? What's she up to on jolly old Obersalzberg?'

Gabriel felt a small seed of panic start to germinate in his stomach. 'You know what she does, Max.'

'But what she does up here makes no sense. Think about it – she's a qualified nurse; they're like gold dust on the Eastern Front and in the bombed cities of the Ruhr. What's she doing here?'

Gabriel spoke slowly to Max as if explaining to a slow-witted child. 'She works in Platterhof Hospital, taking care of battlefield casualties. That's where she serves.'

'But only on a part-time basis. What's that about? She helps out at the kindergarten but I figure she does that because she gets bored. She's here for a reason and it's not kiddies and casualties.'

The seed of panic inside Gabriel grew and its roots twisted around his gut. 'What is she here for, Max?'

'You really don't know?'

Gabriel didn't bother to answer, couldn't answer.

'You're not aware that Lorelei Fischer is on the personal staff of Adolf Hitler? She's his creature as much as his dog, Blondi. You didn't know that?'

Gabriel didn't need to act his reply. 'No.'

Max suddenly shut up when Gabriel needed him to talk.

'What are her duties? Tell me, Max.'

What were her duties? Was she another mistress, he wondered? Was Eva just for his arm? Did Lorelei simply warm his bed?

'Not what you think,' said Max, reading Gabriel's thoughts. 'I made enquiries, bent some arms. Seems the Führer sent for her on account of her command of Japanese. For reasons known only to him, he has need of a patriotic German who is fluent in Jap. There aren't many, she's one – this gives Lorelei Fischer the Führer's seal of approval, and it's this blessing that makes her word your steel alibi.'

Gabriel found his breath returning to his lower lungs. 'You're saying I'm off the hook?'

'Looks like it. Anyway, you don't fit the bill. If the French waiter took the second shot, as seems likely, then that would make you the cross-eyed sniper who missed, and I don't think you do – miss. I think you've got cold hands.'

Max reached and brushed a speck of imaginary dust from the gold Close Quarter Hand to Hand badge on Gabriel's uniform.

As the panic died and withered within him, Gabriel found himself wondering what Lorelei's duties were exactly, what she did for Hitler and why she'd never confided in him? He also wondered if London knew of this other occupation of the Foxley team leader?

'Nothing for it,' said Max. 'We'll have to reel the Old Hares in and see if any of their stories crack under pressure. The ones he didn't send to Berlin with his double, anyway.'

Out of the remaining detachment, there were three Old Hares that Gabriel wanted to investigate, but he didn't want to do it in the presence of Max. 'Don't take this the wrong way but I need to see my Old Hares without you. I want to see each of them alone, Max. They're my officers and they might open up if it feels more of a discussion and less of an interrogation.'

Max looked at him. 'A cosy fireside chat?'

'If I keep it casual, comrade to comrade, they might let something slip. Then I can bring you in to take their story apart.'

'You don't think I can be matey?'

'I think it's the military, Max. You're in a different arm; technically you're a gunner, and, more than that, you're in a different service, the Luftwaffe. They won't confess to suspecting a comrade in front of an officer from a rival service.'

Max nodded. 'I take your point. You do the chat and send for me when you need the cavalry.'

Gabriel needed to see them without Max because of the information that had come from London. He knew an Old Hare had contacted a pastor in Munich after the July plot and only three of the Old Hares had taken a weekend leave pass in that city at the end of the summer. He would look closely at those three: August Korber, Bodo Gelzenleuchter and Emil Maurice.

CHAPTER TWENTY-FIVE

August Korber brought his heels together smartly three steps into Max's office. It was his turn to answer questions. August played the old soldier, doing it by the book – upright, closed off and correct. He sat reluctantly in the chair Gabriel insisted he take.

'On the day of the attempt, did you see anyone else climbing the hill after you heard the shot?'

August shook his jowls. 'I ran from the mess. I didn't see anyone until I reached Bruno Gesche holding the sniper's rifle. I'd been detailed to a close protection duty but the Leader had spotted me. Gave me a flea in the ear and ordered me back to barracks. I'd just got back when I heard the firing.'

Gabriel remembered the incident, witnessing it from above while he waited to take his shot. 'Did you see anything unusual before you reached the others?'

'No, I just ran towards the sound of the guns.' He grinned smugly.

The old cavalry practice of charging towards the sound of battle. August wanted approval for his dash up the hillside. Gabriel was prepared to give it, as he needed to take the Old

Hare off in a new direction with his questions, and a malleable man would be easier to manipulate than a suspicious one.

'You did the right thing. Wolf wants to know the names of those of his Leibstandarte who responded promptly.'

While August preened, Gabriel led the questioning off at a tangent. 'The rifle, being British, must have been smuggled onto Obersalzberg and into Germany somehow. This is a conspiracy involving more than just one madman.'

'You think the Frenchie had help?'

Volfgangu the Legionnaire.

'It's the work of a team that stretches in and out of Obersalzberg. We need to cast our net wide. I see you took leave in July and spent it in Munich?'

August looked confused. 'A few days – but I didn't pick up a rifle and bring it back here.'

'Of course not, I wasn't suggesting that. You're a good and conscientious officer, August. I just wanted to know if you saw anything suspicious in Munich, anything odd, or out of place. Something small that didn't quite fit?'

August gave the question the courtesy of thought but finally shook his head. 'I spent the days helping on a course at the Hofbrauhaus beer hall. Training up the Hitler Youth. They've got to be ready, you know. They'll have to do their bit like men before we're victorious. I told them that – but I didn't get out and about much.'

'Right.'

August's face began to glow. 'Do you know the Hofbrauhaus? That's where it all began, all this, everything. That's where I first saw Wolf. The first time I heard him speak.' August laughed. 'Would you believe, I heckled him? I was a commie then. But his words got to me; he had a gob on him. You see he cared about the betrayal. By god, he cared about the stab in the back, when the Jews and bigwigs sold us out and surrendered to the Frogs and Tommies. I'd been too young to serve in that war but I remembered how that felt. All that blood for nothing but shame; the army not defeated but made to surrender by the Jew-boys and politicians. He understood, the Reds didn't – so I stopped being a communist. Besides...'

He smiled wide enough to show he was missing some side teeth. 'The National Socialists had better street fighters. Wolf was good at that too – led from the front. Back then he always carried a whip and he'd use it. I'm just an ordinary man, but he has made my life extraordinary. He has made Germany extraordinary. I'll be with him in victory or go down with him in defeat. I'm a member of the Leibstandarte, an Old Hare; I didn't get transferred into this unit, it wasn't a posting – I paid the blood price. Mine was Ernst Rohm and Gregor Strasser on the Night of the Long Knives. Do you understand?'

Gabriel did. August had paid his entrance fee to the Old Hares; he had murdered for his Führer.

Bodo Gelzenleuchter, like August, had not seen anyone on the hill before arriving at the attempted assassination site. Having ascertained this, Gabriel asked him about his leave in Munich.

'I don't have family in that city so I go there for a bit of rest and relaxation, if you know what I mean? I've always been a bit of a ladies' man,' he said.

Gabriel wondered if the ladies knew this.

Bodo leered and continued, 'Home is too far away, what with the state of the railways and the terror bombers. And besides, if I go home, what would be waiting for me but a fat wife and screaming brats? So, I hang around Munich, where the girls are shapely, with star-gazey tits, and don't smell of shitty nappies.'

Gabriel returned the man-of-the-world smile of agreement that Bodo seemed to require.

'So – where did you hang out?'

Bodo winked. 'A place I can really recommend. Clean girls, disease free. I can let you have the address for your next leave.'

Gabriel took it. He would need to visit but not for the same reason as Bodo, who was off again. 'You won't believe the underwear, and the minges – soft as mouse velvet. They have rooms you can rent with a discount for the SS, so I just move in for the duration of my leave. Some of the girls pretend to be Jewish and you can fuck them up the crapper.'

Gabriel discovered he wanted to bring Bodo's spiel to an end. 'And that's what you did in Munich?'

Bodo laughed. 'Well I didn't go there to listen to the Frauenkirche chimes!'

CHAPTER TWENTY-SIX

The Oxbridge spy, swaddled by his houndstooth suit, attempted to sprawl in the unforgiving Butaque chair. He inspected the silver-and-enamel badge that Jago had removed from the lapel of his dead, would-be killer. Outside, the traffic softly murmured and seemed almost to be the sound of the Don's mind working. The ugly furniture added to the grey drizzle of the day. Modernism, Jago decided, was not a morning movement.

'Image of an eagle killing a snake.'

The spy chortled into his waistcoat, which had risen up almost like a ruff around his neck. He was a man for whom the straightening of his clothes would seem a betrayal of his intellectual status.

'And the inscription, *Perish Judea*. Thus the eagle is Aryan while we must assume the snake eats only kosher prey. Where did you come across it?'

He offered the badge back to Jago, who took it reluctantly and stuffed it in a pocket, as if the object might contaminate him. 'It fell off a suit worn by a dead man. In Scotland.'

'Ah, Scotland,' said the spy, as if this explained the carnage. 'Did you kill him?'

Jago shook his head. 'Nicky.'

'Yes, well he's good at killing things. Comes with the blue blood, don't you think? Where in Scotland was the fascist dispatched?'

'Peebles – or just outside.'

The Don suddenly beamed with inner knowledge that he was sure wasn't shared. 'And what do we know of Peebles, young Craze?'

Jago suddenly wished the unforgiving chair contained Mrs Cambridge with her no-nonsense, straightforward approach. The Don haggled and bartered knowledge like a peasant. Jago snapped, 'If you've got something to say just say it, otherwise I'm off.' He turned to go, and wanted to be away, out of that miserable flat that was even more dismal than a wet day in Chalk Farm.

'Hold your horses. Steady the Buffs.' The irritating man rose with difficulty from the chair, like a barrage balloon being winched up. He bobbed to the open-plan kitchen to pour some tea that had been stewing there. He offered the pot to Jago, inviting him to join him in a cup, but Jago shook his head. The Don, with difficulty, poured one for himself, and Jago saw that, for some inexplicable reason, the pot had lost its spout. The tea fell like a waterfall and splashed everywhere. Jago found the sight of that tea spewing from the hole the obscenest thing he'd ever witnessed.

'Peebles,' said the Don through the smoke of the cup coming to his lips. 'Peebles is the constituency of one Archibald Maule Ramsey, Conservative Member of Parliament for said Peebles and South Midlothian. Let us not forget South Midlothian.'

He took another sip of tea and Jago waited. Finally, the Don chugged into life again. 'Archibald is now interned for the duration because he'd be happier if the Germans were here rather than the Yanks. The sitting MP is sitting in a cell. In the far-right trade he is what is known as Jew-wise.'

'And what's that?'

'The Jew-wise maintain they are aware of the Jewish conspiracy to rule the world. They are the nincompoops who believe in the ridiculous drivel that is the Protocols of the Elders of Zion. And sadly, there are more of them in Britain than fleas on a hedgehog.'

'Do you mean the blackshirts?'

The irritating laugh came again. 'Dear boy, the grubby shirts are just the tip of the prick. I doubt there's a corner of this sceptred isle that doesn't host its very own Jew-baiting association. There are debating circles, cults, sects, dining clubs, pressure groups, both open and secret societies, leagues, guilds and kinships all devoted to Perish Judea.'

'An exaggeration surely?'

The teacup went down with a crash onto a side table that wasn't there and ended up as a puddle of broken crockery. Jago instinctively leaned to pick up the shards.

'Shit! No, leave it!' The Don was suddenly angry. 'Of course there's the British Union, fascists loved by the working classes and led by a rather lazy aristocrat, all very feudal. But it doesn't stop there, not by a mile of chalk. Every section of society has an opportunity to join a Pals battalion of their peers to battle the Yid menace. The upper classes favour the Nordic League; the smart set are hot for the January Club. The eccentric flock to the White Knights Fraternity, and the animal lovers have their very own Anti-Vivisectionist League, convinced as they are it's the Jew who is responsible for animal experiments. They love Adolf because he's a vegetarian! Let us not forget Margaret Damer Dawson's Women's Police Service; an unofficial constabulary – uniformed, in spite of Henry the Seventh's Statute of Maintenance and Livery aimed at preventing private and political uniformed armies. Peopled by ex-suffragettes, it has a mission to protect English virgins from Jewish depravity. They are firm believers in the non-existent white slave traffic, said to operate from Chinese laundries to supply drugged lasses to Jewish brothels. Jago, there is even a branch of the Ku Klux Klan here, called the Hooded Men. The United Rate-Payers is in existence purely to prevent the pollution of the suburbs by Hebrew blood. Shall I go on?'

Jago nodded bleakly.

'Have you heard of the Christian Defence Movement, a crusader order pledged to rid our shores of the foreigner? The National Citizen's Union, the New Pioneer Group, the British People's Party, the British Council Against European Commitments and Contamination, the Liberty Restoration League, the British Democratic Party – all far right, all anti-Semitic, all pro-Hitler. Dear God, there's the Medical Practitioners' Union, who wish to block Jewish doctors practising here and to prevent them attending our medical schools. The Eugenics Society, who preach death or sterilisation for – yes! – the Jews. There is nothing so innocent in this fair land that it can't be spiced up with a bit of Jew-baiting. For example, the English Mistery. They spell mystery as M.i.s.t.e.r.y. as a banal attempt to sound medieval. Basically, it's a back-to-nature fellowship of fascist allotment holders; no produce sown and grown by English hands should be given or sold to the Jew.'

Jago shrugged and said, 'And yet now there's a war, they all fight. Fight with enormous courage and sacrifice against a people you say they support.'

Jago thought the Don was going to spit. Distaste and anger filled his face. 'They fight for... patriotic reasons. They are a base people who support a team because of its proximity to their home. They are unable to discern what this war is about. They are the biggest joke in the whole shambolic mess. They have fielded a football team to play in a tennis tournament. This isn't a patriotic war. This is a war of ideas. It's not about the defence of Englishness – of village cricket, warm beer and very quiet sex. The real question is: what will stand after the guns fall silent in France? National Socialism? Capitalism? Or International Marxism? They die in droves for causes they can't comprehend.'

Jago felt colourless and bleached by tiredness. 'I think I've heard of the English Mistery.'

'Minor players, not even corps de ballet. Gardeners-against-the-ghetto sort of thing. A yearning for past things, a love of countryside, a fear of cities – home of Johnny foreigner, the Jew-boy and the homosexual.'

Jago fished the badge back out of his pocket. 'And what lot wears this?'

'Oh, a very nasty team, rotters to a man. The real McCoy. That is the badge of the Link. They're a little more dangerous than the gardeners. A middle-class clique of empire loyalists, imperialists, men whose careers – and more importantly whose sons' careers – depend on there being a British Empire. The fate of the Jews weighs very lightly in their scales compared with the pan carrying the Raj. Men of action, colonial policemen and soldiers, they don't hesitate to shed blood.'

'I think they're trying to shed mine.'

'They won't have liked your paper.'

'The man Nicky killed wanted the Walpurgisnacht Plan. Didn't believe me when I said I didn't have it.'

'And you don't?'

'No.'

The Don thought. 'Could still be on its way. Supposed to have been delivered but who knows? Hold-ups, cock-ups, cold feet. Might still arrive. If it does, you will let me know, won't you? If you'll allow us to make the fullest use of this intelligence, I think we can promise to get the Link off your back.'

Tiredness, like a pillow, tried to smother Jago. 'But aren't all these organisations illegal now?'

'In a democracy, I blush!'

The Don affected comic dismay before continuing. 'Some of the leaders are detained – Lady Mosley sports her furs around Holloway Prison – but the structure of fascism is still in place throughout the realm. For them we are fighting on the wrong side, and we have the wrong allies. Their mission is to change that. Link up to Germany and, shoulder to shoulder, fight the Soviets. They'd rather the Yanks just buggered off and dealt with the Japs. They will not tolerate the total destruction of Germany and then the dismantling of their empire by the liberal victors. The establishment of this realm hates Adolf Hitler, not for his views, which, when all's said and done, are their values. No, he is despised because, like an exhibitionist, he has exposed to the light of day beliefs that should be covered. Hate should always be discreet. You wish to save Hitler to ultimately destroy Hitlerism. The English establishment wish to destroy Hitler to preserve Hitlerism.'

Jago looked at the badge again. 'The men who are after me belong to the Link.'

'Next time might be fourth time lucky for them. You have to disappear; you can't go home to Pimlico.'

'Where then?'

'Where shall you lay your little head? Shack up with Nicky for the time being. What's that ridiculous place he has diggings?'

'Albany.'

'Yes, the Albany.'

'No, there's no *the* – just – Albany.'

And Jago was pleased that at last he could correct the Don on something.

CHAPTER TWENTY-SEVEN

'I object to being questioned by a Johnny-come-lately. I'm not the only one to wonder why an outsider was brought in to command the Leibstandarte!'

Emil Maurice was not being cooperative. He twitched angrily and jangled the solid silver Blood Order on his right breast pocket. It had only been awarded to participants of the 1923 Hitlerputsch. The man was a veteran of the Nazi gang. Gabriel sighed. After the comparative ease of the August Korber and Bodo Gelzenleuchter interrogations, the third Old Hare was proving to be a bastard. But Gabriel had the rank. 'Your objections are of no account, Maurice. I was tasked with commanding the Leibstandarte by Adolf Hitler himself. He was sickened by the lamentable state of his closest bodyguard, the many derelictions of duty tolerated by its then CO. The Führer was almost assassinated while the officer commanding was in a drunken stupor. When I took over, I found fat, lazy, waifs and strays, masquerading as SS officers. Stand to attention when I speak to you!'

Even at attention, Emil Maurice still managed to be surly. 'I know who's been stabbing me in the back. The bitch has got it in for me.'

Gabriel wondered if he meant Lorelei, but Emil Maurice was still ranting. 'She might share his bed but Wolf doesn't love her.'

'Eva Braun?'

'Bitch.'

Being able to express his feelings regarding the Führer's mistress seemed to sooth Emil, and Gabriel was able to get some answers. He'd seen no one running up the hill to the scene of the attempted assassination. 'I heard those shots. I heard where they came from. I knew instantly who the target was. Every day he treads that path to the tea-house. I grabbed my sidearm and ran. I was busy buckling it on as I ascended, but you know what that hill's like, you were there. Shrub and cover all the way. I could have been running by your side, I wouldn't have seen you.'

It was true. Gabriel had used growth to approach unseen from the opposite direction and insert himself into the group around the discarded sniper's rifle.

'I need to ask you about your last leave. I believe you spent it in Munich?'

Emil Maurice twisted from his upright *at attention* position and stepped forward. 'Munich? What's that got to do with anything?'

'Answer the question.'

Gabriel stared at him, stared down the protests forming in his mouth. He pulled himself straight again and Gabriel took up a position just behind his back. 'Did you see anything unusual or hear anything out of place in Munich?'

Emil Maurice did not grace Gabriel's question with the courtesy of thought. 'Of course I didn't. What are you talking about?'

He attempted to turn to glare at his interrogator.

'Eyes forward!'

The Old Hare grumbled audibly as he did as he was ordered.

'How did you spend your leave in Munich?'

Gabriel could hear his breath, heavy with impatience. 'I went to church.'

'Don't get smart, Maurice! Answer the question.'

'I did go to church! I'm a Christian. I took my leave in Munich specifically to undertake a spiritual retreat at Saint Lukas.'

'Did you talk to anyone there about our life here on Obersalzberg, our routines; Wolf going to the tearooms every morning for example?'

'Talk? It was a silent retreat!'

Gabriel reported to Max's office and filled him in on the Old Hares' answers. Max grunted. Gabriel didn't know if this was a grunt of acceptance or disappointment; a grunt that signalled he'd have got some answers if he'd been asking the questions. Gabriel didn't share that part of the interrogations where he'd asked the three Old Hares in whom he was specifically interested the Munich questions. But he did want to know some more about Emil Maurice. 'What's he got against Eva Braun?'

Max gave a chuckle that was darker than it was warm. 'He loved a woman that the Führer also loved. That woman, more a girl really, is now dead. Emil Maurice is a romantic and probably feels Hitler should not have replaced this perfect woman with a woman who's blonde on both sides of her skull.'

Gabriel considered this. 'He made a big thing about being a Christian.'

Max pushed a tin of coffee beans around his desk with an idle finger. Inside, the beans samba-ed almost silently, giving out a hushed death rattle. Gabriel wished he'd stop playing with it and make it.

'He would bang a drum about being a Christian.'

'Why?'

'Going to church is so very German, but Mr Emil Maurice is not so very German. Or at least some of his grandparents are not.'

'Are you saying he's Jewish?'

The dark chuckle came again. 'A little.'

Gabriel forgot his need for coffee. 'A Jew in Hitler's personal bodyguard?'

'When it all kicked off in the early days, and the Nazis were just a gang of street thugs, Emil didn't know. He cracked Hebrew heads with the best of them. It was Heine – Himmler – who ran a blood check on all the Old Hares. He found out that Emil, circumcised or not, was kosher.'

'And the Führer didn't dismiss him? What about the Blood-Shame?'

'Wolf is sentimental. He likes dogs and obedience and Emil is an obedient dog. And then there's the other thing.'

Max didn't drop his voice or whisper but it went to a flat monotone that didn't carry and Gabriel leaned in to listen to him. 'The girl who died, the woman they both loved; it was Angela Raubal, they called her Geli – she was Hitler's niece. It was Geli who was the love of the Führer's life, not the simpering tit-head who shares his bed now. But Adolf turned out not to be Geli's prince; she favoured the younger man, Emil.'

'Hitler found out?'

'She's dead, isn't she? Hitler can never come second. Someone kicked her into a rag doll and then shot her through the lung. I was a copper then; I saw the body. Later I read the autopsy report... just before it disappeared for ever. They said it was suicide, but the report mentioned there were no scorch marks around the wound so she'd been shot from a distance. The pistol used was Hitler's own Walther.'

Gabriel had an image of the Walther he'd removed from Volfgangu. The weapon had disappeared under the scanties in one of Lorelei's drawers.

'And no one has ever explained to my satisfaction how she kicked herself to buggery,' said Max.

'He got away with it?'

'His first murder.' Max suddenly made his decision and stood, picking up the coffee tin and heading for the machine on the filing cabinet. 'I remember it very well. I was new to the detective department and they let me have a crack at Emil. They wouldn't normally, I was fresh out of uniform, but nobody else could be bothered.'

Gabriel was confused. 'But it was suspected murder? She was Hitler's niece?'

'That was the problem. My fellow detectives knew that even if we had a thousand eye witnesses there wasn't going to be a trial. The Gob had got too big by that time. So, they let me cut my teeth on Emil Maurice.'

'Did you get anywhere?'

'I sweated him, but he knew he was above the law. He left without charges – but he did it, him or the Gob. And he had an alibi. Emil Maurice maintains he was with Wolf at the time of little Geli's death. Emil loved that girl – but he loves the Führer more and Hitler loves the loyalty of sacrifice and blood. They're bound together. Think of a scab. Fuck it – you make the coffee.'

CHAPTER TWENTY-EIGHT

Albany was a district behind Piccadilly occupied by one mansion house. As such, the building was known as Albany, never *the* Albany. Nicky had talked to Jago about the place, trying to persuade him to visit. Jago had always resisted. Now fear had delivered him to the doorstep.

'The big house was divided into apartments in the eighteenth century, though we call them sets,' explained Nicky.

Nicky's set was on the ground floor, off the Ropewalk. The Ropewalk led from an interior corridor occupied by porters out into the shared gardens in a central quadrangle. Jago thought it resembled a Roman atrium.

Nicky's rooms on the ground floor were everything the self-conscious flat of the spy-don wasn't. Three centuries had lent objects to furnish it, all from other homes of the Godwin family. Jago wondered if there was a single item in it that had been bought specifically for it. The armchairs were all leather and ranged from club to wing, from Chesterfield to bucket.

'I'm sorry to put you out,' said Jago.

'Don't be,' Nicky smiled. 'It's time you stayed for supper and breakfast.'

Jago felt like a girl under an obligation. Nicky had saved his life. Should he offer himself in return? And who would he be if he did? He inspected the set, the location of the seduction that Nicky obviously intended. The rooms were large but few. A spiral staircase in the lobby outside the kitchen led up to what had once been the valet's room, but which the golden boy now used as his bedroom. The original bedroom on the ground floor was the dining room and home to a long mahogany table that Nicky's mother insisted he needed. On one wall, a marble fireplace contained a glowing coal fire that Jago was grateful for; the nights were drawing in. The heat, and the deep chairs with their saggy embrace, were almost his undoing. When Nicky spoke, it made Jago jump. 'What did the commissar have to say?'

Jago yawned himself awake. 'Apparently, the badge we took off that man you killed belongs to a fascist organisation called the Link. The members of which seem to be out to get me.'

'They won't find you here; the most discreet address in London. This is where the sons of the aristocracy have traditionally sewn their wild oats. Byron brought girls back here disguised as pageboys – or was it the other way around?'

The name of one of the right-wing groups had been rolling around his head since the Don had mentioned them. Jago hadn't said anything to him but he did to Nicky. 'Have you heard of the English Mistery, spelled M.i.s.t.e.r.y?'

Nicky had arrived back from Scotland while Jago was with the Don. He'd obviously bathed and was now ensconced in a silk brocade dressing gown, looking as elegant as someone Joshua Reynolds might have painted. In the flickering light from the fire he almost seemed to shimmer, Jago thought, like a mirage, like something beautiful that isn't really there. Something or someone out of Jago's reach.

'The English Mistery, what's that?'

'My late in-laws were members. It's a yeomen-of-old-England sort of outfit, and that was the Dunns. Their home was their garden. They loved the war because they got an allotment. I had no idea it was anti-Semitic or that they were fascists. I just thought they were suburban.'

'Same thing old man. What happened to them?'

'My in-laws? Air raid. The Blitz. House, garden, pond with a gnome fishing, all gone. What did you do with the body?'

'Buried it. Plenty of places to bury a body in the Borders. Beautiful part of the world. Do you know it?'

'Not really.'

'We should go there together, when all this is over.'

Together. Temptation and fear arrived in Jago's heart. He shook himself free by reaching for duty. 'I have to protect my people. I have to protect Foxley. They're over there at this very minute, facing torture if discovered. The Link will do anything to uncover their identities and then they'll tell their friends in the Gestapo. Without Foxley to watch Hitler's back, he'll be killed. There'll be a premature peace and then another war – or perhaps with all these fascist groups, we might just slide into the arms of the Germans and form a right-wing northern European super-state. Or – I don't know, I'm so tired.'

'Poor Jago. It's cruel but it's necessary; I learned that in Spain. The worst time in my life was trudging over the Pyrenees, beaten, the fascists victorious.'

Jago thought the shadows of the flames licking Nicky's face seemed for a moment to be real and consuming him. 'Why did you go to Spain? Why did you cut Oxford? You never seemed political to me, more – if you don't mind me saying – cricket than causes?'

'Why do you say that? I mean what does any man leading a pointless life need but a cause.' Nicky began to laugh then stopped. He looked at Jago. 'I couldn't stay at the university. It didn't matter to me; I'm not a scholar and I didn't need a degree to enter a profession. I'm of independent means. Of course, I'm not really independent; I'm a member of a family. In the Godwin tribe, I'm liked but unregarded. I'm not even the heir's spare as I have two older brothers, both of whom have sons. I'm as far from the succession as the tweeny-maid; even the boot-boy is probably further up the pole than I am. The family were hoping for a girl to make an advantageous marriage alliance. Well they got that and more with my two younger sisters. But what about me, the useless mouth in the middle? I live off the interest of a pot of shares left to me by an uncle, that will on my death revert to the family. I exist in this grace-and-favour set that again belongs to the family, and which will, in the fullness of time, go to house the next Godwin oddball. I was a failure at birth, a mistake, and nothing I can do in life can reverse that under the system that keeps me as a neglected pet. I went to Spain to fight my family – and, of course, for that other reason men run away to war – to forget.'

Jago considered Nicky. 'Someone at Oxford?'

'Unrequited love is so queer, don't you think? I was down in the dumps when I came up. Pleased school was over forever but I wasn't a grammar school boy; Oxford wasn't going to be my big thing. It wasn't going to change my life, it was merely something we did.'

'Did you despise the grammar school lads?'

Nicky shook his head and his blond curls bounced in the firelight, his eyes danced like sapphires. 'They thought we did, but they were wrong. Different cultures, that was all. They were quiet and studious and we were loud and hearty. We were noisier, but we'd grown up in bigger rooms. We were more feral; they were more cherished. But I for one admired what they'd achieved and it was another reason I felt like a useless mouth; occupying a place that someone else might have really valued. Then I fell for one of them.'

Jago waited while Nicky stared away into another universe.

'I never told him and he turned out not to be a grammar school boy. He was one of us, except for some extraordinary reason he'd gone to the girls' public school. Rumour had it he'd shagged himself stupid there. I don't think you had?'

Jago murmured his reply, 'No.'

'I knew I was queer by then. I had a feeling you were, but you sent out the wrong signals. You seemed hot to join all the manly societies. Didn't you take up rugby?'

'Tried to. Eighteen is too old to start putting your head between another man's thighs without feeling a little odd.'

'Then you joined the corps and then the TA proper.'

'Trying desperately to be something I wasn't.'

'I couldn't work you out. You fascinated me. I loved it that you had black hair yet blue eyes. The slight protrusion of your top teeth made me want to hug you and look after you.'

'The girls at school said it made me look gormless.'

Nicky took his hand. 'Your eyes are too awake for that. I don't think I'd seen eyes so alive. Darting everywhere, sometimes landing on me, and then your smile would light up the world.'

Jago smiled. 'I was terrified of you.'

'Same here. We can't share unless we're sure, can we, people like us? It's not just *no thanks*. It's *fuck off you filthy pervert*.'

Jago leaned forward and, against the orders of his more rational self, ran a hand through Nicky's hair.

'Well one day, feeling the ache worse than usual, I took myself off to the cinema. The newsreel showed one of those hunger marches from the north arriving in Whitehall. They flashed a big map up on the screen, showing all the counties they'd walked across, and I sat there, listing all the properties my family had in each of them. They didn't cross a single county in which we didn't have a hunting lodge, or a shooting box, or a fishing beat. We had large stately homes, dower houses, even a castle somewhere. It's not a difficult moral question: should one family own so much, while those families didn't have enough to eat? What was remarkable was that I had been cocooned from that thought for eighteen years. I had been immersed in privilege all my life and I hadn't realised it. I knew then that Oxford had nothing more to teach me. The next item on the newsreel, a story about the civil war in Spain, was a mere footnote to my thought process. Within a week I was there.'

'Forgetting me.'

'Sadly, no. Trying to stay alive. Trying to do my bit. But no, never forgetting you. And as it turns out, unrequited love experienced at a distance is far less painful than it is close to. The memory of you became a comfort to me during some very uncomfortable times.'

How strange, Jago thought; he'd been to Spain in the mind of another. He said, 'Then one day I'm walking down a Whitehall corridor and who's walking up it but you.'

Nicky's face closed, eyes shut, lips pursed, head down. 'I feel so wretched about that. It was a set-up of course.'

Jago had once enjoyed the memory of that meeting – not any more. 'One of the Don's machinations?'

Nicky sniffed. 'The Don, he's a gollumpus. A creature. Clumsy. All head and no grace. There were scholarship boys like him at College House, clever chaps but they couldn't catch at cricket. You probably had boys the same at your school – no of course you wouldn't. Silly me. I expect your chums were tea-party elegant.'

Jago laughed. 'You don't know girls at boarding school. Believe me, they go through a suet-pudding-in-gymslip phase. The mistresses fight the flab with deportment drill and waltz classes. They even organise games specifically tailored to instil a little grace...'

'Be that as it may,' Nicky interrupted, 'your report crossed the Don's desk via the Kremlin and he went mad; bounced off the furniture, danced on the crockery and shouted we needed to talk to you. I wanted to make the approach.'

'Why didn't you?'

'Ordered not to.'

Orders, the lubricant of war.

'The police raid those cottaging toilets regularly. The Don, who doesn't approve of my homosexuality, didn't want a first-rate asset ruined by being exposed as a sodomite. I was supposed to keep my hands clean and Austen, who is more expendable, was given the mission. After all, he'd already ascertained on an earlier meeting that you really were a ducky-boy.'

Jago remembered Austen coming into the gents' half a minute after him. The look. The message in the eyes. Available. Nicky was talking. 'Honestly old man, you could set your clock by your libido. You should be careful. Same time every Friday night – same toilets.'

Jago supposed he was right. A part of his brain was interested in that predictability and wondered how much promiscuous sex was linked to the excitement of ritual.

'Austen said the original liaison had gone well, and that you might welcome seeing him again if the approach was discreet. So, the Don told Austen to arrange a meeting. To begin with, it was all the Don and Austen, plotting and planning. I felt excluded and, well – jealous. Against orders I contrived to bump into you, in that Whitehall corridor.'

'You played your part well.'

'I wasn't acting, Jago. My delight in seeing you, being near you, wasn't pretended. I was hauled over the coals for it but I didn't care.'

Jago had been thrilled too. A man whom he believed hardly registered his existence up at Oxford, was, on their fresh encounter, so happy to see him. He had been flattered, and then almost captured and carried off by Nicky with his physicality and energy. He'd been taken to a small private dining room of a restaurant in St James's. They had talked and talked and this, more than the alcohol, had fuelled the excitement. Jago had been trying to express his admiration for Nicky's war record and had been stopped in his tracks.

'Up off your knees, Jago. I'm not deserving of your homage. There's something about me that would sicken you.'

Jago wondered if Nicky too had suffered a loss of moral fibre, a moment of cowardice instantly regretted. But it hadn't been about battle or fortitude in an open boat. Nicky had told him what he was. Across a table in a room with Regency-stripe wallpaper and a Victorian sideboard that didn't approve of the turn the conversation was taking, Nicky told him.

'You just came out with it, put into words what I could never say,' Jago said.

Before them the fire coughed on a cinder of coal. Nicky looked into the blaze and then back at Jago. 'There was so much dishonesty you weren't aware of. I had to make some present of the truth to you. I needed to give you a little power, so at least I couldn't be a part of blackmailing you.'

It had been thrilling. The small, fussy dining room had vanished. They sat in the clouds. They dined under the stars, or so it seemed. At Nicky's confession, Jago's own had tumbled out. He broke his silence. Jago remembered. 'You took me to your club after, and insisted I join the Rockingham.'

'I knew eventually it would all come out – that you'd been played. But I wanted to make my mark with you before that. I wanted you to judge me on my terms and not the Don's. Impossible I know, but I had to try.'

Nicky sat back away from Jago, as if awaiting a verdict.

Jago felt the heat of the blaze through his clothes. The roasting room reaching down into his lungs. He was a man who had been cold for years, suddenly discovering fire. 'Nicky, I'm so very glad you tried.' They leaned into each other and hugged, a kiss a possibility not realised. Then they sat back, away from each other, and Jago wondered where this was going. And of course, there was still the war.

'You killed that man, Nicky.'

'I think I had to, don't you?'

Jago knew it could be his body out under the turf of the Borders. 'It was the right thing to do. It's just another thing I haven't mastered – the killing touch.'

Nicky sighed a word as explanation. 'Spain.'

'You must have been quite a catch to the communists out there. And you believe it – workers of the world unite?'

'What else is there? The feudal system replaced by capitalism?'

Jago shrugged. 'Democracy?'

'A dead duck, old boy. In its final days. A weak, ineffectual, but thankfully brief experiment in niceness.'

Jago discovered he wanted to do almost anything else but talk politics. He caught Nicky's eyes looking up. Jago understood Nicky's drift before he spoke. 'Time to tread the spiral staircase to the heavens.'

But before they went to the bedroom, Jago took Nicky's face in his hands and said, 'You're not a useless mouth,' before kissing it. Then he allowed himself to be led up the stairs, round and round, up and up, as in some strange dance, a religious quadrille, weaving a spell that ordained Jago should give himself to Nicky.

CHAPTER TWENTY-NINE

The door of Gabriel's room in the officers' mess swung open. He turned, wondering if a girlfriend belonging to one of his comrades had got lost again. The Old Hares were mostly married but kept their wives and families in home towns in other parts of Germany. Girlfriends were a feature of the quarters on Obersalzberg and new ones had a tendency to get lost in the featureless corridors, going to or from the bathroom. But instead of a young girl wrapped in a towel or lover's shirt, Gabriel discovered a giant. The appearance of this monolith triggered in him an ingrained military response. The gargantuan frame and bearing of the visitor snapped Gabriel to attention.

'At ease,' came the response, in a voice as deep as the speaker was big.

Colonel Nicolaus von Below spoke again. 'He wants you.'

The colonel was one of Hitler's three adjutants. When he said *he,* Gabriel knew that meant Hitler.

The force of nature turned and left Gabriel's room, sucking him after, as a leaf caught in the after-draft of a tornado. They crashed down the corridor together and there, ahead, was one of the waifs – blonde, adolescent, hiding her nakedness under a borrowed SS tunic. The girl viewed their implacable advance, which froze the dismay on her face into a mask. She stuck herself to a wall, closed her eyes and tried to disappear as they thundered past, boots crashing on the planking. They continued this progress across Obersalzberg, startling soldiers as they had startled the girl. The men, in a maelstrom of military panic, threw salutes and called out the mantra that Gabriel and the colonel echoed.

'Heil Hitler!'

At the gate of the Berghof, he turned to Gabriel. 'If Operation Watch on the Rhine fails, then defeat becomes almost a certainty. You know what your role will be in that eventuality?'

Gabriel agreed he did. For a moment the giant wavered; his eyes left Gabriel and went up to the mountains around them.

'If the worst comes to the worst…' he trailed away. 'That little girl we passed reminded me of Heidi,' he said. 'I loved that girl in the book. If she had been real, not an illustration, she might have been that young tart in your mess. Did you see her blonde hair, the beguiling timidity? I suppose that's what war does; turns a man into a hero and Heidi into a whore. Don't let him down.'

The giant turned sharply and left, back down the road. Gabriel wondered if he'd talked of Heidi because she was Swiss, reminding him of shared stories and thus a combined destiny. The colonel possibly thought that because, like Heidi and her grandfather, Gabriel had spent his childhood up a mountain, he would identify with her. But of course, Gabriel thought sniffily, the two families had been entirely different: Heidi's had herded goats, his had kept sheep. Only a valley boy would make that confusion.

Gabriel entered the Berghof alone, handed over his sidearm and was shown into the presence.

'When I look at you, I see myself.' The Führer seemed as calm and reflective as the season. The huge window was behind Hitler, turning him into a silhouette without colour. Gabriel felt he was being addressed by a cinder-man; a flint come to life. A malevolent spirit from the mountains. 'This war is your adventure, as the last was mine.'

He indicated the clouds outside, dark and conspiring to unleash thunder.

'We two are children of the storm. Back then, battle made my blood hot.' The silhouette smiled, sudden teeth appearing on the shadow. 'When they told us of the great betrayal, the stab in the back, I was in hospital, recovering from a gas attack that had blinded me. My sight returned, but when they came and informed us that Germany had surrendered, even though the army had not been defeated, the shock took my sight away again. In my blindness and bitterness, I knew I could never trust what I couldn't control. I wouldn't be the puppet of others again.'

Hitler stepped to one side of the window and was instantly illuminated with form and colour, like a slide projected on a wall. 'We were stabbed in the back by Jews. The Hebrews occupy countries as surely as we occupy Norway. But whereas our occupations are honest, open affairs that will ultimately benefit the folk of those lands, a Jewish occupation is as silent and sinister as a cancer. When my sight returned, I knew I must lead a crusade to purge Europe of this Jewish plague.'

Gabriel wondered if he was about to endure an hour-long Führer rant.

'What did Churchill say of the British and Americans? *Two nations but one people.* But the United States is Yid ridden; it should be Germany and Britain who are two nations but one people! The English have been stolen from us. Your Lorelei has the blood of both England and Germany.'

This sudden reference to Lorelei unnerved Gabriel.

'She might be the perfect woman, a fusion of iron and blood – but what if she's too good to be true?' The Führer took himself off to inspect some of the art on his walls. He stopped by the picture of the swan ravishing a woman. Gabriel still found it shocking and knew his father would have put it on an autumn bonfire.

'We think we have to perform miracles to win the ladies, like Zeus here turning himself into a swan to have carnal relations with Leda. The ladies seem to be angels – but then so do the best devils. So do the best deceivers. I asked your woman about a town in Wales and she said she knew this place well, but her stumbling replies, when I asked her for details, convinced me she was lying. Never mind, I thought, small matter; people always lie to me to give me the answers they think I want. Only I tell the truth.'

Gabriel acknowledged this with a small tilt of his head. Inside, his stomach was a knot of panic for Lorelei.

'I meet her again in that charming kindergarten and she regales me with a detailed description of the small town she had known nothing about. Where has this knowledge come from? She can't have paid a visit.' He smiled. 'There's a war on.' The smile went. 'Possibly she researched in the library, so, just to be sure, I have checks carried out. She isn't a member and hasn't visited it, and it's the same for the lending library down in Berchtesgaden. In fact, she hasn't left Obersalzberg since our party on Kehlstein. So, I ask myself, who has briefed her? I know it seems trivial but the passage of information is a map of the world. I understood her motive for trying to cover her previous embarrassing lie, but who told her about Bridgend, the

Upper Town and the Lower Town, the churches and market places? She has been briefed.'

Hitler moved closer to Gabriel. 'I want you to find out. It seems a small matter but you know the children's rhyme, *for want of a nail...* I need to know you're loyal. You might have to pay the blood price and deal with this Anglo-German woman if she is false. Find out – use pillow talk if necessary.'

The Führer left Gabriel and went to his desk and sat. He looked back. 'You're a good boy, Zobel. But like so many of the brave, as I once was before the stab in the back, naive. I wonder, even if Lorelei Fischer proves whiter than white, if she's the right woman for you? You need someone less complex I think, and, call me traditional, but should you be consorting with a married woman?'

Gabriel wondered what hurt more; Hitler knowing something of Lorelei that he didn't, or that Lorelei kept secrets from him. She was married. She hadn't told him. It was a secret. Secrets corrode love.

CHAPTER THIRTY

'How could I have been so stupid?' Lorelei sat on the edge of her bed, her kimono a bright splash of colour on the wall behind her. Her face white and pinched. 'It's the small things, they told us to watch out for the small things. *It will be the insignificant mistake that will kill you.* I can hear my trainer saying it. *Tell the truth whenever it's possible, and don't chatter – stay silent.* What do I do? I gossip with the most dangerous man in the world.'

'He misses nothing.'

She glared at him. 'I know that; even when he's ranting he's watching. Even when he's screeching, he's listening. I should have told the truth. When he asked me about that lousy little town, I should have told him I'd never been there. But no, I had to lie, I had to try and impress him like some fawning virgin from the Band of German Maidens. And when he catches me out in that lie, instead of living with the minor humiliation, I unnecessarily set out to rectify the situation.'

Gabriel stood over her. She was half dressed; top on but still in her knickers and that day's skirt bunched up in her hand. She looked like a child, a small girl interrupted in her careful preparations for school. He resisted the temptation to sit down by her and put his arm around her. The schoolgirl vulnerability was in his head, not hers, he knew that. The self-anger, a necessary cleansing before the calculating and professional Lorelei returned.

'So,' she said, 'how do we repair the damage?' She started to pull on her skirt. I can't now go to the library and borrow a book on small British towns. If I could go to Munich and buy one, it could go on my bookshelf and when they search my apartment – and they will – they could find it and think that's how I researched bloody Bridgend.' The skirt was on and Lorelei, standing, was doing an Hawaiian-type wiggle to straighten it.

'I could go to Munich to get it.'

She shook her head and stroked his scar. 'No, soldier. You can't go for the same reason I can't; they'll be watching us both.'

'London,' said Gabriel. 'Get them to send a second-hand copy of a book. It can come the same way the sniper's rifle did.'

She stared at him. 'It will have to be quick.'

'We have a few days. He's tasked me with investigating you and that takes time.'

'My contact will be on Obersalzberg tomorrow morning. He calls here every day. He has a cover so even if he's spotted it won't arouse suspicion. I'll get things moving.'

She moved in on her make-up purposefully. Gabriel, strangely embarrassed by this wanton application of camouflage, moved his eyes from her to the walls. He looked again at the frenzied line drawings of the Berlin cabaret performers, illuminated with careless dabs of watercolour, and then at the kabuki prints of Japanese actors; grotesque, solid, frozen, mask-like and full of secret thought. Both were Lorelei.

'He said you were married.'

Lorelei paused, with a lipstick about to torpedo her lips.

Her eyes found his via the mirror, then looked back again as the torpedo struck. She worked on herself silently and Gabriel resented the exercise. In his mind he presented his unknown mother to her, someone who, his father had assured him, had never painted her face. 'Well?'

'Yes.' Simply said, before she pouted her lips at her reflection as if she were going to kiss it. The room echoed in silence. The silence of the mountains outside.

'We're both here; just at the moment we don't need a warning device, so do you mind opening the curtains to let in some daylight? I want to check my face.'

The curtains were closed as always, only to be opened as a signal of danger. Gabriel slid them back. Beyond the window, the great houses of the Obersalzberg sailed alongside like a grand fleet. It was a wet day, grey, as if the air had been smeared with battle paint. It was neither autumn nor winter proper; a squeezed day of half-light and tension. There was a melancholy in the murkiness, as the mountains tried to decide whether to have a full-blown storm or not.

'Lorelei, I want to know.'

She abandoned her cosmetics and her mirror and turned to him. Her face, which had been sullen, moved like a shadow into sadness. She said, 'He was an officer in the Imperial Navy.'

'Japanese?'

A small twitch of annoyance at the interruption. 'Of course Japanese. He sailed under the flag of the rising sun. That's always been my favourite flag. Vivid. I thought it was us, our marriage, rising together. I suppose I was ambitious; he was of a good family, and we met and wooed and sealed the knot during the Time of Modernisation. All things Western were considered good, including taking an Otaku – a European trying to be more Japanese than the Japanese – as a wife. Lord how Japanese men love cute, and I was cute, barely out of school with my blonde hair and china-doll blue eyes. But times changed.'

Another silence. Another full stop in her story. Gabriel prompted her. 'He found someone else?'

She sighed. It was a shroud released into the room. Grave clothes. Outside, the rain mourned on the window. 'By now, probably, but not then. His mother came to me; that's how these things are managed there. The Traditionalists had come to power. She told me that marriage to a Westerner was damaging her son's career. I was harming the family. She came with an offer; my father was dead and she offered to buy the business he'd left, his Bierkeller. She'd also pay for Mother and I to return to Europe. I know how it goes in romantic books; I should have thrown her offer back into her face. I would have – if he still loved me. But – he'd already left me. First his warmth had turned cold. Then he just wasn't there any more, not emotionally and finally physically. He was always somewhere else, never our home. I accepted my mother-in-law's offer.'

Gabriel asked the question that he didn't want to. 'Do you still love him?'

She gave him a weak, winter-sun smile. Brief then gone. 'Did I ever love him? Really? I was a child – but no, that isn't fair to me as I was then. Yes, I loved him with the total and blind commitment of the young.'

She touched Gabriel's cuff with the tip of her finger. A glancing blow but one that shocked him with hope. 'I'm a traditional girl; I can only love one man at a time and currently it happens to be you.' She looked into his eyes, into all of him. He was overwhelmed, his defences breached. He hugged her. 'I think I need to finish my story, now I've started,' she said. Lorelei sat back on the edge of the bed. 'Don't lurk over me, soldier.'

He sat. She took a breath.

Gabriel let her talk. He needed to know as much as he could about her. Mystery was not something he was comfortable with – he was Swiss.

'I'd almost completed my training and Japan had started to feel like something that had happened to someone else. I could almost imagine I'd had the German childhood the other student nurses had. In my head I swapped kimono for dirndl.'

Outside, the sun had broken through the cloud, unaware that its appearance in the room was now inappropriate.

'The other day, when he divided the children in the kindergarten – blonde ones stay, swarthy ones disappear – well, it brought it all back. Healthy children stay, disabled, handicapped children... The hospital started receiving more of these children than before, and they started dying in greater numbers. Death rates soared. It was obvious what was going on and in the closed world of medicine it wasn't even a secret. There was no guilt. These children were useless mouths and the Fatherland couldn't afford to be sentimental. You see I hadn't worn a dirndl; I'd escaped what they hadn't – the mad, desperate years. The years of fear. Not all the doctors were members of the Nazi Party but it didn't matter, they were as cold as the ones who were. History had brought them to a place where they didn't need to be ordered and threatened; they did the job conscientiously, as if they had always been waiting for it. The freedom to do away with what disgusted them. The Catholic Church protested briefly but when the Nazis stopped confiscating church property, they shut up. A deal was done.'

A deal was done, Gabriel knew. He also knew that the cessation of property confiscation was only half of it.

'I couldn't be part of it. I went back to London and qualified in a dirty old battleship of a teaching hospital. It wasn't hygienic, it wasn't efficient but, in its way, it was kind. Sentimental perhaps, a wet sort of compassion. I don't think the

British are better than the Germans, the British are just luckier with their history.'

Gabriel understood history, knew as a soldier he'd never been important enough for history. History was a river that ran past ordinary people and occasionally flooded its banks and drowned them.

'When the war came, I could make a moral judgement based on my experience in both countries and I discovered I was British. I thought, as a nurse, I'd be off serving in the forces, but being Anglo-German and fluent in both languages, I received the tap on the shoulder after cocktails at a hotel in Victoria.'

'SOE?'

'The person buying the gin called it Station X. Don't you just loathe the dreadful melodrama of espionage? In Japan the Secret Service is called the Black Dragon Society, very picturesque, but honestly. It was the early days and Britain seemed to have a death wish like the French. I should really have been recruited by MI6, the intelligence gatherers, not the saboteurs, and certainly not sent to Germany, which was MI6's exclusive turf. But pre-war, MI6 had backed the wrong horse; they thought Soviet Russia would be the foe and Nazi Germany the friend. War found them in cahoots with the enemy and compromised like a bishop with a busted fly. All their agents were drinking buddies of their Jerry counterparts and so all of them got picked up. A clean sweep. I couldn't go to Germany as an MI6 agent, as no one knew who was clean and there was no one on the ground. I was on my own.'

Gabriel asked the question that ate at him. 'How did you manage to end up here – in the heart of the enemy camp?'

She shrugged and smiled at him. 'Not my doing. He sent for me. Hitler asked for me. I was wasting my time in a military hospital, listening to soldier talk. I had the opportunity to become a general's mistress, to become a Dakini for the

British, but to what end? The only secrets worth stealing are the ones that will be acted upon. I was just gathering gossip that, frankly, was not worth opening my legs for. Then Hitler took me in his paw, because of my Japanese.'

Gabriel smiled. 'The English wanted you for your German, the Germans for your Japanese.'

'It is a world war, darling. Hitler trusts no one. I mean everyone knows the ambassador from the Chrysanthemum Throne is more Nazi than the Nazis, but the Führer wanted to be sure. Baron Oshima speaks fluent German, but when he addresses his aides he speaks to them in Japanese. Hitler wants to know what he says to them. He wants to know everything. So, I am placed, sometimes making a fourth amongst his secretaries, where I can hear the Baron. I tell the Führer all that passes between the ambassador and his staff.'

She had answered Max's question.

'So, I was ideally placed to head up Foxley and organise the little man's demise. Once I had secured an assassin.'

'And you seduced me.'

'I fell in love with you. Close the curtains.'

CHAPTER THIRTY-ONE

Ealing Broadway faded as soon as the shops closed for the day. Because of blackout regulations, the street lights hadn't come on. Yet Jago felt it was more than the coming of the dark that made the suburb invisible. There was a hush in the soul of Ealing, a respectability that abhorred the raucous. As a spy on a mission, Jago adored its shadows and slumbers.

Blakey's the opticians had closed promptly at five-thirty, as witnessed by Lavender and reported to Jago in the Royal Oak lounge bar, where he waited with Austen. 'He locked up, walked a couple of yards down the road to another door between his premises and Meldrum's Gramophone Emporium. Let himself in and retired to his flat above the shop. Mine's a gin and orange if you're asking.'

Jago supplied the drink. He was still early for his dinner invitation and the pub was warm and seemed to have a supply of spirits.

'Sir...' began Lavender, with less assurance than when she usually addressed him, Jago noted. 'Me and Austen was thinking, if you needed another place to hole up, if Nicky's place got rumbled, well...'

Her brother finished the invitation. 'We got to thinking you could move in with us. In Lambeth. It's not big…'

'But it's ours,' said his sister.

'Thanks to Nicky.'

Lavender shot Austen a warning look. 'He doesn't need to know our business.'

Jago started to agree, when Lavender had a change of mind. 'Perhaps you're right. After all, he's almost one of us.'

Almost, he thought.

Lavender leaned forward and touched his hand with the tips of her fingers; a moment of contact that signalled what was to come was confidential.

'We don't mind you knowing, but I don't think Nicky would like it getting around. It might embarrass him; you know what he's like.'

Jago did.

'He said we'd had a shitty start, pardon my French, and we deserved something better. He took us out of the slum we were renting and put us in a house he bought outright for us.'

'Gave us the deeds; it's in our name, hers and mine.'

'You see, sir,' said Lavender, 'we don't have landlords come snooping. It's a safe house if you need it.'

Jago didn't know what overwhelmed him the most: Nicky's generosity or the offer from Austen and Lavender. He thanked them and offered to buy another round.

'Best not,' she said, 'you're on an operation. Keep a clear head.'

Lavender, ever the professional, Jago thought ruefully, while he was as amateur as a vicars' cricket team.

He left the brother and sister and went down the street to Blakey's door. Jago went over his story again, in his head. The letter had been found in the dead man's pocket, the man Nicky had dispatched. Major Donald Chamberlain had received an invitation to visit Blakey when his business in Scotland was done. The letter-writer had reminded Major Chamberlain that he'd been a comrade of Blakey's late son, Captain George Blakey. The final part of the letter had caused most interest at SOE; it referred to the fact that both the writer and reader were entitled to wear the PJ badge.

The optician was obviously another member of the Link, and from the contents and tone of the letter, he'd never met the major. Therefore, Jago had decided to substitute himself and take up the invitation.

'To what end?' Mrs Cambridge had asked.

'The Link has had a number of pops at ending my life, so I'd rather like to know if there's another attempt in the pipeline. Besides, we need to crack this organisation. Realistically we can't infiltrate our sister agency MI6, but we are aware from Chichester that certain members of the Link know more about the Three Graces than we do. We need any information we can lay our hands on to see if it's possible to deduce the identity of this agent or agents. Then we need to feed it to Foxley, so they can take appropriate steps on Obersalzberg. Somehow I have to infiltrate the Link, and this man Blakey might be the way in.'

Jago had telephoned Blakey and introduced himself. As he'd hoped, the late major had indeed not met the optician. Jago had been invited to dinner and told, on the date selected, that a little after-dinner sport might be on offer. What this meant Jago had no idea but he knew the evening would reveal its secrets.

Jago was finally trying to be the agent he'd trained to be, not in deadly occupied Europe, but in leafy Ealing Broadway. The enemy wasn't the Gestapo but a middle-class network of suburban men. The danger would be to underestimate types who played golf and sipped sherry, and forget they'd murder him as happily as they'd pat a spaniel. He took a breath and pressed the doorbell, which buzzed with the intensity of an ack-ack gun.

Jago's Aunt Esme would have despised the room he was shown into. The large proportions had been wasted in the pursuit of clutter. There was a vulgar display of status via a parade of possessions. The walls were covered with framed reproductions by Lady Butler depicting heroic moments in battle; The Royal Scots Greys charged at Waterloo, and a British infantry square held their ground at Quatre Bras.

At odds with the unrealistic military glory, there were two poignant photographs of the optician's late son. One was of the young man, still in his teens, in the dress uniform of the King's African Rifles. His uniform snowy white, up to the khaki solar pith helmet on his head. The other image showed him, still young, except in the eyes. Less posed than the first, and a scruffier uniform of desert fatigues with a tin helmet up top.

'My son George, my only son,' said Blakey. 'That one was taken the day before he lost his life during Operation Compass. The papers were full of the victory – it was one of the first; pictures of the enormous number of Italians who surrendered. They barely mentioned our own casualties, the fallen who made victory possible.'

Hector Blakey poured them both a sherry from a cut-glass decanter with a silver label bearing the legend *Sherry*. There was a line of identical decanters standing shoulder to shoulder like soldiers on parade, each bearing the name of their regiment in silver. Armed with his sherry, Jago was led through a maze of ornament-loaded occasional tables to a pair of colossal wing chairs in aggressive chintz. They were set too close to each other and Jago and Blakey had to organise knees.

'Mrs Harris is doing us a pie,' he said with schoolboy relish, then added, 'She doesn't live here.'

Jago wondered if Blakey was protecting his housekeeper's honour with this declaration.

'Once she's gone, we can speak freely.'

When the pie was ready, they moved from the furniture showroom to a depressingly similar dining room. The problem wasn't clutter but one enormous table that was just too big for the space. Jago had to wriggle past a carver at one end to make his way to what Blakey called *Midships*. The pie and vegetables were served by Mrs Harris who, Jago thought, could have escaped from a Beatrix Potter illustration – a stocky hamster called the Widow Pie-Crust.

'I'll be off,' she said, 'I'll clear in the morning.'

The pie was good, Jago discovered.

'All done in Scotland?' Blakey asked.

Was this a loaded question, Jago wondered? Did he know of the plan to kill the awkward intelligence officer? But Hector Blakey cast no knowing look with the query; his attention was all on the pie.

'All done. Family affairs.'

'It must be difficult for you bods with two roosts, homes on two continents.'

'To a patriot, home is anywhere in the British Empire,' said Jago pompously.

Hector Blakey smiled. 'Ah yes, of course. I remember that from when I had brown knees.'

The old soldier's definition of service in the tropics.

'You've served?' Jago asked.

'The first show, in the West Surrey's, The Queen's Regiment. Nothing to brag about; truth to tell, I never heard a shot fired in anger. Did my time in India guarding a military hospital. But India; all those natives, millions of the buggers, kowtowing to the white man, to the British. It gave me a sense of our own specialness, our destiny. But that said – I didn't experience the trenches. I've not really done my duty to God and the King Emperor.'

Duty to God and the King? Jago wondered if the young Hector had been a Boy Scout. 'Nonetheless,' he said, 'I'm sure you would have served with distinction and gallantry if so called upon.'

The optician gave a small smile of gratitude and then spoke modestly. 'I have no delusions; my son George was the warrior in this family, not Hector.'

Jago suddenly felt immensely sad for the little man opposite. He was deluded; he'd bought into the South Sea Bubble of destiny. He'd been involved in the great British trek up the class system as surely as Nicky was trying to catch an elevator down. Keep trying, keep plugging away, from trade to profession to gentleman, then all it needed was one outstanding man to make that jump into the peerage. But it was all over for Blakey; he'd made it to profession, his son had been an officer and a gentleman, but now he was dead and so was the family.

'If you don't mind me saying,' said the optician, breaking Jago's thought, 'you're younger than I expected, from all George wrote about you in his letters.'

Jago dismissed his sympathy for the man and got on with the business of lying. 'Commanding colonial troops in Africa ages one. It's not the same as leading white troops; you have to be a father to them, see to every detail. They're not civilised enough, or intelligent enough, to manage on their own. It can be wearing.'

Blakey nodded in understanding. 'For the sake of the poor benighted black races, we mustn't lose the empire, must we? As far as I'm concerned, George didn't die in Churchill's war, he died to save one of our African possessions from the wops. We can't lose them or give them up, as the Reds and the Jew Roosevelt want. My son must not have died in vain.'

His knife went down, and Blakey leaned across the sea of mahogany. 'Major Chamberlain, you're Jew-wise. You know what the Yids are up to. When the dust settles, it is their dearest wish to see European civilisation destroyed, our world reduced to rubble and us the rats. The Hebrew will then fill the vacuum.'

'It's what I fear,' said Jago, meeting his eyes.

'We have to, just have to, make peace with our German cousins before it's too late. I admire Adolf Hitler, but in war sacrifices must be made and he has to go as a sop to the confused. Without him, Churchill and his Jew-lovers won't have an excuse to prosecute this pointless war any further. Then the great alliance can be formed, a reunification of the Anglo-Saxon people; then beware Russia and the United States of Yids, for we will come on!'

It was mid-week and there was to be no pudding, not even a slice of cheese.

'I'm doing my bit for the crusade,' said Blakey. The optician tapped the side of his nose to signal secrecy and whispered, 'Sub rosa.'

'Sub rosa,' said Jago back.

Beneath the rose, the Roman symbol that meant whatever was discussed beneath the dangling flower was secret and not to be repeated.

The small man's eyes glittered with excitement. 'I've been singled out to serve the Link. Top brass has commissioned me to make a very special lens. It's for the telescopic sight of a sniper's rifle. I have to get it off to Stockholm – but I suspect it's not stopping there. Back door to the Reich, know what I mean?'

Jago did and gave him all his attention as the little man prattled on.

'Apparently, the shooter has, at some time in the past, suffered optical damage, a detached retina I expect. He has a cast in his right eye, so the lens has to be ground accordingly. I have a copy of his medical record so I know what I'm doing. With this lens he'll have A1 vision and God help his target.'

Jago wanted to get away, to take this information back to Baker Street, but he fought this desire. Blakey was garrulous and who knew what he might reveal before the night was over. 'Now, I promised you some hunting,' he said.

CHAPTER THIRTY-TWO

Gabriel had a day and, if necessary, a night in Munich to follow three lines of enquiry. He visited the brothel in the morning, as he wanted to be there when it wasn't operating and full of SS officers wondering why he wanted time with the madam and not one of the girls. The establishment was in the commercial district, and looked as if it had once been a small hotel or inn. He went in via a wide-open door that was flung back. There was no sign of the working girls; it was early and Gabriel expected they'd still be upstairs sleeping. The smell of the previous night's extravaganza was leaving out of the windows which, like the door, were all open. He was approached by a cleaner and then shown to a chair outside the madam's parlour, where he sat listening to a conversation going on inside.

'I will deliver you personally.'

'Thank you, Madam Katarina.'

'Not at all. I need to return to our business in Switzerland. One of the perks of our trade is the open border for the likes of us. The need for fresh meat overcoming the security and red tape of our customers. Now Irma, there is one small matter…'

'Madam?'

'You haven't served in my Zürich establishment yet?'

'No, this is my first posting, here with Madam Leonie.'

Prostitution wasn't just the oldest profession in the world, Gabriel realised, it was also its oldest regiment. The conversation continued.

'As it happens, my Zürich house already has a girl working under the name Irma. So, you must choose a different billing.'

'I could use my own name.'

'Which is?'

'Brunhilde – I was named for my grandmother.'

Gabriel heard a tut of impatience. 'And it sounds it. You will discover when you are further into the horizontal career that men, who can be aroused by almost anything, are nonetheless rarely excited by the prospect of a grandmother. Let me make a proposition?'

'Please, Madam Katarina.'

Gabriel heard a chair scrape back and pictured the madam approaching the younger woman. 'You have beautiful dark hair and creamy skin. You could pass for a Jew.'

'I'm not, Madam, I can assure you.'

Gabriel could hear the fear in the young woman's voice.

The madam laughed. 'I know that, I've read your papers. That's not the point. Let's call you Sarah and let us pretend you're a Jewess. A refugee.'

Gabriel felt the girl's confusion through the door. 'To what end, Madam?'

'What did your father do?'

'He worked on the railways, Madam.'

'Let me tell you something about war, young lady. War allows men to have sex with women they could only dream about in peace. It's one of the attractions of conflict for them. It increases their power and diminishes ours. So, you will be a beautiful, innocent Jewess whose father had been a surgeon and whose mother played a cello in the Vienna Tonkunstier

Orchestra. A posh and spoiled little lady, destined for medical school and now, by dint of war, servicing hoi polloi. Men who, in peacetime, count themselves lucky to have sex with a barmaid now get to fuck way above their status; they get to have you, a real lady, and don't they love it? Be shy, tremble a little, weep – they'll adore you. They all want a victim.'

Gabriel wondered if that was true. Did he?

'You're a lucky girl; six months in Switzerland and hopefully all this mess will be over. You'll arrive back here with the Yanks.'

'The Americans? What will they be like?'

'Like men. Be ready midday tomorrow.'

'Yes, Madam.'

The door opened and the girl passed through. Through it the madam saw him and wondered who he was, just as the cleaner returned and answered the madam's silent question.

'He wants a word with Madam Leonie.'

'I'd better see him.'

The madam called him into her parlour. Gabriel saw she was thirty-something, smartly dressed even for the morning, trim of figure and coiffured – not the blowsy slut beloved of the films. She might have been the cashier in a fashionable Salzburg chocolate shop.

'I am Hauptsturmführer Zobel, officer in command of the Führer's Leibstandarte. I was hoping to speak to the madam of this – place.'

A look crossed the madam's face, almost as if she recognised him. For a second, Gabriel thought she was going to say something – but she didn't and sat back, watching him carefully. He wondered if, during leave on some earlier service somewhere in the world, he'd had her. Hired her. But he told himself, if he couldn't remember her, why should she remember him from the legion she'd serviced?

She spoke, 'I'm afraid my colleague isn't available, she had to go to her family in Hamburg. The terror bombers hit it again last night. Perhaps I can answer to your needs?'

Gabriel ignored the innuendo and got down to business. He asked about Bodo Gelzenleuchter and his visit to the establishment and furnished her with the dates. She went to an upright desk in the corner and produced a ledger.

'The Guest Book,' she said. 'The Gestapo insist we keep one. It is the nature of government perhaps, to be overly curious in the bedroom habits of others. Ah yes, here he is – Bodo Gelzenleuchter. Took a guest room and was entertained by a number of ladies over his stay, including Fleur and Mimi, Madam Leonie's French twins. Have you ever had twins, Hauptsturmführer? I can send for them…'

Gabriel ignored the question and the offer. 'Did he leave your establishment at all that weekend?'

'No, he didn't leave – the house, as we call this sort of establishment. We too have our traditions. From the book I'd say Bodo is a regular; this was probably a home from home for him. The other place is where he breeds and is nagged. He didn't set foot outside until it was time for him to return to his duties. Some men think a warm encounter with a Dakini will keep them safe, even from the bombing.'

Gabriel left thinking of the madam's use of the word *Dakini*. He'd only ever met one person before who used it; Lorelei. Had the madam worked in an oriental brothel or hired someone who had? Where had she picked it up? She'd even floated it to him as if he might divine something from it. He shook it from his head and made his way to the Hofbrauhaus beer hall.

Hofbrauhaus was as Munich as a potato dumpling. Its interior might have been the gut of an eighteenth-century man-of-war, all scrubbed wooden boards cleared for action. Tables and benches in neat lines, like batteries of cannon. A quartet of elderly musicians, in hunting-green uniforms, cradled curious brass instruments that seemed to have mutated from more modest trumpets and horns. They talked quietly without music; it was still too early for the lunchtime crowd.

Waitresses, in impossibly low-cut dirndls, stood and gossiped. When Gabriel approached, they challenged him with their eyes, their cheekiness brimming over into giggles like a foaming stein. After they'd had their flirt, Gabriel was directed upstairs to the first-floor dance hall to see the manager, Willy Becker.

Becker was wearing a brown Party uniform, with Party badge, and sporting Great War ribbons on his chest. Around the circumference of the hall were tables, and the manager was putting out chairs around them with difficulty. One sleeve of his tunic was empty and pinned up to the shoulder. He seemed pleased to be able to postpone his chore and to talk.

'We have a dance this afternoon for the pensioners. It's good for morale. I'll let the girls finish setting up.' He patted the stump of his arm. 'You'd think I'd be used to it by now. I lost it at Cambrai, nearly thirty years ago. Means I've lived longer without it than with it. Still pisses me off – taking twice as long to do a simple job.'

Gabriel asked his question and Becker answered without hesitation. 'I know August, known him for years, since the early days.' He touched his Party badge. 'This is where it all began, this very hall. Over there on that little stage, Adolf Hitler spoke in public on behalf of the Party for the first time.' He pulled his head up higher, as if the memory demanded respect. 'And I was there,' he said fiercely. 'In my book that was like being present at the Sermon on the Mount.'

Gabriel looked around the beer hall. He took in the pillars and varnished wood that suggested an aristocrat's hunting lodge and flattered the working men who came to it into partaking of that peculiar Bavarian pastime of beer and politics.

'He came in and stood there and waited while the Reds howled at him. He didn't care, you could see. Then, when he was ready and not before, he spoke and the world was never the same again. Barbarossa was back.'

Gabriel tried to imagine the empty, hushed hall; crowded and turbulent. Tried to imagine the noise and violence in the air. The crashing of steins onto the tables, as competing factions howled out their songs. The shrieks of the groped barmaids. One man stepping into that tornado and controlling it.

'When he finished speaking, there was silence. He had made us listen. In the cheering that began, I saw men like August tearing up their Communist Party membership cards. Throwing them up in the air like confetti, like snow. We formed lines around the sides of the hall, waiting to join the new party, the National Socialists, so we could experience again what we had just heard – the Voice.'

Gabriel wondered if he would have been affected and he supposed he would. He banished the thought and gave Becker the dates of August Korber's leave and asked if he'd seen him.

'He was here, for the whole weekend. He was leading a course for the Hitler Youth. We'd set the hall up like a camp. He taught them weapons drill, let them handle a Panzerfaust. You should have seen their eyes shine. Thirteen years old and hot as a stiffy to get up close and fire their load into the belly of a Soviet T34.' The old soldier lapsed into silence as he stared around the hall, and when he spoke again it was like the whispers in the corners. 'The rotten thing is the poor little perishers are going to get the chance, aren't they? Going to get the chance of going up against a Russian tank, all alone and clutching a tuppenny-ha'penny popgun. Cambrai was where I saw the Tommy tanks for the first time. Terrifying. Coming out of the smoke, going straight over our barbed wire like it wasn't there. Coming for me, roaring and spitting out cannon shells, collapsing trenches on screaming comrades, burying them alive. I ran, threw away my rifle and ran. Ever tried running for your life through thick, sticky mud? It came up behind me, right up, up on its end, then dropped on me. I managed to get most of me out of the way, just left this fellow behind.'

He wagged the empty sleeve.

'August Korber was here the whole weekend with me – putting shit into the heads of kiddies.'

As a child, Gabriel had spent many hours in church, but his god had not survived war. He wondered if it was the same for his father, who went to church not to meet a deity but the neighbours. It had always seemed to him that there were two sorts of churchgoer – the many who went out of habit and the few who were spiritual. The pastor at St Lukas was the latter, Gabriel could tell; the restless energy was there in his eyes, in his bearing the superiority, not humbleness, of faith. The arrogance of the priest. The Vatican had been full of men like the Protestant pastor, impatient with Gabriel's questions. The men who wait on God seemingly have little time to wait on their fellow man.

Pretending preoccupation, Pastor Kalb supervised a party of church volunteers grading donated and salvaged clothes for the bombed-out of Munich. Some were tearing suitable material into bandages. He gave Gabriel a fraction of his attention.

'Yes, he was here for the weekend retreat. A silent contemplation of what God's will for each of us might be.' He turned, almost in a temper, on one of the women helping.

'Sonja, judge the clothes less harshly. The purpose is to keep the bombed-out warm, not to dress a fashion show.'

The resentful Sonja took the discarded coat from the rubbish pile and put it on the useful items stack. The flash of downcast eyes from the female team suggested they felt Sonja had been right in the first place, and they might get on faster and better without the pastor. He turned to Gabriel. 'They'll be back; the terror bombers will return. We have to be ready; it's a terrible thing to witness a child bleed to death for want of a bandage.'

He spoke as if only he, and not Gabriel, had experienced war.

'Tell me Pastor, who was the priest who led the retreat? Was it you?'

'What?' he said distracted, although he'd clearly heard.

'Who led the retreat? Name?' Gabriel snapped the question. He was tired of the churchman's tedious performance.

Sighing at the huge burden his memory was being put through, he muttered, 'Pastor Grunwald.'

The man that London said was part of the plot to kill Hitler. Emil Maurice had been with him on the weekend in question. Gabriel was finished with the polished brass and smugness of the church. He preferred the honesty of beer halls and brothels. He turned and went, ignoring the pastor's last bleat. 'Emil Maurice was with us for the whole weekend.'

Gabriel left the church and its invisible god and decided he didn't need to stay the night in Munich. He drove himself back to Obersalzberg in an open-topped Kübelwagen. It seemed certain to him that the man who had fired the first shot at Hitler and missed was Emil Maurice, but could an SS officer also be so lacking in marksmanship? With the Old Hares it was possible, he decided. They hadn't entered service in the universal way of soldiers, via basic training and then specialist training to arms. They had drifted into uniform as part of the Hitler gang. It was quite possible they'd never even taken a medical, the appropriateness for their service being based on their devotion to Hitler and their mutual history. Gabriel supposed that at some point he would need to kill Maurice, whether at the orders of Hitler, or secretly, he was undecided. That might be a decision for London or Lorelei to make. That brought Lorelei and her problem back into focus in his mind and chilled him more than the cold air rushing at him, as he left the plain and began to climb into the mountains.

CHAPTER THIRTY-THREE

They left Blakey's flat to set out on his mysterious hunting trip, which, he assured Jago, would be fun. Blakey produced a smug Hillman from a garage at the back of his optician's shop. They drove off slowly through the blackout.

'Ridiculous really,' the little man grumbled. 'The bombers don't come any more and the rockets don't find their targets by light. We could illuminate London like Blackpool during Wakes Week and it wouldn't make a jot of difference. This continued blackout is just another aspect of Churchill's melodrama.'

They drove past large houses in prosperous suburbs.

'We're heading for a little bit of Middlesex that's still green, Horsenden Hill.'

It confirmed Jago's suspicion that they were going rabbiting; no doubt there were shotguns in the boot. A bunny probably passed as big game in Ealing. Something for the Widow Pie-Crust to add to another pie.

As they drove, Hector Blakey regaled Jago with stories of Africa, as if he'd actually been there. Jago was reminded of George the Fourth who, when Prince of Wales, told the story of the Battle of Waterloo as if he'd been present at it, as if it was he who commanded the British forces, and not the Iron Duke. Blakey's stories were all gleaned from his son's letters, and Jago understood that the father's inclusion of himself in the adventures was a way of sharing a part of George's life that he'd missed. The anecdotes mostly involved killing things – animals with a bullet, and negroes with a noose.

They passed a push-and-pull station, Perivale Halt, then a large factory. And as they crossed a small bridge over a canal that meandered like a river, they suddenly seemed to be in the countryside proper. The road ahead narrowed and became a lane, trees replaced houses and the moon became obscured by their branches.

'Nearly there. There's a track coming up on the right we could use but we've been asked not to. A mite too much traffic might alarm the prey.'

Instead they pulled up into the car park of a large country pub called the Ballot Box. Leaving the car, they set off up the hill and Jago noticed Blakey had not produced any guns from his boot. Maybe the guns were being provided by others? Walking silently up the hill in the moonlight resembled the gathering of a coven, Jago thought. As they crossed the crest and reached the summit of the hill, Jago saw ahead of them two dark police cars with a dozen men standing around them.

'Watch your step; during the proper Blitz, there were anti-aircraft batteries up here. They're gone now but the concrete placements and steps are still in place. You could take a nasty tumble if you don't take care.'

The shadow men turned and welcomed them into the pack with a whispered share of names; *James, Warwick, David, Eric, Harry, Chalky*.

Jago was introduced. 'This is Major Chamberlain from my late son's regiment. He's one of us. Where's Billy?'

A police sergeant answered Blakey. 'He's taken a section

around the hill and downwind of matey. Cut off their escape. Are we ready, all set?'

They were.

'Right then, no time like the present.'

A driver climbed into each of the police cars and the others, with silent practice, moved up behind the vehicles and began to push them to the edge of the summit.

'Don't want to spook them by starting up the engines prematurely,' said Blakey to Jago.

The cars tipped over the edge and freewheeled away from the pushers down a long slope towards a copse of oaks. The men began to run silently after the cars; Jago could feel their excitement and saw that truncheons and coshes were being produced. Suddenly, shockingly, the cars roared into noise with both their engines and bells. The men following whooped and cheered and one of them yelled *Tally-ho!* and suddenly there was the sound of hunting horns piping in the dark.

The effect on the wood below them was instantaneous. Men began to run from the trees and headed off downhill away from the charge, but as they did so, a line of men suddenly appeared from a hedgerow below, cutting off their escape. Jago heard cries of dismay.

'Good old Billy,' Blakey puffed beside Jago.

The fugitives split and ran right and left between the converging lines, like coursed hares. *Tally-ho!* came again.

'Get the bastards!'

'Kick the fairies where it hurts!'

'Nancy-boys!'

Jago understood. The hunt: it was a queer-bashing party.

Just like a real hunt, there was a bloodlust, a desire to hurt and kill. One of the policemen rugby-tackled a fleeing man. Hunters ran up.

'Put the boot in!'

Sickened, Jago saw them kicking and stamping on the screaming figure on the grass. He ran past and saw the victim was in uniform, he was a soldier.

The ambushing group from below had captured another struggling man, not a soldier this time, just a boy.

'Let's spoil his pretty looks!' said Blakey, running up to him and, without pause, punching him in the face. The others joined in, laughing and encouraging each other. Jago ran on, as about him other policemen and friends pursued men in the uniforms of the armed services, and he felt a surge of outrage that the police, who served so far from the front line, could persecute men who had been there and done their duty.

He ran on, through the cruelty, the hunting horns, the screaming, the laughter. He ran downhill away from it all and in his blind escape he almost blundered into a figure who emerged from the bushes. For a second, Jago thought it might be an escaping invert and he saw the man had the same thought about him as he raised his arms wide to stop Jago. He guessed it was the man they'd called Billy because Jago could supply the rest of his name; William Grogan. Grogan, the man below in Chichester Cathedral, the policeman tasked with being Jago's nemesis. Unable to prevent it, Jago ran into his arms.

'Gotcha!'

CHAPTER THIRTY-FOUR

Jago heard the pleas and screams of the battered men and the cries of pleasure from their tormentors. He felt Grogan's hands holding him, professionally turning him and raising one of his arms up behind his back.

'Please. Don't hurt me. I'm with you. One of you,' he said pathetically.

It was the wrong thing to say. Grogan laughed. 'Bollocks. I don't know you.'

Jago's arm was twisted further up his back.

'No more wanking with this hand,' Grogan said.

Jago was helpless. The pain excruciating. He couldn't talk through the agony.

Grogan slowly, inch by inch, pushed Jago's arm up. He whispered like a lover in Jago's ear. 'I'm going to break this arm, bum-boy. Then I'm going to drag you up the hill by it.'

'Let him go. He's with me.'

Jago heard Blakey's voice. He felt a gush of gratitude. The odious little man was saving him.

Grogan released his hold. Jago fell to his knees on the grass. Instead of relief, the pain momentarily increased. The life flowing back into his bent arm bringing too much feeling. Blakey and Grogan spoke over him. On the ground, Jago felt a shame. He knew for certain now that he would never be able to endure torture.

'Why didn't the silly sod say something?' Grogan said.

'You probably didn't give him much chance, Billy. Come on, let's get him up.'

Jago was lifted to his feet. He tried to straighten himself.

'He'll be alright with a drink in him,' Blakey said.

In the Ballot Box pub, amid the celebrating queer-bashers, Jago listened to them re-enacting their best moments on the hill. All Jago could think of was what if it had happened to someone he loved? Supposing they had got their hands on Nicky? Rounds were brought, glasses clinked. Jago was in the bosom of his enemy. He speculated as to what they might do to him if they discovered he was not Major Chamberlain of the King's African Rifles. Jago wondered if any of his team on Obersalzberg was at this moment in the same position. Drinking with the Gestapo. Holding back the terror behind false smiles.

Lavender had come into the bar alone; that was enough to raise speculation on her status as a *tom*. Lavender had confirmed those suspicions when she picked up Jago on his way back from the toilets. She led him off, to cries of obscene encouragement. In the car park, she smartly stepped away from him and they joined Austen in the car and drove back into London. From Austen's seething silence, he knew they'd witnessed the events on the hill.

Jago knew he'd been damaged by the experience. He felt fear like a wound. Action was for unmarried men and, in the middle of the endless war of an invert with the rest of the world, he had weakened himself with love. He couldn't afford to care. War had made him a refugee with no safe place for his head. He was hiding out in Albany and praying that the Link believed they'd killed him in Scotland. He wanted to stay inside, safe with Nicky. Up the iron staircase in the valet's old room, under the covers in the saggy bed that tipped them into each other in the middle. But life and duty still required that he get out of that bed each day, out of Nicky's arms and onto the streets where he was vulnerable. He avoided his old haunts and SOE and instead spoke on the phone to Mrs Cambridge, when she brought him up to date. 'As you ordered; we informed MI6 of the intelligence we received from Foxley regarding Watch on the Rhine.'

'I don't suppose they were grateful,' he said.

A snort down the phone told him he'd been correct. 'They dismissed it out of hand as a deception operation. Something us amateurs in SOE were bound to swallow whole.'

Jago sighed; the competition between the two agencies just provided aid and succour to the enemy. 'We had to try,' he said.

'But that's not all – some type from 6 turned up at the door at Baker Street and demanded to know all about the assets who had provided us with the supposed intelligence on Watch on the Rhine. He wanted to know if the agents were based on Obersalzberg.'

Jago could hear his own breathing, seemingly coming from the phone he was holding to his ear. The intelligence brief they had sent 6 had ended up on the desk of someone in the Link. 'I assume you didn't hand anything over?' he said.

'Certainly not. I gave him a flea in the ear about just turning up. Pointed out that if 6 wished to take over and inherit our operation, then his boss, Menzies, needed to forward a formal request to my boss, Gubbins. The toe-rag didn't like that. It made me suspicious, that and the fact he was officially a policeman. I know 6 has its fingers in the pies of both the military and Scotland Yard, and uses minions to run its errands, but there was something about this Metropolitan Police inspector I didn't like. Something of the dark.'

'Do you have his name?'

'Of course. Grogan, William Grogan. He had a low centre of gravity. Led with his shoulder, shouldn't wonder if he boxed. Sort of chap I might appoint to act as bouncer in one of my houses.'

'I know him,' said Jago. He felt an invisible hand tightening on one of his arms and pulling it relentlessly up behind his back.

'I gave him the bum's rush and got rid of him.'

Jago sighed. He'd be back. 'Mrs Cambridge...'

'Yes, dear... I mean, sir?'

'It might be a good idea to destroy the Foxley file. MI6 mustn't have the names of our team on Obersalzberg; it would be their death warrants. We have to make this a NOPO.'

A Nothing on Paper Operation.

There was a silence from Mrs Cambridge. She was a meticulous note-taker and a suggestion to destroy records was akin to asking the Conqueror to torch the Domesday Book.

'There's something else, Major...'

'Yes?'

'Remember Foxley wanted a briefing on Bridgend? Well now there's an urgent request for a book to be sent. It either has to be exclusively on that town, or failing that, have a detailed chapter.'

Jago was puzzled. 'They don't just want further information?'

'No, Foxley was quite precise, they need a physical book to plant as evidence.'

To what end, Jago wondered. But he also knew you didn't hold radio operators on air asking reams of questions. You had to trust the agent on the ground to know what they were doing. 'Didn't we glean the original briefing from a volume on British hamlets?'

'*The Primrose Book of Quaint Market Towns.* We sent Nightingale to the Charing Cross Road to pick it up and he was gone the best part of the day. Came back reeking of rum and the wrong change.' It still rankled.

'Send them that ASAP via Switzerland. Plus, they need the information I'm about to give you,' said Jago.

'I'm listening, Major.'

'The sniper employed by the Three Graces has a sight defect, a cast in the retina of his right eye. British fascists are making a special rifle sight and dispatching it via Sweden to Obersalzberg. Tell them they should try to check the medical records of the Old Hares and find out which of them has defective vision.'

'Will do. Oh, and your wife rang. Wants to know where you are.'

Christine, he'd forgotten about her. Why on earth was she interested in his whereabouts? When he called her he found, to his relief, not the great sulk on the other end of the line but someone who almost seemed pleased to hear his voice. She needed to see him face to face, she said. They arranged to meet near her school for lunch.

The Mercury Café in Notting Hill Gate had a table set aside in the corner for dancers from the Rambert. Most of them were impossibly thin girls, but amongst them were young men, boys who still looked too young for the call-up. Both sexes wore coats and long cardigans wrapped around leotards and tights. They were a noisy group and Jago, as he always did, found himself disapproving of the level of campery. The boys were being outrageous and blatantly drew attention to their own perversity. Jago wondered again at the arrogance of extroverts.

The influence of Aunt Esme, who abhorred show-offs, seeped into his anger and fed it.

The noisy effeminacy made Jago anxious. Supposing some workmen came in? There might be a scene. Couldn't they just shut up like him and curl into a cup of tea? His nerves made him irritated that Christine was late. The clock on the wall ticked slowly. He saw the hands jointly holding his mug were shaking. He knew he was terrified. Frightened all the time, his surface serenity a facade. He knew he wasn't brave; his service record showed that he was a coward. He felt himself crumbling from the inside. He smelled again the thick smoke that had choked him in his burning flat. Saw once more the black pit of the barrel of the gun pointed at his heart. He wanted it to stop; the war, his part in it, the shrieking at the other table. He wanted to go away, go to Chichester, see Bishop Bell, and throw himself on his mercy. Claim sanctuary. Give up. Cave in. But he banished this panic with a slow sip of tea. He remembered he'd given in once before; he'd let fear win on the airfield – and peace hadn't followed that decision.

Jago's eye caught one of the young male dancers, who cheekily winked at him, and he surprised himself with a brief smile back. He hadn't asked to play this hand in life, but this was the one he'd been dealt. He'd do his best.

'Sorry, couldn't get away. Grazed knee. Disinfectant job.' Christine taught at a primary school and the playground accident, its normality, even the smell of Dettol on her hands, soothed him.

'What can I get you?' he said.

They had mugs of tea and luncheon meat sandwiches.

Christine was in a good mood; she smiled at Jago. There was even concern in her eyes. 'Where have you been? You haven't been home for days.'

'I told Veronica I wouldn't be around for a while.'

Christine pursed her lips, almost coquettishly Jago thought. 'But Jago, I'm your wife, not Veronica.'

A fact they both usually strove to forget. The disastrous marriage. Such a good idea when proposed by Veronica, so awful when the lie had to be lived out. In fact, it had not survived the wedding itself. The weight of shame that had to be smiled through. The celebration of romance when there was none. Thankfully, both Jago's mother and Aunt Esme were dead by then, but Christine's parents were still alive. He remembered the claustrophobic reception in their semi. The awkwardness of her parents around him as they recognised he was half a class above them. The unctuous mother. Jago trying too hard not to stand on ceremony, but he always did. Of course it hadn't worked. The blessed relief as they drove away, spoiled as Christine broke down and sobbed at the grief of the trap they'd built themselves. The hired honeymoon cottage in Oxfordshire where Veronica waited and Jago drove on to a cheerless B and B. The long, lonely week before he picked her up again and drove her back to London, to her home in Pimlico, where again Veronica waited, and Jago moved into the basement.

'I'm sorry,' he said, 'I should have told you. My work means I can't get home much at the present.'

Christine reached for his hand. 'Work or someone?'

His instinct was to deny, but he fought it. 'Both really. I've met someone.'

'Bravo Jago.'

They basked in the unusual warmth of enjoying being together. Christine worked her way through a bite of sandwich and when it was gone, spoke again. 'I hope this means you've dropped your ghastly plan to go to Switzerland after the war and get cured? I've always hated your denial, the puritan in you.'

Jago still didn't know about that. He changed the subject. 'Do you still go to their allotment?' He meant her parents'.

'I keep it up.'

A sacred duty thought Jago. Christine's parents had been gardeners before all else. Their little plot of land, with its shed, had been their true home, more so than the house in Streatham.

'I go there sometimes after school, it's a sort of refuge.'

Avoiding Pimlico and the phoney marriage. He had the Rockingham; she had the allotment.

'Sometimes, when I'm sheltering from the rain in the shed, I think I can hear them working the plot. Calling to each other, laughing. I even hear them talking to me, as if I'm out there, picking or planting, and the weirdest thing of all is I hear myself talking back and I'm a child. I can hear it in my voice. And then it occurs to me that the little girl I can't see, the one on the other side of the door, is the real Christine. I'm the ghost. If I hadn't married you, I would have been in the house when it was bombed. That was my true destiny, not this lie. Somewhere in eternity I should be helping Mum and Dad on the allotment. Do you think that somewhere you've been truly happy carries the memory of it? That it can be played again and again like a gramophone record?'

Jago decided he hadn't yet been that happy. 'Possibly,' he said. 'It was everything to them, growing things, wasn't it? What was that outfit they belonged to that wanted to green up the country again, reverse the Industrial Revolution? – the English Mistery.'

He saw the thought behind her eyes and the quick sip of tea she took. 'They were good people,' she said, 'but not worldly. They meant no harm but there were elements in the Mistery that were quite sinister.'

Jago let it go, pleased Christine knew of the dark side of her folks' gardening club and was not persuaded.

'So where are you staying?' she asked.

'In Albany, off Piccadilly.'

'Good heavens, that's grand.'

'It's Nicky's set...'

'Nicky the sailor boy?'

'Yes, he's my...'

He couldn't explain his feelings. Then he didn't have to; the young dancer was standing over their table. The performance was gone. The boy was gauche, a little nervous. He was holding something in a napkin, his hands together as in prayer. 'I'm sorry to interrupt, but a friend of mine in the merchant navy has just come home on leave and he gave me two oranges. My landlady has kids so I gave one to her of course.'

Of course.

'And I'm sharing the other with my friends. Well there's more than enough and I wondered if you'd like a segment each?'

He stood there, with the peeled orange nestling on the napkin in his hands. The very colour of it wasn't wartime, the aroma everything that brick dust wasn't.

'Oh, that's so wonderful,' Christine said, reaching to remove her segment. 'I haven't had an orange in years. Thank you.'

'Not at all,' he said. 'You've got to share, haven't you? Sir?'

The orange was offered to Jago, who could barely trust himself to speak as he peeled off his segment. 'Thank you. This is so generous.'

The boy blushed and smiled and then went on to the next table with his orange. Jago and Christine slowly chewed the wonderful fruit in their mouths, releasing a flavour they'd almost forgotten. When he had finished, Jago spoke. 'We have to remember this. This is what we need to take into peace. We must remember how we were, how we shared, this time when greed just wasn't English.'

CHAPTER THIRTY-FIVE

Dolphin Square was just minutes from Jago's house in Pimlico, but it had more of Albany to it than his shabby home. This was not apparent at first sighting; its outline and texture were brutal, far too many bricks Jago thought, but once through its fortress-like exterior, there were gardens. Like Albany, it had a roguish reputation; apartments in one of its blocks being the town homes of many of London's louche elements, or where they parked up their mistresses.

Mrs Cambridge let him in and forestalled his opening compliment on her decor. 'It's stuff I can live with; eighteenth-century wallpaper, nineteenth-century furniture, twentieth-century portraiture. Victorian wallpaper is too incessant, Georgian chairs too fragile and twentieth-century painting is affordable. I'm not short of a bob or two, but unlike many of the other single ladies of Dolphin Square, I'm not kept. I like to have my feet on the ground. I'm in trade and I don't wish for anyone to look at the art on my walls and think I'm trying to pretend I'm something else. No Reynolds-like aristocrats in powder-blue silks, thank you.'

She went to get the office post that Jago had come to collect. 'I make a point,' she called back, 'of never owning anything that might one day own me. If I received a warning not to come home, I could walk away from this place forever without a backwards glance.'

She returned with a folder of military correspondence and handed it to Jago. None of it, he knew, would matter, but all of it had to be read.

'Take my advice, Major; be like me. I think you're another of life's secret agents. You're another shadow, not what you seem.'

In his agitation, Jago transferred the file from one hand to the other for no good reason. 'I hardly think so,' he said. 'I have a college fellowship to return to, and a wife.'

'You're not a scholar. And, well – the people in the portraits on my walls are not my relatives; visitors think they are, yet in reality they're strangers. But their stolid looks help my guests to place me. The real me remains elusive. If I may be so bold, Major, put a picture of your wife on your desk; properly married men always do. Now was it just the mail or was there something else?'

Jago fought down his panic at her words. He couldn't run away, as there was another matter he needed to discuss. Jago wished she'd offer a coffee or invite him to sit but it was obvious she didn't want this Saturday morning arrangement of handing over the post to spread into a social occasion.

'I wonder if you've destroyed the Foxley file yet?'

She pursed her lips; not the question she wanted, thought Jago. 'I have a problem with your request.'

'Request?'

'If you make it a direct order then of course I will comply.'

'May I ask what your difficulty is?'

She sighed and spoke. 'I know you'll think I'm a fussy old maid but I don't like destroying records.'

Jago could think of no woman who resembled an old maid less. 'But in this instance...' he said.

'Yes, yes I know. But what if something happens to us? We're a team of three – Nightingale doesn't count. There have been various attempts on your life, so I don't believe I'm being melodramatic to suggest, say, a bomb under your car that might not just end your life, but mine, and Lavender's. That's a risk I'm prepared to take. But if we're wiped out, what of Foxley? Our replacements will need the file to understand the situation and carry on. Of course Communications will have the radio contact, but can you imagine the situation; *Hello. I'm your new Control. Could you just tell me who you are? How many of you are there? How are you situated? I know you're serving your country in the most perilous fashion possible and risking an horrendous death – but we seem to have misplaced your file.* It's not on.'

It wasn't. 'If we hide the file?'

'The same problem. To keep it safe from the Link and the Intelligence Service means again, if we're rubbed out, the file is effectively lost.'

Jago, uninvited, paced Mrs Cambridge's apartment. 'Supposing...' he said. 'Supposing we treat the file as if it was... well... this flat? A disguise?'

'Isn't that the same as hiding it?'

'It depends. Supposing we keep the file in an envelope next to the out tray. It could be addressed to a friend. When front desk announces the enemy is at the door and on the way up, we drop the envelope into the tray with other outgoing mail.'

'And the friend whose letterbox will receive it?'

Jago had thought of someone. 'My friend Veronica Rawlings. If we're still alive, I can warn her what to expect, and in the event of our demise, she has the intelligence to see the file is returned to SOE.'

Mrs Cambridge nodded, and considered Jago's proposal as if it were her decision. 'Give me her details and I'll see to it.'

Jago did, and as she wrote them down, he looked out of her window. 'Good lord,' he said, 'what on earth is all that iron-mongery?'

The roof of the block opposite was festooned with aerials.

Mrs Cambridge didn't even need to look. 'That'll be Hood House. Major Knight has an apartment in that house. He's with the Box.'

'MI5? Bit of a giveaway isn't it?'

'Giveaway to whom? He's not a spy, but a spycatcher. Besides, everyone here knows what he does and why not? This is Dolphin Square, not occupied Europe. Apparently, he doesn't like conditions in St James's Street, so he works from home.'

Jago was still puzzled. 'But if he's MI5, therefore defending the realm, this realm, security at home – why does he need all that radio equipment to presumably talk to agents abroad?'

Mrs Cambridge tutted. 'Major Jago, if you don't mind me saying, you're talking like an amateur. Where exactly would you say is *home*?'

Jago shrugged. 'This country?'

'Really.'

The wrong answer.

'What then?'

'Haven't you overlooked a third of the world? Remember the British Empire, Major? The Empire is home to an Englishman, whatever far-flung outpost he finds himself in. It's not foreign in the way that France across the Channel is. As such, MI5 is responsible for both security and intelligence-gathering wherever the map is pink.'

Jago felt chastised. 'Of course.'

'And he also works from home to be on hand to feed his animals.'

'Animals?'

'His other passion, besides nabbing Nazi spies, is the animal kingdom. His flat is a regular fug of beasty aromas. I made a point of using the other air raid shelter back in the bombing.'

'Other?'

'There are two. One for owners and pets, the other for civilised people. Frankly, if I wanted a lapdog, I'd get a husband.'

'Ah, he has dogs.'

Mrs Cambridge swivelled him a furious glare. 'No, he doesn't. He has a brown bear and an orangutan. He used to take both of them to the shelter till people complained. He was flagrantly violating the one-pet-only-in-the-shelter rule. So now he just takes the orangutan. The brown bear is female and therefore, of course, better able to cope with the bombing.'

'Extraordinary.'

'Disgusting, I think you mean. It's my intention after the war to get pets banned from Dolphin Square. If people want livestock, they should go and live in the country, or somewhere faux pastorale, such as Hampstead.'

CHAPTER THIRTY-SIX

At some part of the night, Jago, with astonishing unoriginality, likened their togetherness on the large bed to being adrift in a boat. It was an analogy that failed, as Nicky had once spent three days in an open lifeboat on the North Atlantic.

'Cold, but better than the Pacific – fewer sharks and some chance of being picked up.'

'It must have been terrifying.'

Nicky's shape stretched in the shadows and yawned. 'Not really. It was just hanging on, waiting.'

Jago needed more. 'The torpedo? When that hit? Was there a moment when you just couldn't move?'

'I was lucky. I'd already experienced a fair bit of war when the old girl got it. Everything happened so fast there wasn't time to forget my training. My memory of the occasion, the moment when I realised this was it, she's going down, is like a film, lots of images spliced together but with a confusing story. Silent long shots, sudden close-ups with shouted dialogue. A rating sitting on the floor of his mess, resigned to going down with the tub. A lieutenant pushing past me, going back below, shouting in my face he had to get his grandfather's hip flask. Two big petty officers wrestling the old man off the bridge towards a lifeboat. The sea like black India ink. Noticing there was no moon and wondering how the sub had found us. Both fear and courage seemed irrelevant. Most of us just handed ourselves over to the drills we'd practised and practised. You do what you've trained for and, out of hell, you launch a boat and then you endure.'

Jago wished he could go and get a glass of water, his mouth was dry. He asked the question he had been waiting to ask. 'Did anyone behave badly?'

'Of course.'

'What did you think of them, what did you think of the cowards?'

Nicky, realising where this was going, turned to Jago, put an arm around his neck and pulled him close. 'I thought that perhaps it wasn't their day. That on another day, they would have been the cool customers and I the one in the funk. In Spain, at the battle of Jarama, we were ordered to counterattack to win back some lost ridge. The man in charge of our section was a Scot, a man who seemed to me to be the epitome of Scotland the brave. I can't begin to list all the heroic things this man had done. Yet, as the whistles blew for this action, he just slowly sank down onto the dust and wouldn't move. It wasn't his day.'

'What happened?'

'What always happens: someone stood in the breach. Someone replaced him without fuss or words and said, let's go, and we went past him and up the hill.'

'It was you, wasn't it?'

'As it happens, yes. But the point is, courage isn't fixed. It's a movable feast. That day, and during the torpedoing, I was able to behave well, but who knows that up ahead, when I've had enough, when it isn't my day, I too might not take the coward's escape. Listen, a man who hadn't behaved as he ought came to me on the Canadian destroyer that picked us up. He apologised for his paralysis, that he hadn't helped in the evacuation, that he'd frozen. He said he'd let the side down, but he laid his bad behaviour on the fact it was night. He'd been fine until he came up on deck into that moonless night, with the black sea waiting for him. He said had the torpedoing happened in daylight, he might have handled it better. It was the night.'

Jago slid from Nicky, lowered his feet out of the bed and walked off into the room blindly.

'Where are you going, old man?'

Jago didn't know. Away from Nicky, away from love. Away from the things he knew he didn't deserve. 'Shit,' he said softly from the middle of nowhere.

'What is it Jago? Tell me.'

'The night,' he said. 'That night when all I'd worked for came to an end.'

'Come back to bed, please.'

Jago pointlessly shook his head in the dark. 'Possibly,' he said. 'Flying off from an airfield in England to go to somewhere in occupied France is a little like being torpedoed in slow motion. One has glue on one's boots and everything takes forever.'

'Jago, I don't judge you. As I said, on any given day a man can be a hero and the following, with the wrong sort of breakfast in his body – who knows? No one who has been there would judge.'

'Well I haven't been there, so I do, and I find myself guilty.'

Jago heard Nicky sigh and the bedclothes move. 'Where are you?'

Jago shuffled away from his voice, feeling idiotic, as if they were playing some childish game. But Nicky's movement had been for a purpose; the overhead light exploded on, banishing the shadows and exposing Jago. 'Turn it off,' he pleaded.

'Well put a sock in it and come back to bed.'

Jago looked at him. 'Please, I have to tell you. I've told no one else. Let me explain to you what happened – but please put out the light.'

Nicky by the door suddenly disappeared as the blackness returned.

Jago marshalled his memories. He'd been driven across the airfield in Newmarket. There were four in the car: the FANY driving, his *pianist*, another FANY, sitting next to her. He'd been in the back next to his pipe-smoking dispatch officer.

'I'd been quite cool, collected, loading my kit into the boot. I'd seen my *pianist*, my radio operator, trembling. I squeezed her wrist and whispered a reassurance that she'd be alright. She gave me a look of gratitude, the memory of which still crucifies me to this day.'

'Jago…' said Nicky softly.

'I feel so humiliated. I spoke calmly to my dispatch officer as we climbed in the car. He was an older man, probably chosen for his fatherly demeanour. A calming influence. He spoke rugby to me as we drove out onto the field. We climbed out and, dead on time, our taxi, a Lysander from 138 Squadron, dropped out of the sky, landed and pulled up by us. There it was, engine revving, raring to go. Everyone started moving, the ground crew rushed forward to turn it around, my dispatch officer had the hatch up and open, my piano-player was stowing her radio aboard and I – I hadn't moved. I looked at that Lysander. Do you know anything about planes Nicky?'

'Pa took us on a jaunt around the South Seas once, on a flying boat. Preferred when we did it on the yacht.'

'I'd never flown and, as Hamlet says, there's the rub. I stared at that bloody thing that had swooped down beside us. It sounded like some mad professor's invention made out of cutlery and bed springs. Clattering and clanking. I expected bits to drop off. I could see the wing tips shaking. Did you know they did that? Patches covered holes on the fuselage. It was like some monstrous toy, not a proper machine. Not like the car we'd driven to the airfield. I stared at it and I knew in the very depths of my being that it couldn't fly, wouldn't fly. It had got thus far by a miracle but when it took off with me in it, it would break apart in the clouds. And I would fall and fall and fall.'

'And you'd no idea? No inkling you were frightened of flying?'

Jago considered the question. If he'd been sent on the SOE parachute course he would have found out. He wouldn't have been on that wretched field with everyone waiting. Everyone looking at him. 'If the plan had been to insert me by submarine or fishing smack, well, there wouldn't have been a problem. It was the flying – couldn't do it.'

The world had stopped on that field in southern England. No one quite believing what they were seeing.

'I swear to God, Nicky, it wasn't fear of the mission, of being behind enemy lines in occupied France. I just couldn't climb into that contraption.'

He remembered the smell of his dispatch officer's pipe tobacco on his breath as he snarled quietly into Jago's ear to stop making an exhibition of himself and to get the show on the road. He remembered his radio operator looking up out of the rear cockpit, staring at him in the darkness, her eyes bright like a squirrel's. Her hand luminous white as she reached out to him. He remembered her voice, Come on, sir, take my hand – everything will be alright.

He remembered everything. He heard again the disbelief in the voices of the ground crew behind him. *He ain't going to do it. He's shitting himself.*

The pilot's angry enquiry from the cockpit. Is he coming or not?

Not.

His piano-player disappearing down. The cockpit closing like a biblical incident. The Lysander taxiing, gathering speed, growing smaller down the field, fading away in the blackness, hearing it taking off, climbing, and not falling apart.

'There was so much contempt for me. My dispatch officer shook me, cursed me. *You let that little girl go by herself.* The FANY driver saying *I don't want him in the car, sir.* They left me there on the airfield. Drove away in cars and a truck and left me.'

Nicky was by him, his arms around him. 'Come back to bed.'

Jago let himself be led. 'That was that,' he said. 'The end of that life. Naturally I was thrown out of SOE and dumped into the Forgetting School.'

'You're not a coward.'

Jago stared into the blackness. 'I don't know that, do I? I've never been there. I've never been in action.'

CHAPTER THIRTY-SEVEN

Jago had rung Blakey from Albany. It was Sunday morning and he thought he'd catch the optician in. He needed to continue to work his way into the Link and try somehow to discover the identity of the individual or team known as the Three Graces. Blakey had been delighted with the call.

'My dear Major, how lovely to hear from you. I trust you enjoyed yourself after our hunt the other night?'

The last time Blakey had seen him, Jago had been going off with what the optician assumed was a prostitute. 'Thank you,' he said. 'A very satisfactory way to finish an enjoyable evening.'

Blakey chortled down the line.

'You striking lucky put us all in the mood for a bit of rumpity. Billy took us to an establishment he knows off the Buckingham Palace Road. Men have their needs, what?'

Jago supposed they did. Was Blakey any worse than him when he'd lurked around the toilets looking for a cottage?

'Glad you called,' said Blakey. 'Don't know if you're interested, short notice and all that, but there's another get-together tonight.'

Inwardly, Jago groaned; another hunt – could he stomach that?

'Nothing so active as last time,' the optician was saying. 'Bit of a lecture but not dry. Look, I know you've seen active service on behalf of the Link, that business in Scotland – don't worry, I won't blab; no names, no pack drill. Billy had a little too much liquid refreshment at the bordello and, knowing you and I have a regimental connection via my son, he told me you were a cool customer; the man the Link goes to for any wet work, any blood-letting. A reliable son of the Empire, someone who can be trusted. You see we're receiving a briefing tonight from the Earl of Dewsbury, on where things stand with our German friends. Might you be interested?'

Jago knew of the earl; before the war he'd been a celebrated fascist. At the outbreak he'd been interned briefly. 'I'd like to hear him speak very much.'

'That's grand. Could you call at my home at say seven-thirty? Oh, there are no ladies present so black tie, not white.'

Aunt Esme always said it was the mark of a militarised society when civilians found reasons to wear uniforms.

The call had ended and Jago had contacted Austen. He'd need someone to cover him and Blakey and co had seen Lavender. They met for breakfast in Shepherd Market, a front-line area where toff and costermonger could come together and the classes mingled. They had an off-the-ration breakfast in a café that served everything from fry-ups to smoked salmon on scrambled eggs.

Jago took his morning coffee and bacon sandwich to a corner table where Austen and Lavender waited. A greasy plate in front of each told him they'd already breakfasted. Mugs of untouched tea meant they hadn't been waiting long.

'I tagged along, sir,' said Lavender. 'There's something you should know that can't wait.'

Jago felt his appetite draining away. 'What?' he said.

'I expect Mrs Cambridge has briefed you on the Intelligence

Service's visit, occasioned by our informing them of Operation Watch on the Rhine?'

'She did.' Was that all? Jago hoped it was.

'Well there's something she doesn't know. I didn't get to the bottom of it myself until late last night. It concerns Nightingale.'

Nightingale, the bane of Mrs Cambridge's life. 'Go on.'

Lavender took a sip of tea as if it were oxygen and continued. 'We never let Nightingale into the picture about your supposed disappearance. As far as he's concerned, you're absent without leave in Jockland. We do a *we're all worried sick* act when he's around. Well the intruder from 6 obviously spotted Nightingale as the weak underbelly of our axis, which didn't worry us because Nightingale could only spill what we wanted him to; you were missing.'

'So, the problem?'

'You know the system at Baker Street; no unaccompanied visitors wandering the corridors, and one of Nightingale's few jobs is chaperoning our guests. So he leads matey back downstairs and he doesn't come back. Good we think, he's spilling the beans about you being gone. But eventually I go to see what he's up to and I'm in time to see an exchange between them; the man from 6 gives Nightingale some money and Nightingale gives the bloke something in return.'

'What?'

Lavender shrugged. 'Couldn't see,' she said, 'I needed to stay out of sight – the man from 6 had seen me in that pub, the Ballot Box.'

'Bugger,' said Jago. 'What did Nightingale sell him?'

'We were set to find out. I popped back and told Mrs Cambridge what I'd spotted and we lay in wait for Nightingale – but he didn't come back. He does that; disappears for half a day at a time and then turns up like a bad penny with a worse excuse.'

'Did he come back?'

She shook her head. 'I had to track him down – with Austen's help.'

Her brother spoke. 'I know all the naval haunts. All the drinking dens the Andrew hang out in. It took all bloody evening. When I find him, he's nine sheets to the wind, spending his bribe, the swine.'

'And what had he been bribed to do?'

'I had to shake it out of him and threaten him with Mrs Cambridge. He only told me because he was befuddled. He'd let on about Foxley wanting info on Bridgend. Told the geezer he'd been sent to pick up a book on the town.'

Was this dangerous? Jago didn't know, didn't know why Foxley wanted the information in the first place. 'What did he give Grogan?'

'The receipt for the book. The receipt he'd said he'd lost,' said Lavender.

'A receipt is as good as cash to an old tar,' said Austen. 'He was probably going to feed it back into the system using some crook of a purser.'

Jago was at a loss. Was it important? 'It's difficult to know what to do,' he said, dithering and not sounding like an officer.

'We could find out why Foxley wanted the gen on Bridgend in the first place,' Lavender said.

'It takes so long. Better if we just tell them about the book receipt being in the hands of forces who are not supporters of their mission. They'll know how important or trivial that is.'

Jago moved the meeting on to his invitation to the Link's event in Ealing. Austen was up for coming and watching his back. Lavender also volunteered, though this time she told them she had no intention of parading herself as a good-time girl.

Jago smiled, but at the back of his mind he worried about the missing book receipt. Was it dangerous? He came from the academic world. He knew the myth of the disorganised professor with a study of book-strewn chaos. The reality was different. The mayhem was organised. Every document had its place, even on the floor. The secret war was run by men from that world. They didn't misplace papers; they valued them too much.

A book receipt was missing. Was it trivial or not? Jago couldn't be certain, but he felt the first chill of fear.

CHAPTER THIRTY-EIGHT

The hospital at night was a sleeping beast. Gabriel knew from his long months of recovery there that by day it was an insect hive, home to a thousand activities, of scurrying, emergencies, screams and laughter. But at night it was a different creature, a great slumbering whale, down whose interior he and Lorelei walked nervously. The shadows inspecting them. The nurse stations little glowing oases. The smell of the disinfectant intensified by night, like lilies. The tragedies also; the silent muffled weeping from beneath blankets. The grotesque shadows cast on walls from men in traction.

They came to a halt in a coffin of a room; narrow and rectangular. A library table topped in black leather occupied its centre. Around the walls were rows of filing cabinets. Above them, a large clock admonished them with ticks. This was the vault where the medical records of every patient ever treated at Platterhof Military Hospital came to moulder. Silently they went to work, each knowing their task as agreed before, back in the apartment in the ruined theatre.

'We can't hang about,' Lorelei said. 'Iron Arse has her spies. We go in and out and if she asks me next day, I can say I left my handbag behind after duty and I popped in to pick it up.'

She'd hidden it under her skirt and Gabriel, in his nervous state, discovered that as usual before action, he was aroused by small things; this time, Lorelei tucking the handbag into her knickers and jiggling to make it comfortable.

It had been agreed between them that they'd take the records of the Old Hares away with them to study.

'It's Emil Maurice's records I want,' said Gabriel.

'I know, but we'll take the notes on the others as well. Maurice might be the man who made contact with the pastor in Munich, but he might be one of a team like we are. The trigger man, the one with damaged eyesight, might be another Old Hare.'

They'd divided the dozen names between them alphabetically. Now in the gloom they gathered in their crop, sliding out the drawers and lifting the files, while the clock ticked on towards eternity. They gutted the folders and replaced them, putting the paper contents in the handbag that Lorelei had produced, like a semi-erotic magician, from her pants.

Mission completed, they quietly closed the door and made their way out of the sleeping leviathan. When they passed the reception desk, Lorelei held up her handbag to indicate she'd found it. A sleepy nurse smiled back and nodded.

In her apartment, Gabriel discovered he wanted to go where Lorelei's handbag had been and, laughing at his desire, she'd teased him before finally succumbing. There was a holiday mood between them. After a week of awful tension, the book from London had arrived, delivered by the team's *postman,* who was still unknown to Gabriel.

'Thank God they just got on and sent it without wanting to know why we needed it,' she said.

Quietly and conscientiously, like a studious schoolgirl, Lorelei had marked up the relevant chapter with a pencil. As she did this, the tip of her tongue stuck out as a mark of her concentration; something Gabriel found unbelievably tender. She made it seem as if the volume had been used for research, with underlinings and ticks. The book had then been put on her bookshelf and they waited. To their relief and delight, they discovered it gone before their excursion to the hospital.

'I knew they'd search,' she said. 'Now we just have to hope they believe the planted evidence.'

'No reason for them not to,' Gabriel said.

Lorelei's smile lit up the room. 'Then I think we're home and dry.'

CHAPTER THIRTY-NINE

It was an irritable day outside, as if the weather wanted done with autumn. The clouds advanced across the sky like an invading army. Gabriel and Max stepped out through Obersalzberg towards the Berghof; they had been summoned.

'There's something you need to know before we see him,' Max said. 'He wanted me to investigate your lady, Lorelei. Don't worry, she checks out. But in the process I had to search her apartment.'

Gabriel acted his surprise – shock – by coming to a halt. They stood under a bare chestnut tree; a grey lichen covered its bark like a field-grey uniform greatcoat. It made Gabriel think of Russia. Men bent and twisted like old trees.

There was an apology in the tone of Max's voice. 'It's not nice to look through a woman's personal things but I had to do it for her sake. I knew she was alright and I found evidence to convince him. You know what he's like; he wants to believe he's a freethinker, a modern man of the world, but he's not. This is his shire, these peaks and a few fresco-flecked towns under them. He's a man who clothes his soul in lederhosen. He can cope with girls in dirndls, but a German lass in a kimono?

Quite another matter. That's really where his suspicions came from; she wasn't a mountain bunny.'

The gusting wind died to a breeze and the agitated boughs of the bent tree slowed to a gentle pulsing. Gabriel unbent. 'You found evidence that exonerates her?'

Max patted the briefcase he carried. 'It's in here.'

Then he reached out and squeezed Gabriel's shoulder and said with a smile, 'She's in the clear.'

After handing over their sidearms, they were shown into the Great Hall, where they stood, waiting. Gabriel stared at the oversized room and found it slightly absurd. His father had said of their hut that a man should never have more space than he could afford to heat. Looking around the gigantic room, it was apparent that Hitler could afford to heat a world.

The Führer entered, trailing secretaries and aides like stardust. Ignoring Max and Gabriel, he assigned tasks, signed papers and, in the process, gradually dismissed all his entourage until at last he was alone with the soldiers he had summoned. He turned to them where they waited at attention.

'Well?' was all he said.

Max cleared his throat and spoke. 'As instructed, I carried out an investigation of Lorelei Fischer. In all respects the background she described is true. Her father was a sailor in the Kaiser's Imperial Navy...'

Hitler interrupted. 'I know her background is correct. It was checked thoroughly long before you were involved, Major Adler. I want to know about her knowledge of the small British town. How did she come by it?'

Max immediately began unfastening his briefcase. 'Easily explained,' he said. 'I found this book in her bookcase when I searched her apartment.'

He produced a volume in a bright yellow dustcover and held it out to Hitler. The Führer ignored the offering and instead turned his back on them. He spoke away from them towards the mountains in the giant window.

'Tell me about this book, Adler. Is it a 1928 reprint of a volume originally published three years earlier? Can you tell me if the publishing house is Primrose Press, with their distinctive yellow covers? Possibly the front page has a six followed by the letter 'd' indicating the English price of six pence. Am I correct?'

Max checked. 'Yes sir, correct.'

Hitler turned from the window and faced them. 'Below the price there is a stamp bearing the bookshop's name, Babington's, the Charing Cross Road. Well?'

'Yes, sir…'

Hitler plunged on, anger growing in his voice. 'I know I am correct and do you know why?'

Gabriel felt the huge room begin to turn. Fear was taking hold of him. Hitler was waving something. 'I know because I have this! The receipt for this book dated just over three weeks ago. You say you found it in her bookcase?'

'Yes, sir.'

'And yet when I had her apartment searched initially – before I tasked you with the investigation – no such volume was found. Of course not – it was still for sale in London! This receipt arrived on my desk via impeccable intelligence sources we operate in the enemy's capital. Not all the English are members of Churchill's Yid-loving club. Just as not all the people of Obersalzberg are loyal to the Führer and the Party.'

Hitler turned to Gabriel. 'So, my scarred seraph, your little girl seems to be a spy for the British. That is why no doubt she sleeps with you, the officer in charge of my bodyguard. It is why she probably had relations with Goebbels before you.'

The sudden flare of jealousy pained Gabriel, as Hitler intended it should.

'Your alley cat has sex with whoever is close to me, but enough is enough! An unfaithful woman deserves just one reward. I know that, I have meted it out before. So, Hauptsturmführer Zobel, I give you that opportunity. You will accompany Major Adler and arrest this treacherous whore, and you will subject her to rigorous and painful questioning.'

Gabriel's uniform kept him upright. Years of soldiering containing the anarchy within. Inside he was yelling insubordination, refusing to obey orders. But the power of his disguise held true. He was silent. His heels clicked together. He saluted. He left. He went to carry out the Führer's wishes.

CHAPTER FORTY

The chimpanzee stared at Jago, and Jago looked away with a shudder. The chimp was wearing knickerbockers. Jago felt the slight nausea that animals in clothes always caused him. Its teeth were over-white, emphasising its maniacal grin. He wondered if it was someone's job to clean them, to brush the teeth of the six stuffed apes that stood guard on the children's toy and clothes section of the second floor of the departmental store. The tableau of merry primates in sloppy joes and party frocks possibly pleased the visiting child, but Jago, who knew each of them had been shot to fulfil this stuffed destiny, was filled with foreboding. They passed the apes on their way to the furniture section.

'Make you homesick for Africa?' Blakey asked.

Jago played the great white hunter. 'Scream like a woman if you don't make a clean kill,' he said, 'though not as bad as a wounded baboon.'

Was that true, he wondered? Had he read it somewhere? He reminded himself not to lie unless he had to. He was on active service and this after-hours departmental store in Ealing was behind enemy lines. Jago was feeling rather lonely and exposed. Austen had been left behind at the entrance to the second floor, by the panelled stairs and mahogany lift that had smelled of lavender polish. Jago had introduced Austen as his batman-servant. Blakey, who adored the company of men who commanded flunkies, nonetheless felt that, owing to the eminence of the speaker, servants should be left out of earshot. Austen had metamorphosed back into the military man he'd once been; upright, smart and correctly deferential. Like all old sweats used to uniform, Austen wore the evening clothes of café society as if they had been moulded to him. No one who didn't already know would ever have guessed that, under the elegance, he was also armed.

Blakey had introduced Jago to the store's owner, a fellow member of the Link, and they'd all three chanted *Perish Judea* by way of greeting, rather than *Good evening*. Beyond that, none of the dozen men in the furniture corral spoke much. They were too busy acting dangerous times and dangerous men's fantasies. Aping those who truly did undertake hazardous service. The only thing they'd risked, Jago thought, was perhaps indigestion after rushing home from business and pulling on their dinner suits. Now they faced an evening of listening to a higher-up in the Link who was also their superior in society.

'He's of the purple,' Blakey said to Jago, before going on to mutter his mantra. 'No names, no pack drill, but the Earl of Dewsbury is one of the Hengar family.'

Of the purple, an aristocrat. Jago knew a bit about him; besides his fascism, the man had been a go-between in the game of pre-war, playboy diplomacy.

The store owner returned, leading the speaker. The assembled men all raised themselves from the two lines of dining chairs. The man took his place by a small occasional table with a dangling price tag. On its surface was a flask of water and a tumbler. With a curt nod of his head he indicated his audience should sit. They did, each in a middle-class panic that possibly standing had been a mistake.

Jago recognised the man from his famous arrest at the start of the war. He had been detained briefly before his friends persuaded the powers that be he was a harmless eccentric. He was of course elegant in a shabby landowner fashion. He had looks a matinee idol might have killed for, Jago thought – silver hair that was probably too deferential to ever recede, an aquiline nose you could spread butter with and a similar chin covered in a smoky blue shadow. But Jago saw that it was a face of two profiles: the left was impossibly handsome, the right just a little too pointed, too sharp – the effect that of a crafty Mr Punch.

'Gentlemen,' he said, ignoring the store's owner, who had stepped forward to introduce him and now had to scuttle to one of the chairs. 'Perhaps, like me, when you first joined the Link, you wondered at the choice of title. Possibly the image of a chain presented itself to you and you saw yourself as a strong component of it, a link. But you might also have considered that the link could refer to a bridge between two things, two cultures, the blood link between certain nations. Are we linked to the French? God forbid. The Poles? Of course not. The Jews? Don't be vile. We are the English, Anglo-Saxons, that is to say Germanic. Should we be ashamed by our links of blood and history to a nation fighting the Bolshevist menace and to free itself from the poison of the synagogue? We have been tricked into fighting our cousins twice. Churchill is a Marlborough and we know the Marlboroughs are to be trusted – but are we also to trust the Jeromes?'

Churchill's American mother, thought Jago, a Jerome.

'The Jeromes of New York are almost certainly Jewish, or at least tainted with that stain. Do you see the link? Churchill isn't fighting for John of Gaunt's sceptred isle, but for the Hebrew, with his Mitzvah of Challah mixed with Christian blood.'

The agreement at his words was vocal – a long, low growl.

'We have been bamboozled. Yes, we thought our leaders were misguided but we were wrong! They have been guided, guided by the Protocols of the Elders of Zion. This is an insane situation where it is very possible England will win and lose a war simultaneously. How can a man attacking himself ever win?'

He shook his head and displayed his handsome profile. 'Victory will mean the end of the British Empire; our American masters will accept nothing less. You think I exaggerate?'

No one did.

'So we face a Europe occupied by the Soviet Union, a Britain occupied by the United States, an Empire nowhere to be found and the Jew the puppetmaster everywhere.' He paused and Mr Punch was briefly visible. 'Let me tell you what it's like to be the scion of a great house.'

He had their attention, the way a careers master might when hitting upon the secret dreams of a schoolboy.

'A great house is not a single tree in a single field of a single nation. I have relatives in Sweden, Denmark, Germany, Austria and Bohemia. Travelling between the various branches of the house gives the aristocrat a European perspective. It helps us see through the narrow, nationalistic lies of both Churchill and Herr Hitler. What I am about to tell you would condemn me as a traitor to these narrow nationalists. But I trust you, I trust the men in this room, and I trust the English middle classes. Friends, if we are not to lose everything, we must risk everything. Via my family over the water, I can tell you of two events that will happen shortly that are linked. The first will be a huge German reaction to the provocation of D-Day. It may well result in another Dunkirk and, if it does, we must seize the opportunity we missed last time to say enough is enough. Enough blood, enough treasure has been wasted. You and the other men of influence must say this in your communities throughout the realm. We must take a leaf from the Bolshevists' book: organise, agitate, occupy. We must take back our country.'

Grim cheers and stolid clapping.

'The second event will precede the German push in the west and will result in new leaders in Berlin. Reasonable men. Hitler had his chance with Chamberlain but chose not to take it. So be it. To prevent the destruction of Germany, to halt the Soviet advance, to save the Empire and to send the Yanks and their chewing gum back across the Atlantic, I would myself pull the trigger that ended the little corporal's reign of mayhem.'

Nodded agreement.

'Thankfully I won't have to. As it happens, I'm rather proud, as it was a member of my house, on a pre-war visit to our family in Europe, who instigated the actions that will come to fruition before this year is out. Lady Duggan will certainly be overlooked by the history books, but it was this woman who was responsible for establishing a British intelligence team at the heart of the Reich. This team will finish the life of the Austrian house-painter. We must finish the war.'

The speaker had Jago's sudden and full attention. *The Three Graces.*

'I must leave you now. Remember, be discreet but also prepare. We can still save our world.'

There was long applause as the dozen tried to sound like Nuremberg. Dewsbury refused refreshment and left with the store owner hovering after him. Jago wondered how soon he too could make his escape. Brandy was being sloshed out and Blakey was introducing him as a good egg to one and all. Jago was vaguely aware of a latecomer marching in and expressing disappointment at missing the speaker. There was something familiar in the burr of his voice and Jago wanted the opportunity to turn and to see who it was, but Blakey was still busy leading him around.

'This is Major Chamberlain of the King's African Rifles, a comrade of my late son's...'

'That's never Donald Chamberlain,' said a voice by Jago's head.

He turned. The old dug-out and pretend policeman from the Scottish Borders looked at him with disbelieving eyes. 'You're supposed to be dead,' he said.

He turned to the others, as Jago froze. 'This is the man Donald was to have dealt with. It's the traitor, Jago Craze.'

There was a brief silence, then a cry of petulance that grew into a shout of anger. Jago was grabbed and his brandy glass dropped, the spirit sploshing. Suddenly the head of the chimpanzee in knickerbockers exploded into sawdust, and the sound of a shot filled the furniture showroom.

CHAPTER FORTY-ONE

Gabriel and Max saluted and marched from the drawing room. Through the giant window the mountains watched them go; from behind his desk the Führer didn't. Heinz Linge, Hitler's valet, let them out of the room. There was no sign of his aides. In the waiting room they recovered their sidearms but, before they could leave, Martin Bormann waved them to one side and ordered them to wait. He then disappeared down the corridor through the doors at the end. Gabriel was desperate to follow him, to get out of the Berghof and to get to Lorelei's apartment. He knew she wouldn't be there yet and he could set in motion the warning system they'd devised. If he was late she'd be back and Max would arrest her. But Bormann wanted them to wait and without explanation.

Opposite, in the corridor room, were the Führer's secretaries; Traudi Junge, Christa Schroeder and Gerda Christian. They were turned in on themselves, having a private conflab and taking neat piles of documents from a stack on a table by them.

Max said, 'Those little girls know where all the bodies are buried.'

Gabriel didn't care, he wanted to stamp his heel in

frustration. He needed to go. The three secretaries turned, took in the two silent men opposite them across the corridor and smiled.

'Good morning, gentlemen,' said Traudi, still looking like an ivory angel in her black widow's weeds.

'Ladies,' said Max.

The double doors at the far end of the narrow room flew open and Martin Bormann returned at the head of a military convention. Gabriel and Max stiffened into attention and brought their arms up into the Party salute. A glitter of Reich Marshals marched past with Hitler's own aides and adjutants in attendance. Apart from the crash of their heels it was a silent group, precise and Prussian. The valet must have been listening from the other side of the doors to the Great Hall, for upon hearing the heel tattoo, the doors flew open and the marshals swept past and into the Führer's presence. The aides hovered briefly, picking up and taking documents from the secretaries, then they too went through the doors, which were then closed, this time with Heinz Linge on the outside of the room.

'All safely delivered,' he said and the people in the corridor visibly relaxed, except Gabriel, who set off immediately. Max was just behind him, talking. 'Did you see that SS Obersturmbannführer in the second rank, behind Model and Rundstedt? I recognise him but I can't recall his name.'

Gabriel could. 'Joachim Peiper. He has the 6th Panzer Army.'

'I thought they were on the Eastern Front fighting Ivan? If the staff want a briefing from him why not the Wolf's Lair? Why bring him all the way west to Obersalzberg?'

'Perhaps he's being re-tasked. Eva told Lorelei that Hitler was planning something big on the Western Front.'

'Bloody women, always chattering.'

They left the Berghof and went towards the ruined theatre.

'You up for this?' said Max.

Gabriel nodded. 'Better me than some fat gangster from the Old Hares, leering and touching her up as he searched her.'

They approached the theatre that Gabriel thought once again looked like it had been stepped on by a passing mountain troll.

'Will she be in, d'you know?' Max asked.

'Should be,' Gabriel lied. 'She had a night shift yesterday, so she climbed into bed this morning as I climbed out. That's where we'll find her.'

But he knew this wasn't true. Before he'd left, Klara the kindergarten head had arrived and begged Lorelei to cover for a sick nurse. Wearily, Lorelei agreed to help out. She was due back at midday and Gabriel needed to warn her off.

They moved through her apartment, Max letting Gabriel take the lead. Gabriel headed for the bedroom as if he expected to find her there, even calling her name. 'Lorelei?' He went past the empty unmade bed and through the stuffy air and pulled back the curtains and opened a window. He had set the signal.

'Where is she?' Max asked, carefully skirting some of her discarded scanties on the floor.

'I don't know,' he said. 'She should be here catching up on her sleep.'

It was after midday and he knew she'd be on her way back from the kindergarten. If she followed tradecraft she'd check her bedroom window from a safe place. The open curtains would tell her she was blown, that she had to run for her life. There was a plan in place, Gabriel knew, but what that contingency plan was, he did not. She had kept it from him on the assumption that if they were after her they might already have him, and be torturing him for her whereabouts.

Max spoke. 'We'll wait. Let the mouse come to the cheese.'

He glanced again at the knickers on the floor. 'But not in here.'

In the sitting room, Gabriel sat but Max paced. 'This is not looking good for you, sunshine.' Gabriel didn't reply, so Max carried on. 'Well?'

Gabriel grunted. 'My woman turns out to be a British spy. Can't help that.'

'She could also be the sniper.'

It was a clumsy attempt to trap him. 'She was in that room, in bed with me when the shots were fired. I didn't lie.'

Max said nothing but sunk down into a chair. 'The fact remains, the person furnishing your alibi turns out to be a traitor. Who's going to accept her word? You're up shit creek. And when push comes to shove, what can I say Mr Zobel? You're not even German.'

'I've taken the blood oath.'

'So had the generals who tried to murder the Führer in July. For want of a better word, you're a mercenary.'

Gabriel tried to present the fear that gripped him as outrage. 'I have never been a mercenary. The Holy Father in Rome did not consider me a mercenary. My father fought for the Fatherland, the land of his language. German-speaking Swiss want an Anschluss. My greatest hope is that my children will be born in Germania.'

Max brought his hands together in a soft mockery of clapping. 'Bravo,' he said, 'bravo, but Gabriel, just spiel. You bring me your tart cuffed and crying and I'll start to believe you, but I don't have time for speeches. The enemy is at the fucking gate. Adolf might be an arsehole but he's our arsehole.

We don't have time to fanny around looking for an alternate leader like some effeminate democracy. We're in this together; the Party, the people, the military. We break apart and Ivan will be through our front door, shooting Granddad and raping our little sister.'

Gabriel leaned into Max's face. 'I understand that. I fought Ivan for two years.'

Max carried on as if he hadn't heard Gabriel. 'There's only one man who can deliver the miracle we need to survive, and as far as I'm concerned, anyone trying to kill him is organising my sister's rape. I'm not Party, I'm not Jew-wise, Germania sounds like a medicine to me, but what I am is family. And you Mr Zobel are not a member of my family.'

Someone knocked on the door. They looked at each other and then moved quickly to it. Max threw it open. They were faced with a bunch of ferns and twigs, and the odd late-flowering rose. The young soldier-messenger looked at his superior officer as a rabbit might have viewed a wolf it had blundered into.

'What the fuck is this?' Max screamed.

The flowers were plucked a second time that day, but on this occasion from the hand of the boy. Max shook them and then the bouquet hit the ground and was kicked.

'What are you doing lurking around a woman who's clearly marked *officers only*?'

The blushing boy tried to back off, changed his mind and came to attention, changed it again and continued the retreat.

'You repeat this dereliction of duty and you'll find yourself in a punishment battalion on the Eastern Front!'

The young soldier actually ran down the road, skipping out of the path of the milkman's horse, slowly coming the other way.

'You know about him?' Max demanded of Gabriel.

Gabriel shrugged. 'He has a crush on her. He's harmless, just a boy.'

'Is that all it is? Could be a cover. How often does he pitch up here?'

The same thought had occurred to Gabriel. The young soldier might be the *postman* in the Foxley team.

'I've only seen him once.'

'Well you won't be seeing him again.'

But then Max's attention was caught by the passing milk cart.

'He's late. He's been and gone by now most days.'

Max waved at the milkman to stop. Reins were pulled, and the horse humphed. 'You still up on the mountain? Something happen?'

The milkman clambered down from the cart, an action that displayed his inflexible wooden leg. His real one, he told people, he'd left in Poland. 'I've been up once already. Leave that!'

His horse had begun to inspect the wrecked bouquet on the road.

He lugged a feed-bag from between the wooden crates filled with empty bottles, and hung it around his horse's head. The dull-eyed piebald began to chomp, more out of duty than appetite, Gabriel felt.

'Got back to the yard and didn't even have time to unload the empties. Had to come straight back up, didn't I?'

'Did you?' said Max. 'Why?'

'Orders from his bit of fluff, Eva. She's doing a picnic for the Führer and some bigwig from Japan. Dish of the day is going to be Jaegerschnitzel. The ladies of Obersalzberg are going to collect the wild mushrooms. Me, I have to provide the cream. Buckets of it according to blondie. I told her my supplies are limited so she said she could give me requisition forms to commandeer cream from the other milkmen of Berchtesgaden. So back up I had to come to get them.'

The horse stopped munching and stamped its hoof impatiently.

'I know, Lily,' he said to the nag, 'it's a liberty, up this mountain twice in one day.'

For the first time the disgruntled milkman looked at Gabriel. 'She wants to be safe in her stall back at the yard.'

CHAPTER FORTY-TWO

The glass eye of the chimp rolled across the floor towards Jago and came to a halt looking up at him. Austen held the smoking Webley in both hands, feet spread evenly.

'Don't move, gentlemen. Major Craze: to me, sir.'

Jago tore his eyes away from the exploded head of the stuffed chimp. By his side, Blakey stuttered like an alarm clock no one was going to switch off. 'Craze? But this is Captain Chamberlain...'

The Peebles policeman didn't think so. 'Take it from me, this isn't Chamberlain – I expect Chamberlain's as dead as that monkey.'

Jago shook himself and moved to join Austen but Blakey stopped stuttering and stepped in front of him. 'We can't let him go. I told him about the telescopic sight I modified. Grogan said it was top secret.'

'Get out of my way,' said Jago.

Blakey glared at him. 'Bloody traitor!'

Jago put into practice the fighting skills taught to him on the unarmed combat course. He discovered this unused talent was waiting for him when he needed it. He drove his right heel hard onto Blakey's instep. As the optician squealed and raised his injured foot, Jago swept Blakey's uninjured foot from under him. Blakey crashed to the floor on his bottom and sat like a shocked schoolboy.

'Come on, sir!'

Jago joined Austen without further trouble. They walked quickly towards the lift. The voice of the Peebles policeman followed them. 'You won't get far. Billy Grogan has all his boys out looking for you.'

The whole queer-bashing team, Jago thought bitterly. Men who could have been doing their duty overseas at the sharp end of the war, instead kept at home on a safe but malicious remit – to act as a British Gestapo.

When they reached the lift, Austen suddenly and unexpectedly put two shocking rounds into the elevator-summoning mechanism.

'Dear God, you could have warned me.'

'Sorry guv. I don't know if that's buggered it or not. Anyway, I've reminded them I've got this.' He waved his weapon.

They raced down the mahogany-panelled stairs, and out onto the street. Jago looked around wildly and saw the dark shape of the Riley move like a mollusc in the blackout gloom. They ran to meet it, pulled open doors and fell in. Having scooped him up, Lavender gently accelerated without fuss and started the process of returning to central London and of evading pursuit.

Jago spent a fretful week kicking his heels at Albany. It wasn't until Saturday morning that he could put his plan into operation to pursue the identity of the spy known as the Three Graces. To that end he needed to see his old boss. He decided to beard Smedley at his home in Oxford, where the major retreated at weekends. He couldn't risk going to him in Whitehall: too many eyes. Besides, Jago knew he needed to address the scholar in Smedley, not the soldier, and Oxford was better than London on that score. He needed to appeal to that academic duty, that responsibility to aid a fellow of the same college in their research if paths of enquiry crossed.

Horace Smedley shared a home with his twin brother Hugo. It was a large Oxford house with a garden that Aunt Esme would have desired, and his Quaker mentor lusted after few things, Jago thought. It was the brothers' passion away from their studies: the trowel, the trug, the torture of weeding. A stately magnolia, caught bare in the early winter, twisted its branches in embarrassment at Jago's approach down the front garden path. The wisteria that covered the house in a purple mist in summer was closed up for the season, protecting the old brickwork from frost.

Though it was still early on a Saturday morning, the path looked swept and Jago was willing to bet that, although arriving back late the night before, Horace had been up at first light with a broom. Then moments before Jago reached the front door, he spotted Horace Smedley. He saw the insistent wig first, then the face under it, staring out of the front window with an expression that suggested the wearer had just spotted one of the Four Horsemen of the Apocalypse coming up the garden path.

In a room that was so typically an academic's study that it might have been designed by a stage artist, Jago sat in a faded velvet armchair that must have been bought by Horace's mother while still a young wife. Smedley still suffered from the agitation that Jago's sudden appearance in Oxford at the weekend occasioned him. His hands flapped and his lips muttered: he simply didn't know what to do – call the authorities or offer tea.

'They're after you,' he said.

'I know,' said Jago and left it there. Horace needed time to settle. He travelled the room in fits and starts like a disturbed crane fly. He came to rest by a bookcase, replacing a book that seemed to have been serving time as a coaster on an occasional table. He looked balefully at Jago, as Jago slowly recounted his story from the beginning, explaining the attempts on his life, the Link and going once more through his reasons for thinking a premature peace would play into the hands of Britain's enemies.

There was a silence at the end which both of them held in stillness. Jago knew Smedley was thinking and he gave him space to do it.

'People do these things, don't they?' the academic said suddenly. 'You think you know someone, admire them even, and then they do something so morally bankrupt that you realise you never did know them after all. When I was first a fellow, before your time, a chap I considered a friend stood for some minor college post. The sort of responsibility that usually might have gone begging. But on this occasion two young fellows perceived it to be the first step on a long ladder that might eventually lead to the Master's Sanctum. In the event my friend secured the responsibility, because the day before the interviews his opponent had pulled out of the race. Apparently his much-loved Labrador had been taken ill and subsequently died.'

Smedley at last sat down. 'Some months later, while socialising in the Bird and Bastard, my friend, who'd had far too much to drink, laughingly confessed to me he'd poisoned the dog to nobble his opponent.'

He sat back, his eyes somewhere else. 'I still remember the shock of it. There's so much cruelty in the world, don't you think?'

Jago did, but stayed silent, waiting.

'Boys can be so very cruel, I know that. But when we grow to man's estate, surely we put childhood monstrousness behind us? But some don't, do they? I realised this man I took to be a pleasant companion would do anything to propel his career. Whitehall is full of men like him. If there's a dog to be poisoned, lead them to the arsenic.'

Jago cleared his throat. 'When I asked you to pass my report upstairs you refused. I wonder why?'

Smedley scratched a knee covered in Manchester corduroy. 'I thought you were one of them, a self-server. Up to a point I still do. You're ambitious and I don't like that. Academics shouldn't have careers: it's vulgar, and more importantly it can cloud the truth. The fruits of research must be revealed, whatever the implications. We must be prepared to go to the stake for the truth. We take ourselves out of society into a university so that we can work with clean hands. But I now believe that your arrogance is the fruit of the original thinker, not the self-server.'

'How can you be sure?' Jago wasn't sure himself.

'Because you don't kowtow my boy. The dog-poisoner put into your predicament would have thrown in his lot with the appeasers and fifth columnists. Truth requires sacrifice. You believe your report to be true?'

'I don't know. I was an appeaser. In a world without Adolf Hitler I'd be a pacifist. But I can't deny he exists and that the best hope of a long and lasting peace is that he continues to exist until the bitter end. A premature peace, though momentarily wonderful, would I believe, with time, prove a curse.'

Smedley nodded, climbed to his feet and wandered to the fireplace, above which was a sepia photograph of a young officer in a Great War uniform. Around the frame was a black ribbon, fading to grey with the passage of years. Smedley straightened it. 'The war to end all wars. The job half done.

All the sacrifice wasted. It mustn't happen again. What is it you want of me?'

Jago also stood. 'Not you, sir – your brother. I need the help of Hugo Smedley.'

CHAPTER FORTY-THREE

It was a week before Gabriel felt safe to come down from Obersalzberg. Seven days when he'd watched his back constantly, expecting to feel Max's hand on his shoulder, arresting him. But the scarred seraph was in the clear. Hitler believed in the mountain boy's naivete, just as he was equally convinced that all foreign-born women were perfidious. But Gabriel waited because he knew war was all about waiting.

He parked the Kübelwagen in the centre of Berchtesgaden, and wandered into the communal space beneath a fresco misty with gold. He sauntered into a bar, sat with his drink in a corner and watched the world to see if any of the world was watching him. The bar was quiet and subdued, as if it was listening for the end of war. He drank up, left and strolled across the town. He moved through the interconnecting squares and arcades, moving north. He re-joined the road that ran through the town at the point where it inclined sharply upwards – a rise Lily, the milkman's horse, must have resented on their return journey each day.

Gabriel studied the plate-glass windows of the closed shops, watching the reflections of the small town, looking to see if he was being followed. He wasn't. The town seemed to be the setting for a sad costume party; everyone Gabriel passed was in one uniform or another – forest rangers, female auxiliaries, Hitler Youth, railway police and Feld gendarmerie with metal gorgets hanging around their necks. In spite of the people the place was muted, as if the war had sucked away the last of the merriment from its night-time streets. The young men who might have caroused were all away or home again in shrouds. The garrison on Obersalzberg avoided the graveyard atmosphere and stayed up the mountain, using their own messes or canteens.

Gabriel passed a pair of men in civilian dress who saluted with nods. Ex-soldiers. One was on crutches swinging a stump, the missing leg something he'd left in Russia or the western desert, or somewhere Hitler played his games. The other's jacket had an empty sleeve pinned up. They passed Gabriel talking football eagerly. They weren't downcast but they nonetheless depressed Gabriel. They were coping, but could he? He touched his scar. Would that be it – the price? Or would the war give him one last surprise? If he was to lose a limb, would he be able to go home and manage to climb his mountain with a crutch? Or tend a struggling sheep with one arm? He walked on, watching his back and contemplating his future.

Certain that he was alone, he turned down a lane on his right, walked to the dairy and entered the yard. The milk cart, empty of crates and bottles, stood strangely naked. A pair of dark eyes watched him from over a stall. Lily snorted a greeting, or was it perhaps a warning? Gabriel went to the door beside the stall and rapped on it. It opened immediately. Gabriel knew that the milkman had some way of watching who came into his yard. He was ushered into a small scullery with a sink, stove, table and some hard chairs. There was also a spare leg with dangling straps standing, minding its own business, in the corner.

They viewed each other without a word; the milkman and the SS officer. The *need to know* had worked well, with only Lorelei aware of the identity of both of them. Gabriel understood but found it strange, like playing in an ice-hockey team and only being introduced to the goalie at the end of the season. And it was the end of the season: Lorelei's exposure as a British spy had seen to that. So now the milkman knew who the trigger man was and Gabriel knew who the postman was. Not the young Luftwaffe messenger with his ridiculous bunches of flowers that he had suspected, but the gaunt, weatherbeaten man standing in front of him.

'Where is she?'

Gabriel was led through another door and taken to a narrow flight of steep wooden stairs. 'Up there.'

Gabriel looked up at the glow that was escaping from under a door off the landing and wondered if that room too would stink slightly of horse shit.

Lorelei was sitting on a bunk carved like a piece of furniture found in a building made of gingerbread. She sat with a Madonna smile. 'This was the children's room. Herman, the milkman, grew up in this room,' she said. 'After losing his leg he finds it easier to sleep downstairs in what he still calls his mother's room.'

Gabriel, who'd waited out ten lives in the last week, was at a loss for something to say. She understood. She understood him. 'I'm afraid this bunk is tiny. I'm not sure there's enough room to make love – unless you have an inventive position in mind, soldier?'

He drew her up and kissed her, his arms so far around her he felt he could have tied her in a knot with them. He kissed her repeatedly, wanting to reassure himself that she was really there. That he was with her, that she was safe.

'I opened the curtains,' he said.

'Thanks.'

They sat side by side on the bed, still wrapped in an arrangement of arms, still reassuring each other with their eyes.

'How did you get off the mountain?' he asked.

'Prearranged signal, like the curtains. There's an out-crop of rock with a holly bush on top. You can see it from down here, from Herman's yard. I tied a piece of red rag in it, one of the kids' aprons from the kindergarten. He saw it and came for me.'

'So when Max stopped him…'

'I was on the back of the milk cart, cowering down behind the crates.'

Gabriel felt his fists stiffen, felt his arms ache. He saw clearly what might have happened; Max was conscientious enough to have searched the cart. If he'd discovered Lorelei, Gabriel would have had to kill him. Could he have done it quietly enough? He touched his SS dagger in its sheath on his hip. 'We need to get you out of Germany,' he said.

'All in hand. There's an exit plan in place. I have fresh papers with a new identity and profession. I'm down as a working girl, a tart.'

Lorelei's language shocked Gabriel, as it often did. 'Lorelei,' he said wearily.

She squeezed his hand. 'Don't worry, it's only a cover. I won't actually do anything naughty.'

She laughed like water splashing over pebbles. 'Your face, soldier.'

She gave him another kiss and said, 'It's good that you care for my reputation.'

He nodded grimly and she continued. 'Herman can

get me to Munich in an old van he borrows. He has what he calls a dairy passport. He goes there to get the delicacies that Eva Braun desires. The travel papers cover two people in case he needs help on account of his leg. Once in Munich, I'm to hole up in a brothel. Then the madam, who makes regular trips to Switzerland, will take me and another girl to a bordello in Zürich, and transfer two girls from there to Munich. They swap them around regularly; the punters like a fresh face or something. It's been going on for years, no one notices any more.'

'Are you sure you'll be alright? The girls in those places can be hard.'

'Darling, you of all people know I'm not a shrinking violet. I can play the Dakini, the sacred whore, with the best of them.'

Gabriel knew she could. 'How soon can you go?'

'Not yet,' she said. 'I want them to think I'm long gone before I in fact depart.'

'Supposing they search Berchtesgaden?'

She shook her head. 'They won't. This is Adolf's home patch. Here he likes to pretend he's a country gentleman and not the great dictator. He won't upset the locals. As usual he'll defy his congregation to dislike him.'

Gabriel knew waiting was the best tactic; in evasion, success went to the patient. He wanted to lie back on the bunk with her, but behind them on the covers were the contents of the hospital files.

'I thought you'd taken this stuff back?' Gabriel said.

'I did. This isn't the stuff on the Old Hares. By the way, they all have A1 sight according to the medical bumf. If Emil Maurice fired the first shot, he missed because a rabbit bit him.'

'So whose are these?'

Gabriel picked up a sheaf and read the name on the front. 'Martin Bormann?'

'I took these away when I put the others back. I hid them in my locker in the kindergarten. When I saw the open curtains, I went straight back and got them.'

'Never go back for things. You should have run straight away. Leave stuff and people behind. That's what you taught me.'

She pulled a contrite face that involved a lot of eyelash. 'But darling, I needed these. The work goes on. I wanted to see if anyone else close to the Führer has an optical problem. I lifted the records of his aides, secretaries, staff, even his double.'

'Weler? He's been sent to Berlin. According to the press the Führer has been in the capital for months.'

'But Weler left after the assassination attempts. He was on Obersalzberg for the first, and remember he was in the Kehlsteinhaus during the grenade attack.'

Gabriel nodded and Lorelei continued. 'I'm going to look at everyone, and I'm going to find him.'

'Or her.'

She looked at him, less eyelash this time. 'Yes, or her. I'm going to look at everyone and I'll find him. And when I've discovered who it is, well you can kill him – or her.'

CHAPTER FORTY-FOUR

'In you go, Prof.' The guard at the gate waved them through. Hugo Smedley, a regular visitor to Rollright Abbey, touched the accelerator on his rickety station-wagon and drove Jago towards the trifle mould of a building that was the stately home of the Hengars. Professor Smedley had told Jago the family would be absent as the estate in north Oxfordshire had been commandeered by the military to serve as a training ground for tank warfare.

'Visiting officers and the training team are billeted in a wing of the great house, other ranks in converted barns and stable blocks. They won't get under our feet,' he said.

As they roared up the long drive, they passed small groups of men wearing the coal-black berets of the Tank Regiment, but there didn't seem to be much activity; there didn't seem to be many tanks. Jago knew the rumours; there was nothing left. Britain had used the last of her reserves to cross to France on D-Day. Everyone who was eligible to be in uniform was, and serving in one of Britain's seven armies placed around the world, or was in her gigantic navy, or in the air armadas that nightly destroyed more German cities. There was simply no one left to train. If the British suffered another reverse of the

Dunkirk sort, they would have to wait for another generation to grow up before they could try again. When they crossed the Channel to land in Normandy, they'd crossed the Rubicon.

Rollright Abbey had originally been just that – an abbey and one of the many religious houses that Henry the Eighth had removed from Rome. It was gifted to the Hengars and they had cannibalised the stone to create for themselves a Hampton Court of the Midlands.

'They were a family before the Conquest,' the professor had told him. 'Jute aristocracy settled on captured lands in northern France. They spread by sword and marriage. In the aristocratic world, the Hengar family is known as the ermine rash.'

The document room was right at the top of the house under the eaves, with the snouts of dragon-like gargoyles visible through the leaded windows. Jago hadn't wanted to visit in person but the professor had been adamant that he wouldn't remove any documents from the family archives. 'It might be a very big house,' he'd said, 'but at the end of the day it is still a home and I don't rob other people's homes. You are, however, welcome to accompany me and have a snoop.'

'That's alright is it, to snoop?' Jago said a little sarcastically.

'I think so. A family that likes to swim at the high tide of history must expect some public interest. I can point you in the right direction but beyond that I don't think I can be much help. For the past twenty years I've been cataloguing their vast correspondence. I've made it from Hastings to Waterloo but I'm nowhere near the contemporary stuff. You'll have to delve for yourself.'

Jago viewed the jumble sale. Long oak tables were covered in envelopes of all sizes. It looked like the sorting room of a central post office serving a sizeable city. At the far end, where the oldest correspondence lurked, Jago discerned a sense of order, where Professor Smedley's twenty years of labour had resulted in neat piles and less clutter. Around the walls, mahogany filing cabinets that clashed with the oak everywhere else now stored most of the ancient epistles, the professor had told him. The long rectangle of the ceiling was interrupted at regular intervals by gable windows, under which were desks craving the natural light.

'This is the table with the documents you need to peruse, the pre-war bumf.'

The two of them separated both in space and time; the professor going to the far end of the room and the early nineteenth century, Jago to the higgledy-piggledy pile of the mid-twentieth century. Jago checked the date stamps; he wanted those letters written as it slowly dawned on the British that their next war would be fought against the Germans and not the Soviets. That time when, short of intelligence assets, they tasked those natural travellers, the aristocrats, to be go-betweens and information-gatherers. He was also looking for any letter penned by Lady Duggan. She was the peer named by the speaker to the Link in Ealing as the woman who had discovered the Three Graces. Jago knew there was little chance of finding the spy's real name there in black and white on any of the letters but there might be some clue. He needed some tiny piece of information that he could follow up. So, he began to ferret, slowly and meticulously.

The room was unheated and, as the day wore on, it became bitterly cold. Something the professor, armoured in academia, seemed impervious to, but that ate at Jago's bones like acid. He opened letter after letter until he found he could recognise Duggan's handwriting. The woman wrote like a schoolgirl gossip and Jago soon found he wanted to slap her. There was a mountain of drivel about people with ridiculous nicknames such as Binky and Bruin. Jago's breath started to leave him like fog. His hands were numb and refused to come back to life however hard he rubbed them. Fingers withdrew cooperation. He cursed and struggled as he discarded a page, when he spotted a name on the freshly exposed sheet before him: Clive Roberts.

Jago retraced the story of the letter and started again, with a small excitement fighting the cold for his attention. Was this Roberts, a deputy head of the British secret service, MI6 – or possibly a different Clive Roberts altogether, one who might sell superior hams for Christmas? But a line told him it was the right sort of Roberts. Lady Duggan was staying with a Swedish branch of the family and had occasion to visit a doctor's surgery in Stockholm.

My toe was still giving me gyp, after that troll, Gustav, stepped on it at the Frost Ball. But in the quack's surgery I met someone who has a relation close to the Austrian Corporal. The sort of chummy we were asked to look out for by that chap in 6, Clive Roberts. I'll explain all to him when I return for the shooting. No names, no pack drill but for reasons that amuse me, I'll call this 'friend' the Three Graces.

Jago's eyes lifted from the page. He looked out of the window and into his own thoughts. Dusk was creeping closer across the north Oxfordshire fields. The darkness sliding past the ancient arrangements of the Rollright Stones. One of the groups was known as the Whispering Knights, and Jago could almost fancy he could hear them sibilantly calling him, warning him not to meddle, to stay apart and anchored, detached and uninvolved in the affairs of men. Another noise pierced them and drowned the ancient whispering. It was the engine of a car. He corrected himself; of cars. A convoy of cars was coming down the long drive. Dark shapes, as if the Whispering Knights had uprooted themselves and now were coming for him.

The lead vehicle pulled up below on the gravel. A door opened and a man stepped out smartly. He looked up and it seemed to Jago that Billy Grogan was looking into the very window he was looking out of. As if their eyes met in the darkness.

CHAPTER FORTY-FIVE

Jago quickly checked the envelopes in front of him, putting all the correspondence in Lady Duggan's handwriting into his briefcase. He buckled it closed and found Professor Smedley leaning back in his chair watching him.

'You're stealing historical research materials.'

'Sorry – war effort.'

'My brother is right; you're not a scholar.'

Jago didn't have time to debate this. He knew that Billy Grogan would be inside the house looking for him. He took his bag and left. Prior to infiltrating Rollright Abbey, he had studied an interior map of the stately home and had planned an emergency exit should it prove necessary. Upon leaving the document room, instead of taking the stairs down and risk meeting Grogan coming up, Jago continued to ascend, up the short flight to a door with a bolt. He shot this bolt, opened the door and went from inside to out onto the roof. He was at a front corner of the house beside a domed folly that he knew from his map was a *desert*, a place to which younger people could desert the dining table and take their pudding. A snug for sweet things and for flirting, canoodling and – for engaged couples – respectable petting above the waist. The *desert* was balanced on the other corner of the frontage by a similar-shaped building that Jago knew to be an observatory. A facility for all the stargazing needs of guests. Jago didn't cross the front of the house towards it; instead he followed the gangway on the roof above the east wing towards the rear of the house.

He scuttled along next to the crenellations, with Oxfordshire dark and owl-hooty beneath him. Somewhere out there in the darkness the Whispering Knights sighed, and somewhere behind him Billy Grogan was coming. But the night also held the promise of Nicky. Jago hurried on. He saw the park stretching from beyond the rear of Rollright Abbey and the silhouette of a large beech tree that by daylight would be copper coloured. It grew near the curtain wall of the estate. On the other side was a sunken lane, and on the lane would be a parked Daimler, with Nicky waiting inside in case things went tits up and Jago needed a getaway vehicle.

He descended via a staircase in a rear tower. At the base, on ground level, he crossed the north wing of the house, which was the ruin and remains of the original abbey. Dark shadows pretended they were black monks. Ghosts didn't worry Jago; the man leading the hunt for him did.

He left the tumbled masonry and lost prayers and went down into a ha-ha that had perhaps been a defensive moat from the times the abbey had been both a house of religion and war. He crawled up the other side, handicapped by his briefcase and feeling slightly absurd because of it. He crested the far side and entered the park. No shout came behind to indicate he'd been spotted. He ran towards the wood where the copper beech lurked. In the shelter of the trees he startled roosting birds that flapped off, crashing through the branches with calls of alarm. Jago hated those cowardly, stupid birds that threatened to alert his pursuers. He was aware that the further he got from capture the more panicky he became.

He blundered in the undergrowth that clutched at him, as if it too was a member of a sinister organisation that wished him apprehended, or better still dead. He passed the beech, too lofty for the affairs of men, and arrived at the wall. The incredibly filthy ivy he climbed treacherously unpeeled itself when he trusted it, and scratched him when he did not, clutching it too hard. The dust and grit made him sneeze, without an available hand to deal with the snot. He felt wretched as he pulled himself up and dragged his bag after. He clambered over the top and fell, rather than descended, to the other side. He lay winded on the grass verge and Nicky's face appeared above him, like the moon with the stars behind him in the purple sky.

'Hello old man.'

Nicky's amusement at Jago's state had irritated him. They drove in silence as Jago regained his breath and his sense of humour. Nicky took a hand from the wheel and squeezed Jago's thigh, and Jago found he was able to reward Nicky with a grin. Through the roar of the engine and the exaltation of escape, Jago felt the joy of life and snuggled into the warmth and aroma of Nicky. Nicky leaned across, merging with Jago, and leaned towards his ear. 'I love you.'

Was it Nicky or the Whispering Knights that hushed those words into his ear, Jago wondered? Those three words. The girls back at school had used that expression; *those three words*. Used them in respect of boys they'd met during the hols at parties or on impossibly romantic beaches under tropical moons: *did he say those three words*? 'I love you' being too delicate a declaration to voice in conversation, words to be saved and savoured only in their true utterance. Now Nicky had said them for real and Jago had heard them for the first time in his life. Someone loved him romantically. *I love you*, Nicky had said, and Jago discovered, however much he wanted to, that he couldn't say those three words back. The silence stretched ahead like the road.

Nicky moved away, sat upright, like a megalith.

They drove in silence. The winter trees, doing an Arthur Rackham thing, spread their fingers in a knuckly way that seemed to be telling them to stop, of danger ahead. Nicky changed down a gear to negotiate a corner, before accelerating on the straight and changing up again.

'After the war – are you still planning to go to Switzerland, to have that cure?'

'I don't know.'

Nicky laughed but it wasn't a happy sound. 'I'm so bloody stupid; falling for a man who's contemplating curing himself of me.'

Jago shrugged pointlessly in the shadow-deep car. 'I'm trying to think what's best.'

This time there was no laughter, just a noise of anger, and the car went faster.

'That's just bollocks. Your mind can do many things, Jago, but it can't direct your heart. Love marches to its own beat. You can't hear it because you're too busy thinking.'

Jago was lost. 'All I have is my mind.'

'Believe me Jago, there is something truly unedifying in the spectacle of a pragmatist in pursuit of love. It's like a man in an off-the-peg suit at a good restaurant. Slice and cut your politics any way you wish but you can't do the same with your heart. You're still frightened of flying.'

'I know.'

Nicky threw the car about down country lanes, past trees in frozen screams.

'Dear God, why do you want to be normal? Where's the attraction in that? What sort of a man do you want to be?'

Jago shook his head but nothing moved inside it.

Nothing came, no answer. 'I don't know who I want to be. I suppose I don't really know who I am now. A pragmatist? Possibly. I'm not an idealist like my Aunt Esme. I'm not a scholar, someone told me so earlier. Not a real man; my dispatch officer told me that on the airfield after I'd funked it. Am I a queer for all time and in every way? I assumed I'm odd because I'd been effeminised by a childhood spent amongst girls, that if I'd had a normal education, I'd be heterosexual. I thought I just needed to tune myself. Certainly lavatory-creeping never brought me any joy, just a temporary numbness. Then I meet you and happiness seems possible – and now I don't know.'

But he did. Somewhere in him, hanging on like a tumour, was the need to be as normal men were. To have in his life no possibility of humiliation, even if that came at the cost of love.

They drove in silence and parted the same way.

CHAPTER FORTY-SIX

'I use it as a sewing room,' Lavender said. 'I'll move my patterns off the bed.'

She was stowing Jago in the tiny box room of her home in Lambeth. He'd spent the night in a service club but he knew he needed a deeper bolthole, so he'd come south of the river. On the endless, awkward drive it had been agreed that Jago had to be separated from the Hengar correspondence. Nicky took the letters with him back to his set in Albany, to go through them carefully, looking for any further clues as to the identity in Sweden of the person Lady Duggan thought might be useful to MI6, the agent known as the Three Graces.

The Link knew that Jago was still alive and working against them. Whitehall and the West End were places that were deemed too hot so Jago had phoned Lavender to ask her to take him in.

'I've emptied the top drawer for you,' she said, as she indicated a tallboy almost as high as the low-ceilinged room.

'There's a nail in the door with a hanger for your uniform.'

Lavender in her tiny house south of the river. Almost a doll's house and Lavender a child playing with it. Jago looked at her, reminding himself that the little cockney had fended for herself behind enemy lines on two missions in occupied France.

Back downstairs, Jago saw that Austen had brought a hard chair in from the kitchen to place between the two armchairs before the fire in the parlour. Austen took the kitchen chair for himself and insisted Jago had a soft chair. Everything was cosy and homely; there was a mirror over the mantelpiece where Lavender bobbed her hair in the light from the window. The framed sepia wedding photograph of their parents the only photo on the distempered walls, balanced by a homemade calendar, made out of a compilation of images of a bearded seaman from Senior Service cigarette packets.

Jago had been tucked away safely. The cell advised him to stay in; a commissioned officer a rare sight in Lambeth. When his hosts left Jago alone and went to their work, the voices of street kids playing outside provided a better radio drama than the ones acted out on the squeaky wireless. Their skipping songs became his music; the good ship apparently sailed on the *alley-alley-o.* The brash immediacy of their contact with each other was so spontaneous and without side that Jago felt he was in a strange land, not just south of the river.

Lavender brought him tales from the far land he'd once lived in. As he knew, in the corridors and committees there had been no interest in Foxley's intelligence of a possible German assault in the west.

'6 shot it down, sir, Mrs Cambridge says. Reckoned it was tainted info, a deception operation that we in SOE didn't have the analytical grey matter to see through. They said, Hitler's major problem is the Eastern Front. If he was planning an offensive it would be there.'

The next day, Lavender returned again an hour after leaving for Baker Street.

'You've got to come in, Mrs Cambridge says. Orders from

the top. She'll tell you properly but you've got the boot. You're being replaced by that geezer you used to work for.'

'Major Smedley?'

'That's the one.'

Mrs Cambridge ushered Jago into his own office, followed by Lavender. Nightingale was sent to rustle up some tea.

'Has Lavender told you?'

'I'm being replaced? Yes.'

'The order has come down from upstairs.'

Jago considered Mrs Cambridge's words. Was there more? 'I don't really understand why I needed to come in.'

He saw the look between the two women.

'Commander Godwin has been arrested. I wanted to tell you to your face.'

Nicky, they had Nicky. Jago felt nauseous, felt that the grey light seeping in at the window was poisoning him. The crackle from the burning coal on the open fire not comforting but ominous. He felt the older woman watching him. Did she know Nicky was more than a mate? More than someone who had been putting up a friend in an emergency?

Mrs Cambridge continued, 'He's been charged with immoral soliciting in a gents' toilet.'

Jago came to. 'That's not possible, that isn't Nicky, not in a public convenience – he hates that sort of thing.'

Jago didn't want to believe it. He didn't want to think Nicky needed the casual caress of a stranger when he had Jago. Or had his disappointment in Jago caused him to go out and act rashly?

Lavender spoke. 'They came for him at his place, Albany. The porter told us, and the constabulary asked after you.'

Jago was confused. 'Me? Why didn't they arrest him at the scene of his alleged immorality?'

'No idea,' said Lavender, 'but the porters tipped Nicky the wink when the rozzers showed up. One of them made a fuss about letting them through, and the other hared ahead to warn Nicky what was occurring. He bunged this porter one of the Duggan letters and told him to bring it here.'

Why did they ask after him at Albany, Jago wondered? How did they know he'd been living there, would still have been there but for the row? Who told them Jago was staying with Nicky?

'Where's this letter?' he said.

'As it was red hot I decided it should be passed on pronto, before the new man arrived to betray all our secrets. So I popped it into the envelope with your address in Pimlico, the one containing the Foxley file, care of Miss Veronica Rawlings, as agreed.'

'Might have been better to readdress it to Lambeth.'

'Lambeth is our safe house. I want to keep it that way and I don't want Lavender involved if things fall apart.'

As they were in the process of doing, thought Jago.

'It's in the post?'

Mrs Cambridge nodded sharply. 'Of course. I gave it to Nightingale with instructions to take it out of the building and to post it in a public box on the street.'

Jago looked at her, 'Nightingale?'

The thought formed a bridge between them; Nightingale the lead-swinger who did no job properly. Jago turned around and stepped back into the outer office. There in the out tray was the buff envelope with Veronica's name and Jago's Pimlico address. Mrs Cambridge arrived by his side.

'Blast the man. I specifically told him to go out of the building not just dump it in the nearest tray. Idiot!'

The admonishment, Jago knew, was for herself because in

the rush of removing the item before the office was occupied by the enemy she had trusted in a man who was untrustworthy.

There before them was a silent epistle that seemed to Jago to be throbbing with red warning lights. If Nicky had removed a letter from its fellows and sent it in, then it had to contain intelligence. It just might hint as to the identity of the spy known as the Three Graces.

Jago took a step towards the dusty wicker basket that was the out tray, as the door from the corridor opened and Major Smedley stepped in. Entering behind him, with a smile as wide as Whitehall, came Billy Grogan.

CHAPTER FORTY-SEVEN

Mrs Cambridge attempted to conduct a last-ditch stand. 'Has that man any right to be here?'

She meant Grogan.

'The inspector has a duty to perform. I am the new commanding officer of this operation, and I order you all to cooperate. Inspector Grogan has some questions for my predecessor.'

Major Smedley's eyes didn't meet Jago's, but Grogan's did.

'Information has come to us,' Grogan said, 'that you illegally purloined property belonging to the Hengar archive. Most of the letters have been recovered but the Earl of Dewsbury informs us that there is still one letter from his sister, Lady Duggan, missing. Where is it?'

'I'm also required to hand over all information regarding an ongoing intelligence operation called Foxley,' said Smedley.

Jago couldn't speak; in the corner of his vision the envelope lay in plain view.

'Well?'

Major Smedley suddenly rounded on Jago. 'The Hengars have banished my brother. They blame Hugo for introducing you to their home. You've ruined years of his research.'

Jago, still a little bit the scholar, felt guilt. 'I don't have it. Yes, I was at Rollright Abbey; I conned my way in, convincing Professor Smedley I was involved in some academic research. Please tell the family he was not to blame. I took the letters that the police have now recovered. I can't offer an explanation as to the missing one, only to repeat: it's not in my possession. Either I lost it leaving in haste, or it's still there amongst the piles of correspondence. The latter is more probable in my opinion.'

Mrs Cambridge spoke again. 'Major Craze believed that in the pre-war letters of a member of the Hengar family there might be some indication of a threat to our operation on Obersalzberg. Protecting our people in the enemy heartland, and servicing their needs, is his job. Major Craze was doing his duty.'

Smedley, uncomfortable in this awkward interview, turned aside and Jago clearly saw him register the envelope in the basket. He stared at it.

'It won't wash, Craze,' said Grogan.

Jago stiffened. 'Major Craze to you, or sir. Acknowledge the rank, Grogan.'

The policeman's face, empty of emotions, trailed a small smile at the corners of his lips that threatened to flower when the time was right. 'Sir,' he said quietly, 'we searched your place in Pimlico. I have to say I found your domestic arrangements rum. So…'

The smile started to blossom. 'Just how friendly are you with Commander Godwin?'

The smile fully bloomed.

'Why wouldn't I be a friend of Nicholas? He's a comrade in arms, a fellow officer. He's worthy of respect, having two gallantry awards. While you – what are you, Inspector Grogan? A stay-at-home copper whose methods resemble those of the Gestapo.'

The smile gone; winter was on the face of Grogan.

'Well maybe there is something in that, Major Craze. Me and some of the lads think we could learn from Jerry on that score. They don't pussyfoot around with their Vaseline men; it's straight into a concentration camp with them. They put a pink triangle on 'em to show the world the wearer is a bum-boy. Should you be wearing a pink triangle, Major Craze, sir?'

Before Jago could answer, the door opened and Nightingale slid in, holding a tray of tea things. 'Char,' he announced gloomily.

Jago, still trying to outstare Grogan, registered several things happening simultaneously. He heard the tea tray smashing to the floor, and saw Major Smedley's service cap fly across the room.

'What the devil?' Smedley shouted.

Jago, turning to the seat of the kerfuffle, saw the major's wig land in the open fire and begin to burn. Smedley, now as bald as an egg and incandescent with rage, turned on Nightingale.

'You madman! You lunatic! Why did you do that?' He turned to them all. 'He threw my hairpiece on the fire.'

Nightingale vehemently shook his head. 'I didn't, sir. He's having a turn. He smashed my tray to the floor and threw his own wig on the blaze.'

'Liar!' Smedley stepped towards the flames, where the consumed wig could still be seen in a web of orange lines, like veins on an illustration of a dissected body.

'Five guineas that cost!' he shouted.

All eyes were on him and the fire. Jago was barely aware of Lavender stepping forward from the corner by the door, where in her silence she had almost been invisible.

'I never done nothing!' Nightingale wailed.

'Be silent!' Mrs Cambridge snapped.

Jago heard the door to the office close quietly.

'I'm going to have you arrested,' Smedley said.

'Assaulting a superior officer is a serious crime,' Jago tossed into the fracas.

'It wasn't me,' bleated the unfortunate Nightingale.

It wasn't, thought Jago. Horace Smedley, the shit-slicer, had come down from his ivory tower like his father before him, and done his bit. The out tray was empty. Smedley's distraction had worked.

Grogan tried to restore order. 'Alright, settle down. Never mind the perishing wig – hang on, where's that FANY gone? The one in the corner?'

His question was answered when the door opened and Lavender returned, leading one of the military policemen who lurked in the corridors of SOE headquarters.

'There he is,' she said, pointing at the shell-shocked Nightingale, 'Take him into custody.'

The MP looked around for advice and Smedley gave it to him. 'Get him out of here, he's having some sort of breakdown.'

Nightingale was led from the office, still shaking his head at the unfairness of events, his world sunk as surely as if it had been torpedoed. Grogan, using the rating's exit as an opportunity, took command of the situation.

'Right, here's what's going to happen. First, I'm going to search your person, Major Craze, for the missing materials. If you don't have them about you, I shall summon help and we'll take this office apart.'

'Are you arresting me?'

'Not until we find the evidence,' Grogan told Jago.

'In that case, after you've searched me, I shall take myself off for some lunch.'

Grogan wasn't happy but there was nothing he could do. He

searched Jago roughly and, when he found nothing, Jago left. Lavender was waiting for him on the stairs.

'I wanted to get it out of the building but they had a man downstairs on the door.'

'Where is it?' Jago asked anxiously.

'The post room sack was due to go, so I put it in there. It'll be in the system by now. Central London to Central London, it should get to your place in Pimlico by second post today.'

CHAPTER FORTY-EIGHT

Jago had bought the house in Pimlico in another age. There had been a peace, there had been hope, and in it Jago had secured his first home. He'd grieved for his mother to the same extent as she might have grieved for him; the missing of someone familiar, getting used to them not being there, but there had been little love. He had felt guilt that there'd been no keening pain, and guilt at his excitement over his inheritance. The house, and the plans for it in his head, had come to nothing. War had arrived instead, and then Christine. Both had spoiled it for him. And now there was Nicky, and now he never wanted to walk down the shabby street again. He wanted to make his way home to Albany and to have Nicky waiting for him with a smile and a hug.

Late afternoon and Jago's heart was dipping with the day. He let himself in. The hall table empty. No post yet. He felt them rather than heard them. Out of habit he almost called for Veronica, to tell her he was about the place, but then he remembered the last warm meeting he'd had with Christine in the Mercury Café and so he called her name.

'Christine, it's me, Jago.'

However, it was Veronica who came along the hallway from the kitchen. 'What are you doing here?'

There was to be no welcome.

'We've had the police; do you know that? It was frightful. They turned everything out. They knew about Christine and me, guessed from our sleeping arrangements. They laughed at us and said dreadful things.'

She shuddered. 'It was as if they owned us, these men from Clapham and Battersea, with their horrible fingers stained yellow with nicotine, going through our drawers, handling our underclothes, believing they owned us. That they could say anything to us because we were of no account and they were our masters.'

Veronica didn't cry; she began to shake. Jago moved close to hold her but her hand prevented him. 'No. None of that.'

'I'm so sorry,' he said.

Veronica shook her head bitterly, as if to shake him and the memory of what happened out of it. Without her heavy make-up, she seemed naked and vulnerable, like the schoolgirl Jago first knew.

'Damn you, Jago, why couldn't you play the game? Why couldn't you just keep your head below the parapet? Survive like the rest of us? Why do you have to sacrifice us just to make you special? Whatever you do won't make you one of them. Go ahead, save the world, but they'll still think of you as a nancy-boy.'

Jago knew this, but a childhood of solitude – ignored by his mother, abandoned by his father, being preached to by Aunt Esme – had brought him to a place where he discovered he needed to be heard, to be reckoned with. To his surprise, he found it wasn't in him to stop now, whatever the cost. Jago had come into manhood without realising that he was ruthless.

'Sorry,' he said. It was as empty and echoey as the hall.

A crash came from the kitchen.

'What now?' said Veronica. 'It's dreadful in there – she's having some sort of breakdown.'

Jago followed her.

In the kitchen, he was reminded of a Greek tragedy. Christine looked as if she had been violently raped. She squatted on the quarry tiles, her legs apart. Crimson jam moved down the pleats of her skirt. Clumsily, she tried scooping it up with a shard of broken glass. Her thighs and Aertex knickers were on display. In her misery, Christine seemed not to notice.

'It's gone everywhere,' she wailed. 'I dropped it.'

Veronica knelt beside her. 'Don't, you'll cut yourself. Leave it.'

Jago saw an open suitcase on his mother's table, with a dozen jars of jam inside. A neat line that, for some reason, disturbed Jago. He turned back to Christine and found her watching him with over-bright eyes and the crazy grin of the clown.

'I'm leaving you,' she said. 'We're going to live in the country.'

Veronica sighed. 'We're not, darling.'

'The man said, the policeman…'

'He was lying, stringing you along. Getting what he wanted from you. I'm afraid it's what men do.'

Christine looked woefully at the jam. 'I've ruined this skirt for nothing, haven't I?'

Veronica held her tight. 'I rather think you have, my darling.'

Christine looked again at Jago, as if he might have some explanation. 'He seemed so nice.'

'We saw a different side of him today.'

Jago asked, 'Are you talking about Inspector Grogan?'

'He came to her a couple of weeks ago and filled her head with nonsense.'

Christine stirred. 'He knew Mummy and Daddy. I trusted him. I don't trust you, Jago. Never did.'

'What did he want?'

She giggled like a small child as she cuddled Veronica's arm and shared the conspiracy. 'He wanted to know where you were. He said you'd vanished off the face of the earth. He told me if I found out where you were hiding I'd be rewarded. It was logical, he said: once you were removed, I'd get this house, could sell it and move to Nettlebed.'

The location of her parents' honeymoon, scene of subsequent family weekends. The place Christine had chosen as her English Eldorado.

'What did he mean by removed?'

'Jago, don't get melodramatic,' said Veronica. 'He's a policeman when all's said and done, I'm sure he just meant prison, locked up for a bit.'

'No.'

They both looked at Christine. 'No, not locked up; dealt with.' She pointed her fingers at Jago in the manner of children playing cowboys. 'Bang,' she said.

'Christine!'

She ignored Veronica and squirmed on her bottom towards Jago.

'We always hated people like you,' she said. 'Mummy, Daddy and me. People whose woolly ideas will destroy our Empire. Daddy said your lot thought the blackies were equal with the whites. He said the socialists would pass a law that made white women marry buck niggers and Delhi wogs.'

'You were all in the Link?'

She nodded. 'Mummy, Daddy and me. But then they were killed in your stupid war. I'd be all alone but for the Movement. I showed them your paper; that upset a lot of people so something had to be done. They almost got you with the fire – I wasn't happy about that; my property could have been damaged. We had another pop in Scotland but you still turned up like the bad penny. I told them you were still alive but they didn't believe me at first – I'm just a woman.'

Jago knew she disliked him but had put it down to the claustrophobia of their situation. 'Why on earth did you marry me in the first place?'

'She made me.' Christine indicated Veronica with a look. 'She said there had to be some way of wresting this house away from you once we were married.'

Veronica's head went down. It was true.

'Veronica,' he said.

Her head came up. Her eyes angry. 'You have no idea. You have no idea you stupid little man, what it's like to be a woman. Don't be so bloody superior!'

She looked for words and they arrived in a rush. 'Do you have the merest inkling what it's like to be a woman with no money? A woman who under no circumstances can take up with a man and be provided for? It's like being naked on the street. Even with a good job, a woman won't be given a mortgage. Women like me are stateless in our own country. We're forced to use guile and evasion just to survive. So yes, I wanted this place one way or another.'

Jago appealed to her. 'It's not been easy for me, either.'

Her laugh took the last warmth from their friendship. 'Look down, Jago. Haven't you noticed? You have a prick.'

Christine made an announcement as she heaved herself up. 'I'm the Queen of England and this is my jam.'

Jago went. Inside the wire letterbox on the front door, an envelope with Veronica's name protruded. It had arrived after him. He took it, let himself out and went down the cast-iron stairs from the pavement to the basement. The door had been scorched into toothy shapes. He pushed it open and went into his burnt-out flat. In a pool of the day's last light, he opened the envelope and took out the single sheet that was the Foxley file, and a folded letter in Lady Duggan's handwriting.

CHAPTER FORTY-NINE

Jago sought some daylight to see the letter clearly. A burnt rocking horse watched him, its dapples now paint blisters. The fire had cleansed him of the clutter of childhood. All those inherited things – his mother's Bible, the notebooks of Aunt Esme's poetry, the photograph albums – all gone and no longer a burden to him.

He found the light he required in what had been his bedroom. By the charred frame that had been a window, he read the letter. He went through it twice. The writer didn't name the person they'd recruited on behalf of 6, referring to the asset as the Three Graces, but when he read it, Jago, who had attended a public school for girls, knew the secret.

In the letter, Lady Duggan complained about the noise her three girls were making in the corridor outside her study while she was trying to write. They were apparently playing the *Grace Game* and Lady Duggan wrote that she hoped her Three Graces over the water were a little more discreet.

The Grace Game. The very words brought a world back to Jago. *Play up, the house!* rattled round his head again. It was a sport that existed nowhere outside of an English girls' boarding school. Huntingdon School, like many of the others, ran a tournament named the Grace Game. Jago had quite forgotten this obscure winter term cup, when teams of three competed with other teams of three, using rods and hoops. It was a keenly fought competition, and the teams were selected from pupils who had a special relationship with each other. That relationship informed Jago of the identity of the MI6 agent. And now he knew, it was vital to get this information to Foxley.

Intelligence that couldn't be passed on and acted upon wasn't intelligence. It was dead knowledge. Jago knew he could hardly now use SOE radio to contact Foxley in Zürich, but he had a plan. He just needed a *piano–player* and a rocket attack on London. The V2s were falling nightly, so Jago felt he could rely on the dependable Germans.

As he made his way to the telephone kiosk, Jago held back the concern that threatened to swamp all others: Nicky. They had Nicky. Beautiful, lovely Nicky was in the hands of men who pathologically despised what he was. Policemen, who had the double reward of an aristocrat and a queer to torment. Jago ached to give them what they wanted, not destroying the evidence. He could bargain for Nicky. But Jago walked through these temptations, trying to block them out. He needed to put together a team. The priority was Foxley and getting a message to them.

There was almost a full moon, what had been called in the Blitz a bomber's moon. But rockets didn't need natural light to find their targets – they were blind and implacable – and Jago knew he was right. The war had to be brought to a final conclusion with the total and unconditional surrender of Germany. Otherwise, on a night like this in just a few years, a rocket would fall on London with God knew what explosive in its cone.

Jago used a telephone kiosk on the edge of Warwick Square. He rang both Lavender and Mrs Cambridge and set things in motion. When he left the box he found Billy Grogan and his team waiting for him.

'We turned over your office to no avail, so I think it's time we stopped pussyfooting around, don't you?'

They took him to a police station on Rochester Row, and to a small, windowless office below ground.

'Fetch a bowl, Nolan,' Grogan said, and one of his men nodded and disappeared. Then he opened a drawer in the only desk in the room and threw a face flannel onto the surface of it. The other detective moved the desk chair to the centre of the room and guided Jago firmly into it. Jago felt vulnerable with Grogan's henchman lurking behind him. The third policeman returned with an enamel bowl, water sloshing around in it. He carried it to the desk.

'Careful,' Grogan said, as it was put down.

Grogan dropped the flannel into the water. Jago wondered if he was going to freshen up before a long interrogation.

'Where's the Foxley file, and where's that blasted letter?'

Grogan spoke with his back to Jago, working the flannel in the bowl.

'I've no idea what…'

Grogan spun around and the wet flannel smacked across Jago's cheek. The pain was almost as intense as the shock. 'What the hell…' He saw the flannel coming back from the other side, heading for his un-smacked cheek. He lifted his hand to protect it, but the detective behind grabbed it and held it clear as the flannel smacked home.

Grogan hit him three or four more times in quick succession, while Jago's arms were held. When he was released, he instinctively jumped up. Jago realised too late he was expected to do this, as Nolan, the detective who had fetched the bowl, hit Jago full in the belly with a balled fist. He fell, trying to gasp and throw up simultaneously. He lay there as they talked football.

Apparently Brentford, an unlikely team, lurked near the top of the league.

'Only because there's so many pro footballers stationed in London. When peace breaks out they'll all go home up north and Brentford'll go down the table as is right and proper,' said Nolan.

'Back to the Third, where they belong,' pronounced Grogan.

They all nodded in agreement.

'Right,' said Grogan, the break over, 'get him up.'

Jago, sick and faint, was lifted off the floor and put back into the chair. The flannel cracked again, and the dance was renewed. Before too long, Jago found himself back on the floor, gasping like a stranded fish and hardly able to remember a time when he wasn't in agony and consumed by fear.

Grogan bent down by him. 'You will run out of spunk. You are going to tell us where you've hidden the letter and the file.'

Jago was slammed back in the chair and it began again; the slaps, the punches, the collapse.

'What about putting the boot in?' suggested Nolan.

'I don't think we need to. Remember, this is a ducky-boy, not a real man. Okay sunshine, where's the stuff you nicked?'

And so it went on.

'What letter?' he would say occasionally, through lips caked with blood, and, 'Please, I don't have the file.'

Sometimes they would halt the assault to taunt him.

'Are you a bum-boy, Craze? Has Commander Godwin had his willy up your arse?'

Lying on the ground, Jago became aware of something; that he could take it. Their violence, so shocking to start with, hurt less with each round. A terrible tiredness gripped him and he wanted to be left alone to crawl into a ball and sleep, but their efforts were the torments of unimaginative men. Jago found a place to go in his mind to plot and plan.

Grogan was speaking in his ear again. 'Not so pretty now, are you?'

Jago stayed silent. His lips felt they belonged to someone else, fat and badly attached. Blood, trickling from his nose, climbed them and spilled down into his mouth. His stomach throbbed, his sweaty hair irritated his eyes.

'Well?'

'I've probably looked better.'

Grogan punched his stomach hard and he slipped from the chair back onto the floor.

'Get him up. Let's take him to see lover boy.'

Jago, dragged and stumbling, was taken out of the office, down into the arse of the station, down into its Victorian bowels. They came to a door as solid and respectable as the age it was made in; it wore its studs with pride. A huge key was turned and the door swung back. There inside was Nicky.

CHAPTER FIFTY

When Jago had viewed his mother for the first time at the undertaker's, he'd thought for an instant that he'd been shown the wrong body. It didn't seem to be her. His reaction to seeing Nicky in the police cell was the same. Even though he was still alive, the face didn't appear to be his. Some elemental part of him had gone. He remembered Nicky talking of the brave Scottish sergeant who had come to the end of his courage on a day that *wasn't his.* Jago saw that this wasn't Nicky's day.

'Hello Nicky.'

The stranger looked up, the face of a tired old man, the eyes vacant.

Jago was to see Nicky alone, and Grogan let himself out of the cell as discreetly as a parent softly closing a bedroom door on a sleepy infant. Jago understood that this wasn't a kindness but a further torment. An opportunity for Jago to fully savour, without distractions, what they'd done to Nicky.

'What's happened?'

Nicky didn't answer but slid his eyes off Jago and returned them to the wall next to the bunk he was sitting on.

'Are you alright?' Jago sat next to him and gently touched his wrist. 'What's wrong? Tell me.'

Nicky sighed a soft, long breath that grated as it turned into a groan. His eyes returned to Jago's. 'They brought my father in.'

Jago didn't know if this was a good or a bad thing. 'Is he going to help you? Help you get a solicitor, hire a brief?'

'He's disinherited me. I'm no longer family.'

A small, wan smile moved across Nicky's lips briefly and was gone forever. 'He's a funny old bugger. He took the opportunity of giving me the sack to tell me I'd always been his favourite son. Me, the useless mouth.'

'Nicky...'

Jago's comforting hand on Nicky's shoulder was gently removed.

'He told me I was a disappointment. He accepted I couldn't help being what I am, a Vaseline man – but to be caught, trying to do it in a public lavatory... He said the family name would be dragged through the Sunday papers.'

'Did you tell him you were framed?'

Again some secret humour, too deep to share, briefly flared and faded around his eyes. 'How do you know I was framed?'

'Nicky...'

'Perhaps I am a pervert who haunts shitters.'

'That's not you, Nicky. You have too much style.'

'Style?'

The word floated away like a balloon. Something from a lost world. A word whose meaning had become incomprehensible.

'Grogan targeted you to get to me.'

But Nicky was fighting other battles. 'I've had this war, Jago. I've had it up to here. Win or lose, my side never had anything to gain. We're cannon fodder for the bigots. I did convoy duty in the Atlantic, I did the Malta run in the Med, I've been to Archangel and back a few times. Good grief, I was torpedoed and they gave me another decoration. But to Grogan and my pa, that all counts as nothing. I tried to do my bit, but my bit was never big enough to compensate for what I am: one of the pansy fraternity. Men like us Jago, we're the common enemy of the British police and the Gestapo. We're the one thing they can agree on: the persecution and eradication of the effeminates.'

Jago sought around in his head for some raft of hope to offer Nicky. 'You have your political beliefs.'

This time the smile was open but not happy. 'I'm not a fool. I believe in a fairer system but revolution is for the immature; things will evolve, improve, but not in a hurry. It's always too slow for people who need something different just to survive. Whatever's up ahead, it's too late for me. This is Dunkirk and I'm not going to get off the beach.'

The harsh crash of a cast-iron lock being turned shattered their complicity. They moved apart as Grogan and his two detectives entered.

'You little girlies holding hands? Cheering each other up?' Grogan was back.

They ignored him. He moved in on them. Jago didn't want to look at him as he stood above them, but he feared the unexpected blow, so he did, and saw that Grogan was grinning.

'Major Craze vehemently denies he's a... what does the judge call this sort of deviant, Cooper?'

One of the detectives spoke. 'Homosexual, guvnor.'

'Ah yes, a homosexual. Are you a homosexual, Major Craze?' Grogan asked.

Jago wanted to say yes, and to damn them. He wanted to be free of the lie he was forced to live behind. He felt like a Jew denying his race to the SS. But there was Foxley. He had a duty to a world beyond the men who policed it. There was no god in Jago's life, no divine purpose. There was just a belief that the war should continue until either Germany or Britain be crushed into concrete dust. Judged impartially, without the blinkers of patriotism, Jago thought British society was marginally better than Nazi Germany. For that margin, he gave Grogan the lie. 'I am not a homosexual.'

'Have you ever indulged in homosexual activities?'

'No, the thought disgusts me.'

'Disgusts you, does it?'

'Yes.'

'Let's get this straight – queers disgust you?'

'Yes.'

'Commander Godwin has confessed to being a homosexual. Does Commander Godwin disgust you?'

Silence. Jago hoped it would provoke an attack, wanted to feel again the sting of Grogan's slap. Nothing happened. The world ticked on, waiting.

'Well?'

Beside him, Nicky spoke. 'Tell them, Jago.'

Give them the lie, Nicky was saying.

'Yes,' said Jago.

Grogan tutted and shook his head. 'No, what I want you to say is, "Commander Godwin disgusts me because he is a homosexual."'

Jago despaired. He had wanted Grogan to keep the torture simple. He was prepared to have his arm twisted again. To scream as it was broken. He would endure. He just didn't know if he could cope with betraying Nicky.

Jago took a breath. 'Commander Godwin disgusts me because he is a homosexual.'

Grogan beamed. 'Now try, "Commander Godwin disgusts me because he is a bum-boy."'

Jago felt as if he'd swallowed acid. 'Must I?'

Two things happened simultaneously. Grogan yelled, 'Do it!' And Nolan stepped up to Jago and kicked him hard on the shin. He cried out in pain and Nicky said, 'Give them what they want.'

Jago breathed the pain away into an ache and spoke. 'Commander Godwin disgusts me because he is a bum-boy.'

'You choose one, Cooper.'

'Nancy-boy, guvnor.'

'Now you Major Craze, you know the form.'

Jago stared at the green-painted brickwork and spoke, 'Commander Godwin disgusts me because he is a nancy-boy.'

'Your turn, Nolan.'

'Shirt-lifter, guvnor.'

Jago repeated it flatly like a schoolboy echoing a lesson learned by rote. 'Commander Godwin disgusts me because he is a shirt-lifter.'

Grogan brought his hands together in a single clap. 'My turn again. Perhaps one of you two gentlemen has a request?'

They sat in silence.

'No? Well let's try this one. Commander Godwin disgusts me because he is a shit-stabber.'

'Commander Godwin disgusts me–'

But Grogan wasn't happy. He wanted to refine the torture. 'No, Major Craze, not out into the air. Look at him and say it. Don't give him his rank or name because he doesn't have either any more. Look him in the eyes and say, "*You* disgust me because *you* are a shit-stabber."'

Jago found Nicky's eyes waiting for his. Throughout occupied Europe, captives had faced this problem, that of saying one thing out loud and meaning another in their heart. He needed to tell Nicky just how much he loved him with words that were as gangrenous as the green cell. He spoke softly. 'You disgust me because you are a shit-stabber.'

The bridge between them was broken by Grogan suddenly intervening and dragging Jago from the cell. 'All done!'

In the office upstairs, Jago was given a cup of milky tea by Cooper. 'No gin in it,' he said by way of levity.

Grogan looked at Jago with concern. 'That Commander Godwin is in a bad way, but fear not,' he said theatrically, 'all is not lost.'

Jago sipped the tea and guiltily realised he was enjoying it. Nolan and Cooper left the office. He watched Grogan over the rim, through the steam.

'This can still be hushed up. We can give Commander Godwin breakfast tomorrow and send him on his way. No appearance before the beak, no conviction, no name in the Sunday papers. Maybe a place for him back in front of the family fire. You give us that file and letter you stole, and the Walpurgisnacht Plan you've got tucked away somewhere, and a whole heap of problems vanish as silently as the spinster's fart. You give us that stuff and, if you keep shtum and don't cause no more trouble, well you might survive this war, Major.'

Jago sipped the tea. 'By us, you mean the Link?'

Grogan laughed. 'Silly name. It's the war; coughs up rubbish labels like there's no tomorrow. The Link is a society forged by an open secret, that the British admire the Germans. We admire the German prowess at fighting. We admire their discipline, and order, and love of the Fatherland. Their food doesn't stink of garlic. They're our people, not our enemy.'

'Do you want us defeated by them?'

'God, no!' Grogan slapped his desk to emphasise his words. 'I want us fighting on the same side. I want the Brigade of Guards marching shoulder to shoulder with the Potsdam Grenadiers against the Reds. All we have to do is remove Hitler from the scene to make our friends across the North Sea respectable again. Then we can begin our war.'

Our war, thought Jago. How many wars were there? A war for every person.

Grogan was speaking again. 'You'd be able to move around freely again, without fear, without worrying who's behind you on an Underground platform. You'll be safe.'

Jago discovered he wanted to be safe. Wanted that feeling, so unappreciated while in possession of it, and so missed when lost.

'We have some big guns in the Link and I've been authorised to say that if you give us the letter, the file and the plan, then after the war there's a career waiting for you in the Diplomatic Corps. A little bird has told us that's what you want. It's not much of a choice is it? Give us Foxley, people you don't know, strangers at the end of the day, and your friend goes free without a stain against his character. Hand over that letter and the Jerry plan and you won't get pushed under a District Line train, plus you get entry into a top-notch profession. What do you say?'

Jago put down the teacup on the floor beside him. 'I'm sorry, but this is the truth. The Walpurgisnacht Plan never reached me. However, the Foxley file, which is one sheet of paper, and the letter are wrapped in a waterproof wallet and stuffed into a jar of homemade jam. The jar is stacked with others in a suitcase that was on the table of the kitchen in my house in Pimlico.'

CHAPTER FIFTY-ONE

'Billy Grogan had better come back with that letter or you'll be brown bread,' said Nolan.

They were alone together in the office. Grogan had taken Cooper with him to Pimlico. Jago could imagine the scene, a bloodbath of jam. He'd brought more trouble to Christine and Veronica but it hadn't been deliberate, just the first hiding place that came to his mind. And all too soon Grogan would return in a fury. Nolan seemed to sense his fear.

'If you've been wasting our time, it'll be the poof down in the cells who gets it. Billy will kick his balls to beetroots in front of you. He won't even begin to question you again until he's had his fun. Big mistake to lie to the guvnor.'

'I haven't.'

But he had. He had a clear recall of the soot-stained lavatory bowl in the burnt-out flat. Of the impossibly white flakes of paper floating down into it as he tore the report and letter into pieces. He'd used a charred segment of a picture frame to stir the bits into a dark, glutinous mass. Now he'd told Grogan the lie to buy time, that most precious commodity they'd said in his SOE training. Time for something to happen, for someone to turn up. Jago had made a little time, but for what?

The sudden sound of the air raid siren made him start.

'Here we go again,' said Nolan. 'Come on, petal.'

Nolan lifted Jago out of his chair with a huge hand under the armpit.

'Where are we going? To the cells?'

A locked cell would be the end of hope.

'It'd make sense you'd think, the cells being underground. But technically, unless you've been charged, I can't lock you up in one during an air raid.'

He led Jago out of the office into the corridor. The sound of a distant explosion confirmed it wasn't a false alarm, that London was being hit again.

'Rocket attack,' said Jago.

'Sodding Jerry, why doesn't he lay down and die.'

Jago repeated his question. 'Where are we going?'

'The Military Police let us use the shelter of their TA hall opposite.'

The dark street was empty and silent, a rocket attack being different in that respect from the bombers of the Blitz, when wave after wave of aircraft had been the background growl to an hysteria of sirens, ack-ack and fire engine bells. A rocket attack was silence, punctured by sudden and noisy devastation, before an eerie quietness returned and all waited for the next one.

Nolan, in the process of hustling Jago across the street, leapt when the second rocket struck much closer than the first.

'Jesus!' he yelled.

Jago saw the van, a dark shape without its headlights, rushing down the road towards them. The driver trying to outrun the raid and preventing them from crossing the road.

'Come on, you bugger.'

Nolan plainly didn't like rocket attacks. As he fidgeted in agitation, Jago, without warning, barged the detective onto the bonnet of the passing van. The force of the collision threw them both up and back onto the pavement behind. Nolan had taken the brunt of it and, through the larger man's body, Jago had felt the echo of the blow. Slammed down on the unforgiving paving stones, only Jago was moving. He heard the van's brakes screech and Nolan's soft moans, as if he were having a very private nightmare. Jago felt the grip of panic as he realised he couldn't breathe, but with that realisation, he suddenly heaved and air rushed back into his lungs. With huge protesting gasps, he pulled himself up. His trousers were gone at the knees, an elbow and wrist on one arm throbbed, and his ribs felt like a busted parrot cage. Leaving the still gently groaning Nolan, Jago staggered off, as another rocket hit London.

Bare chested, Jago sat in the back of the Riley, as Austen finished fastening a very tight bandage. 'I don't think any of them are broken. Badly bruised, though,' he said.

Jago felt bruised was an understatement. His ankle throbbed from the kicking. His cheeks felt swollen. He felt he needed a proper check-up and then bed. Instead he had to stay on his feet and carry on.

Austen helped Jago on with his shirt before rummaging in the first aid box for some disinfectant to rub on Jago's bloody knees. Jago winced.

'That stuff's supposed to be for victims of air attacks,' said Lavender.

She drove them carefully through the blackout and rocket attack towards Dolphin Square. Since they'd picked Jago up, he'd been aware she was not in the best of moods. And while he had little to do with the personal aspects of women, he wondered if it were her time of the month. School, not marriage, had acquainted him with this phenomenon; when he'd walked the corridors, trying not to decipher the various codes the girls used. That so many girls had an Aunt Flo, who visited them regularly, had confused him for ages. Of course, given the prevalence of horsey girls at his mother's school, it had been no surprise that *back in the saddle* was the most commonly used term, and occasionally the fairy tale version, *riding the cotton pony*. Strangely, in his lonely way, Jago had envied them that fraternity of *the curse*, before he discovered he also was a member of a cursed fraternity. Whether Lavender was suffering from her monthly affliction or not, her temper was certainly foul, he thought.

'Is Commander Godwin alright?' Austen asked, as he dabbed disinfectant onto Jago's knees.

'That stuff stinks,' Lavender complained from the front.

Jago ignored her. 'No.'

A sudden series of angry blasts on the car horn filled the car. Jago looked out – he couldn't see the cause of them.

'Well he's only got himself to blame. Carrying on like a bloody Frenchman, in the middle of an operation, what was he thinking of?'

Austen spoke quietly in Jago's ear. 'She's been like this since she come back from seeing the Don.'

Jago wondered if it were another biological imperative that had caused Lavender's mood, not hers but the spymaster's? Veronica had told him that all men were delusional where women were concerned and could, if the wind were coming in the right direction, confuse *do you want a cup of tea?* for *let's have sex*. Had the Don tried it on, was that it, he wondered? If the Don had been sordid, it would explain Lavender's anger. Beside him, Austen, rashly in Jago's opinion, questioned his sister's attitude to Nicky's situation.

'I don't think Nicky was done for looking for fun. Not in a lavatory, not him. He was framed.'

Austen's words seemed like petrol on the fire of Lavender's temper. 'Do me a favour! Listen, framing him's only possible because everyone knows he's that way inclined. Roll on the revolution, I say.'

Even Jago had to question that. 'What's the revolution got to do with this?'

'Because after we get a Marxist–Leninist government of the proletariat, there won't be any deviants.'

Jago's sudden anger seemed to exacerbate the pain from his bruises. 'You're going to put us up against a wall and shoot us, are you?'

'Won't be necessary,' she said, taking a corner too fast. 'Sexual perversity is a symptom of capitalist society. When we cure society, we cure everything else, everyone. Austen will have a normal life with a wife and kids, not a half-life doing what he does.'

Jago wanted to tell her that what she'd said was horrible, but Austen spoke first. 'I can't help it.'

Lavender swung her eyes from the road ahead to turn to her brother. 'Of course you can!' Then her eyes swung back as she muttered, 'Dad would be so ashamed.'

Around them in the dark the raid continued. Explosions, muted by distance, that nonetheless brought tragedy and the end of things for all time to the people caught in the blast.

They reached Dolphin Square in a silence that Jago broke. 'There are two air raid shelters; Mrs Cambridge will be in the one that doesn't allow pets.'

'I'll get her.'

Lavender went and Austen turned to Jago, embarrassed he'd witnessed the family scene. 'I'll make up with her later.' The two of them approached Hood House. On the roof, the dark sculpture of the twisted aerials was in silhouette.

Mrs Cambridge arrived, brisk and businesslike, as if burglary was a nightly experience for her. Jago had briefed her on the phone before he'd been picked up and she knew what was required.

'Up these stairs,' she said, as they entered Hood House. 'I should warn you, Major Knight keeps a brown bear in his rooms. Normally it's harmless, a pet, if you like that sort of thing.' Mrs Cambridge plainly didn't. 'But one doesn't know how territorial the beast is going to be, whether it will cut up rough at the scent of intruders. We must be prepared for it to be vicious on its home turf.'

'Great,' Lavender muttered.

Jago too considered the prospect of an unsympathetic bear bitterly. They had the air raid that had removed Knight from his apartment into a shelter but, in his absence, they still faced his Cerberus.

Jago picked the lock and, as officer commanding, did his duty and entered first. A deep rumble welcomed him and told Jago this was a conscientious bear, one not asleep on duty. A dark shape loomed towards him. The shadow grew in height and the rumble sharpened into a growl of outrage.

'Stop that! Bad bear!' said Mrs Cambridge. The animal froze at her words. 'Naughty girl. Stop showing off, Bessie. Go to your bed.'

The silhouette before Jago shrank like a concertina and slunk back into the shadows.

'That's how he talks to the creature,' she said. 'Like a nanny.'

The bear's den was under a long mahogany dining table, which the intruders skirted cautiously. Lavender made her way to a transmitter on a desk, the surface of which also bore an aquarium of fish.

'It may take a while,' she said. 'This isn't a regular call time and if the receiver was in occupied Europe there'd be no chance of a link-up. The *piano* would be packed away and hidden. But Switzerland? Who knows, maybe the pianist keeps it out and on. We may get lucky.'

'We have to try,' said Jago. 'We have to tell Foxley the identity of the Three Graces.'

'You're sure you've identified the right person?' Mrs Cambridge asked.

Jago thought back to his schooldays and the Game of Graces, and that very specific rule regarding the make-up of a team. 'Yes,' he said.

'Right,' said Lavender. 'I'm about to start tapping out love's old sweet song. When I do, every home security detector van will pick me up and start homing in on us here.'

'Will they bother? Won't they think it's Major Knight?' her brother asked.

She snapped at him, still angry at something. 'Don't be stupid. Signals have to be logged in advance. Something out of the blue will upset the bloodhounds. Now clear off and do something useful.'

The taps began, and sounded extraordinarily loud in the claustrophobic flat, with its fug of animal smells. Time passed, and no acknowledgement came from Switzerland. They stood unspeaking, trying to block out the stink and waiting.

'Can we have a window open?' Lavender asked, bent over her task.

Her brother opened one but the blackout curtain in front of it prevented any meaningful invasion of fresh air. However, the gap allowed in the sound of bells ringing frantically on an emergency vehicle.

'Coppers or an ambulance?' asked Austen.

No one could tell, but the sound grew more insistent as it

came closer, and, as if connected, the intensity of the rocket attack increased.

'I'm not getting through,' Lavender muttered. 'Come on, come on, pick up!'

The ringing outside got louder.

'I thought so, they're coming here,' said Austen.

'Right,' said Jago. 'We need to give Lavender as much time as possible. We need to divert them. Austen, we need the police to see us on the roof so they think that's where we're sending from. If they storm up there we can try to hold them back for as long as possible.'

'Right, skipper.' Jago noted he had been promoted in Austen's head, but the man was still speaking. 'Even after we're arrested it might take them a time to twig the roof isn't the site of the transmission.'

'It could still be an ambulance,' Mrs Cambridge ventured. But they all knew it wasn't.

Jago and Austen reached the roof via a small flight of stairs. Every step was agony for Jago. Around them was the weird and wonderful copse of aerials, frozen as in the middle of a frenzied dance to music by Stravinsky, fingers up in ecstasy. Jago and Austen acted out the pantomime of popping up and down by the aerials, trying to give the impression of subterfuge. The show was timed to the arrival of the detector van and police car.

'Up there, on the roof!' came a voice that Jago thought might be Detective Cooper's.

'I knew that rogue signal was him,' Grogan could be heard saying.

There had been no way of locking the door to the roof and

nothing to block it with but their own bodies. The two of them braced themselves against it, waiting for the assault.

'We need to buy time,' Jago said.

'She'll get through. She's a good girl.'

Why Lavender's moral standing might make it inevitable for her message to be received, Jago wasn't sure.

Distracted as Jago was by pain and nausea, he was unprepared for the crash when it came. The door smacked him on the nose he'd left too close to its surface. His eyes streamed, and he cursed as they pushed it back the few inches they'd surrendered. Jago's ribs screamed at him, and his knees asked not to be thrust against the door, but they were ignored.

'Open this fucking door!' came Grogan's voice from the other side.

A series of thrusts were choreographed from the other side, each gaining some territory, before relinquishing it again as the defenders dug in. But numbers told and the door was forced back, inch by inch, until Jago and Austen gave in to the inexorable pressure and jumped back. There was a moment of silent movie comedy as the policemen ended up in a pile by the open door.

More slapstick followed, as a Keystone Cops-style chase happened across the flat roof of Hood House, Jago dragging his body through one last torment. He knew that, below, Lavender was desperately tapping her Morse. He intended to buy her as much time as possible. It wasn't long; he went down onto the tarmac, rugby-tackled by a brute of a policeman. He almost fainted with the pain as the last of his resistance went. Someone hauled him up. He was dragged to Billy Grogan. Austen was frogmarched over. Grogan ignored them.

'Well?' he called across the roof.

'Can't find the transmitter,' a voice called back from the gloom.

'Keep looking. It's up here somewhere.'

He turned to Jago. 'You bastard. You've finished Nolan's service. A wife and three kids and he might never walk again.'

Might never put the boot in again, Jago thought, but he said, 'These things happen in a war.'

Jago didn't mean the official one. Grogan nodded and understood. 'Well it's all one. Casualties on both sides. Talking of which,' he spoke with a false concern that awakened in Jago the beginning of fear, 'we reckon your chum's dad smuggled in a weapon. Well, your average British rozzer won't search an earl. A Smith and Wesson revolver, one bullet up the spout. Gentleman's way out. The honourable thing to do – Commander Godwin took it.'

Grogan's words were the worst that Jago thought he would ever hear.

'Nicky?' It was worse than all the punches and kicks. It hurt more than the van he'd collided with. He hadn't known pain until this moment.

'Dead. Brains all up the wall. Duty sergeant at the nick not well pleased.'

Shock was a world of ice where Jago wanted to stay, numb and protected from the heat of grief. The homosexual pursuit of love wasn't a romance of ships that passed in the night, he thought. It was the Silent Service, two submarines seeking each other blindly, in a minefield. Jago became aware of a uniformed constable in front of him, like something emerging from a fog. The man had crossed front teeth. He was grinning at him. Nicky's death had pleased this man, had given him pleasure. From the ice and before the pain, Jago discovered there was another stage he had to travel: rage.

Grogan was speaking again. 'The commander had been sitting on that gun all the time you were slagging him off. What did you call him? A shit-stabber?'

Jago flew at Grogan, his sudden fury taking a policeman holding his arm by surprise, but Grogan had been expecting it. He'd been goading Jago and, as Jago reached him, he hit him hard in the face. Jago fell backwards to land with a sudden intensity on his bottom.

The police laughed at his pratfall, but another figure detached himself from a captor and careened into Grogan. Austen had been brought up in the school of hard knocks. Grogan's fist found nothing this time, as it swiped around the empty air where Austen's head had been a moment before. Austen bobbed down, hoisted up the shouting Grogan and set off at a run, carrying him like a giant child. None of the policemen later said they made out what Austen yelled, but Jago, who knew the context, did. As Austen jumped to his death off the roof of Hood House, taking the screaming Grogan with him, he shouted, 'Boy, First Class.'

Jago rushed to the parapet. Below, on the crazy paving path, were two very still bodies. Behind them, on the roof, the access door opened again and Lavender came through it.

'I've done it. Message sent and received. Foxley has acknowledged.'

The triumph faded from her face, to be replaced by a flicker of confusion. 'Where's my brother?'

CHAPTER FIFTY-TWO

Devils gathered by the hunting lodge on Lake Königssee; men who held the carved wooden Satan masks they would wear when the fun began. The women were dispersed throughout the trees, gathering mushrooms, their locations revealed by glimpses of the pure white dresses of the Perchten. The white signalled the innocence that the devils in their masks were so attracted to. How many remained pure at the end of the Krampuslauf, the devil's run, remained to be seen. Even Iron Arse, who Gabriel supposed was technically a maiden, was in a white dress.

'She's a pig-dog, an absolute pig-dog.'

As Gabriel picked mushrooms, he explored the expression in his mind; both a pig and a dog, and meaning a glutton. A person without any dignity or restraint around food. Ilse Braun meant Iron Arse. 'We do all the hard work collecting the mushrooms and she thinks we don't see her guzzling half of those she's supposed to be slicing.'

'Raw mushrooms are good for her. Roughage.'

'I'm tempted to slip a death cap toadstool in. That'll give her roughage.'

Ilse Braun was less fluffy than Eva, Gabriel thought. Maybe

that was the way with elder sisters. Angular, shrewd and opinionated.

'Here we all are; foraging to make a disgusting glop of mushroom and cream, creating a midwinter Krampuslauf in the forest, with string quartets to provide the chase music. It's all so crude and Bavarian, like our leader. Mr Hitler likes to think of himself as a sophisticated modern man, an artist – well rubbish. There's more of the town hall clerk to him than the creative. I come from a family that appreciates the arts; we went to concerts all the time, never the ghastly opera. Many of our friends were Jewish and most had more appreciation for the finer things than the Nazi Party ever had. We didn't have to wear lederhosen and eat like harvest mice to listen to music.'

They moved on through the woods.

'And all because he lost his mother at Christmas and Eva thinks he needs cheering up. Lord knows what the Japanese ambassador will make of our peasant dishes. Do they eat fungi, do you know? Probably do, no different from us I expect, just smaller. Do you know they have their own Krampuslauf? They call theirs Mamahage. I think I learned that from your ex. Almost exactly the same festival apparently; men wear devil masks they've carved themselves and chase maidens. I suppose it's universal; the need for a man to smack a pretty girl's bottom in the name of tradition.'

Ilse grumbled on. He held the basket, as she delved and decimated mushroom plantations under bushes and trees. All the spare officers had been dragooned into helping the Braun sisters and the Führer's female staff. It was the social activity of a peacetime military force, except there was no peace. The world was at war, and the Krampuslauf just a diversion to amuse the man who started it. Everyone was pretending: the laughter of Hitler's secretaries too ready when teased by the men; the officers too charming as they swished through the woods, as if in the opening scene from a light opera when the curtain rises. Gloves were slapped on thighs, maidens span coquettishly, the comedy troll stole food in full view and the audience waited for the entrance of the star.

A peal of laughter shocked the sombre trees about them. Traudi Junge in a black dress between the two white ones worn by her fellow secretaries.

'She's quite forgetting herself. Those three young secretaries of the Führer's are the end, cavorting in the woods and canoodling I shouldn't wonder. Mr Hitler won't like it, he's a jealous man. Have you seen the way they hang off him, in front of my sister sometimes? All simpering and sweetness, and Traudi a widow, though not much evidence of that – the merry widow more like. You don't talk much, do you?'

She looked at him and he smiled. 'Enjoying the woods,' he said.

'Eva says you've had your heart broken. Sorry, have I said the wrong thing? Women like to talk about these things but of course men don't. Silly Ilse, don't listen to me. Take my arm. Just to say, I know what it feels like. There, subject finished. May I call you Scar like the other women? I'd love to have a male acquaintance called Mr Scar, so may I?'

He smiled. 'Scar without the Mister will do.'

She held his arm and butted it with the side of her head. 'Pleased to meet you, Scar. God, I hate this war. I hate this: pretending to be a Bavarian bunny and foraging food squirrels have peed on. Scar, tell me you prefer café society to this folk business? I'm cosmopolitan for heaven's sake, I fell in love with a Jew. Does that shock you? No, I thought not. He was a doctor, is a doctor. He got out – before the war, to Sweden. Mr Hitler allowed it, facilitated it, because of my sister. I still visit him. It isn't easy. Mostly it's rotten. You see, I told you I know about heartbreak. I hope we dance later.'

She was gone, joining the end of a giggling queue, to empty her basket onto the mountain of fungi that was waiting for a sea of cream. Ilse Braun seemed a woman apart from the white frock brigade. In white, but it was as if she wore the colour for mourning. Gabriel knew that, because of her relationship with a Jew, the eldest Braun sister was rarely welcome on Obersalzberg.

The string quartet played Strauss, accompanied by a burble from the guests. The three secretaries were besieged by the Old Hares August Korber, Bodo Gelzenleuchter and Emil Maurice. Martin Bormann, Hans Lammers and Wilhelm Keitel were with the grand ladies of the Party – Ilse Hess, Annelies von Ribbentrop and Magda Goebbels – while the Führer's adjutants – Nicolaus von Below, Albert Bormann and Karl Puttkamer – entertained Eva Braun.

Gabriel saw the milkman. Gretl Braun was taking a crate of cream from him. The milkman moved off back to where his horse waited on the track. He seemed not to notice Gabriel as he produced his hanky and wiped some dust from his boot. Gabriel understood and followed him into the woods.

Lorelei came out of the bushes. Gabriel was appalled. 'Are you insane? What are you doing here?'

She ignored Gabriel's anger and spoke calmly. 'London has been in contact; they've discovered the identity of the Three Graces. And there are three of them.'

'Who are they?'

Before she could reply, the milkman shushed them from where he was watching on the track. A file of Luftwaffe gunners passed, holding crates of wine. They waited while the noisy airmen went on out of earshot. Gabriel held Lorelei's eyes, willing her to speak. As silence returned, she took a breath and told him.

'They're here,' he said, 'to run in the Krampus. But we need to know who their trigger man is.'

'We do,' she said. 'The mistake we made checking the medical records was looking for an injury caused in conflict. Platterhof is a military hospital after all. But he wasn't treated for this injury here, he was treated in North Africa. When I couldn't find anything initially, I started again and went right back to their childhoods. It was all there under their service records, a mountain of it for everyone. It took forever. So much detail of tonsillitis and whooping coughs...'

'Lorelei.'

'Sorry. It wasn't a war wound, so it got lost at the bottom of the file with the kiddie stuff. It was a civilian traffic accident. Smashed up his leg and, although he didn't know it at the time, it detached the retina of his right eye.'

Gabriel knew. 'Max,' he said.

She nodded and said, 'Today's the day of the hit. The Krampuslauf has been planned for weeks. They know Hitler and his stupid need for operatic theatricals; he's coming up Lake Königssee on the prow of a boat, like a figurehead, the easiest target in the world for someone on the bank.'

They both heard it. The baleful sound of a lonely flugelhorn, blown on the Führer's boat and seeking echoes from the surrounding cliffs. It announced the imminent arrival of Hitler, but it was a voice behind them that made their hearts lurch.

'Scarface and Nurse Fischer! Traitors!'

Iron Arse had found them.

CHAPTER FIFTY-THREE

Iron Arse stood staring at them across the clearing. Shaking the bushes that framed her as she turned to fetch help, instead she ran into the milkman.

'Oh no you don't,' he said, as he grabbed her in a choke hold; one arm holding her arms behind her, the other across her throat, suffocating her scream. Lorelei ran the short distance to her and, with fingers pointed like a spear, stabbed Iron Arse in the solar plexus. The matron collapsed in the milkman's arms, eyes rolling, mouth opening and closing like a landed fish.

'I'll take her. You find a death cap toadstool,' Gabriel said as he took her from the milkman and secured her in a full nelson.

'You're going to force a toadstool down her throat?' Lorelei asked.

Gabriel shook his head. 'Too slow. Use your pill.'

Lorelei knew he meant her suicide capsule. She reached down under her top, and brought out the small, flat tin in army green that she always carried. She flicked it open and carefully took out the strychnine pill.

Iron Arse saw it, gasped 'No' once and clamped her mouth closed, as she began to writhe in Gabriel's arms.

'Hold her steady,' Lorelei said.

Gabriel tried to, but Iron Arse was dense and heavy and fighting for her life. Lorelei stabbed another vicious finger jab into her stomach and, against her will, Iron Arse opened her mouth to gasp. It was all Lorelei needed; she stepped in, pushed the pill into the wet mouth and, with both hands, forced it shut.

Iron Arse screamed from behind her lips, her eyes wild and pleading. Gabriel felt the poison hit. SOE maintained it was instantaneous and so it proved. She convulsed as in a seizure. Gabriel felt he was holding someone experiencing an electric shock. Her inner screech became siren-like and the terror did to Iron Arse what the laxatives had failed to: she lost control of her bowels. She died in her own mess, a sudden lifeless baggage in Gabriel's arms. He lowered her onto the grass. The milkman ran back, holding a red-topped death cap toadstool like a tiny umbrella.

'Still need this?' he asked.

'Mash it up with some regular mushrooms. Quick.'

They all three frantically scoured the glade for the fungi. Gabriel took them and, using a flat rock and a large stone, mashed some innocent mushrooms up with the deadly toadstool, leaving its red crown intact. Then he scooped it up and plastered it in and around Iron Arse's mouth.

'They'll think it's death by incautious gluttony. The fatal mistake of a pig-dog.'

Then he turned to the milkman. 'Get Lorelei away.'

Lorelei started to leave but turned to give a final order. 'Max – get him before he gets the Führer. Save Hitler.'

The quartet had expanded into a band and were playing the Radetzky March. Military officers clapped along, or kept time with the single glove they carried, the other being lost in the mists of the traditions of the old Austro-Hungarian Empire. It had grown colder and most of the women wore furs or a coat over their light Perchten dresses. The men were experimentally putting their monster masks on and adjusting the strings. Soon they would be running through the woods, top coats abandoned, and screaming or roaring depending on their sex. In the excitement, there was an impatience for things to begin, but the Krampuslauf couldn't start without the chief devil.

Lake Königssee stretched out, away from the party, like a long finger, the water an almost impossible shade of green. The fringe of trees and rocks was perfectly mirrored in the still waters that seemed to be waiting. Snow was coming; Gabriel could feel it in his bones, smell it on the air. A smell like clean rust.

The moose-deep sound of the horn came again, and there was the launch bearing the Führer, chugging up the lake, cleaving the water like a knife cutting a sponge cake and releasing the cream in small bow waves. Gabriel knew that somewhere close Max would be waiting, waiting to line up his shot, confident that the adapted sights on his rifle would do the job this time. Gabriel tried to blot out the waltz music and think where he would place himself for the killing shot. Higher, he thought.

Behind the hunting lodge, a giant had, at some time in the primordial past, tossed a pile of boulders onto a small rise. Trees, like nervous skaters spreading their legs wide, clung to the low, rocky summit with outstretched and exposed root systems.

Gabriel decided it was up there he'd place himself. He'd have a clear view of the launch as it approached the mooring dock. He knew the shooter could be higher or more distant, but Max had missed once. Gabriel knew that this time he'd want to be close. He ran to the rocks and climbed.

The summit had been weathered into a small arena. A space for a pagan ritual, a sacrifice. Max was looking over the lip down on to the lake. In his arms he cradled a Mauser rifle with telescopic sights. He turned to greet Gabriel.

'Come to watch the show?' he asked.

'Put the rifle down, Max.' Gabriel covered him with his sidearm, a Luger.

Max seemed unconcerned by Gabriel's sudden appearance, or the pistol pointed at him. 'Come on, you want him dead too. Was it you who took the second shot?'

Gabriel kept still; the Luger unwavering. 'It's over, Max.'

The smile left Max's face. 'We can still do it. We can still win this war. Without that clown and his Fred Karno army with their custard pie tactics, we can do it. Split the Allies and deal with them one at a time. First the Ivans, and then we can do what God failed to do last time – punish the English.'

A bush of dead and dried beech leaves applauded in a breeze.

'Lower the rifle…'

'No, Scar,' the voice came behind Gabriel, 'you put your weapon down.'

Gabriel looked over his shoulder as Emil Maurice slid out from behind a boulder. He was pointing his own Luger at Gabriel's back.

Gabriel said, 'Were you the Old Hare who approached the pastor in Munich?'

'He made me,' he indicated Max.

Gabriel turned to him. 'How?'

Max seemed the most comfortable of them, sprawled on the grass, propped up by the rocks. 'Blackmail. I told you, when I was a young detective I questioned Maurice about the death of Hitler's niece – well, this piece of shit confessed to me that he'd put a bullet into little Geli Raubal. Got a signed confession, I did. So why wasn't he arrested? The times. Hitler was discovering he could get his flying monkeys to commit murder with impunity. That confession wasn't worth the paper it was written on. But I kept it, put it somewhere safe, so if the war ends with defeat and law and order return, Emil here will finally stand trial for the murder of that little girl.'

Maurice bleated, 'It wasn't murder. I put her out of her misery. Wolf had made a mess of her. He made me do it. My punishment, to kill the thing I love to serve him.'

Gabriel spoke, 'Why send Maurice to make contact with the British? Why not go yourself?'

'He was a good cut-off – if things went tits up and the pastor proved patriotic and brought in the Gestapo. I'd have used him to pull the trigger as well but you know how it is, Gabriel: few men are born to be snipers; most suffer from the shaking hand. Maurice is a shaker, only up for murdering girls.'

The sound of the brass horn came again from down on the lake. This time much closer.

'Here he comes,' said Max and he rolled back onto his front and raised the rifle.

'There's something you should know.'

'Not now, Gabriel,' Max said.

'About the sight. The sight that's been ground to allow for the damage in your retina. The telescopic sight sent by your friends in London. The sight made by an optician in the West London suburb of Ealing. We know everything.'

Max was still; Gabriel knew he was listening. 'You think you have a sight tailored to your needs but that isn't so. The package was intercepted. The thing on your rifle has a run-of-the-mill lens. Look down it and squeeze the trigger and your shot will go wide. Believe me.'

Max turned to him, his face hot and angry. 'You're lying.'

'Maybe he's not,' said Maurice.

'I'm trying to save your life, Max. I don't want you strung up on a piano wire. Take that shot and miss and they will murder you.' He half turned to Maurice, 'And skin you alive.'

'Shit,' said the Old Hare.

'If it helps, I can even tell you who the sight went to in Sweden. Who brought it to you on Obersalzberg.'

'Go on, tell me,' said Max.

Gabriel did. Max turned from the lake and stared at the rifle in his arms. Gabriel felt Emil Maurice twitching behind him. 'We can't risk it, Max.'

Max made a decision. 'We can. You've been too clever, Gabriel. Now I know I can adjust the sight to allow for my cast.'

He pulled out his Luftwaffe dagger and used the point to adjust the screws on the sight.

'Bit rough and ready,' said Gabriel over his shoulder.

'Don't risk it, Max!'

'Quiet.'

Max finished adjusting the screw and threw the dagger point down into a tree stump. He turned and lay on his front, boots crossed at the heels. He breathed out slowly and sighted the Mauser.

'Wish me luck,' he muttered and squeezed the trigger.

The sound of the shot was lost in another mournful bleat from the launch.

'Well?' Maurice asked in a whisper.

'Missed,' said Max.

'Shit.' The Old Hare turned and ran from the small arena.

'I don't understand,' said Max.

As Maurice crashed away down the hill, Gabriel moved forward and pulled Max's dagger from the stump. The band began *Das Lied der Deutschen*. Below, all stood straighter. By the time they reached the second bar, Max was dead. Gabriel was removing the blade from below his friend's ear. For the first time ever, Max did not stand for the German National Anthem. Gabriel came to attention over him.

'Shouldn't have trusted me, Max. The sight was true.'

He looked down onto the lake. The launch was approaching the small stump of a pier and preparing to dock. On the prow, the Führer was raising his right arm in the Party salute but with that peculiar modification of his own; his hand was turned flat, fingers back, palm to the sky, as if trying to hold the clouds up. Behind him, a young Japanese naval officer was raising an umbrella over Ambassador Oshima. The flakes were like blossom falling on the lake, but it was snow.

CHAPTER FIFTY-FOUR

Von Below and Albert Bormann stood over the body of Max as if pondering a use for it.

'We mustn't let this spoil the day,' said Bormann. 'We'll inform Wolf later.'

Carry on as normal: the mantra of war, Gabriel thought. He looked down below to where the Krampuslauf was about to begin. The women in white flocked together and bleated like sheep before a dip. The men in their devil masks were selecting silver sticks from the bunches offered to them by the widows and mature ladies. The devils swished their rods and the women dutifully wailed in delighted anticipation. Hitler smiled and bobbed and warmed his hands together as if they itched for a goad. By his side, Ambassador Oshima, in his tails and top hat, seemed almost a snowman of soot. Gabriel saw that his aide, the naval lieutenant, was wearing a Mamahage mask, an oriental devil as ally to his Western cousins. Suddenly, the aide turned and looked up at Gabriel, seemingly looking straight into his eyes, the demon reading him, Gabriel wondering why he was filled with a foretaste of dread. Then, with a whoop, the women were away, like flapping sheets caught up in a hurricane. They blitzed the settled snow with their hems and caused small tornadoes in their wake. The men, like dogs of war, were hot to be unleashed. But then Gabriel's spying was interrupted.

Admiral Puttkamer arrived, brought by the Old Hare August Korber. His comrade in arms, Bodo Gelzenleuchter, guarded the track. Below, the band played on. Bormann took the admiral to view Max. Having glanced and grunted, the admiral came over.

'That swine damn near pulled it off. But for Hauptsturmführer Zobel...'

'Yes, he'll get a gong later,' said Von Below.

Another piece of tin, thought Gabriel – it seemed a poor exchange for Max.

Gabriel hadn't told them of Emil Maurice's role in the attempted assassination; he knew Gabriel was working for London, and as Gabriel hadn't had the chance of silencing him permanently, it was better he showed a clean pair of heels. He was probably running for the Swiss border. Later it would be assumed he was just another cowardly deserter.

Gabriel returned alone to Obersalzberg in his Kübelwagen. He parked and made his way through the trees towards his mess. He wanted to sleep for a week. He wanted to remove Max from his head. He found himself asking the question people all over Europe and the wider world were asking: how much longer would the war take to bleed out?

Automatically, he glanced at the ruined theatre. He came to a halt. Lorelei's curtains were closed. Gabriel suddenly fired up into rage. Instead of going back to Berchtesgaden with the milkman, she'd slipped back into her old apartment. Angrily, he made his way to her.

He invaded her apartment without knocking and found Lorelei standing in her lounge in her underwear. It was the sort of underwear he knew she called *laundry*. She also had underthings she named lingerie – small clothes of satins and silks, meant to be seen before being removed. The laundry she stood in was cotton and white and comfortable, somehow more private.

'Gabriel,' she said.

For an eternity there didn't seem much more to say: the silent man in the winter uniform of the Imperial Nipponese Navy seemed to dry the air of conversation.

'Gabriel,' Lorelei began again, 'this is Lieutenant Toshikyo Amori – my husband.'

Gabriel had taken rounds to the body before, and just like the times he'd been shot, he wanted to drop, to curl on the floor and slip into never-ending sleep.

Lorelei's husband gave a sharp, shallow bow, and Gabriel's heels, seemingly with a mind of their own, automatically clicked together in response. He saw that the man was the ambassador's aide from the launch; the umbrella holder. They stared at each other.

'Well,' said Lorelei, 'I seem to be doing the marriage thing again. I'll obey convention and finish undressing in private.'

She scooped up the discarded clothes at her feet and took them with her into the bedroom. As she went, her words *doing the marriage thing again* took control of Gabriel. The door closed behind her and he realised he was to be shut out forever. Whatever access he'd enjoyed to her nakedness, to her touch, to her love, was over. The Japanese naval attaché could saunter past him and enter Lorelei's sanctum because he, and not Gabriel, was her husband, and Lorelei was doing the marriage thing again.

'The ambassador admires the assistance you gave Mr Hitler.'

Gabriel met Toshikyo's eyes. Could they talk? Shouldn't they be brawling? The lieutenant's impeccable manners and courtesy seemed to make violence an impossibility, and anyway, he was the cuckold, Gabriel the lover. Yet he had been deceived, and therefore it was Gabriel who felt aggrieved. His stomach nursed acid and he wanted to start an argument that could climax in a fight.

'And yet,' Gabriel said, 'until September we were attempting to *kill* Mr Hitler. Something I assume your ambassador approved of then?'

Toshikyo nodded his agreement and slid past Gabriel to inspect his wife's cabaret art on the walls. He shook his head occasionally in disapproval. But there was a softness in his censure that seemed to come from a long knowledge of his wife and her tastes, that came from a history of intimacy. There was a tenderness in it. Gabriel felt his heart would rupture. Toshikyo spoke.

'Japanese policy is fluid. Strategy is a floating world. We have two parties with opposing views on how to prosecute the war. Before the conflict, the land party was for declaring war on Russia and wresting Siberia from her, as we had unsuccessfully attempted in 1939. Whereas the sea party was for going south, across the Pacific, and creating an empire by displacing the effete and defeated European imperialists. Of course, this latter option meant war with the United States, and that unfortunately was the path chosen. It soon became apparent that America was not going to conduct a limited war of the sort we had traditionally waged with Russia. The United States was fighting an unlimited total war. Japan realised it needed to extricate itself and the belief grew that the death of the Führer would allow us to make the same deal that the German generals hoped to do; an armistice without occupation.'

Gabriel needed Lorelei, needed her presence, needed her out of her bloody bedroom and answering his questions about them, not the war. But because he couldn't discuss *them* with her husband, he goaded him.

'Kill Hitler, don't kill Hitler. Do you have any idea what it's like to serve behind the lines? Living on your nerves while your masters can't make up their minds how to get you killed?'

The naval lieutenant nodded. 'I have done this sort of work. I understand. We are powerless; Bunraku puppets moved by men in black. The land party disagreed with the sea party and their analysis of the situation. They feared that if Mr Hitler died, we would not be able to make the same deal with the Allies as the German generals. That the United States would still want revenge for its humiliation at Pearl Harbor, and similarly the European imperialists. Plus, the West would need to win a war somewhere for reasons of prestige; they would need to intimidate Soviet Russia. This became the prevailing thought and, upon it becoming policy, it was decided we dare not risk the death of Mr Hitler.'

Lorelei entered from her bedroom, not fully dressed but in a sheer silk slip that wasn't laundry. Her husband said something to her in Japanese that Gabriel thought was an admonishment for her undressed status.

'I know, I'm sorry,' she said, 'I can't concentrate. I need to talk to him. I need to explain to Gabriel. We owe him that, don't we?'

Toshikyo thought about this and then, without a gesture or a bow, turned and went wordlessly into the ruined theatre. Lorelei watched him go, then turned to Gabriel.

'I'm sorry.'

Gabriel felt he was a bottleneck, with too many emotions and not enough words to break through. 'Lorelei…' was all that came out.

'I tried not to hurt you, believe me I tried. That was the last thing I wanted.'

Gabriel stared at her as she became someone else in front of him. 'Everything was a lie.'

She shook her head sharply, almost looking annoyed. 'The only lie was the stuff you made up in your head. Words I never said. Things I didn't promise. A future I never referred to.'

A word of his father's came into his head. 'You behaved like a whore.'

She sighed, a sound echoed by her silk stockings as she turned from him, as if all of her were sad. 'Gabriel, your values aren't mine. I tried to tell you; the Dakini on the temple steps, the courtesan of the imperial court, the geisha in old Edo, these are me.'

His father controlled his tongue. It was his voice in Gabriel's head. 'Oriental decadence.'

She huffed and laughed simultaneously. 'Really? And what about those SOE girls from good homes who, when parachuted behind enemy lines, don't hesitate to give their bodies to the enemy to prise out his secrets? They know what duty is.'

'Was I your duty?'

She accepted the challenge of his question. 'Yes. If you want the truth, yes. Japan is my country and I will serve the Chrysanthemum Throne in any way I can, with whatever I have. Men like you shed blood to win honour; women like me shed honour to save blood.'

He wanted to hurt her. 'You've had me in your mouth, the mouth you'll kiss your husband with. There's no honour in that.'

He had succeeded; she was hurt, wounded. She moved from him with the face of a misunderstood child. 'Toshikyo said you wouldn't understand. You're a European.'

She turned back to him. 'I want you to understand,' she said. 'I want your – good opinion. When I was offered this mission, to leave my husband and everything I loved and go to

Europe to infiltrate British intelligence, I went with a heavy heart. I knew I would have to put aside things that are precious to a woman. But I was helped by knowing that whatever I did in pursuit of my mission would win honour not just for me, but for my husband and his family. Admittance to the Black Dragon Society comes at a price for a woman; traditionally, its female members were prostitutes who won back their names with sacrifice.'

Gabriel looked about him, around the apartment, at the cabaret performers in the art, and they all seemed to be laughing at him. 'Did I ever mean anything to you?'

Another sigh, another rustle. 'Let's say loving you wasn't a chore. But I'm married. Sorry, soldier.'

And she reached to stroke his scar, but he turned his head.

She tried to open him with her eyes, but his were impregnable with hurt. She turned to leave.

'Where are you going?'

'I think we're finished and I need to dress.'

'You can't just walk out of here. You're a wanted woman.'

She'd opened the door to her bedroom and stood in it, like a picture in a frame.

'That's being dealt with. The ambassador is presenting me to the Führer as a Japanese intelligence asset, someone who was secretly working to save his life. Toshikyo is going to ask you to verify that, by the way. The story is that I approached you at the Krampuslauf and warned you that Max Adler was a sniper who was about to try to end Hitler's life. I'm to be presented as a double agent.'

Gabriel turned to her, wanting to hear the answer he knew she wouldn't give.

'And then, when you're off the hook? What about us?'

'No,' she said, a small word that killed his hope. 'I shall be making the long journey home.'

'Japan?'
'Home.'

CHAPTER FIFTY-FIVE

It was Gabriel's turn to wait in the ruined theatre while Lorelei briefed her husband, telling him of Gabriel's reduced status in her life. Giving Toshikyo what she wouldn't give him. He stared at the wrecked auditorium, those places where the collapsed roof met and rested on chairs that had once been velvet. The destroyed grandiosity of the building. The great plans, the exciting seasons brought to nothing by snow. By relentless snow. Snow as weightless as air, falling and falling until the roof broke and the dreams collapsed.

Gabriel could hear Lorelei's voice clearly, but it wasn't the German girl he had known. This Lorelei was Japanese. Her fluency in that language pushed him away as if it were clenched fists in his chest. Then there was silence. An obscene image came to his mind of them in the bedroom, re-cementing their marriage carnally. Unable to help himself, he went back into the apartment. They hadn't gone anywhere. They were standing and staring at each other. Not speaking. Looking into each other's eyes, Gabriel invisible to them. He had seldom felt more ceremonial. He had stood by the Pope, in feathers and helmet, but as invisible to the Holy Father as he was now to Lorelei.

She had finished dressing and Gabriel had never seen her look lovelier. She was wearing a dress that she had once told him was cut on the cross to show off her tiny waist. On her head was a pillbox hat, at a crazy angle, and rescued from levity by a fringe of severe black net.

Outside, a car horn sounded. They came to at the summons and left Gabriel without a word, as if he no longer existed. He followed them out to the road where the ambassador's car waited. It felt like a funeral.

Inside the Berghof, Gabriel and Toshikyo were divested of their sidearms, and the lieutenant also handed over his sword. As was the practice, Gabriel was allowed to keep his ceremonial dagger, and the Japanese officer his short *tanto* blade.

The Great Hall of the Berghof was full. Hitler had been taken back there after the Krampuslauf and it was here that his three adjutants had told him of the foiled attempt on his life. It was as if the Führer was a magnet. At this time of treachery, those close to him and wanting to show their loyalty came and stood by him. All the uniforms were there: the Party, the SS, the Wehrmacht, the navy and the Luftwaffe. Even Traudi had put aside her widow's weeds, so the trio of his young secretaries were in their identical charcoal skirts and white, boiled blouses, and looking as if they were in uniform.

Everyone waited while he stewed the information: Major Adler, a would-be assassin, dead. Emil Maurice, the Old Hare, missing, and the body of Matron Irmgard Gunther found. All, like the audience at a concert, were waiting for the first opening bars of rage. Into this set-piece, the Japanese party entered, trailing Gabriel like a supernumerary.

Ambassador Oshima conferred quietly with Martin Bormann, before Bormann brought him to the Führer. Hitler had his back to the room, staring from his window at the mountains sliding into shadow as the afternoon packed up shop.

He was obliged to turn and acknowledge the ambassador, before turning back to the window, listening while his eyes watched the avalanche of darkness rolling silently and inexorably towards him.

Men became aware of Lorelei, the British spy, standing without shame or fear, seemingly one of the Japanese party. And they waited, wondering if they would be called upon to arrest her, and stretch her pretty neck, and look up her skirt as she danced on the end of a piano wire. However, the ambassador started by explaining Lorelei's role in the affair. He revealed that it was she, in the guise of a double agent, who had uncovered the identity of MI6's assassin. Lorelei who had communicated this vital information to the commanding officer of the Leibstandarte, Hauptsturmführer Zobel, that Major Adler was about to attempt to kill the Führer. Her information had been acted upon and the traitor dealt with. Gabriel, when it was his turn to play his small part, confirmed this.

Hitler nodded and thought and stared into the black mirror of the window as night stared back. Somewhere on the edge of his vision, Gabriel saw Martin Bormann gesture, and lights suddenly started to illuminate the giant room. They came on line by line, advancing and pushing back the darkness. Hitler turned and stepped away from the blind window and his secretaries moved in smartly to draw the heavy curtains.

The Führer regarded Gabriel. 'That fat hospital woman who was found dead?'

'I just dealt with Major Adler, sir.'

Von Below, the adjutant, spoke, 'We think her death is unconnected to the plot. She seems to have eaten a poisonous toadstool.'

The Führer tutted his annoyance. 'She was a glutton, that was obvious. Probably a Prussian – they don't know their mushrooms from their toadstools.'

A general nodding followed this pronouncement, but his eyes were back on Gabriel. 'Emil Maurice is missing?'

'After I'd dealt with the traitor, I went to find the three Old Hares on duty at the Krampuslauf. August Korber and Bodo Gelzenleuchter were in place, but Maurice had vanished.'

Hitler sighed. 'He was with me from the beginning. Set in motion a search for him.'

Von Below spoke again. 'We've already instigated one. He'll be apprehended.'

Gabriel doubted that. Maurice would have his escape route planned, would have MI6 agents to hold his hand and get him to Spain or Switzerland. Emil Maurice would disappear from history.

The fury never came. The Führer had escaped death again and this fed into his sense of destiny. The Japanese ambassador took the opportunity to cement Lorelei's innocence.

'Lieutenant Amori's wife wishes to apologise for any and all deceitful actions she was forced to conduct in regard to the Führer's safety.'

Upon her cue, Lorelei stepped forward and, in a graceful movement, spread herself on the floor before Hitler. An oriental act of contrition. Gabriel could see that the seam of the black stocking on her left leg was crooked and he felt an almost overwhelming urge to straighten it, to stroke those shadow legs of spider silk. He was aware of the Führer speaking, forgiving her, his uncle voice charming her and the room. He urged Lorelei to stand and, as she did, one of her high heels was nearly her undoing. Gabriel saw her stumble and her ridiculous hat slip onto her cheek. He watched as she reached, seemingly to secure it, but instead reached under its brim and produced a small Walther PPK pistol.

Volfgangu's pistol, Gabriel thought, as it also occurred to him that the floating world of Japanese policy had tilted again and, once again, Hitler had to die. Lorelei was going to sacrifice her life. She hadn't meant Japan when she said she'd be going home. He saw the short barrel of the Walther coming up towards the Führer. Gabriel knew the men in the room would butcher her if she took the shot. He stepped forward between Lorelei and her target, knowing she'd never harm him.

Gabriel saw her look – the irritation at his action – and then she shot him twice in the chest to clear her way to Hitler. But he had bought that second of time needed for the other men, who also threw themselves between Lorelei and her target. He saw her look of hopelessness, as they formed a wall and began to draw their daggers. Her husband caught her from behind, and she seemed to bow her head in supplication, her long, beautiful neck exposed. *Let me introduce you to the back of my neck.* Toshikyo Amori, using his short *tanto* sword, with one stroke virtually severed her head.

Gabriel lay on the floor, watching her blood creep towards his, and he knew this mingling was another lie, Lorelei's last. Then it felt to him as if they were switching off the lights again. Darkness covered Gabriel in a soft blanket of night.

CHAPTER FIFTY-SIX

The snow had made the cemetery featureless, and an unmarked grave the norm. The unshriven ground of suicides' corner was further drained of outline by the rule that there be flat tombstones only; the angels and crosses reserved for the respectable dead. Nicky, freshly planted, had not settled yet. A small hillock under the snow, a fold on the earth Jago had been directed to. It was as if Nicky had one last breath to expel before he could be compressed into eternity. He'd taken the *honourable way out* but Nicky's father still hadn't made a shelf available in the family crypt. Possibly, Jago thought bitterly, that space at the Godwin necropolis was at a premium and none could be found for a useless mouth.

Austen, too, had gone alone into eternity. He'd been buried without ceremony in an unmarked grave behind the walls of Wormwood Scrubs Prison. As a murderer and suicide, his body had not been released to his family. Lavender had grieved where she could; in all the familiar places their lives had touched together. She had survived the loneliness of being an orphan because she had the love of one other person. On a visit to Jago, the pragmatic Mrs Cambridge had declared that the lost brother must be replaced by a new man. War had stripped

Lavender naked and left her like a raw nerve. A bandage had to be found. Jago knew that Austen's name would never find its way onto a war memorial. No poppy would be worn to honour his sacrifice, but he knew that Austen had kept Churchill's maxim: *Take one with you.* Billy Grogan, the British fascist, was dead.

A tree on the edge of the cemetery shuddered in the cold and shed frost like silver leaves. Jago came back to where he was. He stood and looked down at the snow and the snow wasn't Nicky. The situation failed to work. He grieved every day, woke up to grief and lived through it every minute, but near to Nicky, near his last resting place, Jago felt nothing. The bleak acres, bereft of mature trees and bleached of detail, defied any spirituality. It was a place to challenge the faith of a pope, a car park of the dead. The place just knew there was no hereafter. It was a municipal dead end.

Nicky was gone, just as Jago's footprints in the snow would be gone in a thaw. If Nicky was anywhere, he was in Jago's head – the memories he would hoard like a miser, the time they'd shared growing smaller in proportion to the time Jago would exist without him. An oasis of brief happiness in the desert of what was to come. A love affair at a time the world went mad. Nicky had been Jago's first love and Jago had decided he would also be his last love. Love was a jealous god, only for those who gave without reserve, without other priorities, who didn't try to segregate their emotions into separate locked cells.

Love, he knew, demanded the truth, even at the expense of status, ambition, and even anonymity. To be openly himself, even if it made him available for love, would mean he would become known for what he was and not what he might do. He would become the property of lesser men, the butt of their jokes. It was not possible for him to say out loud what he was;

he knew he therefore lacked the moral fibre for love. He could not do his bit. He must stay on the lonely airfield by himself.

Jago consoled himself; he knew he had gifts and that, as he was a good man, they might benefit society. His industry would enrich mankind rather than loot it. Therefore it was almost a public duty for him to serve this silence. He could not ask of himself that which he'd plotted for Germany. He couldn't be ground into dust, destroyed, just for the opportunity to begin again. His ambition ticked too strong and loud in his head. Besides, he was to be given another chance and he hadn't the sort of courage needed to waste it.

Jago felt he should go and not come back. Nicky was dead and, in his way, so was Jago. But he found he couldn't move, not yet, not this way. He stood and his mind meandered. It was a bitter time in Europe. SOE's intelligence of Hitler's planned assault in the west had gone unheeded. The Armageddon that followed was being called the Battle of the Bulge. The Americans had triumphed eventually but suffered terribly in the process. Jago knew that if the Yanks ever had knowledge that the British had had warnings of the attack and failed to pass that on to their allies, then, the man from MI6 said, the fat would be in the fire.

After Austen's sacrifice, Jago had been taken into custody and locked up. Mrs Cambridge and the grieving Lavender had been released under the excuse that they were only obeying orders. Uncharged, Jago was kept caged while the police waited to find out what the secret world wanted them to do to him. Hitler's winter mayhem changed everything.

Jago's silence had been bought. The Link had vanished with the American victory and the crossing of the Rhine. Now the result was inevitable, nobody was Germany's friend. Everyone was seeking the final reduction of her forces and the destruction of her society with bomb, shell and bullet. German civilisation was being razed into rubble, its daughters raped into submission, its fathers humiliated into an undead that could no longer protest or protect their families, and still the bombs fell. But Jago, who had helped make this possible, was not being dragged down into hell but offered a new job.

When the dust finally choked the last German in Berlin, Jago would be plucked from the Forgetting School. Clive Roberts, the man from MI6 and the Perish Judea crew at Chichester Cathedral, had come to him, and, for his silence over the Battle of the Bulge, had promised him an opening in the Diplomatic Corps. Jago was going to be a diplomat, something both he and Aunt Esme had dreamed of for him.

He came back to himself in the cemetery, feeling guilty at his wandering mind. A low moan of wind pushed a line of soft flakes across the surface of the compacted snow, like the slow advance across a continent of an invading army. *Blessed are the peacemakers*, Aunt Esme had always added to any conversation on the Diplomatic Corps. He was to sit a board exam but he'd been assured the result was a foregone conclusion.

He cursed himself: his mind was like a balloon floating away, when he had come to say goodbye to Nicky. He knew the problem was that he couldn't face the pain of his grief; that letting Nicky out of the grave would tear Jago apart. That last terrible time in the police cell had been Grogan's final curse. He had come to apologise, to say sorry he didn't damn the world and proclaim his love for Nicky. Nicky had died alone in more than one way and Jago took that on himself. He considered crying and falling full length in the snow, hugging the earth that was Nicky's blanket, but he couldn't. Trapped by the rules, even alone. He considered telling Nicky he loved him, but it was too late and the crows would laugh at him. He was alone on a square mile of snow.

The man came to him across the cemetery, inexpert in the

slush, skidding and swearing. He came not to visit the dead but the only other living person. His dark overcoat had an Astrakhan collar which would have suited it if his head covering had been a Cossack hat of the same material. Instead his head was encased in a woolly balaclava that made his plump face resemble a schoolboy's. His breath left his mouth as smoke that seemed to signal his dangerous intent.

The Don from the Isokon Building arrived beside Jago, removed a glove and offered a hand for shaking which, when ignored, was re-encased.

'Can't you leave me alone?' said Jago.

'You're a hard man to speak to these days.'

Jago didn't want any company, least of all his.

'You're to be offered a government job,' said the Don.

'None of your business.'

'Excellent,' he said, as if Jago had agreed with him.

Jago knew he should walk away, cross the white desert and go back to Lavender's. 'Why excellent?' he asked instead.

The Don opened his gloved hands wide. 'Because you can continue your work for us after the war.'

'Fuck off,' said quietly, said as low as the sound of falling snow. Said with a tiredness that ate at Jago's bones.

The Don manoeuvred himself next to Jago and looked down, as if they were jointly mourning Nicky. 'Nothing's changed,' he said, 'just because this one took the coward's way out. Let's face it; you're still a sodomite. A word in the wrong ear and you can kiss the Diplomatic Corps goodbye. You'll be out on your arse. Do you have any choice? I said the same to Lavender the day her brother tried to fly.'

'What?'

'I mean the silly girl thought that little house of hers was – well, really hers. I told her the Party needed it.'

Jago remembered her anger, her harshness to Austen.

'You needed it, you mean. Having to give up the flat in Hampstead, are you?'

The Don grunted angrily. 'The damn man is coming back from the States now the war is all but over. Wants his place back he says. I told Lavender, but she wasn't sympathetic. I explained to her property is theft and so, while Nicky might have given it to her, it belonged to the Party. My word, she was stubborn; give a woman a house and her vision diminishes. She sees no further than new curtains. I had to be quite blunt with her: she either had to make over the house to me, or I'd make sure her neighbours knew her brother had been kicked out of the navy as an effeminate.'

Jago understood. She thought she'd lost the house. 'But now her brother's dead?' he said.

'The little cow isn't budging.'

'Nicky wouldn't have let you get away with it.'

'Yes, well he's brown bread, isn't he? And the dead don't get a vote. Now you'll do as I say. You'll work hard as a diplomat, climb the sticky pole to positions of responsibility. But all the time you'll be our creature. I mean you don't have any choice, do you?'

CHAPTER FIFTY-SEVEN

Christine made small molehills with the snow, a whole row of them. Sometimes she would take a step back to check the line was straight. Occasionally she talked to her mother, who wasn't there, and occasionally to Veronica, who was. Jago was ignored. He stood in the lea of the shed, seeking what shelter he could from the bleak day. Veronica shivered by his side and whined with the wind.

'I've tried getting her help, but all they offer is an asylum. If she goes into one of them they'll never let her out, they never do.'

'But she's having a breakdown?'

Veronica glared angrily at a point beyond the allotment – the wide world.

'Nerves. The doctors call it nerves, and mention in passing that, when they're trying to help men who've had their limbs blown off, or chaps who have had their skin fried to a sizzle, a woman suffering from her nerves is less than important.'

Christine padded past them without a word, and went into the shed. She reappeared immediately with a handful of canes. She hummed to herself as she went back to her line of snow hills and planted a pole in each of them, moving slowly and purposefully, doing the pointless task with precision.

'I'm not going to apologise,' said Veronica suddenly.

'No,' he said.

'Then why are you here?'

How to explain, he wondered. 'The last good time I had with Christine, a young dancer gave us both a slice of his orange.'

A low wind moaned; it might have been Veronica wanting him to get on. So Jago did, he took the plunge. 'I'm giving you the house, both of you.'

Veronica looked at him. 'Both of us? Not just Christine? Giving it to us? Why?'

He shrugged inside his greatcoat. The movement barely made it to the surface. 'I want you to have some freedom, Veronica. Some life without gratitude. I don't think you should be owned again the way your guardian owned you, when we were children.'

'It's your inheritance?'

'That's exactly what it is. Payment received for a rotten childhood. I clutched at it the way my mother held onto her school, and not me.'

Veronica spoke the catechism automatically. 'It's not easy for a woman on her own.'

Jago sighed and then spoke angrily. 'I know that, Veronica. Anyone spending half an hour in your company would know that.'

His voice had risen more than he intended and Christine had turned towards them. She started a soft wail of alarm, like a siren warming up.

'It's alright, darling, we're just talking. Go back to your gardening.'

They watched her as she watched them, but finally, as there

was no more shouting, she turned back to her poles and began to tie the tops with ribbons she produced from her overcoat pocket.

'The whole house is too much. Why not keep the basement flat? You can have it rebuilt after the war.'

He shook his head. 'I'm one of those people who can't own things. It brings out a side of me I don't like.'

She acknowledged this with a mute nod. 'Thanks – I'm not sure I deserve it.'

'Who gets what they deserve? Men die because they're in the wrong place at the wrong time, not because of some divine judgement. Everything is arbitrary. You need it and I want rid of it.'

Christine headed towards the shed again.

'I need to ask her something,' he said.

Veronica gently halted Christine as she opened the shed door and let out a faint smell of creosote.

'Darling,' Veronica said.

Jago echoed her soft tone. 'Christine…'

She looked between them both with the innocent eyes of a child. 'Time for tea,' she explained.

'Christine, did something come for me? Was a letter or package delivered to me in Pimlico that you – put to one side?'

The childlike face clouded over and closed down.

'Tell him, darling. He's giving us the house, so if you have something of Jago's, it's only fair to give it to him.'

Christine suddenly opened her eyes alarmingly wide and said to Jago, 'Naughty.'

'I've been naughty?' he probed.

'An Irishman rang the doorbell. We don't like the Irish.'

She meant her parents.

'He asked for you; Captain Jago Craze. He seemed very shifty. He became very nervous when I said you weren't in, and so he gave me the envelope. He almost ran off down the street and that made me suspicious.'

'What did you do with Jago's letter, darling?'

'I opened it, Veronica. It was delivered by hand, and you're always saying that official things get given to the man, when it's the wife's business as well.'

'What was it?' Jago asked.

Christine actually wagged a finger at him as she said, 'Bad boy. It was in German and Jago had no business getting things in German.'

He tried to catch her eyes with his but they slid away.

'Did you give it to the friends of your parents?'

She shook her head and pursed her lips. 'They thought you had it. They were cross. But I decided not to give it to them because I knew if they had it, they might not bother doing away with you. I did so want to be a widow. It's heroic to be a war widow, and it even comes with a small pension.'

Jago felt colder on the inside than out in the snow. 'Where is it?' he asked.

'Tell him, darling.'

Christine went past them into the shed and they followed. It had been her late father's domain. There was one armchair facing a bell-stove with a pipe that went up and through the roof. An old scullery table down one side balanced a kitchen dresser on the other. Across the walls were framed photos of cricket teams that had creeping stains on the mounts, where damp was insidiously invading.

Christine took one of these team photos down and turned it around. Stuck to the back was a large buff envelope. Jago removed it with difficulty.

'I used flour paste,' she said proudly.

He struggled to unstick it. Christine had perfected her paste over years in the classroom. Jago reflected ruefully that she could have stuck the wings back on a Lancaster bomber with the stuff. He ripped the envelope free, leaving half of it still attached to the back of the frame. He opened what was left and slid out the papers. He saw the German script, he saw the crests and stamps, the eagles and the swastika. It was the generals' plan for how they would prosecute the war after they'd killed the Führer – now as useful as an appeaser on the first day of war.

'What will you do with it?' asked Veronica. She meant would handing it over bring trouble down on Christine's head.

Jago went outside and burnt the Walpurgisnacht Plan in the incinerator used as the final solution for bindweed. The papers twisted in the flames and turned from white into shadows of themselves. They broke apart and became ash. The brief bonfire over, Christine and Veronica left the pyre to return to the shed for tea. Jago wasn't invited but he didn't mind. He had an interview to prepare for.

The board exam had gone well. They'd even volunteered that Jago was the cut of the men they were seeking for post-conflict diplomacy. The world, they said, must learn to trust to talk again. The talking cure. Jago could have been happy, had he not known he had snow on his boots. He was still living a lie.

Jago had told them his marriage was coming to an end, but this had caused no shocks.

'Lot of it about,' one of them said. 'A wartime mistake?'

'Yes,' said Jago, 'a mistake.'

'But no scandal?'

'No.'

They ended with a routine question from the chairman. 'Is there any reason – anything in your personal history – that might prevent you carrying out your duties as a diplomat to the best of your abilities? Anything we should know about?'

Members were already starting to fold things away and gather up papers. Jago sat facing the line of them. One more lie. Jago opened his mouth but no words came out, no assurance. Instead a sound grew in Jago's head. The sound of a small monoplane filled him. The Lysander swooped and landed between him and the men packing away. It hovered and quivered in front of him, dripping oil and shaking. The impossible plane. He was a rational man and he knew it couldn't fly. Knew it would break up and plunge from the clouds. But the cockpit was open and a figure was beckoning Jago – not the FANY, but Nicky. Nicky had come for him. Nicky was smiling and saying *Come on old man, you can do it.* Jago took a step towards the unfeasible contraption. He protested to himself that it wasn't possible, it wasn't fair, too much was being asked of him. But in his mind he took another step. Nicky, with his impossibly blue eyes, as blue as the sky behind him, was smiling and saying *Bravo, Jago, learn to fly*. And Jago's mouth was working.

'There is one thing,' he said, 'One scandal...'

The packing up ceased; he had all their eyes now.

'The reason my marriage ended – well for a start it was never consummated, and that's because I'm a homosexual. Yes, that's it I suppose, I'm a homosexual. I always have been and I always will be. A homosexual, yes.'

CHAPTER FIFTY-EIGHT

Gabriel had semi-conscious memories of nurses singing carols. Little choirs of them, like angels, singing 'Silent Night' at the end of his bed. They had their cloaks reversed, displaying the more seasonal red of the lining. Then Christmas was over and Gabriel returned to the land of shadows and uneasy dreams.

As, gradually, the hospital became real once more around him, he learned that Operation Watch on the Rhine had failed, and the Allies were calling it the Battle of the Bulge. The ward around him was crammed with casualties, the nurses no longer sang and the nights were no longer silent. Sudden screams, groans and desperate prayers were now the midnight music.

Gabriel, incapable of movement, lay there and listened as the wounded talked. They had nearly pulled it off, nearly driven a line between the Yanks and the British, nearly reached Antwerp and the North Sea. Nearly, but not quite. An American parachute brigade had dug in and fought like demons in the woods at Bastogne. They had halted the advance long enough for the fogs to clear and the tank-busting fighters of the Allies to return to the skies. A massacre had followed. Then the fuel promised by the Führer dried up and the adventure was over, all bar the pain of the wounded and the grief of the widows.

As he lay and listened, Gabriel felt confusion. The British knew of this attack through the Ardennes, so why were the Americans unprepared? Why hadn't the Foxley intelligence been acted on? He lay there in confusion and grief. And as he listened to the misery of the wounded around him, he was weighed down by a heavy blanket of guilt. He felt the shame of wearing a false uniform among men who knew their duty.

He'd close his eyes but Lorelei was waiting for him on the other side of his lids. Her eyes looking into his, honestly, openly, lovingly, but all the time using him. Stroking his scar and calling him *soldier*. Perhaps, he thought, the only time she'd looked at him truthfully was the moment before she shot him.

The nurses gossiped to him, even when he was too weak to respond. It was medicine of course, part of the treatment to bring him back to the land of the living. He was told how the Japanese ambassador and her husband had distanced themselves from Lorelei's action. How they had prostrated themselves at the Führer's feet and apologised. Hitler had accepted their contrition, and the gift of the short sword that Toshikyo had used to nearly sever his wife's head. Hitler apparently kept the blade on his desk. Everyone now knew she'd been a rogue agent, someone who had reverted to her mother's race and become British.

Then, as he swam slowly towards the surface of life again, up to where the light was, he had a visitor. Toshikyo Amori came and stood by his bed in his dark naval uniform, bowed his head sharply and then stared into the distance. Gabriel was at a loss. His head was clearer than it had been for a month – he knew this apparition was no dream – but what the man wanted, and why he stood by the bed silently, Gabriel had no idea.

Toshikyo made a small grunt, as if he'd made a decision, or had arranged the jumble of words in his head into some sort of order. 'Hauptsturmführer Zobel, I wish to speak to you as the husband.'

The husband. Just the husband. Not as a naval officer or a diplomat but as the partner in marriage of Lorelei.

'Alright,' said Gabriel, wondering how it would play out. Was Toshikyo aggrieved, angry, bitter over his wife's adultery?

Suddenly his eyes swung to Gabriel's. They were dark but very readable and Gabriel saw in them a sort of desperation that confused him. 'Well?' he prompted.

'I want to thank you for looking after her when I couldn't.'

He bowed again, but this time it was far lower and he took longer to stand again.

'I didn't know she was married,' Gabriel said. It sounded weak.

Toshikyo gave him a look that was almost European in its spontaneity. 'Would it have made a difference?'

Gabriel shook his head slowly.

'Of course not,' said Toshikyo. 'Men are men.'

'We were on a mission, we grew close.' Gabriel realised he wanted to talk about her, wanted to remember her in words, even with *the husband*. But perhaps Toshikyo felt the same, the need to keep her alive just a little longer, even if it meant sharing her in memory, as he had in life, with his wife's lover.

'I think you must have a poor opinion of me,' Toshikyo said. 'A man who prostitutes his own wife.'

'She wasn't a prostitute.'

Toshikyo considered this. 'No. I was a student in San Francisco and I would say the principal difference between the occidental and the oriental is the position of honour. The American young people owned their honour; it came from within and no government could order them to do something which they felt compromised this belief in their own values. In Japan, honour flows from above, and no action, however distasteful, taints the doer if they are doing their duty. In fact the reverse is true; paradoxically the woman who prostitutes herself for the nation is revered above the virgin.'

Hard duty, Gabriel understood. It was the same for soldiers. The good soldier obeyed the difficult orders and shot the wounded, or the prisoners, or the women. And officers patted them and gave them whisky and cigarettes. But at the front, the soldier who remembered his peacetime code of ethics was resented, seen as a liability; a bad soldier.

'Shooting you didn't mean that she didn't – care for you. You just came between her and her duty. She had a difficult decision to make. A hard choice.'

'Lorelei knew she was going to die, didn't she? She must have; she couldn't expect to shoot Hitler and walk out of his house to a life of love with you.'

Toshikyo looked around the ward at the beds with their cargoes of wounded and dying. 'How many miles and miles and miles of hospital beds are there in the world right now, all bearing men and women bleeding for their leaders?'

He turned back. 'When you returned to her apartment, we were discussing the nature of Lorelei's death, how to end her story. Should she put two bullets into the Führer and the third into her own head? She wished for something different. She desired the honour of what men call *seppuku*. For a woman, it's *jigai*; not the male ritual of slicing the stomach, but a cut to the neck that can be administered by a *kaishakunn*, a helper. You entered just after she had offered me the honour of being her *kaishakunn*. I accepted. She died as she had lived, a great woman.'

Gabriel saw the moment, her head down not in defeat but

to offer her neck to her husband, for a clean stroke. Her death sacred, something in which he had no role to play, the angel on the outside.

'But why did she need to kill Hitler? We'd just saved him.'

'Policy,' said Toshikyo. 'Is there anything more redundant in a war than a diplomat? And yet they are men of energy, of enterprise – so they circle the fighting dogs, seeking some way to influence the outcome.'

Gabriel looked at him. The man hidden behind the uniform. 'What are you? A naval officer, or a spy, or a diplomat?'

'I have been all three. But now I am an aide to Ambassador Oshima, so currently my weapon is diplomacy. In this capacity I have met both Mr Hitler and Mr Stalin, and in undiplomatic terms I can tell you the difference between them: the Führer is a fantasist and the Marshal is a paranoid–realist. As you know, Japan is not at war with Soviet Russia and an initiative was floated with them; that the Soviets consider making peace with Germany. We were open about our interests: the Americans and the British taking on Germany, without the help of Russia, would absorb all their forces, so relieving pressure in the Pacific.'

Gabriel was confused. 'Why would Stalin want to let the Nazis off the hook now?'

'Stalin no longer fears Germany, but he does the Western Allies. He suspects they are letting Russia take the brunt of beating Germany so that when finally East and West come face to face over the body of the Reich, the democracies will launch their true offensive against an exhausted Russia. Having Germany as a buffer state has its attractions for the Marshal. They had a pact before.'

'But Hitler?' said Gabriel, meaning *why did Lorelei have to die?*

'We approached Herr Goebbels, knowing him to have the

ear of the Führer and to be someone intelligent enough to see the advantages of this peace proposal. He grasped it immediately, as a starving man snatches at food. He himself said Germany has never won a war on two fronts. He wrote a carefully worded memorandum for the Führer.'

'And?'

'Mr Hitler read it, put it in a drawer apparently. He never referred to it again. He was wedded to the ridiculous nonsense of his offensive in the Ardennes – the result of which you can see about you. It was decided to remove him from the game. Without Hitler, the remaining Nazis, or the generals, would jump at the opportunity for peace in the East. The war in the Pacific would wind down. Space could be found to bring things to an end there, by diplomatic and not military actions.'

'Do you believe that? You killed Lorelei because of a plan? Some failed diplomacy?'

Toshikyo closed his eyes. He seemed to be speaking to himself. 'We don't know what's ahead. It's impossible to know what fate awaits Japan. What retribution the Americans will wreak upon us. What the blood price will be. My wife thought her death mattered little in the scheme of things. I disagreed. But Lorelei was always her own woman.'

'She's dead and Hitler's still alive.'

For the first time, Toshikyo's shoulders seemed to bend, as if the weight of the thoughts in his head had become too much. 'I know,' he said. 'Had I been able to see Lorelei before the festival, I could have told her. We could have let the German major kill Adolf Hitler – and my wife would still be alive. I'm taking her ashes home. Our son should see them.'

Once again, Gabriel struggled with a world that attacked him with its secrets. 'She was too young to have a baby when she left Japan?'

'Our girls marry early. Lorelei was fourteen when I took her as my bride. Akihiro was born within the year; what we call a honeymoon baby.'

Around him, the hospital rattled and clattered. A voice called out for a nurse, another voice asked for permission to die. Gabriel was a pillar of silence. He wondered if he would ever speak again. There was to be no ending to this pain. She had a child. Another secret. More acid on his heart.

CHAPTER FIFTY-NINE

The mysteries of Lorelei curled around Gabriel's soul and tormented him in his loneliness. Once, in his half-sleep in his hospital bed, he thought he could smell her perfume. The scent of her leaning over him as he recovered from an entirely different and earlier set of wounds. But it wasn't her; the perfume was wafting out from another woman's neck. He woke and they talked as she stood awkwardly. Chairs were absent in a military hospital.

'It's being here,' he said to her. 'Where we met.'

At the hospital, Lorelei had nursed him, wooed him. Had it all been an act? Had he been selected as a possible sniper, or did she like him for something that was just him?

'It takes time,' the woman by his bed said. 'But life will begin again.'

Gabriel knew this, but then again, he didn't. It didn't seem real; this life without Lorelei. Without anyone. Alone in his hut on a mountain. Life could only go on if he had a life.

A nurse arrived with a chair for the visitor, who was too important to be left standing.

'Did you go to her funeral?'

She shook her head. 'Not allowed to. I went to Iron

Arse's, Matron Gunther's. A pitiful turnout. None of the big-wigs and very few nurses. I understand she wasn't popular. Did you kill her?'

He nodded. 'Yes.'

'You're one of the SOE team, aren't you?'

'What's left of it.' Gabriel stared at her. 'And you're one of the Three Graces.'

Eva Braun agreed, 'Myself, Gretl and Ilse.'

'SOE warned us you were MI6's agents on Obersalzberg.'

'It worked well,' she said, smiling brightly, hair still fluffy but with eyes that were strong and piercing. 'I'd tell Gretl Mr Hitler's pillow talk, or anything of interest he'd broadcast in one of his tedious rants. Gretl would travel to Berlin, where she'd pass the intelligence on to Ilse.'

'And she would take it to Sweden?'

Eva tutted and set about rearranging the bunch of tiny snowdrops she'd brought and were stacked in a mug, the only vessel found that was small enough for them.

'Winter flowers, the last winter of the war, I hope. Yes, Ilse would travel to Stockholm. We hid her in plain sight; the liberal dissident with a Jewish lover whom Mr Hitler tolerated because of me. She'd slip away, supposedly to see this man, a doctor, but he was long gone. He emigrated to the United States before the war. The man masquerading as him in Stockholm is a British intelligence contact. That's where it all began. Ilse met Lady Duggan in his waiting room. She was our introduction to the spying world. Lady Duggan christened us.'

'The Three Graces.'

'From the Grace Game, a silly sport played by teams comprising three sisters. Much loved in English girls' boarding schools. Lady Duggan told us about it. Only the English wouldn't comprehend the symbolism. Hoops thrown about by virgins to be stabbed by others wielding sticks. And they call us pagans.'

'Do those schools have that many sets of three sisters?'

Eva shrugged. 'Lady Duggan said so. She had three daughters who were hot for the game, and I think the schools bend the rules a little and allow blood cousins to join a team of two sisters. Girls who have recently left are invited back from finishing school, or the hunting season, to make a third with younger siblings. The English upper classes like big families; look at the Mitford litter. The schools work it out somehow; the important thing is to show the three ages, from child to girl to young woman. The grace.'

She smiled at him. 'And of course, it was the perfect nom de plume, as only a woman who has attended a British girls' public school can ever have heard of the Grace Game, and women aren't employed in the offices of counter-espionage. Poor Mr Hitler, he has no idea what's going on under his nose.'

He looked at her and saw Lorelei. 'Do you love him? I mean, did you ever?'

Eva shook her head. 'But then, truth to tell, I don't think Hitler really loves me. Little Geli was the love of his life and he kicked her to death, before making sure with a bullet in her heart – so perhaps I'm lucky that I'm only an extended fling.'

There was something Gabriel didn't understand. 'Operation Watch on the Rhine, you knew about it. You talked about it to me when you visited Lorelei. Surely you passed that intelligence to London?'

She pursed her lips. 'Actually, no.'

Gabriel was confused, 'Why?'

She thought about stacking the snowdrops again but then abandoned them to their huddle. 'Too dangerous. I had my sisters to consider. If we'd warned the Allies and they were waiting, the resulting bloodbath would have warned the Abwehr there had been a leak. The Three Graces gave intelligence on the mood and thoughts of the Führer. A specific military secret, of the magnitude of the assault in the Ardennes, would have set alarm bells ringing. Instead I just blabbed it around in my fluffy way with unguarded chatter. The hope being that someone in the rival British team, which we knew was operating on Obersalzberg, would pick it up and report it to London.'

'We did, but they couldn't have believed us.'

'Heard it through the wrong ear, I suppose. We weren't happy when London made us team up with their assassination squad. It wasn't what we did.'

He brought the talk back to Lorelei. 'Did you suspect her?'

Eva smiled. 'I didn't, for the same reason no one suspects me. We were two feckless females of loose morals and no political convictions. But in reality, I open my legs for a cause.'

Another Dakini, he thought.

'I've shocked you,' she said. 'But a woman is a small country. An unimportant nation surrounded by great powers. Men make the rules and the rules suit the men. Sometimes a woman has to break those rules just to survive.'

An ache rolled back through him as regular as a tide. 'Lorelei broke the rules and she didn't survive.'

Eva reached across the bed and took his hand. 'She's made a mess of you. It happens in affairs of the heart. But you're not one of those men who are better alone. Believe me. Silent maybe, but not solitary.'

'You think I need a little wife?'

She laughed and then checked her eye make-up in a tiny mirror, speaking all the while. 'Not little. There's nothing little about you, Gabriel. You're a hero from another age and you need a mate of the same proportion. Another hero, but perhaps less complicated. When this mess is over, don't try to live alone. You'd make an awful misogynist. Give one of us ladies another chance to win the prize.'

He had no energy left for romance, he knew that. But he also knew that life was a death march: you either found the strength to put one foot in front of the other, again and again, or you gave up and died there and then. Gabriel just didn't know if he'd reached as far as he was going.

'I've got to go to Berlin,' she said. 'He's sent for me. Because he thinks life is an opera, I'm supposed to say he's forbidden me to join him in the capital because it's too dangerous. But, gallant little Fräulein that I am, I go to be by his side anyway.'

'Why? Sit out the war here. Wait for the Yanks.'

She sighed at the temptation but shook her head. 'I've been doing this job for a dozen years and I'm half afraid it's become an addiction. Peace frightens me – does it you? What on earth will we do when the guns fall silent?'

Gabriel had no idea.

Eva turned as she was going. 'He asked after you. Mr Hitler. He told me to visit you before I depart. He wants to know if you're on the mend. Are you?'

CHAPTER SIXTY

The siren seemed to be a magic sound that froze the people of the magic kingdom. Night after night, sirens had sounded across the rest of Germany but never before in the Bavarian mountains. The war had arrived in the shape of a great air fleet, a dragon whose intention was to destroy the town below, not with fiery breath but with blast bombs and incendiaries.

As he stood in the hospital grounds, listening to the rise and fall of the electronic wail, Gabriel thought of Max. Max, who had planned to leap across his battered BMW motorbike if the sirens sounded and roar off to his Luftwaffe anti-aircraft batteries. Those havens of peace, full of soldiers grateful for a posting far from the hot war. He remembered those dugouts, domesticised with empty shell casings used as vases for wild flowers and each gun crew with its own adopted dog. Lazy days in the sun, cosy days in their shelters, listening to the rain.

Max had been a man Gabriel liked, but he had killed him without a thought. Not to save Hitler but because of what Max wanted – more war. More and more war. As the bombers approached, Gabriel envied him his belief in something. Max had been a patriotic German. Gabriel was beyond flags and drums, without fellowship in a lonely landscape.

Searchlights pierced the skies. People on the terrace behind him, looking up, shared the hope that the bombers were just passing over on their way to a bigger target. Gabriel heard the rising panic coming from inside, as the wards were cleared and patients were rushed to the shelters below. He would have helped but he could still barely stand. The terrace emptied and people called for him to come inside and take shelter but he ignored them. He was where he wanted to be. He was handing over to a god he no longer believed in. He had no idea what to do with the life he was in possession of, so if God wanted it back, so be it.

The first drone of an aircraft sounded, faded, came again and then was joined by others. The amphitheatre of the mountains batted the sound back and forth and then a searchlight skidded across the fuselage of a bomber before losing it again. The stick silhouette seemed impossibly high and Gabriel also now wondered if the fleet above was on its way elsewhere.

The searchlight found another aircraft and held it in a cone of illumination as a slow trickle of bombs began to fall from it, as if it was crapping on them, Gabriel thought. He knew the bombers' tactics: first would come the high-explosive bomb to tear the facade off a building, and blow out the doors and window frames. Then would come thousands of incendiaries to fire the wooden roofs and expose the guts of the houses to heavier incendiaries. If enough buildings were torched, oxygen would be sucked into the sea of flames and, in the resulting fire storm, trees would be uprooted and people upended and all pulled into the furnace.

The air above thundered with hundreds of bombers and their bombs rushed to meet Gabriel with shrieks of joy. The carpet of grass beneath his feet began to bounce as if being beaten. The searchlights above ducked and weaved like crazy worms. The inexorable drone from the heavens was the sound of vengeance, and the bark from the guns ineffectual in response. The bombs became a rain and Gabriel found himself, without being aware of falling, full length on the grass. The sirens still wailed pointlessly, as if Obersalzberg itself was shrieking. Around him night became day, screams were ignored and paradise became hell. Gabriel waited for God's decision.

The air raid left Obersalzberg a smoking ruin. The Nazis abandoned the town and Gabriel was left behind with the wounded. Within days of the pull-out, an American airborne battalion arrived, wearing eagles as their divisional flashes. Gabriel, with the last of his military vanity, changed from hospital pyjamas back into his SS uniform. It won him no friends among the conquerors. He was put into a POW cage – as the saying went, into the bag.

The Americans created a prisoner of war compound with wire and tents on the edge of the bomb-blasted town. From it, Gabriel could see the Berghof, ironically one of the few buildings left relatively unscathed by the air raid.

The paratroopers were wary of him. His SS flashes, ash-blond hair, blue eyes and duelling scar made him seem the essence of all they were fighting. He was given death stares and called 'arrogant bastard' if he strayed near them from his side of the wire. Then one day, he found himself looking at a woman who had wandered into his line of vision as he watched the horizon.

'Hello Gabriel,' she said. 'I'm Mrs Cambridge.'

The Americans put him into one of their offices alone. When the woman came in, she was accompanied by a younger woman in a British Army uniform. Mrs Cambridge took a file from her.

'This is my driver, Bangle. She's a FANY, which is a regiment that just uses surnames, not ranks. I'm sure you understand.'

Gabriel did. The military was a tribe wherein all manner of peculiarities flourished.

Mrs Cambridge was still speaking. 'I'll introduce you properly later.'

The younger woman gave him a brief smile and left silently. Gabriel mused on a military force staffed by officers who introduced their drivers. Mrs Cambridge was looking at him, as if she could read his thoughts.

'I've a lot of time for that young lady. She's been there, like you, working behind enemy lines.'

Behind enemy lines, he thought. This was to be the reinventing of Gabriel Zobel. Not a man who willingly volunteered for the SS, not an idiot carried along by events, fused to a situation he'd wandered into without foresight. Now he was to be someone with a side, a cause, someone like Lorelei. A believer.

Mrs Cambridge opened the file and began to tell him about his life now. 'You're going to have a commission in the French Army, in one of the Foreign Legion regiments. It will be backdated to 1940. So you're Free French, understand?'

Gabriel did and nodded.

'The Frogs are short of heroes, so the commission comes with a Croix de Guerre, and by the way, we're giving you a Military Cross.'

More tin. He seemed to hear her as if she was speaking to him over the radio. Her voice came and went, his head full of smoke.

'We told you about the assault in the Ardennes,' he interrupted her. 'We warned you.'

'Possibly, but that's something that need concern you no longer, and it's a matter you can't share with your American hosts. Do you understand?'

Gabriel did.

'Now,' the woman continued, 'we've located you, Herman Koch the milkman and Katarina Sporrier the courier...'

Gabriel interrupted. 'I never met the courier; Lorelei kept her identity secret.'

Mrs Cambridge smiled softly. 'Actually, you did once.'

Had he? He hadn't known. He wondered where and when.

'Which brings us to Lorelei Fischer. She hasn't surfaced?'

Gabriel breathed deeply. 'She didn't make it. The bombing.' He didn't want her memory turned over and investigated and pulled apart.

Mrs Cambridge wrote something silently in her folder with a slim, gold pen. She finished and looked up. 'We'll get you out of here into somewhere more comfortable. My driver will stay in Bavaria in case you need anything while I get things moving. For a start, I'll need your measurements for your new uniform. Do you know Gieves and Hawkes?'

He didn't.

'Tailors. Rather good at military togs. You'll look quite dashing as a major in the Foreign Legion. Very Beau Geste.'

His father's spirit would be happy. His son was in the Legion, as he'd been. He banished the thought; he knew he had to stop serving the ghost.

'With a uniform and papers, you can move about freely. Oh, and you're owed rather a lot of back pay by the French, and a resettlement grant by the British. You won't be financially embarrassed.'

He was still thinking about serving in yet another army. 'When will I have to report to this French regiment?'

It was all beginning again.

Mrs Cambridge smiled and shook her head. 'The commission is to give you a history, not a future. Bide your time here and in a month or two you'll be decommissioned. Gabriel,' she said, using his first name to gain his eyes. 'It's over, you've survived. No more postings, no more duty. You're home and dry. Free.'

The word was too big to take in, alone.

'War,' Mrs Cambridge said, 'burns ambition faster than buildings. Millions of men will return home with no more desire left in them than to have a square of lawn to mow at the weekends. They will have come through the storm and will believe their patch of grass is enough, but they'll be wrong. They'll wake up one day and find the world is being run by lesser men.'

Gabriel, who had no idea what to do with this new word *free*, listened.

'This last year, all we've heard from above is that victory requires one final push, but actually it's peace that requires that final effort of the will. It will seem wrong, inappropriate, ungrateful to survive and yet want something more. But Gabriel, you will need to do something with yourself. Do you have any ideas, plans? A dream?'

The dream was dead. Plans were something you did over a map. And ideas hadn't been encouraged so far in his life.

'I thought I'd go back home, to Switzerland. To my hut.'

'And do what?'

He shrugged. 'Sheep,' he said.

He sensed her inner shudder at the suggestion of sheep.

'Forgive me, but I think that will be a mistake. You'll sit down by a log fire in your Shangri-La, doze off and when you wake up you'll be middle aged. Too late for anything and trapped. My driver, young Lavender, is the same as you.'

Lavender, Lorelei, Lorelei, Lavender. He bounced the names around his head and listened to them echoing away.

'She's suffered a bereavement and it's knocked the stuffing out of her. All she wants to do is sit in her house in Lambeth and lick her wounds. But the girl is top notch and I can't bear to see another good woman wasted. I've got her to agree to go to Canada. To pick up the threads of life again there. It's a big country with new opportunities. I think you should consider Canada, Gabriel. If you still want snow and cabins I believe it has them, but it also has cities and the whole place is raring to go. Europe will be in mourning for a generation, a shell-shocked continent drowning in ghosts and shades.'

And unquiet spirits, he thought.

CHAPTER SIXTY-ONE

Gabriel stayed on Obersalzberg and moved into Lorelei's apartment in the ruined theatre. It, too, had escaped the bombs. He felt like a drunk, compelled to return again to his favourite bar. He knew that if he stayed in Europe he'd live on in places like this, where the voices in his head would own him. Ostensibly he was waiting for his new uniform, but sometimes it seemed to him he was there to stare at Lorelei's kimono, pinned to the wall. Left behind, forgotten, like a pelt on an abandoned barn. He didn't know whether to take it down and store it with his things, or leave it to be looted.

He tried to gather his thoughts as he waited for a chance to speak to Mrs Cambridge again. Lavender told him that she was away, visiting a business she'd had before the war in Hamburg. A lace factory and shop. Mrs Cambridge wanted to get it up and running again now Hamburg had been taken.

'Apparently she thinks there'll be a demand for lace among the soldiers of the conquering Allies,' Lavender said.

They were walking in the woods above Obersalzberg, avoiding the American soldiers. 'They're nice blokes, don't get me wrong, it's just my regiment. They read my cap badge and get silly.'

Gabriel looked at it, the simple cross in a circle of steel. Embossed at the top, the letters WTS. 'For the Women's Transport Service. That's not the problem, it's underneath,' she said. Gabriel looked at the word at the base of the circle; FANY. 'To the Yanks a fanny is a rude word for a bottom.'

She reminded Gabriel of a nice girl he'd seen bothered by a coarse boy at his village school. A punch on the nose had sorted out the problem then, but he thought it might be difficult for him to hand out the same punishment again to the entire division of paratroopers. Instead he said sniffily, 'Americans.'

'No,' said Lavender. 'Mostly they're lovely, and the boys back home in Blighty are just as bad. I can't tell you what the word fanny means in their slang. It's just – I see the combat wings they get for jumping into action and I want to say, I've been there, I've done that, I'm one of you. But they don't give us women wings, or commando dagger badges. They say *I'm a para*, or *I'm a commando*, or *I'm a fighter pilot*, but what do I get to say? *I'm a FANY.* It just gets a laugh and it shouldn't. People don't understand what this maroon on my shoulder title means.'

Gabriel looked at it, at the word FANY in blue on a maroon background.

'Most of the girls have a khaki background, but if you've been an agent in occupied Europe you wear the maroon. But men don't know this, don't get the significance and just make anatomical jokes. I don't mind for me, but I do for the girls who went and didn't come back. They deserve better.'

'Tell them, then.' They'd reached the edge of the wood. The green lake where Gabriel had killed Max was below them.

'Does that colour mean it's rancid?' she said, then sighed. 'Hark at me getting all aerated about the Yanks, and most of the time they're so sweet. Why should they understand the traditions of the British Army when most of us Limeys don't either? And anyway, some men are alright.' A memory lightened her eyes and she spoke on the edge of a smile. 'Have you heard of the Ritz Hotel?'

Gabriel hadn't and Lavender explained. 'It's one of London's grand hotels. For a girl like me, from my background, entering a posh place like that was as daunting as going behind enemy lines. But there's this tradition in the FANY – before we went on our missions, we had one last really good bath. In barracks there was never enough hot water, but one of the girls had been taken to the Ritz before the war, and she started the fashion for us going there for our final bath. We had a second one if we were lucky enough to make it back. Our ritual: top and tail the mission with a soak. Very girly. Of course, we couldn't afford a room with a bathroom each so we had this ruse: one FANY would check in to the Ritz and the rest of us would *visit* her, and have a buckshee bath. The only problem was towels, never enough.'

Gabriel supposed there weren't. But Lavender was talking again.

'You know what an unexpected knock at the door does to your heart when you've served time undercover. There we all were, giggling in the luxury of this posh bedroom, and suddenly someone's banging on the door and we just knew we'd been rumbled. I goes to the door and opens it and there in front of me, in all his glory, is the manager of the Ritz; frock coat and more authority than a field marshal. And I think, now you're for it girl. And then he says, *We're rather afraid we've neglected to supply this room with enough towels*. And blow me, he sort of beckons and two maids slip by him with the biggest piles of the fluffiest towels you've ever seen in their arms. He lifts a bath sheet you could wrap around the world off one of the passing girls, and, with a little bow, he gives it to me and he says,

There's always hot water for one of our girls. One of our ladies of the maroon. I can't tell you how proud we are at the Ritz, that you heroines choose our hot water. You see he knew. I'd just got back from my second tour over there and I knew I'd never have to do another. I felt relieved and guilty all at once, and this elegant git who should have been shouting at me smiled – like I was a little girl and he was a dad. I didn't cry. I gave myself an order; *don't let the girls down.* So I didn't boo-hoo, but I shook, shook like a leaf, and he saw and he spoke to me gently, *You've made it, my dear – this is your home-run bath.* He escorted me across that hotel room like I was a queen, popped me in the bathroom and closed the door behind me. Closed it on all that terror and fear, all over. I'd like to live in a grand hotel. It's a place where you can feel safe.'

Gabriel wondered about his home-run bath – what he'd have to do to feel clean again. He thought about his future. He felt like a schoolboy asking himself what he was going to do when he left school. Back then that question hadn't occurred; it was always assumed he'd follow his father's footsteps into the military and then shepherding. Now he sought around in his head for some indication. His thoughts turned to Max and his stories of being a detective in the Bavarian police. Gabriel knew enough about himself to know that he needed the camaraderie of a way-of-life job. He wasn't a nine-to-five man. He wasn't a soldier any more but he wasn't quite a civilian.

His ruminating and wandering, and occasional coffees and walks with Lavender, were punctured by brief spells of raucous joy from the American paratroopers, such as when news of Adolf Hitler's death had reached them. It wasn't just triumph that the beast was dead; they knew it couldn't be long now, the war was almost over. Then the hooting from the jeeps came again ten days later, accompanied by the illegal discharge of weapons into the air, and singing, and it was all done; the war in Europe had been suffocated, snuffed out.

An impromptu party began in the Berghof, to which Gabriel and Lavender had been gathered up and delivered by Americans whose eyes were as bright and shiny as their teeth. A piano played, a few army nurses were danced off their feet by the many men, and alcohol was drunk copiously by young men who had perhaps never tasted it back home on the farm.

Gabriel supposed there were parties like it going on all over Europe. And in all these parties, at a certain point, when the quiet person in the corner had become invisible to the euphoric people in the middle, the anonymous shadow would slip away from the noise. Not in protest but in memory, in the full knowledge that their melancholy would always separate them from the party. Across Europe, on that night of nights, the bereaved made their way from the celebration to quiet places, to look at the stars or an empty armchair.

Gabriel and Lavender chose the stars. They sat on a hill, sharing the new greatcoat that had been delivered to him. Buttoned in together against the chill of the evening in the mountains, they resembled a two-headed troll. Both were still heart-bruised and Lavender needed to talk.

'I'd been so good. I never gave him a bad time about being a ducky-boy. I always knew what he was. It was part of him being Austen, I accepted it. When the navy kicked him out, I was on his side. I didn't blame him. It was the two of us together, always. Then on that day, the last day – I said horrible things.'

She went quiet as, behind, the party reached a new pitch of madness. 'I have this little house – I've told you...'

She had. Lavender had given him the whole story; the gift from a fellow communist in the party she'd now left.

'It was a present to me and Austen from Nicky. It was nothing to do with the Communist Party. But then there's this git, I mean he's been sitting pretty in a big flat in Hampstead, but then he gets his marching orders from the flat's real owner. He's another comrade-bigwig who sat out the war in Bermuda, and now it's nearly over he wants his place back and the git out. Nicky's been arrested and because he's out of circulation, the Don says the house belongs to the Party and he's going to occupy it, and me and Austen must make other arrangements. Hop it, he says, and don't dilly-dally on the way.'

Gabriel felt the heat of her anger raise the temperature inside the tent of the coat.

'I told him to sling his hook. I said it was my house. He said property was theft. I said he was a trespasser. I was raging, angry. I was furious with Nicky because at that point I still believed he couldn't keep it in his trousers and had got himself into trouble. And...'

She swallowed and took in the stars before she continued.

'And then the Don said he'd tell the neighbours Austen was a homosexual if I didn't move out. That was his trump card and I didn't have anything to match it. We couldn't cope with the shame if it got out onto the street. I thought I was going to lose my little house. I became so angry with Austen for being one of them. I blamed him. For the first time ever I had a go at him because of it, said rotten things.'

Gabriel could see her eyes running like wounds.

'I never had the chance to say sorry. What I said was really horrible, and now he's dead.'

Her shoulders shook and Gabriel took her as she turned into him. Her hair tickled his nose as she looked up at him with a drowned face. 'What am I going to do, Gabriel?'

He didn't know. Behind, the celebrations seemed to grow louder. Below in the valley, in Berchtesgaden, people would be trying to deal with the enormity of defeat. Gabriel, with no words of comfort to offer Lavender, told her instead about Lorelei, all of it. She listened carefully and then spoke.

'It's what they call a love affair, isn't it? Passion and beds but no wedding ring. I've always thought that sort of thing was more fiery and consuming than conventional love. In occupied France, there was this Resistance man, really cheeky. A communist, he recruited me, made me think about capitalism. You know what the danger does; you get to know people in double-quick time. I had it in mind that I might be falling in love with this man. Thing is, he was married and I liked his wife. So, it wasn't on, not for a girl like me. Coming out of an orphanage you only own two things – a sense of humour and your honour.'

Confusion screwed up her face. 'It's all more muddled than they tell you in church. There are men and women, and then there are men like Austen and women like Lorelei. I expect in her way she was always true to her husband, to the one she really loved. You just have to accept it wasn't you, Gabriel. I think I admire her: in spite of loneliness and terror she stayed true to her mission, and because of that she kept faithful to him in her way.'

In her way. Gabriel knew that, knew he'd only had the echo of her love. The stars that had looked down on six years of war now looked down on peace, and seemed no different.

'You're going to Canada,' he said.

She nodded. 'I need to get away from the memories. I asked Mrs Cambridge if she had a job for me abroad, in one of her lace factories, but she said lace wouldn't suit me. She made another suggestion – police work, in Canada. If I tell you what department, you'll laugh.'

'I won't.'

'The Mounties.'

Gabriel laughed.

'I know,' she said. 'You can't imagine me in jodhpurs.'

Gabriel thought about it and discovered he could.

'Oi!' Lavender said. 'I can hear what you're thinking. Anyway, jodhpurs and scarlet coats are just the ceremonial clobber. The Royal Canadian Mounted Police are going to be the FBI or MI5 out there. The fact I've apparently had a good war, got the George Medal, speak French, I've worked undercover, and most importantly I'm one of the few women who can drive a car, makes them want my services as soon as I'm demobbed.'

Gabriel smiled at her. 'You might meet a French Canadian without a wife.'

Lavender smiled back. It was a nice smile, he thought, but she didn't say anything.

A new tune began behind them on the piano, and a smoky voice sang a softer song, 'As Time Goes By'.

'She wants me to go to Canada as well,' Gabriel said.

'Why not? Start life again.' Lavender swayed gently to the slow rhythm of the song and whispered the odd line from memory, and Gabriel became aware of his arm around her waist. It had been there since they'd buttoned themselves into the coat and sat on the cusp of the hill. He'd put it around her because there was no space between them, but now it seemed to him, it was there for another reason.

She whisper-sang into his ear and out into the universe of the stars, the song the pianist was playing; 'As Time Goes By'.

CHAPTER SIXTY-TWO

Mrs Cambridge was speaking with her head round the door of Jago's room. 'I must say, it reaffirms one's faith in civilisation to discover an Englishman who, having spent the night in a brothel, has done so clad in flannel pyjamas.'

Jago, who had been up till nearly four in the morning serving drinks in Mrs Cambridge's Munich House, was not as merry as his employer. She had woken him with a bang at his door. 'Is something wrong?' he asked. 'Is it a delivery?'

He meant wine or beer. It had been explained to him that part of his duties was to unload alcohol when it arrived.

'Get dressed,' she said. 'There's someone downstairs I want you to meet.'

She closed the door and went, and Jago pondered their changed circumstances as he pulled on some clothes. Both had played the Battle of the Bulge card, each promising to carry to the grave the secret that the British had prior warning of the assault in the Ardennes. Jago had blown his opportunity for advancement, while Mrs Cambridge hadn't. She had transferred from SOE, which obviously as a sabotage service wouldn't survive peace, and entered the Secret Intelligence Service, MI6. Her *lace* business was seen as a magnet for information, as men of all uniforms, when they were out of them, tended to be less than discreet in the ambiance of a bordello. Jago, on his uppers, had been taken in by her and offered a job as a barman.

'You speak German fluently, barely drink and won't chase the girls. You're ideal.'

And so Mrs Cambridge became the superior officer and Jago rubbed along the bottom, as a sort of Nightingale. In a strange way he felt his life had turned full circle, from being the only boy in an English girls' boarding school to being the only resident male in a German brothel. All things considered, he could find little to choose between either institution except in the matter of profanity; the prostitutes swore considerably less than the schoolgirls.

In fact everything about the house was more restrained than he had imagined. The nights were less raucous, and the alcohol consumption was low, as the men were there for a different vice. Unlike the films, no honky-tonk piano crashed out boogie-woogie to the shrieks of gartered floozies in their undies. The girls wore pleasant frocks, which apparently inflamed the men more than tartery. The music was provided by a retired piano teacher called Fräulein Becker, who soothed the debauchery along with Mozart and Liszt. In her breaks she liked to sip a glass of sweet white wine and practise her English on Jago. Both agreed they had seen better days.

The salon downstairs was occupied by Mrs Cambridge and a British Army major nestling under the maroon beret of the Airborne Corps. After six years in uniform, Jago felt slovenly in his civvies, and he was conscious that he hadn't washed or shaved.

'Major Thom,' she said formally, 'may I introduce Mr Craze to you?'

Hands were shaken.

'Right, I'll rustle up some coffee while you two get acquainted.'

Jago felt a moment of alarm as she swished off. Acquainted? Was she now playing Cupid as well as patron?

'Mrs Cambridge speaks very highly of you, Mr Craze.'

Jago was at a loss. The major saw his confusion.

'I'm sorry. I've had you roused out of bed and now you've been left with a stranger without any explanation. Let's start again. I'm Major Thom, currently serving with T Force.'

Jago knew of T Force; it was an interesting outfit charged with securing, capturing and even kidnapping German scientists and engineers who might be useful to post-war Britain. They were in competition with the Soviets and the Americans. Jago imagined them out scouring the burnt-out hulk of Germany with large butterfly nets.

'And before T Force I was an intelligence officer in Airborne.'

Now Jago had him, Jago could place him. He knew he was talking to a legend. The name had seemed familiar to him at introduction, but in his sleep-befuddled state the connection had eluded him. In intelligence circles it was known as Thom's maxim: Only give a general or politician intelligence if it's the truth. Never give them merely what they want.

Thom had delivered the unpalatable truth to a general of Airborne: that the parachute drop the general was planning was fatally flawed, after two Panzer divisions moved in close to the landing zone. The general had not wanted to hear this and had sacked Thom. The jump went ahead with disastrous results.

'I've heard of you,' said Jago.

'And I you. Your board for the Diplomatic Corps has passed into legend.'

Was he being mocked, Jago wondered, but apparently not. 'By god you told the truth that day, whatever the cost to yourself. That took guts.'

Around them the sleeping brothel slowly roused itself. The cleaners silently ignored them as they went behind the bar to fill their buckets from a sink there. They heard Mrs Cambridge enter the vicarious madam's office to ask if she too wanted coffee. Upstairs a lavatory was flushed.

'Thank you,' said Jago. 'But as you can see, I haven't exactly landed on my feet.'

The major stared at him. 'Contrary to popular belief, there is always a need for men of integrity. My little shindig with the blimp in Airborne brought me to the attention of people who had been charged with overseeing the set-up of something called the United Nations. Have you heard of it?'

Jago had; the phrase had been used throughout the war to describe the alliance of nations fighting the Axis. Then the order had come that, henceforth, the alliance was to be called the Allies, as the term United Nations had been chosen as the title of a new international talking shop.

'It's to be the successor to the League of Nations, isn't it?'

'If it ever gets off the ground. Everyone is losing interest now the war is over. But we have to keep talking, we have to find a better way to manage things in the future.'

Jago found something stirring in him, something that had almost been smothered in the shame of his dismissal from the army, when he had been requested to resign his commission. It was the optimism that he could do something useful. 'You know what I am?' he said.

'I know what's important,' said the major. 'There's a mountain of work to be done to get the United Nations up off its knees. On every level the team entrusted to do so will encounter graft and corruption, indifference and cynicism. I need people with nothing to hide, who will negotiate with clean hands. You, Mr Craze, have all the right qualifications and, as I said, you come highly recommended.'

'Mrs Cambridge.'

The major smiled. 'Not just that good lady. The United Nations in all its glory is currently located in some classrooms of Westminster School, in Dean's Yard behind the Houses of Parliament. We're going to get Church House when the Lords move out. I was taking a shufti at that accommodation when I was accosted by one of the staff. I think she was a secretary. Had a face like Cleopatra…'

'Veronica Rawlings,' said Jago.

'That's right, Miss Rawlings. She knew of the United Nations and my brief and that I was recruiting a team. She asked if she could be cheeky and recommend a friend. She told me all about you. She said if I were looking for men of integrity then look no further than Jago Craze. I was intrigued and followed up her suggestion, which led me to Mrs Cambridge and more plaudits.'

Veronica, he thought. 'Are you offering me a post?'

'If you're willing to travel. Don't worry, we won't be staying in Dean's Yard. Initially they wanted to plant the new United Nations in Switzerland, like the League of Nations, but that won't do. The new place has to follow the power and that means the United States. Of course, the Yanks don't get it yet; they're so big, isolation comes naturally to them. It can't go to Washington; they can't be seen to own it politically.'

'So where?' Jago felt his excitement rising.

'San Francisco for another short let and then we hope to New York. It's the most exciting city in the world and so career diplomats will lobby their governments to be sent there.'

New York. Jago thought about it; a new beginning

for the world and for him. Aunt Esme had hated the place – without ever having been there, of course. Jago discovered he was sick to his soul of being English, of the smell of unwashed English bodies, of English stodge that passed as food, of English accents that betrayed class with every syllable. He writhed on the memory that once he would have sold his soul for leather club furniture in the English style. Surely, he thought, the only positive aspect of a war was that, after it was over, space might have been gained for something new to happen. Every fibre of his being seemed stale and he ached to be fresh. He needed the balm of being an exile. He wanted nothing more than to live and work in Manhattan. 'You really need me?'

'Yes.'

In the silence of the acceptance, the voices of the madam and Mrs Cambridge were heard clearly. Brothel business.

'Are the French girls recovering from their ordeal, Katarina?'

'We have found wigs for them and their hair will grow again. We removed with bleach the swastikas the Resistance drew on their foreheads.'

Mrs Cambridge's snort of contempt almost rattled the building. 'Resistance, my arse. Most of those swine were collaborating until the day before the tanks rolled into Paris – then they joined the Resistance. Bullies, that's what they are; shaving a poor girl's hair off when all she was trying to do was survive and feed her elderly parents.'

Madam Katarina's voice dropped slightly and the air of conspiracy this generated drew in the eavesdroppers too. 'Do you know what one of the girls said to her tormentors? Gentlemen, like yours my heart is French – sadly my cunt is international.'

The woman laughed and the men smiled and Jago

noticed that, like him, Captain Thom was slightly flushed at the use of the 'C' word. They had come through a war of unspeakable violence and seen, in person or on newsreels, images of unimaginable cruelty. Men had lost their gods, states, surety, but one English innocence remained: the ability to blush when a woman swore.

Major Thom spoke through his embarrassment. 'I expect we're all in the same boat as that poor woman; if we want to survive in the post-war world our hearts might beat to an increasingly irrelevant love of motherland – but our arses are going to have to become international.'

They smiled across a gilded table at each other and moved on.

'Everything's happening at a rate of knots. I'm finished with T Force and being shipped home. I'll get your travel papers sent here, shall I?'

'Yes.'

'You're going to hit the ground running, so if you've any unfinished business this side of the pond?'

'No,' he said, and then he thought. 'Well perhaps. In my last job, I ran an operation called Foxley, situated on Obersalzberg.'

'Hitler's lair?'

'I think I might just like to visit it once, before I leave – a sort of pilgrimage.'

The major gave Jago the once-over, taking in his stubble and creases. 'I can get you into a uniform of some sort. Might make travelling easier than pottering about in mufti.'

Jago smiled and shook his head. 'Thanks. I'm not being ungrateful but I think I'm finished with soldiering. I'll go in my civilian suit.'

CHAPTER SIXTY-THREE

The American soldiers had stopped obeying orders. Gabriel could hear their NCOs shouting at them and the officers reasoning. He overheard, through the open window of what he still thought of as Lorelei's apartment. He listened to the news that emerged from the argument beneath. The men had taken a vehicle without authorisation and planned to go to Munich or somewhere *swell* to celebrate the end of war. The end of all wars, for all time. Then, when they returned from the party, they wanted to be repatriated immediately to the United States. The NCOs blocked the road with their bodies; the officers leaned into the jeep and tried to persuade the men to climb out of it.

'But sir, you heard the news; we dropped two bombs on Japan and the place ain't there no more. The man on the radio said the atomic bomb makes war obsolete. So when can we go home?'

Gabriel could feel their impatience coming up from the road outside. He had it himself. Wanting to be away. Wanting to catch a military flight to England with Lavender and then board a troop ship to cross the Atlantic with her to their new life in Canada.

'When? When? When?' came a voice from below.

When, when, when? echoed Gabriel's head.

Everything was in order and in place. Mrs Cambridge had secured a commission for him in the police, who were to be Canada's new security and counter-espionage service. The West already knew that the Soviets were about to devote a great effort to attempting to subvert Canada, and have an ally sitting on the head of the United States. The call had gone out for experienced intelligence officers and Gabriel apparently fitted the bill.

But Gabriel couldn't leave yet. He haunted the old Nazi Eldorado of Obersalzberg. Preparations were being made to demolish the Berghof, to prevent it becoming a shrine for those who would wish to worship the devil. Gabriel wandered the deserted and looted building at the same time every day, as agreed at the meeting on the Eagle's Nest. The bombing raid, while leaving the roof untouched, had blasted out the giant window in the Great Hall. Gabriel stared at the damage and thought it was strange that it was the glass that had made the window remarkable. Without it, the window became a mere hole in the wall. Through it the mountains seemed closer, more threatening, as if they could now get in. A breath of wind did and passed over him like a shadow. And out of its whisper a voice came, mimicking the softness of the breeze.

'Only the mountains are constant. People will always fail you. How are you, my scarred seraph?'

Gabriel had heard someone enter after him, heard a door creak below. He turned around. The toothbrush moustache was gone, as was the side parting. The hair was now swept back. Gabriel caught a glimpse of pink skin at the top of the head where he had shaved it; the bald patch of a monk, as befitting the robes he wore.

'Hello, Wolf,' Gabriel said.

He saw the discomfort in the eyes. His world in ruins, Adolf Hitler would have preferred the rank of Führer to the familiarity of a nickname.

'You waited.' Hitler spoke in the same soft, beguiling tone he reserved for manipulation. 'I knew I could rely on you. I knew you would keep the faith. I was right to trust you.'

A memory like a dried leaf blew through Gabriel's mind; the Führer in that very room saying something about trusting and dangerous men. Then Hitler was speaking again.

'How do you like my outfit?'

Hitler, almost effeminately, twirled the habit.

'A good disguise,' said Gabriel.

Hitler latched on to the faint praise as the last resonance of a Nuremberg cacophony.

'Even in the 1930s I was planning for this eventuality. Even then I suspected the German people would let me down, prove unworthy, not iron enough for the struggle. I had foresight; I struck a deal with the Pope. I guaranteed the sanctity of Church property, and they promised to create an underground railway to smuggle the Party faithful out of Europe if the people betrayed us.'

'What do you want?'

Hitler ignored his question. 'I moved my command from Berlin on one of the last flights.'

Moved his command, Gabriel thought bitterly. He'd run away, leaving his child-soldiers and elderly men to face the Ivans. He also knew it was the remnants of his old unit, the Nord, that had been fighting to the last around the Führerbunker, a division consisting of foreign volunteers. In fact, the doomed, forlorn hope dying in that rubble had been mostly made up of Frenchmen. Gabriel was suddenly struck by the illogical futility of the battle in Berlin: French soldiers in SS uniforms, protecting an Austrian holed up in the German capital that was besieged by Asiatic soldiers, serving a Georgian who controlled Russia. There had to be, he thought in a moment of levity fuelled by his despair, a better way to promote foreign travel.

Hitler interrupted his thoughts. 'I made my lair in a monastery.'

'Who died?' Gabriel asked.

The blue eyes blinked. 'Instead of me? Gustav Weler, my double of course – and the silly cow.'

'Eva,' Gabriel said, remembering her at his hospital bed. She'd played the great game to the last and lost. Her addiction had killed her.

'She'd always been expendable. I even married her to validate the supposed suicide pact.'

Suddenly Hitler seemed almost overcome, suddenly pathetic. He stared at Gabriel as if seeking forgiveness. 'Scar, I had to kill Blondi. Poison.'

The one death that seemed to cause him guilt, Gabriel thought, the death of his dog. Then he brightened again. 'As you can see, I am indestructible. I survived the fall of Berlin as I survived the generals' bomb in the Wolf's Lair. I even used the British to protect my back.'

Now he had Gabriel's attention. 'The British?'

Hitler nodded and grinned. 'When your friends threaten, you must enlist your enemies. After the July plot, a lowly English captain wrote a report to the effect that my generals would prove a bigger menace to the future than me. It landed on my desk courtesy of the Abwehr; I saw it presented me with an opportunity and I fabricated some evidence in support of the man's theory.'

'What evidence?'

'Goebbels called it the Walpurgisnacht Plan, a trifle melodramatic but he had a feel for that sort of thing. It purported to be a document mapping the generals' sinister intentions if they managed to destroy me. We delivered it to the English captain using our friends in the Irish Republican Army. With that evidence in their hands the British couldn't afford to let me die. That my turncoats didn't manage to finish me off is, I'm sure, because of British intervention.'

The grin was back briefly, before Hitler moved on. 'But enough of the past. The future will be ours, eh? Tomorrow belongs to the strong. We must leave this worn-out continent that has been bled of its spirit by the Jews. The ranch is waiting in Patagonia. From there a new struggle will commence. The Catholic Church is seeding my people all over that continent. That will be my base for a new world order.'

Gabriel almost hit him. The delusion was monumental. He wanted to beat him again and again, chanting it's over, it's over, it's over!

Hitler touched his arm conspiratorially. 'It's still too soon for me to attempt the journey, even with this disguise and my false papers. But by next spring the world will be sleeping again and then I will go. I have a Swiss passport. I just need a safe bolthole. I can't wait out the winter lurking around a hotel every day, and now the Allies have become suspicious of the Catholics and are watching the churches, I daren't risk another monastery. I want your help, Scar. I need the use of your hut in the clouds for the winter. You'll take me there and keep us supplied. In the spring, when the world has forgotten me, I will come down off the mountain and fly to Argentina.'

The world would never forget Adolf Hitler, Gabriel thought. It would forget the names of the children who died under the bombs, and the men who fought and died bravely for the wrong side, but the evil icon would live on.

'When do we leave?' Gabriel asked.

'Tomorrow. It'll be quite a hike from here to Switzerland, but we're both mountain boys, eh? You the son of a hunter.'

He was the son of a hunter.

CHAPTER SIXTY-FOUR

Hitler came along the familiar track, the one that led past the Mooslaner Kopf tearooms. A soft wind blew. Choughs called. Gabriel lined up the crosshairs of his telescopic sight on the head of an icon. He allowed for the breeze that seeped in through the gap at the valley end. He breathed in, he breathed out, stilled himself, and squeezed the trigger. The shot was a short bark, lost in the hunter-heavy hills of hungry people seeking meat. Hitler's head jerked back and he began to shake. Gabriel knew he'd destroyed Hitler's nervous system and the Führer had lost control of his movements. Gabriel remembered the newsreels the Americans had screened of the Victory in Europe celebrations in London. Cockneys had been doing a dance, walking forwards and then backwards; they called it the Lambeth Walk. Adolf Hitler, as he died below on the track, performed his own ridiculous Lambeth Walk. Jerking forwards, then twitching into reverse. He fell on his back, his legs twisted, his mouth open, as if to begin one of his interminable rants. But the Gob was finally silent.

Gabriel went down to him, breathing air back into his lungs. He'd chosen this particular spot on the path for the kill for a reason. Just off the path was a manhole cover to the giant sewer that served Obersalzberg. He removed it and the warm scent of ordure rose to greet him. He threw in the rifle and then he threw in Hitler. There was a satisfactory sound as the Führer hit the shit.

'King under the mountain,' said Gabriel softly, as he replaced the cover.

Gabriel returned to the apartment in the ruined theatre and took down Lorelei's kimono, barely looking at the red camellias, refusing to remember their significance, the flower of grace and death. He crushed the silk crepe into a kit bag, suppressing his thoughts as he did so. Then he went to the Berghof to wait. He arrived as another man was going in, an Englishman by the cut of his civilian suit. As they passed each other, the man acknowledged Gabriel's French uniform.

'Bonjour,' he said.

'Good morning,' Gabriel replied. Then they moved past each other, onto other and separate lives.

Lavender came for him driving a jeep. 'Ready to go?' she asked.

'Ready.'

She looked at him, the man she'd let into her life. 'I think a journey like this, the beginning of *our* journey, should start with a kiss. What do you think?'

Gabriel agreed.

Afterwards, Lavender drove them away from Obersalzberg, down off the mountain. Gabriel felt as if he was driving through a series of images, like hoardings spread across the road, torn in half by the jeep; the bishop in Spain, the Russian soldier running towards him with his Stalingrad spade, Hitler pinching his cheek like a sweet uncle, Max staring at him at the moment of death and Lorelei – mostly Lorelei – smiling and stroking and calling him *soldier*. Ghosts. He blinked his eyes and blinked them away. And as he did so, the words of the American soldier who had taken the Japanese surrender came to him; *these proceedings are at an end.*

THE END

Unbound is the world's first crowdfunding publisher, established in 2011.

We believe that wonderful things can happen when you clear a path for people who share a passion. That's why we've built a platform that brings together readers and authors to crowdfund books they believe in – and give fresh ideas that don't fit the traditional mould the chance they deserve.

This book is in your hands because readers made it possible. Everyone who pledged their support is listed at the front of the book and below. Join them by visiting unbound.com and supporting a book today.

Hanna Abts
Alison Arbuthnot
Dylan Arrowsmith
Jo Ashcroft
Annette Badland
Jason Ballinger
Brigid Battiscombe
Alan Baverstock
Sarah Baynes
Dan Berlinka
Tim Berry
Olivier Blanc
Nicholas Bourne
Dermot Boyd
Amy Buscombe
Mellie Buse
Marcus Butcher
Dirk Campbell
David Cantor
Suzanne Carr

Matt Carter
Catherine Chatterjee
Greg Childs
Pat Collis
Tim Compton
Tony Cooke
Emma Cope
Peter Cork
Prue Corp
Kim Crowther
Avril Danczak
Maddy Darrall
Jane Dauncey
Hugo de Melo
Nicky Dean
Robert Eardley
Susan Elkin
Caroline P.B. Fewkes
Ericka B Gairy
Charlotte Gascoyne
Paul Gerstenberger
Graham Gibbs
Will Gillham
Alison Grade
Helen Grafham
Angela Griffiths
Andy Groves
Samuel H
Ed Harris
Julie Harris
Paul Harrison
Simon Heath
Matt Hemley
Adam Hughes
Alison Hume
Karen Inglis
Chris Jarvis
Helen Jenkins
Lydia Jones
Paul Joyce
Ian Kellgren
Julian Kemp
Dan Kieran
Cas Lester
Jan Leventhall
Brian Lighthill
Nest Madden
Emma Manton
Best Martin
Sally Martin
Hannah Mason
Mica May
Helen McAleer
Dez McCarthy
David Mercatali
Claire Miller
John Mitchinson
Chie Miyadera
Silvana Montoya
Mary Morley
Sophia Morphew
Karina Murphy
Brendan Murray
Rhel ná DecVandé
Carlo Navato
A M Nightingale
Jeff Norton
Bob Nunn
Himanshu Ojha
Andrew Oldbury
Georgina Ongley
Charles Palmer
Gill Partridge
Krupa Pattani
Tim Patterson
Kate Paxton
Scott Payne
Avice Pearson
Patricia Phillips
Katherine Pile
George Poles
Justin Pollard
Miroslava Rattley
Beryl Richards
Mick Robertson
Evelinka Rose
Lewis Rudd
Robyn Rush
Chris Sanagan
Chris and Danielle Sanagan
Julian Scott
Alan Shannon

Leah Skipper
Melanie Stokes
Michael Towner
David Tucker
Laurence Tuerk
Juliet Tzabar
Tom Vanson
Mary Walker
Maureen Walker
Lee Walters
Tony Weston
Ivan Wheatley
David Whitney
John Willcock
Hannah Williams
Mark Wilson
Antony Wood
Andrew Woodruff